The Discourtesy of Death

The Discourtesy of Death

William Brodrick

Little, Brown

LITTLE, BROWN

First published in Great Britain in 2013 by Little, Brown

A CIP catalogue record for this book is available from the British Library.

ISBN HB 978-1-4087-0472-1
ISBN CF 978-1-4087-0473-8

Typeset by Palimpsest Book Production Ltd, Falkirk, Stirlingshire

Printed and bound in Great Britain by Clays Ltd, St Ives plc

Papers used by Little, Brown are from well-managed forests and other responsible sources.

MIX
Paper from
responsible sources
FSC
www.fsc.org   FSC® C104740

For my father, who met disability and
terminal illness without complaint.

Acknowledgements

My warm appreciation goes to Ursula Mackenzie for companionship while handling the rapids of difficult moral questions and guidance in shaping the subsequent novel; to Richard Beswick, Iain Hunt and Philip Parr for help in preparing the text for publication; to James Hawks who, turning to W. B. Yeats, found the title; and to Françoise Koetschet, Christine de Crouy Chanel and Sabine Guyard, old friends of Anselm, for their unwavering support.

Her heart sat silent through the noise
And concourse of the street;
There was no hurry in her hands,
No hurry in her feet.

Christina Rossetti

Prologue

The man in the tweed jacket knelt down and pulled back one corner of the bedroom rug, a large, expensive thing, handmade in the uplands of Kashmir and sold by a connoisseur of elegant home furnishings from a tiny shop in a back street of Cambridge. The pile was bright red, with an involved gold and blue design, its twists and turns suggesting an obscure meaning known only to Gurus not quite of this world. There were countless animals beneath arching branches. It was called 'The Tree of Life'.

The man's scrubbed fingernails settled into a groove of planking. He pulled, gently, and the floorboard lifted like a lid onto a box of old tools. His hand entered the dark space, feeling for the Billingham camera bag that hid a small seventies tape recorder and the Browning Hi-Power 9mm automatic pistol with silencer. The magazine capacity was fourteen rounds. Four had been fired in quick succession thirty years earlier: BAM-BAM, BAM-BAM. Ten remained: one up the spout with nine ready to go. The safety catch was on. The silencer was detached, wrapped in a yellow cotton duster.

'You can't hesitate,' came the low West Belfast voice down the years, dark like the damp sitting room in Ballymurphy where Army handler and informer had met for the last time. 'You move quickly. He has to go down. You do the job.'

The man in the tweed jacket stared at the complicated pattern in the carpet. He'd once been a captain in the British Army, dressed in jeans and a bomber jacket. He'd shaved infrequently and he'd worn his hair long.

1

'There's no other way,' said the informer, holding out the gun. Liam knew what he was talking about. 'All the thinking's been done, hasn't it? If you want peace, you'll have to pull the trigger.'

The man blinked and swallowed. Liam's voice faded and with it the dim light of that tenement house in Northern Ireland. The Troubles were over. Birdsong came from the trees in the quiet Suffolk garden. Autumn sunshine lit the panes of polished mullioned glass. Shadows drifted across the neat lawn towards the trimmed garden hedge. Beyond, a red tractor rumbled along a quiet lane.

Resolved, Michael Goodwin (clean-shaven now, with short, neatly parted hair) replaced the plank and smoothed the rug home with his foot. Opening a drawer on a dressing table, he took out his two passports, one British the other Canadian, and slipped them into the opposing inside pockets of his jacket. Sliding the drawer shut, he picked up the three framed photographs of Jenny and laid them in the small suitcase packed that morning by his wife. She was downstairs, waiting; edgy, like the informer in Ballymurphy; sure and convinced, like the man he once was, the man who could pull a trigger when it was necessary.

'I'm ready,' said Michael entering the kitchen.

Emma turned around. Her right hand moved a stray hair above one eyebrow. Smoke from a cigarette lodged between two long fingers made her wince as if she couldn't see properly. She stubbed it out, breaking the unburned length.

'Don't know why I bother,' she said, languidly. 'I thought these things were meant to calm the nerves' – she nodded towards the open pack by the *Sunday Times* on the table – 'all I feel is seasick. Waste of time and money. Should've had a stiff drink but I thought it's far too early for a slug of gin. Didn't want the headache. Damn thing always comes when I booze before lunchtime.'

She paused to watch him shrug on his Crombie overcoat. His movements were slow and deliberate; irrevocable. One after the other he pushed the buttons through the eyes.

'Actually, there's no gin left,' she said. 'Finished the bottle last night.'

Her matey fretting was just a performance – they both knew it. She wasn't worried about the job, not as such. Her only concern was that her husband's nerve might fail. That he might hesitate. The banter was just a kind of loving shove towards the door, urging him to get the necessary over and done with. For everyone's sake.

'Don't worry,' he said, pocketing his trembling hands. 'I'm ready.'

Their eyes met across the long breakfast table. Emma's outline was dark against the windows above the sink, but Michael knew well the shades of feeling in that fine-boned face, the deep hollows that held her tortured gaze, the wide half-open mouth. He'd watched the changes for thirty-five years. She'd been happy, once; like him.

'Just think of Jenny,' she blurted out.

'I will.'

'Keep her face in mind.'

Michael nodded.

'She deserved a better life.'

Emma reached for the cigarettes, stamped on the pedal bin and dropped the packet in the hole as the lid opened. They were silent. Husband with his hands in his pockets, wife with her back to him, her shoulders juddering, her breathing like a kind of suppressed insane laughter. She snatched some kitchen towel to wipe her face. When she'd mopped up the spilled emotion, her voice was quiet and assured.

'People bring dogs to the surgery. They've bitten someone . . . I mean the dog, not the owner . . . and I put it down, quickly and painlessly. I have to. Because it might bite again. You can't talk to a cross-breed. You can't bring a pit bull round with a warning. There's something wrong with their minds. The thing has to go down. And, you know, when it's lying there on the table, no longer dangerous, it looks peaceful; simply asleep. Grateful that it's all over. No more chains around the neck. No more bloody postmen to ruin its life.'

Emma turned from the window and walked the length of the beamed room to Michael. They faced each other, staring hard. Their hands locked.

'Peter is not a good man, Michael.'

'I know.'

'Before they locked him up he was mouthing off on the radio about morality.'

'Darling, I remember.'

'He went to prison for the wrong reason.'

'Yes, darling.'

Michael seemed to stumble out of the kitchen into a memory. He saw Jenny after the accident, lying on her back in the orchestra pit. He saw again the splayed feet of his fallen angel, the failed ballerina. *Don't move her. Just wait for the ambulance.* Bright stage lights flashed off the brass instruments as the players in rumpled black grouped to stare at the crippled swan.

'He never cared for her.' Emma was angling her head, coming closer to Michael, drawing him back to the matter in hand. 'And yet he got all the sympathy and praise.'

'Emma, darling, I don't need reminding.'

'You do, over and again.' She kissed him violently, as if she might suck the pain once and for all out of his life. 'You do, because you're a good man who'd never harm a fly.' She reached for the table and picked up a book off the breakfast table. 'Here's Peter's present. It'll keep him in his chair for hours.'

Michael read the title to himself, feeling Emma's angry satisfaction.

'Well chosen,' he said, without smiling. 'He won't be able to put it down.'

They walked arm in arm outside into the warm sunshine, Emma shouldering the camera bag, Michael carrying the suitcase and the book. It was like their wedding day, only there was no guard of honour from the regiment, no cheery guests; they were starting this particular adventure on their own. On reaching the blue Volvo hatchback Michael said, 'I'll call tonight.'

'Okay.'

'After that, it's lights out. No contact. I need to be completely alone.'

'I understand, Michael. I'm ready, too.'

'You only ring to confirm he's out of prison and back home.'

'I remember.'

'Use a coin box. Become someone else to make the call and then leave that someone else behind, in the phone box. Go home as if you'd done nothing.'

'I will.'

Michael put the bags in the boot and then examined his hands. The tremors and shakes had gone for the moment.

'They're good, clean hands, Michael,' said Emma. Like the informer, she had the impatient energy of the person who had to stay behind and wait; the fussy authority of the accomplice who'd planned but wouldn't act. 'I know I'm angry . . . that I'll always be angry, but this is not about vengeance, Michael. Our feelings about Peter are irrelevant. We're doing this for Timothy, Jenny's boy . . . our grandson. To give him a better future. We can't leave him with Peter, not after what he's done.'

Michael drew her close and pressed his lips against her forehead. He left them there and closed his eyes.

'Everything's going to be just fine,' he said, quietly. 'Just go back to work and heal some cats and dogs.'

He opened the car door, seated himself and wound down the window. Emma was holding out some letters. She'd been clutching them in her free hand during their slow walk from the kitchen to the driveway.

'You forgot these,' she said, affectionate and scolding. 'There are some of mine, too. Remember to pop them in the post, will you? They're urgent. Should have done it myself when I bought those awful cigarettes, but I had other things on my mind.'

It was a desperate gesture to be normal. Doing what ordinary people do when their other half heads off to work. Michael glanced at her in the rear-view mirror as he turned into the empty lane. She was standing tall and remote, just like on the day Jenny was lowered into the ground. One hand was covering her mouth.

Michael drove to the post office, bought some tulips from a florist and then made for 'Morning Light', a thatched cottage in Polstead. Jenny had found it shortly after she'd moved in with Peter. She'd been captivated by the lemon colour-wash. She'd said, 'Dad, I want to live and die here.' It stood empty now, waiting for the surviving owner to finish his custodial sentence. Michael went through the usual motions: he opened some windows; he raked up the leaves; he shut the windows again. For the umpteenth time he counted the number of steps from the fuse box by the back door to the sitting room, halting two yards before Peter's chair by the fire. Twelve quick, silent paces. These tasks done, he then departed from the established routine. First, he placed the captivating book on the armrest; second, he put the wheelbarrow by the back door. After one last look at the chair by the fire, imprinting the image in his mind, he locked up.

Feeling strangely weightless, Michael walked to the graveyard and laid the tulips on Jenny's grave in Saint Mary's. He then motored to the Slaughden Sailing Club, just south of Aldeburgh, where he kept *Margot*, his small yacht. He put the Billingham bag in the cabin and then drove south to Harwich, using his British passport for a crossing to Holland. On reaching the Hoek, he went to Harlingen and the holiday home bought with Emma's inheritance. It was from here that the family had sailed around the Frisian Islands, mooring here and there to hire bikes and cycle along the long, deserted lanes. After the quick promised phone call to Emma, he went to bed but didn't sleep. After breakfast he hired a Citroën with a spacious boot, purchased a large tarpaulin and then took the road back to the Hoek, where a customs official barely glanced at the proffered Canadian passport. Heading north, he retrieved the camera bag from *Margot* and drove the remaining few miles to his final destination: the Southcliff Guest House, a charming Victorian property on the promenade at Southwold. He was a single man on holiday, exploring the wind-swept coast of north-east Suffolk. Jenny had loved it as a child.

Part One

1

'There is no God,' murmured Anselm.

'You're going a bit far, there,' replied Bede, Larkwood Priory's tubby archivist.

'No, I'm not. This is one of those moments of insight that sent Nietzsche over the edge.'

Anselm stared in horror at the open pages of the *Sunday Times*, laid out for all to see, on a table in the monastery's library. The title ran: 'The Monk who Left it All for a Life of Crime'.

'Bin it.'

'I can't and won't.'

'Why?'

'The Prior said not to.'

'But it's . . . embarrassing.'

'It's about you. The Superman. It's about Larkwood. It goes into one of my binders.'

Several brother monks had already read the article. Only 'article' didn't do justice to the author's exertions. It was more of a biopic. A careful examination of the unusual twists and turns in a strange man's life. Anselm had come running to the library after hearing a few loud guffaws in the calefactory.

'Bede, everything's out of proportion.'

'You can make annotations, giving the right dimensions.'

'Get stuffed.'

Anselm leaned over the table, his wide eyes skimming down the columns of print, culling facts and quotations. French mother,

11

English father. Quirky at school. According to John Wexford, headmaster of the day, *Charming fellow, but he could never see the wood for les arbres.* Graduate in law from Durham University. Called to the Bar at Gray's Inn. No academic distinctions to speak of. A barrister for ten years in the chambers of Roderick Kemble QC.

Bede's chubby finger appeared.

'This is my favourite,' he purred, stroking a paragraph. 'Let's read it quietly together.'

They did:

> 'A rare breed of man', argues Kemble, one of London's most distinguished criminal lawyers. 'A loss to the Bar when he became a monk. I've rarely come across such a remarkable combination of brilliance, sound judgement and disarming humility. The top corridor of justice is a colder place for his absence.' Great men have great flaws, I suggest. Kemble frowns, obliged to acknowledge a certain kink in the character of his former protégé. 'Well, as the Good Book says of King Solomon – another fine jurist – he loved many strange women.'

'I'll never forgive you,' breathed Anselm and, addressing Bede, 'He's joking.'

'Manifestly.'

With an oath, uttered in French, Anselm moved onto 'the hidden Larkwood years' and the 'quiet eruption of unreported forensic activity'. Each investigation was explored in some detail, culminating in a hymn of admiration. To give it prominence Bede cleared his voice:

'"After the closure of each case, this reticent sleuth returned to Larkwood, refusing interviews, disdaining praise. But justice had been done in places beyond the reach of the law. He resumes a quiet life tending bees. To this day he repudiates any—"'

'That'll do.'

'It only gets better. Try this—'

'Belt up.'

They were quiet for a moment while Anselm chewed his lip. The call from the *Sunday Times* had come without warning. Having pieced together some old and scattered headlines, a journalist with an eye for the unusual had glimpsed the larger canvas. He'd called wanting an interview. In the nicest possible way, Anselm had declined to oblige, following which he'd assumed the matter had died a quiet death. He hadn't imagined that the journalist might contact key witnesses, let alone examine his life prior to Larkwood. There was one small mercy.

'Thank God he didn't speak to one of my old clients.'

'On reflection, perhaps you were right,' came Bede, purring once more.

'What about?'

'Nietzsche.'

Bede turned the page ceremonially as if it were a revered text. The chubby finger tapped a name in the article's concluding paragraph.

'Mitch Robson.' Anselm murmured the name.

The insurance man who'd run a jazz club. The trumpet player who'd tweaked the rules of harmony. His two acquittals at the Old Bailey on charges of theft were memorable high points in Anselm's career. A man of good character had been scandalously blamed for the slipshod accounting system of a ruthless employer. The lambent phrases (used twice) returned to Anselm's mind. In a fancy, he glimpsed the jury's indignation. He'd passed it on like an infection.

'Don't be churlish,' scolded Bede in reply. 'He speaks movingly of your gifts . . . your high character.' The archivist paused to salt the wound. 'You were close once, it seems.'

Anselm snatched the paper. He couldn't bear the commentary any longer. He read on, with growing dismay:

Despite this double vindication, Mr Robson remains aggrieved. 'The law doesn't always mesh with reality,' he explains at home, an old pleasure wherry moored on the Lark. 'One moment you're driving on the right side of the road, and the next you're in court battling to put your life back together. Thankfully, I knew Anselm. He winkled some justice out of the system.' Mr Robson is not surprised that his one-time advocate became a monk, or that the monk then returned to the quest for justice. 'He's somewhere between this world and the next. That's why he sees a little bit further than everyone else. That's why anyone in a hopeless situation should give him a call. There's no one quite like him.' Mr Robson is right. And surely that makes this reclusive monk one of the more unusual detectives in England.

Give him a call? thought Anselm in disbelief. *I'm not free to do anything.* He appraised his brother monk, seeking sympathy and a recognition that things had got out of hand.

'C'mon, Bede, this makes me into something I'm not.'

'Undeniably.'

'Let's put it where it belongs.'

'Okay.'

'In the bin.'

'Nope.' Bede rose and carefully folded up the paper. 'No can do,' he said, locking it beneath one chunky arm. 'This is history. My job is to preserve it for the instruction of future generations. A cautionary tale, perhaps.'

'I'm not sure I like you, frankly,' whispered Anselm. 'I do my best, you know, for the sake of the Kingdom, but I've always thought there's something . . . *Vichy* about you. You're an ally of dark powers. Just wait till *your* name appears in print.'

'That day will never dawn.' The archivist had reached the door. He turned and gave the newspaper a reproving slap with the back of his hand. 'Like most of us at Larkwood, I keep out of the public eye. It's called being a monk.'

Anselm stared out of the window. He could see fresh green tree-tops behind the blue slate of Saint Hildegard's where the apples were pressed and the mash recycled into a hideous chutney reserved for communal consumption. Bells rang, punctuating moments of importance, but Anselm didn't move. His mind meandered through remembered conversations. He picked his way over the rubble of another life, listening intently to guarded disclosures. At one point he groaned out loud, wryly noting the curious symmetry between his former life as a barrister and his present existence as a monk: so much of what he'd been told lay protected by a solemn promise of confidentiality. He could never repeat anything he'd heard until it was already public knowledge; he couldn't voice any previous suspicions until they'd been openly confirmed. His role as a listener was a kind of prison, shared with the person who'd sought his counsel. After an hour or so, he left the library and went to his cell. He had letters to write, beginning with a few ill-chosen words for Roddy Kemble and ending up with a salvo to the editor of the *Sunday Times* to the effect that the hidden life is best left hidden.

2

The first letter arrived for Anselm's attention on Tuesday morning. Three more came on Wednesday. Eight on Thursday. Twenty-six on Friday. By the following Monday, Sylvester – Larkwood's frail Doorkeeper – had been obliged to fill an old shoebox, obtained for that purpose and stored in the nearby mail room. He glowered at Anselm when he appeared, all sheepish, to collect the morning's intake.

'I've got better things to do than heave that lot around.'

'I didn't write them, Lantern Bearer; I merely receive them.'

'I can't hold the fort and fool around in reserve. There are external lines, internal lines, buttons and switches. What am I to do if one of the phones rings?'

'What you normally do, with that same, touching patience.'

Sylvester sniffed, nodding at a vacant chair. Larkwood's receptionist was one of the community's founding fathers, a thatcher who'd helped restore the ruin donated to a group of winsome ascetics after the Great War. The oral tradition regarding his contribution to the English Gilbertine revival was unequivocal: he'd talked twice as much as he'd thatched. The written account was mercifully threadbare, largely because Bede hadn't yet turned up with his files and folders.

'No one writes to me any more,' he mooned.

'Why's that?'

'Pushing daisies, the lot of 'em.'

'Too busy, I suppose.'

'Mmmm.'

Anselm took the shoebox.

'You're the last of your kind,' he said, sincerely. 'A scout among cubs.'

Like Merlin, Sylvester youthened with age. It was impossible to judge his years. His flimsy hair was gossamer white, his bones protruding and somehow soft.

'What do they all want, anyway?' The old man peered at the sealed envelopes with the same curiosity that sent him on tiptoe to any closed door.

'Help I can't give,' replied Anselm, wondering if today's requests would be any different. 'So far, I've been asked to find a cat, contact the dead, tackle the Chinese on Tibet . . . you wouldn't believe the range of things that blight peoples' lives. Thanks to a throwaway line in that article, the friendless and cornered think I'm some kind of magician. A link between earth and heaven. What can I do?'

'Go to the Prior.'

'Why?'

'I just remembered. He wants to see you. And don't forget Baden-Powell: "Be prepared." He's got the Moses-eye.'

Which was Sylvester's way of saying the Prior had that sharp look of vigilance that appeared when he feared someone might go astray: in the instant case – Anselm surmised – through a venture into self-engendered public acclaim.

'I've been waiting for this,' muttered Anselm, rising. 'He thinks I've had a hand in that blasted article. He thinks I might take it seriously . . . that I might even dance around my own image and likeness. I'd better explain.'

Anselm set off for the Prior's study. When he reached the arched door to the cloister, he swung around to face the old scout: 'If I'm not back in half an hour send out Peewee Patrol.'

During a moment of shared reflection the Prior had once declared that Anselm would always be freed from his monastic routine to help people who'd fallen between the cracks on the pavement to justice. The promise was, however, grounded upon three unspoken principles. First, an element of secrecy, in that Anselm was expected to work behind the scenes and without public acknowledgement; second, any such release would be the exception rather than the rule; and third, the kind of case he'd be allowed to accept belonged to a limited class: grave matters that touched upon the community or, by extension, people known to it. Such conditions kept Anselm firmly lodged in the cloister rather than the world. It did not take a Desert Father to recognise that the *Sunday Times* article had offended the first of these principles. Anselm had become a household name, if only for Sunday morning, but that was bad enough. The Moses-eye had grown increasingly troubled throughout the week following publication and Anselm, drawing up a chair, knew exactly what the Prior was going to say.

'I tried to put him off,' began Anselm. 'It's the last thing I expected to happen, but you can't stop these people. They've got to find something to fill out the paper. They chose my past.'

The Prior, lodged behind his desk, adjusted round, cheap glasses. They were almost alone. To one side stood a headless statue that had been unearthed by a plough in Saint Leonard's Field. Old parts of monastic history were forever turning up like this – smashed decoration, sections of pillars, capitals: the waste of a once violent, reforming zeal. The figure seemed to watch with a patience acquired over centuries.

'And now I'm receiving letters from people who need a solicitor, the police or a doctor,' continued Anselm. 'They're from decent folk who think I can do something these others can't. And, of course, it's just not possible. I appreciate that. It's not my place in life. It's not Larkwood's, either. I'll be telling them all that they need to understand the limits of—'

'A letter came for me, too,' interjected the Prior, the Glasgow grain shining through the Suffolk sheen. He held up an envelope. 'They can't go to a solicitor. They can't call the police. It's too late for a doctor. They think you can help them. I understand why. I'm minded to agree.'

Anselm took a mental step backwards.

'You're not vexed about the article?'

'No.'

'The attention it's attracted?'

'No.'

Anselm lifted the shoebox into view. 'The requests for help?'

'No, though Tibet will have to wait.'

The Prior pushed back his chair and walked to a window overlooking the cloister Garth. His voice was uncharacteristically ponderous, as if he were speaking to the generations of monks who'd come and gone, shuffling beneath the arches down below. Anselm listened, like Sylvester at a door.

'I've been brooding on something I'd never thought possible,' said the Prior. 'It's about the very identity of this monastery. Larkwood doesn't exist for itself or any number of pilgrims. We provide a place where anyone at all can look clearly – at themselves and the circumstances they've left behind. They discover a kind of flickering light.' He paused significantly. 'There are many who might never come here. I'd like you to take that flame beyond the enclosure wall.'

Anselm sensed the Prior had much more to say; that he'd been turning over the mulch in his mind and come to a decision with implications beyond the request in the letter on his desk. Anselm listened with subdued anticipation.

'There comes a time in a monk's life, Anselm, when he can go back to the world he left while somehow remaining apart and different. He's travelled that most difficult of journeys. He's become something of a recollected man, a sort of birdwatcher attuned to the mysterious forest of the human heart. He returns to the familiar as a kind of stranger; an outsider within the ordinary. He can enter deeply into what he once knew, only deeper than before. He can see things to which he was once blind. He can hear things to which he was once deaf. And, most importantly of all, he hasn't the faintest idea that he hears or sees anything in a way different to before. He just finds himself bemused in a place he once recognised without complication. But it's that . . . *being puzzled* which permits him to probe the hearts of men and women, seeing what they would hide, even from themselves. He has an eye for the bright and the dark, for he has seen the light and shadows in himself, and not turned away.'

This was considerably worse than the *Sunday Times*. Anselm shifted uncomfortably. Something didn't feel quite right.

'Of course,' continued the Prior, 'this is a journey you have yet to travel.'

Anselm made a thin smile.

'You've only just taken to the road. But I've been persuaded that in certain circumstances, it is right to learn en route.' The

Prior turned from the window, smiling indulgence and the natural worry of a father. 'You've always been a lawyer in a habit; a man of two worlds. It's only right that you should serve them both, and sooner rather than later. So I've decided to formalise things, for the benefit of people who'd never come to Larkwood but would turn to you when all other doors are closed. Henceforth you are at liberty to accept cases from anyone who contacts you, subject, of course, to the exercise of sound judgement. I'll try and help in that regard. You must always give priority to those on the margins of hope.'

Anselm didn't know what to say. For a man bound to monastic life the decision was momentous with significant repercussions. The exception had just become the rule.

The Prior returned to his desk and took the letter out of its envelope. 'Do you need time to reflect upon what I'm asking or a shove to get on with it?'

'Is there a middle road? Something vague and indecisive?'

'No.'

'Fair enough. I'll take the shove.'

3

Without further ceremony, the Prior handed the letter to Anselm. There was no address, no name and no date. The author had used a typewriter. Anselm angled the page to the light, reading under his breath.

Father Prior,
I read with interest the article about Father Anselm. As it happens, I've followed his career wondering, on occasion, why his services were not more widely available and why his clients were only friends or those

with a special connection to his past. What of those who are strangers to your world? People on the margins of hope? People with nowhere to turn because no one would believe them? Are they to be forgotten?

'That's an interesting point,' observed Anselm. He'd also noted that phrase about hope; it had burned Larkwood's protector.
'I know,' replied the Prior, still feeling the heat.
Anselm continued to read:

I write on behalf of Jennifer Henderson. When she was alive she made no cry for help because she didn't see the danger. Neither did I. Nor did anyone else. We didn't read the signs properly. Now it's too late. She's dead. There's no point in going to the police because there's no evidence, and without evidence there's no suspect and no crime. So I come to you speaking for her. Find out what really happened on the day she died. Her husband knows only too well. That's why he snapped in Manchester and ended up in prison. You've got two weeks before he's released. What does the future hold? It's obvious: he'll snap again. Only this time he might just take his own life. Why not help him, for the sake of the living and the dead? Why not extend Larkwood's reach?

That was the end of the letter. Anselm turned the page, looking in vain for some stray clue to the writer's identity.
'You know who the husband is, don't you?' he asked. 'It's Peter Henderson, the philosopher from Cambridge, the celebrity commentator. Always on television and the radio. *Question Time* and the *Moral Maze*. Did you follow the case?'
'No more than anyone else.'
Anselm thought for a while.

21

'I met her once . . . years back. She was in hospital having some routine tests. I was filling in for the chaplain. I told you when I got back . . . don't you remember?'

The Prior didn't. But that was no great surprise. His memory was strangely selective, favouring the details that everyone else tended to forget. Anselm made a forgiving sigh and then read the letter once more. Looking up, he said:

'Is this why you've extended my mandate? This plea on behalf of the forgotten?'

'Yes.' The Prior gave a self-reproving laugh. 'It was Mr Robson who first set me thinking, when he spoke out for the hopeless. And then I received the letter . . . from someone I've never met and who, like Mr Robson, doesn't know our ways. But from that place of unknowing they raised the most important question of all: the scope and nature of Larkwood's reach. Isn't it strange: if you'd asked me yourself to be released without restriction, I'd have said, "No". It took a vindicated man and a stranger to show me that the time for change was upon us both.'

There was nothing more to be said. The decision had been made. Anselm had already embarked upon a changed life. As if nudged to start work, he examined the author's phrasing.

'This is an allegation of murder.'

'It is.'

'Only the word itself isn't used.'

'It isn't.'

'Which means they're not sure.'

'Yet sure enough to write in the first place.'

'They suspect Peter Henderson but they don't accuse him. Which means they're not sure of that either. They're a disturbed bystander who can't make sense of a woman's dying. They can't accept that no one's to blame.'

They were quiet, watching each other, and then the Prior leaned on his desk, fingers knitted.

'Normally, when it comes to legal exegesis, I'd defer to your better judgement.'

'I make no lofty claims—'

'But on this occasion I sense you've latched onto what is important, while missing the *importance* of it, do you get my meaning?'

The Prior made it sound like a surprising achievement.

'Not really.'

'Look at the wording again,' said the Prior. 'They may well be a confused bystander, they're also a sure voice, inhibited by an understanding and respect for the law. They don't accuse anyone, because they don't have the evidence. They don't allege murder, because they know it can't be proved. The importance of the matter is this: they still *know* that Peter Henderson killed his wife. They want that rare justice which lies "beyond the reach of the law". This is why they've come to you. No one else would even try to help them. Perhaps no one else could.'

Anselm wasn't so sure the Prior's reading of the text was entirely different from his own. The Prior had identified a note of certainty, Anselm an agonised hesitation. They were separated by a hair. On either understanding the author wanted Anselm to prove that Jennifer Henderson had been murdered: whether that end was achieved by confirming a belief or dispelling a doubt hardly mattered. Anselm's mind began to wander:

'They're holding something back.'

'What?'

Anselm had seen the lie. 'They knew Jennifer Henderson was in danger but they didn't take it seriously. They failed to act. And now they live with a secret guilt. They want it purged.'

Anselm thought of his shoebox and the little heap of despair, mischief and last-ditch pleading. Only someone with nothing to lose would write to a Monk who'd Left it All for a Life of Crime. In there, folded neatly, were serious attempts to hit back at the sadness and tragedy of life; attempts to bring someone on side who might make a difference. Anselm felt curiously light-headed. Through an anonymous letter, Larkwood's Prior had heard those joined voices.

'There's more than guilt here,' corrected the Prior. 'There's pity, too. They might speak for Jennifer but they also care for Peter. They've seen the signs, and understood them. Now he's a danger to himself.'

'And this time they've decided to act,' agreed Anselm.

'Exactly. So get started immediately. On their behalf. You might want to thank Mr Robson first. He helped me to understand how I might best direct your talents.'

Anselm said he would, colouring slightly – for praise and indebtedness made him restive – and then, with a tentative exploratory voice he ventured a novel idea:

'Normally I operate alone, but on this one occasion do you mind if I bring Mr Robson on board as an assistant . . . if he's willing? In the circumstances, I think it would be more than fitting.'

The Prior approved, but when Anselm had reached the door on his way out, he called him back.

'Bring Larkwood's flame into this family's hidden tragedy . . . only be careful.' He'd been arrested by an afterthought of great importance, something he should have seen earlier and mentioned at the outset, only, being a Gilbertine, he'd come to it by accident and at the last moment. 'Bring the flame but take care not to burn yourself or anyone else. We view this troubled world by a wavering light. Don't impose the truths you think you see.'

Bemused by this obscure warning, Anselm straddled his scooter thinking of Peter Fonda in *Easy Rider*, the outlaw who joined up with another fugitive to discover the taste of freedom. On reaching the public library in Sudbury he consulted the newspaper archives and did some adroit Googling, research that generated a handful of photocopies and print-outs that he placed in his leather satchel, a childhood relic more proper, now, to the discerning bohemian than a monk who wrestled with crime. Wanting an appreciation of the wider issues, he glanced at an entry in the *Encyclopaedia Britannica*, only to confirm his initial expectations: the ancient Greeks had thought of everything (though – and this was new to Anselm – the first suggestion of a code of conduct for health professionals was to be found in Egyptian papyri of the second millennium BC).

Back at Larkwood, brooding on the healing craft, Anselm mumbled his way through Vespers, afterwards pushing food around his plate in the refectory while Father Jerome read out some twelfth-century text entitled 'Awareness in the Heart'. Unfortunately, Anselm was so taken by the title that he couldn't follow the reading itself. The very notion intrigued him, suggesting as it did a kind of insight parallel to scientific enquiry. The heart as the seat of conscience. He was still turning over the phrase throughout Compline, during Lauds the next morning, and while he walked along the west bank of the Lark, his feet wet with dew. Two miles upstream he saw the pleasure wherry and slowed, wondering how best to express himself. If Anselm was going to start a new life, he wanted a clean slate.

4

The *Jelly Roll* was moored to a wooden landing stage. A black canvas sail hung lowered, leaving the stout single mast among taut cables, their clean lines sharp against the morning sky. The hull was black with a white nose, the long cabin section a rich cedar brown. Anselm came on board by a companionway that divided the living quarters in two, descending the few steps to a door that had been left ajar. He pushed it gingerly and entered.

The interior was beamed and low. Drawers and lockers separated cushioned benches, all built into the surrounding wood panelling. Brass instruments of navigation, almost certainly of no use on the Lark, adorned one wall. At the far end a row of copper pans hung above a devastated kitchen. Sunlight broke through small round windows, igniting months of dust.

'Good morning, Mitch,' said Anselm, when he'd reached the middle of the cabin. 'It's been a long time since we talked about right and wrong. In those days it was about notes. And bending old rules. Bop and be-bop. You favoured them. I didn't. Shall we delve a little deeper, now?'

He was talking to the figure slumped in an armchair. A silver trumpet lay on a nearby table, along with a bottle of water and a torn packet of aspirin. Mitch had come back late from his club, it seemed. Too tired to get undressed, he'd blown himself to sleep. Anselm looked around. There were no signs of wealth. No hint of ill-gotten gains. The room glowed with old wood, crafted when people still went to work by foot; when shire horses nodded along the churned-up Suffolk lanes; that simpler, ruder time.

'C'mon Mitch,' said Anselm, loudly. He gave the sleeping man a nudge with his foot. 'It's time to wake up and face the day.'

The two men eyed one another across the years.

'I never thought I'd see you again,' said Mitch, with his soft Northumberland lilt.

He'd showered while Anselm made strong coffee. Seated now at a table, they found themselves evoking other, less fraught meetings, held long ago in Anselm's chambers. They'd talked about Earl Hines over damning evidence: heaps of paper demonstrating slow but sure enrichment. The first time around, forensic accountants had calculated that £113,268.32 had disappeared in settlement of small, bogus claims. No one had signed them off. Though one of a team, only Mitch Robson had worked on each of the cases in question.

'I read about you in the *Sunday Times*,' replied Anselm. 'I thought we might tie up a few loose ends.'

After the second trial, concerning the alleged theft of £174,189.84 from a previous employer (by identical means), Anselm had never set foot in Mitch's club again. He'd let their friendship whither without saying why. Professional etiquette had prevented him from speaking plainly, as friends must. He couldn't say that he'd blushed at the improbability of his closing speech, when he'd twice blamed missing secretaries and the honourable dead (juries like to think the upright had merely concealed their corruption). He couldn't say that he'd never accepted either of the rogue verdicts.

'Where do you want to start?' teased Mitch. 'Where we left off?'

'No. To put our parting in context, I need to go back to the beginning . . . to when I first came to the bar. Will you bear with me?'

Mitch gave a willing nod. He had the worn look of a man who lives by nights, not altogether caring what happens during the day. His hair was silvered, cropped close to the scalp. He was dressed in black: a rumpled T-shirt and faded jeans: the uniform of musicians and vendors of *Socialist Worker*, devoted acolytes of art and protest. His face was lined from too much frowning. All those high notes, fancied Anselm. Or maybe it was the worry. He was pale, too, from only working when the sun went down. Brown eyes flickered with curiosity. Anselm said:

'When I first entered a courtroom, I thought that winning a case was all that mattered. If I lost, well, it was just hard luck; or maybe I just needed to learn a few clever moves . . . you know, the tricks of the trade. It took me years to realise that winning had nothing to do with finding the truth. More often than not I went home pretty sure the jury had got it right. But sometimes, especially during a winning streak – like with you – I was convinced they'd got it wrong. And these were golden moments, because I'd pulled off the impossible. I'd persuaded twelve decent people that in the exceptional circumstances of this most difficult case, two and two make five. I'd done nothing wrong. I'd followed the rules. But I'd ended up as part of the crime. I went home with a taste of ash in the mouth. This wasn't why I'd come to the Bar. Not to win a game. Do you understand what I'm trying to say?'

Mitch gave the matter careful consideration. Then he reached for his trumpet and played an Ellington refrain, *forte*: 'I'm Beginning to See the Light'. He was a cautious man. Even now he wasn't going to incriminate himself.

Anselm continued:

'You, Mitch, belong to the ash. That's why our friendship ended. But I've come back because I've selected you for a special role. On the scale of criminals I helped along the way, you are roughly in the middle. You're an average player. And that makes you a fitting symbol for the rest . . . for all the people who walked free but should have been sent to Wormwood Scrubs.'

Mitch couldn't think of a rejoinder so he just worked the valves. In a way, it was a gesture of appreciation; and sarcasm.

'I've got a proposal for you,' said Anselm. 'But first I need to ask a few questions, starting with the obvious. Why steal the money? You needed nothing.'

'There Was Nobody Looking'. Mitch had blown another Ellington line, *pianissimo* this time.

Anselm persevered: 'The police couldn't trace a penny. Will you tell me where it all went?'

Mitch gave a shrug and played 'Undecided', a Dixieland standard, but Anselm cut the tune short: 'Have you gone clean? I need to know for sure. No fooling around this time.'

Mitch thought about the question long enough to persuade Anselm that he was being serious, and then he began 'Keepin' Out of Mischief Now'.

It was one of Fats Waller's funny promises. And an appropriate note to end on.

Broadly speaking, these guarded 'replies' had completely exceeded Anselm's expectations. He'd foreseen a spat and some trading of insults. But instead, Mitch had cut to the chase with a candid confession making sure, however, that it could never be used to initiate a fresh prosecution. He'd been honest, retracting with the Gilbertine the lies he'd told the lawyer. As if acknowledging that the first half of this peculiar conference was over, Mitch put his trumpet down and said:

'You mentioned a proposal.'

The sun had climbed high, moving shadows round the boat as if to rearrange the furniture of light and dark. Something important had changed. Nothing looked the same. Mitch swallowed a couple of aspirin and finished off the bottled water. He was smiling faintly. A kind of forgiveness had come to his pleasure wherry. And he was important now. He was a symbol.

'Up until this morning I was a beekeeper,' explained Anselm. 'I also picked apples, washed bottles, and waxed floors. On occasion, I was released to help those who'd come unstuck with the law. This arrangement has come to an end. You are partly responsible.'

'Me?'

'Yes. You invited readers of the *Sunday Times* to contact me should they find themselves in a hopeless situation. That's a large category of people and a surprising number took up the offer. My Prior thanks you. He's also asked me to respond in the name of the community. For me, it's a new beginning. And like everyone who starts a new venture, I want to clean up the past. I'd like you to help me.'

'Me?'

'Yes.'

'As a symbol?' Mitch was amused, failing to appreciate that Anselm wasn't even remotely smiling.

'At Larkwood we use lots of symbols and rituals to express

things that can't be put into words. We also use them to enact important changes in direction.'

'You have something in mind?'

'I do.'

'And?'

'I want you to help me solve a case, just one example of the need for justice. I'd like you to contribute something to the system you flouted. Because whether you like it or not – remorse and forgiveness aside – the law is our only means of restoring order to a disordered world.'

Mitch was no longer flippant. The creases in his pale face, the lines of worry or concentration, had deepened.

'There's an element of reparation, too,' persisted Anselm. 'Call it a fine, but I want you to meet any expenses. And since you twice before took me for a ride, I'd like you to provide the transport. We'll use the boat as our office. That's everything. If you think about it, I'm not asking much.'

'And what's in it for you?'

'Like I said, you represent all the others, from the greatest to the least. All the liars, thieves and killers. Back then, I could only offer a route off the charge, not knowing whether it should stick or not. Now, with your help I want to uncover the truth regardless of what anyone says and whatever the cost or implications. Working with a former client who should have been convicted will be my one small act of reparation. It's not much either, but it's something. That's what symbols are for.'

When the silence grew heavy, Mitch went to the kitchen and made more coffee. He was quiet and absorbed, mulling over Anselm's outlandish proposal; reviewing their friendship, the sudden break, and now this surprising offer of reconciliation. Before each jury the greater part of Anselm's speeches had dwelled upon good things, things known to be true: Mitch's blameless past, a jazz club that raised thousands for charity, the history of glowing commendations from his bewildered employers. All that

good faith had survived. It was still there. The only shadows –
back then and now – had fallen from the two indictments. When
Mitch came back to the table Anselm spoke again. There was a
need for absolute candour:

'I'll be honest, Mitch, I'm hoping that once you become
involved in the search for justice, once you've seen how we need
rules to protect and save, you'll answer for yourself without hiding
behind a trumpet. I'm hoping you'll tell me why you stole the
money and what you did with it. I'm hoping you'll hand yourself in and face the consequences.'

'As a symbol for all the others?'

'No. For your own good.'

The grooves along Mitch's forehead buckled and Anselm
wondered if there wasn't an element of bitterness in those crooked
shadows; a deep and abiding disillusionment. Mitch's brown eyes
rose inexorably, settling onto Anselm with a kind of livid pity. Or
was it frustration? An exasperation with do-gooders who don't
understand their own rhetoric? He seemed to accept a challenge:
there was tension in his voice, born of the longing to be proved
right:

'Maybe at the end of this expedition into joint atonement, you,
too, will learn something about law and the complexity of life,
and how rules don't always protect or save.'

Anselm held Mitch's gaze: there was fire in there, and resistance.
The spat and the insults weren't that far away after all. Anselm
said, lightly:

'I take it you accept my offer?'

Mitch's anger subsided. He slumped back in his chair, regarding
Anselm with an old familiarity. They'd spoken like this about bop
and be-bop. They'd said hard things to one another; unforgivable
things. And then Mitch had got charged. They'd spoken politely
about the evidence, never once exchanging a cross word.
Everything had gone smoothly. Smiling mischievously, he reached
for his trumpet. Assenting to Anselm's proposal – and looking

forward to the rewards of conversion — he closed his eyes and belted out 'Oh When the Saints'.

Anselm was jealous. He coveted the wherry and its place on the Lark. He'd always been drawn to rivers and the sea and their shared element, water. It was cleansing but dangerous, sure but unpredictable. At night, listening to 'Sailing By', he rode imagined waves, feeling the swell of the deep, wondering what tomorrow might hold. Humming the tune, he followed Mitch on deck to a bench on the prow. The morning glow had vanished off the fields. Cattle tugged at the grass. Fish snapped into the air.

'I have a case already,' said Anselm, watching ringlets spread and vanish. 'There's no evidence of any crime. Finding out what happened will require both grit and imagination.'

'What do you expect from me?' said Mitch, uncertainly. 'I'm just a musician.'

'And I'm just a monk. Perhaps you could improvise with the facts.'

They watched the cows slowly eating, sticking close together as if they might get lost.

'But you're not just a monk, are you?' qualified Mitch, to distinguish the conductor from the player. 'You're a detective.'

This time Anselm was the one with a lined brow, shadows cut into skin that had once been smooth and free from cares. He almost felt the Lark lift with anticipation.

'I'm not sure the term meets the demands of the moment,' he said, rather quietly. 'Think more a solver of puzzles. A troubled explorer in a wilderness of moral problems.'

5

Michael moved resolutely down the stairs of the guesthouse, past the dining room and out through the front door. A cold wind struck his face like a wave on a desolate beach. Orange-rimmed cloud, violet to black, smeared the vast expanse above the complaining sea. Michael didn't linger. He had a job to do. He'd picked his target during the previous days' dawdling, after confirming that the corner shop was still there, flanked by a pub and lighthouse. He'd checked the opening and closing times. He'd found out when the streets were deserted. The informer had told Michael to practise.

Look into the eyes of someone you love. Turn out the light with a flick of a switch.

Someone you love. There was no one to hand. But Michael had a loved memory of a loved place. A tiny shop two hundred yards from the shore. He'd first gone there with Jenny when she was a child . . . after he'd come back from Northern Ireland. A sign on the window had warned customers that the proprietor used the old imperial weights and measures. Pounds and ounces. A Union Jack had been drawn on the bottom as if it were the seal of Her Majesty. There'd been two counters inside, one for children, the other for adults. To the left, jars of sweets containing Liquorice Allsorts, sherbet lemons, wine gums and sticks of bright pink rock. To the right, carved pipes, pouches of tobacco, cigars, cigarettes and matches. In the middle, a kindly man with a wide smile, always wondering which way to go. Michael had smoked in those days. A pipe. To give age to his permanently young appearance. Jenny would drag him along the pavement, one step ahead, her mind on the large jars of many colours. Even in those days she'd held his hand very tight, as though fearful something bad might happen if she let go. They'd enter the shop, Jenny facing the tobacco, Michael facing the sweets. The kindly man, hair short, sleeves rolled up, all homely in his long brown apron, would hesitate, not knowing who'd speak first. He seemed to be teetering, his face alight with expectation.

'A box of matches, please,' Jenny would say.

Followed by Michael: 'And two ounces of jelly babies.'

He'd expected crossfire . . . Jenny right to left, Michael left to right, but they'd tricked him. When he got used to the pattern, they'd swap it round, just to knock him off balance. Just when he was sure the child at the tobacco counter wanted matches for her father, she'd ask for bon bons, sending him the other way, like a goalkeeper wrong-footed in a penalty shoot-out.

'Don't let go, Daddy,' she'd say, as they stepped into the street, failing to appreciate that she, now, was trapped by a choice between two directions: the security of her father's touch or having a free hand to dip into the paper bag. Back then, the choices had been so much simpler. It hadn't mattered if you got it wrong.

The shop was still there. The kindly man was now a kindly old man. He stood in the doorway watching life go by. There were trestles on either side of the entrance holding crates of fruit and vegetables. The windows were clean, the frames painted white. Inside – Michael had only glanced while scouting from the other side of the road – there was only one counter. The tobacco side had gone. It was all sweets now . . . but still in those big jars. The shelves along the sides and the back were crammed with them. Jenny would have loved it.

You have to be calm.

Michael rounded the corner. The sea lay behind him, restive, advancing, withdrawing, endlessly rolling forward and sweeping back. Ahead were the lighthouse and the pub. Dwarfed and open for business stood Number Nine St George's Green. The locals had bought their fruit and veg for lunch. The kids were now at school. The streets were empty. The old man had just stepped back inside, limping slightly, an empty crate between his hands. He was still wearing a brown apron.

His eyes are full of surprise . . . you can see it, just before you kill him. It's the look of a newborn . . . and you can't hesitate. You turn out his light.

The gun chafed against Michael's spine. The flush of sweat on his brow had dried in the cold morning air. His heart was beating hard, hitting out at the ribs, wanting to escape and pump life into another less tortured body. Michael crossed the road, looking right and left. The old man was bending down, placing the crate beside the wall. In seconds he'd stand upright, place a hand on his back and slowly turn around – Michael had watched him, he knew the man's routine – and Michael had to get there at the moment he turned. Moving with determination – not speed or nervous haste but with a cold purpose – he stepped onto the pavement, one hand slipping through his open overcoat and reaching behind his jacket. His fingers slid into position just as the old man looked over his shoulder. He didn't show a hint of recognition. Just a faint glow of surprise.

6

'Does the name Peter Henderson mean anything to you?' asked Anselm, documents in hand. 'Philosopher. A regular on the *Moral Maze*. Radio 4.'

'Nope.'

'He was once billed as a new voice in search of a new morality: someone trying to find a modern classification of right and wrong that doesn't appeal to the failed systems of the past. That's what he said in the *Radio Times*, anyway.'

'I like him already.'

'You're not alone.' Anselm held up a photograph taken from a university website. 'He's based at University Campus Suffolk where he holds a Chair in Contemporary Ethics. Prior to that he was at Cambridge. Speaks with a refined vocabulary that often hides the unsettling implications of his argument.'

And when it didn't, he wouldn't flinch from politely desecrating people's sensibilities. Anselm had once heard him outline the circumstances in which the torture of children may well be a moral obligation. He'd brought the same challenging candour to a number of other questions . . . political assassination, animal rights, global warming, terrorism ...

'He's a sort of Jack Bauer of the Academy,' postulated Anselm. 'Only he doesn't shout and shoot. He just quietly thinks. But the conventionally minded are scared rigid of what he might say next.'

'Jack Bauer? You've seen *24*? In a monastery?'

'No. Someone told me about him.'

Anselm walked to a cork noticeboard on the wall and pinned up the photograph. Stepping back, he appraised the man's features: a high, rounded forehead; black, unruly hair; dark stubble; hungry eyes; a confident smile.

'I recognise the face,' said Mitch. 'I don't remember why.'

'Maybe because he ended up on the front page for his behaviour rather than his ideas.'

Anselm remained standing. He'd mastered his brief. The facts were straightforward.

'A few months back he was in the BBC studio in Manchester for a recording of the *Moral Maze*. One of the other panellists quipped that making an appeal to Peter Henderson's conscience was rather like searching for Atlantis. It might not exist. Ordinarily, the soft-voiced philosopher would have hit back with some cleverness. But not this time. He stormed out of the studio.'

Fate or chance – explained Anselm, authoritatively – has a way of goading the man who's ready to fall. Gives him an otherwise innocent nudge to push him over the edge. It can be anything . . . a pencil that snaps on touching the paper . . . a diligent traffic warden . . . a tube of toothpaste without a cap. In Peter Henderson's case, a few of them lined up to bring him crashing down, acting in concert with a sort of malicious delight.

'He was striding towards the station when his passage was blocked by council workmen replacing some brick paving outside a baker's shop. He couldn't get round immediately because the remaining section of pavement was occupied by a pushchair and a young mother who'd dropped her shopping bag, spilling the contents everywhere. On the road itself an articulated vehicle was making a delivery. So he had to wait. According to one of the lads with a shovel, Peter Henderson swore violently and then his eye latched onto a boy who was watching him from inside the baker's. Two customers testified that a staring contest ensued with Peter Henderson glaring through the window in an aggressive and threatening manner. If only the HGV had pulled away at that moment. If only the young mother had parked her pushchair just a little to one side. Peter Henderson would have walked to the station and taken the next train to London. As it is, he snapped and was taken, in due course, to the Crown Court.'

Anselm came over to the table and picked up a newspaper report.

'He was brought before Her Honour Judge Moreland. A friend of mine, as it happens. Recently appointed.'

Anselm read out her judgement in the kind of voice he might have used if he'd ever been elevated to the bench – slow, ponderous and vaguely sad:

You are a well-known figure. You stand high in the
public eye. You have – by fortune, talent and ambition
– assumed a position of considerable importance in the
civic life of this country. Even an eleven-year-old boy
recognised your face. You have made moral problems
and their analysis your special territory. You have not
flinched to make stirring judgements about the actions
of politicians and churchmen. You have sentenced many
to ignominy, arguing that example is the touchstone of
integrity. For this reason your own conduct falls under
special scrutiny. Everyone understands the frustration
caused by street works, spilled shopping and snagged
traffic. We can all imagine that being recognised in the
street might not be a welcome adjunct to celebrity.
Everyone in this courtroom cannot but fail to have
profound sympathy for your personal circumstances.
But your response to these trials was nothing short of
astonishing. You picked up a brick. You hurled it through
a window at a child who dared to face you down. You
broke his jaw and collar bone. You might have killed
him. You traumatised all those present. You damaged
property. You have, in passing, shattered your reputation.

Mitch thought for a moment while Anselm placed the report
back on the table. 'Is this the new right and wrong?'

'I doubt it. He asked for no mercy.'

'Bloody right. Didn't deserve any.'

'He did, actually. But to understand why, you have to go back
to the days when he'd just begun to make a name for himself.
Before he'd found notoriety.'

Anselm picked up another photograph, copied from a newspaper
article.

'This is Jennifer,' he said, pinning the picture beside that of her
husband.

She had that alarming vulnerability captured by Degas. The same athleticism. A certain tiredness linked to fabulous energy. Her facial bones were clean cut, her eye sockets deep and dark. Anyone sitting in the back row couldn't fail to notice her.

'Started out as a dancer with the Royal Ballet but packed it all in just after she'd won her place. A career cut short. According to some, a Fonteyn in the making.'

'Why stop?'

'Motherhood. Shortly after meeting Peter she had a boy, Timothy. Never performed with the company again. Stayed at home looking after her son while Peter's star rose higher in the firmament. School runs and the like until, ten years later, she opened a dancing school in Sudbury – nothing high powered, just something for the kids to do after school and at the weekends, but serious enough to pull in a brass band for a summer show. We'll never know Jennifer's true ambitions because things didn't work out as planned. She put herself on the programme to give the mums and dads an idea of where the hard work might lead if Jack and Jill ever took dancing seriously.'

'What happened?'

Anselm became ponderous. 'It had been a long time since Jennifer had captivated an audience. Maybe she got carried away. Maybe she'd failed to measure her steps. Whatever the reason, she fell off the stage and broke her back.'

'And?'

'She was paralysed from the chest down.'

Mitch didn't respond, but the control revealed something deep and compassionate, the knowledge of pain that brings everyone together when a tragedy occurs.

'Aged twenty-nine,' said Anselm, as if Mitch had asked a question.

Peter – by now a celebrity – abandoned his media commitments and took an open-ended sabbatical from teaching. He became her nurse, on hand by day and night.

'I imagine both of them thought that things wouldn't get any worse,' surmised Anselm.

'They couldn't.'

'Well, they could and they did. After eighteen months or so, Jennifer was diagnosed with bowel cancer.'

'*Cancer?*'

'Advanced and terminal. Five months later, she died at home . . . on her birthday.'

Mitch grimaced. 'So that's why he snapped.'

'So it seems, though – curiously – not straight away. He returned to the classroom and the studio and then, two years later and out of the blue, he almost killed a boy who wouldn't look in the other direction.'

Her Honour Judge Moreland had ordered the preparation of pre-sentence reports from a psychologist, a doctor and a social worker. All of them maintained that the only explanation for the defendant's behaviour was the tragedy that had engulfed both him and his family. But Peter Henderson himself had refused to endorse the conclusion. He'd refused to cooperate with the court's attempt to find a meaning for his outburst of violence, maintaining a studied silence on all questions of importance. He'd simply wanted to be sentenced for what he'd done without reference to any mitigating factors.

'His most vocal supporter was Emma Goodwin, Jennifer's mother,' said Anselm, selecting a cutting from a veterinary surgeon's website. 'She spoke to the experts and eventually to the court. She appeared frequently on the television, in the papers and on the radio. Sympathetic to the victim, she nonetheless stressed the extraordinary pressures to which Peter had been subjected, empha-sising his contribution to the thinking life of the country, his dedication to her daughter and his devotion to their only child.'

Having added the portrait to the others on the noticeboard, Anselm paused to consider the picture. She had a sympathetic face, with the fine bones of her daughter. She had the same smooth forehead, too, and the deep-set eyes. Being imaginative, Anselm saw not an animal doctor but a choreographer, one of those artists of the human body who know how to move people around; how to get them into position, making it look completely natural. She'd been adroit with the press and the court. No doubt she'd nudged others around, too. Cutting short this interesting but irrelevant meditation, he turned to Mitch and said:

'A quieter presence was Emma's husband and Jennifer's father, Michael Goodwin. Couldn't find a decent photograph anywhere. He's always got his head down. A broken soul, I suspect. Grief's like that. Hits people in very different ways. Emma became energetic whereas Michael sank deep into sadness. The most he could do was hold his wife's hand while she spoke for Peter and pleaded for mercy.'

Mitch made another grimace. 'But he nearly killed a child.'

'Judge Moreland's observation before she sent him to prison.'

The presentation over, Anselm sat down and helped himself to cold coffee. But then, being a man who liked to put things in perspective, he said, 'There was a memorial service for Jennifer in Polstead, a pretty village near Ipswich. Do you know it? Famous for its cherries . . . Polstead Blacks.'

'No.'

'Famous, too, for the Red Barn Murder of eighteen twenty-seven.'

'Never heard of it.'

Anselm gave the soft tut of a disappointed local historian. 'A young girl eloped with her tomcat boyfriend,' he explained, patiently. 'Or so it was thought. But the stepmother – another tenacious woman; another Emma Goodwin – dreamed that the girl had been killed and buried in a grain storage bin at the rear of a barn. So the dad – a quiet molecatcher – took his spade and went to have a look, and sure enough, he found his daughter's body. The authorities tracked down the missing lover, tried him and hung him from the gallows in Bury St Edmunds. Used his skin to bind the court proceedings. Scalped him, too, and left his body to a dissecting class from Cambridge. All of which is by the by, save to say that a murder can be solved even when there's not a trace of evidence on the table. All it takes is someone who can dream about the truth.'

Mitch watched Anselm expectantly, glancing occasionally at the photographs on the board; the close family bound by fidelity and tragedy.

'And this is the case you want to solve?'

'Yes.'

'But there's no crime. It's just a really sad story.'

'That's what everyone thinks,' agreed Anselm. 'But then, thanks to you, someone wrote a letter on Jennifer's behalf, marked for my attention. Gives her side of the story. Changes your under-standing of why a man might throw a brick through a window.'

7

The Spinning Mule had once been the comfortable residence of a wool merchant. He'd run a smallish operation transporting rolled fleeces to chosen weavers along the Lark. Hence the landing stage at the end of his garden. Following the decline of textile manu-facturing, the house had passed through several hands until a couple with vision and a passion for real ale had stumped up a deposit to buy the place. They'd sold the rights over the river to Mitch, along with the mooring and an access route, providing their neighbour with a glorious location to dock his floating home. The small talk over, Mitch read the letter sent to Larkwood's Prior.

'You take this seriously?' he said, on finishing.

'I do.'

In the absence of mischief and malice, Anselm didn't think an allegation of murder could be easily ignored.

'Peter Henderson will be released next week. Between now and then I hope to find out if the accusation is anything more than fanciful.'

Mitch folded up the letter, listening carefully while Anselm continued his exposition. The view of the media and the courts was that Peter Henderson enjoyed the unqualified support of his dead wife's family. Not one of them had ever raised a word against him. When he fell to be sentenced, no friend or neighbour seized the opportunity to yell from the gallery or feed a line to the press. But someone had now broken rank.

'They belong to the inner circle,' said Anselm. 'They have the confidence to speak in Jennifer's name. They knew her well enough to say that she had no appreciation of the danger to which she was exposed. They know sufficient, with hindsight, to recognise that the risk to her life was plain to be seen. And now they're telling themselves that they should have seen it coming; that they should have done something to protect her. The implication is that Peter Henderson murdered his wife.'

They were seated at a small table in a quiet nook far from any windows. Warm light flickered on the flagstones. The walls carried prints of paintings, evocations of rural life when windmills ground local wheat into flour. Horseshoes and black implements from a farrier's yard had been fixed to the beams and stonework. Anselm pursued his point:

'You can't kill someone without the dead body answering back. There are signs left as clues for the trained eye. Sometimes they're minuscule. But they can't be removed. It's a real problem.'

'So what are you saying?'

'Someone very powerful in our society helped Peter Henderson.'

'Who?'

'A doctor.'

Mitch arched a brow. 'You mean that Peter Henderson came to a chummy arrangement with a GP to finish off his wife?'

'Just look at the implications of what we know already,' rejoined

Anselm, patiently. 'Jennifer Henderson is dead. Someone says she was murdered. If that is true, then a doctor must have written out a false death certificate attributing cancer as the sole cause. Any expression of doubt would have generated an investigation by the coroner, which would have opened the door to the police. For all I know the doctor was blackmailed, threatened or tortured according to a new morality – I really don't know. The fact is – accepting the allegation in this letter – Jennifer Henderson was buried, along with the true cause of her death. Only a doctor has that kind of power. And it saved Peter's skin. As the author of the letter says, without evidence, there's no crime; without a crime, there's no suspect.'

Mitch savoured his beer as if it was a touch too bitter. 'Doctors can be fooled, you know. There are some pretty weird herbs in an English country garden.'

'And they all leave weird signs on a body.'

Mitch didn't seem impressed, but he moved on. 'If he killed his wife, why throw the brick?'

'That's the key question. The experts only gave half the answer because they only knew half the facts.'

'You have something to add?'

'Yes. In my line of work, one gets to recognise . . . the signs . . . though, interestingly enough, you come out of it strangely unmarked.'

'Well?'

'Guilt. I'm not talking about the shame stoked up during infancy by your parents, that unhinged priest or the culture you're born into, I mean the primitive reaction to what we do; that turning in the stomach . . . it's impossible to avoid.' Anselm drank some beer. 'Peter Henderson was accused on air of having no conscience. He walked out of the studio. And then he found himself trapped. All he could do was look around. And what did he see?'

'A kid with nerve.'

'No, Mitch,' replied Anselm, confidently. 'He saw himself.'

'Come again?'

'A window is like a mirror. It is unforgiving. Peter Henderson was staring at the man who'd killed his wife. That's why he reached for the brick. He couldn't take the shattering simplicity of self-accusation.' Anselm came closer to the table. 'It's why I don't think the writer of the letter is mistaken. The allegation of murder is the only compelling explanation for Peter Henderson's behaviour. That's why he rejected any mercy from the court. He wants to pay because he knows he's guilty . . . only he can't own up. The price is too great. How do you explain yourself to your son?'

Mitch nodded thoughtfully. 'So you've all but wrapped it up, then. Two years ago Jennifer Henderson is murdered by her apparently loving husband, assisted by a compliant doctor. All you need to do is find out how and why, and that will give you the evidence, and the evidence will give you proof of the crime.'

Anselm returned the nod, noting – uncomfortably – that Mitch's summary had a slight jingle about it, as if the configuration of data had been ever so slightly predictable. The Prior seemed to appear at Anselm's shoulder, congratulating him once more on failing to appreciate why the important is important.

'Would you like me to improvise with the facts?' offered Mitch, sympathetically.

Anselm didn't. 'Please do,' he said, warmly.

Mitch picked up the letter and read it once more as if to make sure of where he was going. Then, placing it to one side, he said: 'I see the plan for a second murder.'

8

It was almost midday. Time for a pint before lunch. Only Michael had no appetite. He walked along Southwold beach close to the daisy chain of small, wooden beach huts. They were brightly coloured, the paint fresh or peeling, the aggression of the sea air seeming not to tolerate any intermediate state of decline. The wind pulled at Michael's hair and lifted the flanks of his overcoat. He was rehearsing – yet again – his encounter with the proud trader.

'Can I help you?'

Michael stared at the kindly old man, unable to respond.

'You can have some of these tomatoes, if you like. Half price. Local produce. No chemicals.'

He wore a cloth cap the colour of heather in bloom. It threw a mauve shadow over his face from the fluorescent strip lighting in the middle of the ceiling. But Michael could still see his eyes. They were brown with green specks. His life wasn't passing across them. Just a faint hope that he might sell some of the veg that were losing their sheen.

'They're fruit, not vegetables. Did you know that?' He smiled as he'd smiled long ago. 'Everyone thinks that tomatoes are vegetables. I put them with the fruit and everyone tells me I'm losing my marbles. But I'm sharper than they are. Tomatoes. They belong to the nightshade family. Originally from Peru . . . not these, of course. I get them from a market gardener near Bramfield. He actually talks to them. Says "Good morning". Are you all right?'

Michael swayed, his hand still behind his jacket.

'Problems with the lower back?' The old man removed his cap and slapped his thigh. 'Me, too. I wear a corset now. Still gives me gyp. Especially getting out of bed. You have to put up with it. None of us are getting any younger. Some carrots? They're a vegetable. From Iran. If you plant them side by side with the tomatoes, the tomatoes go raving mad. Odd, isn't it? You don't look too good, to be honest.'

Michael steeled himself and with one, swift movement he gave a tug and whipped out his hand.

The old man frowned and said, 'Fruit or veg?'

They both looked at Michael's outstretched arm, his fingers gripping a wallet pulled from his back pocket.

'A box of matches.' Michael's voice was low and it cracked.

'Sorry. Don't sell them any more.'

'Really?'

'Yes. I used to . . . before my wife got cancer. She's fine now. It wasn't the matches, of course. Benson and Hedges. Her lungs were smoked like kippers from Craster.'

'Sherbet lemons,' whispered Michael.

'Sorry?'

'Sherbet lemons. Two ounces.'

'Good God . . . but I've gone metric. Well I never. You're one of the few Englishmen to cross the threshold since we surrendered to Germany. I held out for as long as I could but in the end they took me to court. Not the Germans. The council. Do you want to sit down?'

They both looked at Michael's shaking hand.

'No, I'm fine.'

'If *I'd* been in Number Ten, we'd've stayed imperial. And I'll tell you something else. I'd've kept the ten-bob note and the shilling, too . . . along with the tanners and threepenny bits. But I'm just a nobody. I don't even run Number Nine St George's Green any more. They confiscated my scales. Said I'd have to go to Brussels to get 'em back. Two ounces of sherbet lemons coming up. And don't you worry: I could judge the weight in my sleep. There'll be no charge. Hang on a minute . . . you don't take them for old gyp, do you? I've never heard of that one. Beats a corset, I can tell you.'

Waves rushed onto the shore, stealing back the broken shells and sand.

Michael had been examining the replay ever since their friendly confrontation. Like Foreman watching Ali after the Rumble in the Jungle, he was trying to work out what had gone wrong. The whole thing was meant to have been over and done with in a jiffy. Hand in, hand out . . . nice and steady.

You move quickly. There's nothing to hold you back.

But there was. He'd been stopped in his tracks. As he'd reached the pavement, feet away from the unsuspecting patriot, Michael had shifted zones of time and place. He no longer saw the old man in a brown apron ...

He was at a farm gate in a remote valley, part of the Blue Stack Mountains of Donegal. He saw the rutted pathway winding down to a stream lit by a summer moon. He saw the cottage surrounded by ling and bell heather. He saw the smoke rising from a stub of chimney. He saw the low orange light giving shape to a small window. He saw the two other gates – three in all upon the track – between him and the man whose death could change everything for the better. Instantly – with an explosion of speed and remembered anxiety – he was on the far side of all the barriers . . . at the farm door . . . it was opening . . . he saw the puzzled dog at the far end of the corridor, he heard the thunk-thunk of a grandfather clock, he heard the moan of a kettle . . .

'Can I help you?'

The farmer had used the same words as the trader . . . he'd looked at Michael with that same strangely infant surprise, and all at once Michael was back on the pavement in Southwold, arm behind his back, one hand on his wallet.

'You can have some of these tomatoes, if you like.'

The beach huts had names. Enticing names, commemorating a loved one, proclaiming a creed, giving a view onto life, tantalising the curious with an enigma. Private jokes, too, Michael suspected. The huts fronted the beach, seeming to talk to the sea and the children on their knees in the sand. Jenny had liked to read out the names, walking a few steps and then stopping, ignoring the pull from her father's hand. Michael had gone half mad. It had taken an age to go anywhere. He'd had to find roundabout ways of getting from one end of the beach to the other. He wanted that time back, now; to linger and hear her voice: 'QUEENIE . . . SUMMER'S LEASE . . . ALBERT . . .'

Michael's eyes blurred. Tears spilled onto his cheeks. He looked around at the deserted beach, the immense blue sea, the chain of huts on either side. He felt utterly alone . . . abandoned. Jenny had gone, leaving behind the sound of these other names. His voice burst from his lips. 'Why? Why? Why?'

Why had Jenny ever met Peter? Why had she fallen? Why had she been left . . . a crumpled marionette?

'LIFE'S A BEACH.'

Only it wasn't. After leaving hospital Jenny had looked just the same. All the strings had been in place. None of them had been tangled or frayed. But there was no life in them. Her limbs wouldn't move. God had refused to pick up the handle to which all the threads had been attached. She'd just been dropped in a heap among the toys that weren't much fun any more.

'RETURN TO SENDER.'

Michael read the nameplate out loud several times, joining his voice to the memory of Jenny's. After reflecting for a long while, staring at the blue lettering above the entrance to the hut, he moved on, wiping his face on a sleeve. At last he recognised what had gone wrong the night before. There was no point in watching the replay any more. He knew what he had to do. He had to go back ...

Michael had come to Southwold intending to stick on the surface and go through the motions . . . touch that gun . . . get used to its weight again . . . feel a trigger on his index finger. Fend off any memories. He'd planned to rehearse the operation: to walk through the streets while armed (not an easy task when you think everyone can see what you're doing, when you expect to be stopped by the police at every corner); to approach a target as if it were Peter; to pull out his wallet instead of the gun. He'd hoped the shaking would stop after a week or so. That he'd manage to defeat the old hesitation, the crippling last-minute wavering that he'd been warned to avoid. But he couldn't even bring his arm from behind his back . . . because every time his hand went near the Browning, he was back in Donegal, by the first of three gates.

But now he understood.

If he was going to hold that gun again, he had to deal with 1983. He had to go back to that shocking meeting with a traumatised, sobbing priest in Belfast . . . where it had all begun. He had to walk down that rutted pathway to the farm. He had to face everything that his later breakdown had concealed. It was the only way to steady his hand. Ultimately, as a final blazing purification, he would have to listen to the tape. He'd have to press PLAY. He'd have to hear the clang of a pot or a pan.

By the same token, if he was to pull the trigger, looking Peter straight in the eye, Michael had to revisit his memory of Jenny's voyage from distress to calm and the anger he'd felt at Peter's treatment of his daughter. It was the only way to summon the belief that he must act once again against his most basic inclinations . . . with the same depth of conviction that had enabled him to creep along a furrowed trail in the Blue Stack Mountains.

Michael paused. He was astonishingly calm. The recognition of what he had to do – handling the past in order to handle the future – had brought a numbing inner peacefulness. He breathed in the moist air. He gazed over the sea, listening to the rush of shingle, the sand and stone sucked off the shore. He turned round and stared at the beach hut immediately behind him. He frowned as if a foreign voice had interrupted a dream:

'WHOA STOP.'

9

'You once said that evidence has more than one interpretation, do you remember?' Mitch was leaning back, sitting slightly to one side on the short bench. 'That we had to move the facts around to build the most convincing picture, using every piece on the table?'

Anselm remembered using the image. It had been a favourite. Now it made him flinch. He'd made so many false pictures in the name of justice. He'd even preferred some of them to the truth. They'd been far more credible.

'First, we'll assume that Jennifer Henderson was murdered,' said Mitch, warming to the game. 'But second, we'll suppose it wasn't Peter who killed her. And third, we'll suggest that the person who did is the author of this letter.'

Anselm spoke from behind arched hands. He didn't know whether to be bored or annoyed. 'Go on.'

'We'll now imagine that Peter knows this author. We'll call him X. We'll further imagine that Peter knows what X has done because, in a way, X did it for Peter. You see, Peter the philosopher can argue that killing is necessary – even a moral obligation – but he couldn't actually do it himself. So he turned to someone who could. A relative. A friend. Someone who didn't like the idea of the cancer and what it can do.'

'What about the doctor?'

'He didn't like it either.'

'So they're agreed, all three of them? Peter, the relative or friend and the doctor?'

'Yes.'

'This is ridiculous.'

'Do you mind if I finish?'

'Sorry, carry on.'

Mitch took an injured breath: 'Now, Peter has just brought national attention to himself by nearly killing a bairn in a Manchester bread shop. Like you say, his conscience has accused him. He's wondering if the cancer should have been left to do its worst. But X doesn't agree. And he's seriously worried that Peter might fall to pieces. He might talk. Which means our killer has to kill again.'

'This is complete nonsense.'

'It's what the letter might mean,' replied Mitch, testily. 'If this guy runs the risk of being exposed, he'll have to act first. So what does he do? First off, he sends a letter to a well-meaning monk who'll come running to the destitute and abandoned, because, frankly – thinks X – these otherworldly types are pretty easy to wrap around your finger. He's confident the monk will believe whatever is written to him in confidence.'

Anselm mustered some patience. 'I don't see how a letter to Larkwood might silence Peter.'

'It wouldn't. That's not the point. The only reason you're drawn into the scheme is to provide an explanation for Peter's later disappearance.'

'*Disappearance?*' Anselm tried to sound engaged.

'Yes.' Mitch was unmoved by Anselm's tone. He'd played to many a sceptic audience. 'Just look at the wording. There's a flaw. It's the insinuation of time pressure. You've only got "two weeks". After that Peter Henderson walks free to end his own life. It was written to twist your Prior's arm. To make him put you on the case. Because X wants a man like you to go searching for evidence of Jenny's murder . . . because he knows it isn't there. But it also reveals the wider game plan: what he intends to do as soon as Peter gets out of prison. For now he just wants to get you digging, knowing that all you're going to find is evidence of a man's unredeemed regret. Reasons to substantiate the suicide that hasn't happened yet.'

'And then what?'

'When Peter Henderson goes missing and everyone wonders why, you turn up on cue with an envelope and your explanation. Short version: "His behaviour matches the allegation of murder in the letter. He threw that brick out of guilt. I got involved because I feared he might take his life out of remorse." The Detective Inspector nods and when you've gone he says to his team, "We'd better have a word with the doctor." Which they do and, as you'd expect, the doctor says, "She died of cancer. I should know." And so they all head back to Martlesham for some instant coffee. Six months later, the police are still looking for Peter's body and maybe a note for Timothy. But it's Jennifer's story all over again. There's no murder to investigate. The file lies on a different kind of desk. Missing persons. Downgraded in importance. Everyone gets on with their lives . . . except for a rogue cop with scruples. But X has thought of him, too. And he's not overly concerned. Because after some soul searching the doubter joins his colleagues in the canteen. Why? He sees the light: there's no one to catch. Jenny's killer went and topped himself.'

With that snappy conclusion, Mitch reached for his drink, took a mouthful and waited.

'Completely fascinating,' applauded Anselm, dutifully, marvelling – genuinely – at the breadth of Mitch's imagination. 'I'd never have been able to come out with that lot in a million years. But – no offence – we're engaged in a serious investigation and I think we'd better stick to the notes on the page.'

'I just played it as I saw it.'

'Absolutely,' affirmed Anselm. 'But we've got to be practical. Frankly, it's not that kind of case.'

The jazzman didn't reply. He wasn't offended. Improvising

was a hit and miss activity. You put yourself on the line and sometimes it worked and sometimes it didn't. Instead he suggested lunch. He was always hungry after a performance. Even a bad one.

The sausages were excellent (enthused Anselm). Home-cured pork, prime cuts. At Larkwood there was a consensus that the bulging chipolatas served on feast days contained eyelids, earlobes and nasal hair collected from makeshift abattoirs throughout East-Central Europe. A ghastly image of the production process came suddenly to Anselm's mind and, transfixed, he dropped out of the conversation, leaving Mitch to ruminate over the death of Jennifer Henderson. When Anselm came around, the jazzman was still chewing over the same theme: why murder a paralysed woman with terminal cancer? What was in it for the killer? What was in it for the doctor? All they had to do was wait. Her death was already guaranteed.

'What motive could they possible share?' wondered Mitch.

His tone was disingenuous, as though he had a good idea, but Anselm didn't favour him with the invitation to speculate. He said: 'I appreciate that's the question investigators always pose but in my experience people do very strange things for even stranger reasons. Best leave motive till last. For now let's stick to the facts. Plain, boring facts.'

'But no one's going to give us any. You said so yourself. They've closed ranks.'

Anselm had already considered the matter. Perhaps it was his monastic training, but notwithstanding the acclaim set forth in the *Sunday Times*, he didn't especially rate his own importance, let alone his abilities. If Anselm was the last resort – he'd concluded – there must have been a first one.

'The writer of the letter believes that Jennifer Henderson was murdered. I'm inclined to think that they are not alone. My guess is that someone did, in fact, go to the police. I refuse to believe that Jennifer Henderson died without anyone raising the alarm . . . even timidly. So that's where we begin . . . where the timid left off.'

10

Anselm had first met Detective Superintendent Olivia Manning at the outset of her career, an opera buff who couldn't understand Anselm's obsession for jazz. They exchanged CDs in the hope of finding common ground. The venture failed and, in time, they stopped meeting for coffee or lunch. Things that might have happened didn't happen. But not just because of their differing tastes in music. Fate or chance – those goading imps who'd vied to ruin Peter Henderson – placed them on opposing sides in a string of significant trials. Trials Olivia had cared about and lost. Trials that Anselm had won. Sitting in her office on the second floor of Suffolk Constabulary HQ in Martlesham, they'd steered away from victory and defeat; and what might have been.

'So you're a detective, now?' she asked, wryly.

'I prefer "fretful explorer into the dark places of the human conscience".'

After digesting that mouthful, Olivia's expression seemed to quip, 'Did you bring a compass?' but she held back. After all, her old adversary had become a monk. He'd placed the search for truth above all else.

'I ought to have cautioned you,' she said, feigning regret. 'But you know the score. Just remember anything you say from now on may, and will, be given in evidence.'

Olivia hadn't changed much. Her hair was still short and jet black though responsibility had turned a few strands into silver. They fell from the crown like neatly trimmed piano wire. Long black eyelashes moved slowly as she spoke. Her voice was hard without being harsh.

'You'll be listed in Yellow Pages?'

'No. I'll rely on word of mouth.'

'A public service?'

'Yes.'

'For those who can afford it?'

'No, for those who can't.'

She made a shrug, but the indifference wasn't entirely convincing. Sensing an open door and a softening of memory, Anselm spoke plainly, addressing the past and the future: 'This time I want to do something completely different. I don't want to shift evidence around trying to make a pretty picture. I want to get it absolutely right . . . even if no one likes what they see. This time the client is the situation. I'm no longer taking sides, not for any price.'

Anselm produced the letter. He explained its background and his thinking. He made no reference to Mitch's fantasy that the author had tasked him to uncover evidence to support a verdict of suicide; that another murder had been planned. This was not the time for laughter, even for the purpose of completeness. The real problem with this case was not a fresh, unfolding drama, but the stale and settled history. The past had been left undisturbed for years. It had become compressed and solid. Anselm's difficulty was to find a crack on a seemingly smooth surface.

'I'm imagining that back then someone approached the police. Since they've never made any public declaration, I'm guessing they wanted an off-the-record meeting. I'm hoping they had an irrational distrust of junior detectives and came to someone senior. Someone with the power to act behind the scenes. Someone who shut the case down because there was no evidence of any crime.'

Olivia's stern face slowly relaxed and, for a moment, Anselm thought they were in a wine bar near the Old Bailey. They'd just exchanged confidences, shyly: *Tosca* by Puccini for *Lady in Satin* by Billie Holiday; different takes on love and dying. Things hadn't quite worked out. It had been difficult explaining why because a murder trial had lain between them. This time, the vibes felt promising. Olivia couldn't quite suppress her amusement. She, too, had been warmed by the remembrance of wanting to be understood and to understand, recalling, too, the unexpected disappointment. And now, when the shape of their lives had changed beyond recognition, they were moving in the same direction.

'I know who wrote the letter,' she said, smiling.

Had there been a wine bar in Martlesham, they might have gone there to reclaim even more of the past; to toast (perhaps) a strange and unforeseen fulfilment. Instead, Olivia made tea. She'd always had a passion for tea, keeping in her locker a private stock of mysterious blends from Asia and the Orient. Her interest bordered on the religious. She'd tasted aspects of revelation.

'A couple of years back I got a phone call from a man who wanted to see me on "a matter of some delicacy".' Olivia used two fingers to open and close the quotation marks. 'They didn't want to talk on the phone so I suggested they come here for a meeting.'

'Who was it?'

'Nigel Goodwin.'

The first name meant nothing to Anselm and his face said so.

'Jennifer Henderson's uncle,' explained Olivia. 'The brother of Michael, her father. Estranged brother, I should say. Turned out they hadn't seen each other for years. There'd been some sort of dispute or breakdown in the past that had never been resolved. Your territory, I imagine, not mine.'

'Then why come to you?'

'He was also Jennifer Henderson's godfather. She'd died three days earlier. He wanted to know if the police had the power to request a post-mortem examination notwithstanding the existence of a death certificate. Whether it could be done without the consent of the immediate family. Whether it could be done secretly.'

'No, no and no,' replied Anselm with a flourish, though not entirely sure about questions one and two. He reflected for a moment. 'A *post-mortem*?'

'Yes.'

'Did he say why?'

'No.'

'A solicitor could have answered his question. Why come to you?'

'He wanted to make an allegation without making an allegation. To report a crime without naming a crime. He was distressed. As was his wife. I got the impression she had something to say . . . that she wanted to interrupt and give her point of view. But she just sat there, letting her husband do the talking. He's a man who's used to running the show.'

Anselm drank some Gorreana, a tea from the Azores. Olivia had branched out from the mysteries of the East; she'd looked closer to home for enlightenment. The thought came to Anselm like a welcome distraction, because in this desperate meeting between godfather and police officer lay the first and last opportunity to obtain concrete evidence of any crime before the burial of Jennifer's body. It would have been there . . . faint abrasions on the neck, a chemical in the blood . . . however it was done, there'd have been some signs of forensic significance; and those indicators would—

'You can't act on this kind of thing,' she said, quietly, following Anselm's thoughts. 'He had a suspicion . . . but it was based on nothing he was prepared to reveal. He wasn't even involved with the Henderson family. He was a stranger to everything that had happened after Jennifer's accident. I sensed he was kicking himself for not having sorted out the problem with his brother.'

'As if that might have made a difference?'

'Perhaps.'

Anselm placed his cup on the edge of Olivia's desk. As with *Tosca*, he couldn't see what the fuss was about. Perhaps his palette lacked refinement. That's what Olivia had managed to say when Anselm had given back the recording. He'd lost the booklet that had come with the box. Worse, a killer had been acquitted earlier that afternoon. He'd shaken Anselm's hand afterwards and asked if he could have one of the autopsy photographs.

'He should have spoken up while he had the chance,' continued Olivia, trying to reach the brooding monk; she'd lost him, suddenly, and felt the separation. 'If he'd said something specific before the burial, I could have responded appropriately. But he said nothing. And he's saying nothing now. He came to me in secret and now he's come to you in secret. But behind all this is a simple, tragic, all too human story. It often happens when people enter retirement. They look for something to do. Something meaningful. And Nigel Goodwin . . . he's a distant uncle who feels he let his niece down. She was sick and he didn't pull his weight. To make up for his absence while she was alive, he's become her saviour in death. He's lost his way.'

Anselm retrieved the letter. He looked at the words without quite reading them.

'This is not a case you or I can investigate.' Olivia was leaning on her desk, hands joined, her almost black eyes levelled upon him. She was saying to Anselm what she'd probably said to Nigel Goodwin and his subdued wife. 'There's no evidence and no crime. Just a broken husband.'

The killer had got off because Anselm had found a small hole in one of the prosecution's forensic reports. An innocent slip. He'd picked away at it with smart, technical questions, making it seem far bigger than it really was. The distinguished author had been outraged and the jury had confounded righteous indignation with the bluster of incompetence. Now, remembering that great triumph, Anselm vowed to trap his man. There was no forensic evidence against this other killer, no hole in the paperwork, nothing for a scornful barrister to pick wide later on. And that was all to Anselm's advantage.

'Have you heard of the Red Barn Murder of eighteen twenty-seven?'

Olivia blinked slowly. 'Yes. The case began with a dream . . . a nightmare.'

'And the evidence came afterwards,' observed Anselm. 'Sometimes we just have to persevere, especially when we can't sleep easily any more.'

Olivia walked Anselm to the main entrance. She'd given him Nigel Goodwin's address. She'd warned him not to expect much when he got there. They stood beside each other in the sunshine, wondering where the years had gone. They spoke of judges, counsel and detectives, people they'd both known, seeking points of contact. There weren't many, because Anselm had been out of the field for a long time. It was like they were trying too hard to be nice. Time seemed to run out and anyway, Mitch was right in front, waiting in his rusted Land Rover.

'I want to make up for the cases I should have lost,' said Anselm, abruptly.

Olivia made another unconvincing shrug. 'Then you've a lot of work to do.' But then she seemed to turn a page, more interested in what was to come than in what had already happened. 'Why not just . . . do your best, again?'

Anselm could settle for that. He said goodbye but then surrendered to an afterthought.

'Just out of interest, is Nigel Goodwin a doctor?'

Olivia made a slight start, impressed that this 'fretful explorer' had discovered a man's profession through the simple exercise of his imagination. It was a promising beginning.

'He is, actually. But I wouldn't trust him to treat the common cold.'

The condemnation unsettled Anselm. It had been harsh,

suggesting there was more to this man than troubled grief. Mitch (emboldened, now) begged to differ. Clunking through the gears, he improvised once more and Anselm, disinclined to put much store on his assistant's judgement, stared out of the window, barely listening. His mind soon drifted away from the inept doctor to the haunted brother, the quiet man with the lowered face in all the photographs. What had happened to Michael Goodwin that he'd chosen the shadows? Grief, on its own, wasn't a sufficient explanation.

Part Two

The Diary of Timothy Henderson

~

It's very quiet in the house. Except for the clock. There's a clock in the sitting room that ticks really loud and I'm wondering why it carries on like that. It just keeps going as if nothing has happened. Tick tock, tick tock. My mum stopped breathing yesterday but the clock's still working. It's like someone walking past. Doesn't even slow down. My mum's dead. And the clock's still working.

My granddad gave me this diary after my mum's accident. He told me to write down my feelings because otherwise they'd get stuck like leaves in a drain. But they didn't. Because my mum was still with me. She's gone now, though. Everyone's saying she died of cancer but that's not true.

★★★★★★

16th June

My granddad was right. He knew what was going to happen two years ago. I'm all blocked up, just like he said. I've been like this since the night my mum died and it's getting worse. So I'm going to write down what's happened and what I feel.

My dad was sent to prison last week because he threw a brick at a boy in a bread shop. They all reckon it's because he feels bad about my mum's death. They're all wrong. He feels bad but he can't tell them what he did and why. When I saw my dad in the cells before they took him away, I could see it

65

in his eyes. He was glad. He wants to be locked up. It's the only way he can get away from me. Because most days, there's one of these moments. He looks at me asking himself just how much did I hear and see. I don't say anything and he doesn't say anything. We just look at each other and I can tell he feels bad. But now he's in prison. He's glad and I'm glad. My grandmother's glad, too.

23rd June

My grandma doesn't realise it, but she stares at me while she talks. She's worried. She's got questions but like my dad she's afraid to ask them. She puts down animals at work. She's no idea how many cats and dogs she's killed. Must be hundreds. She doesn't feel a thing when she does it.

My granddad never asks any questions, not any more. Instead I ask him and he doesn't have any answers. I watch him avoiding the truth and I wonder if I should even stay and listen. He keeps two passports. Like the others, he's two people.

Uncle Nigel wanted to know who saw my mum after he left on the night she died. He knows something happened but he'd never guess what it was.

7th July

I just want my mum back. I loved her and I still do. The paralysis and the cancer didn't change her. She wasn't any different, not to me. She was still my mum. Everyone else felt sorry for her and said she didn't have much of a life. But I didn't, not once, and I'm unhappy because she's gone and I miss her every day. No one understands that even though she was ill, I didn't want her to die. They all said, 'She's at peace now,' as if that changed everything. Well, it doesn't. She was given peace but mine was taken away.

11

Michael lay on his bed. He'd kept on his overcoat as a kind of protection, a thick skin against the awful cold he was about to remember. When he'd come back from Northern Ireland, Danny, the army psychologist, had told him to lie down on a bed and listen to some tapes – chimes from a Buddhist monastery, the sound of the wind in the trees, the sighs and murmuring of the sea. The idea – advanced for the times – had been to help Michael relax; to calm the anxiety so that his suppressed anguish could surface . . . in the imagined mountain air, in the dreamed-up woods, on a make-believe beach. He'd tried his best but with each foray into the subconscious he'd simply fallen asleep. When he'd turned up for the interviews, taking his seat by the table with the box of tissues, he could only yawn. But now he was savagely awake, his senses sharply attuned to the crash and sudden lull of real waves upon real sand. The tide was coming in. Michael let himself go back to that terrible late November. Eyes wide open, heart beginning to race, he watched Captain Michael Goodwin act and speak; watched himself as though he was a disembodied spirit observing the preliminaries to the unforeseen catastrophe. Everyone was acting normally, even though their nerves were frayed . . .

'Where is he?' asked Michael.
  'He'll come.'
  'When?'
  'Soon.'

'You're sure?'

'I'm sure. Relax. He said he'd come.'

'It's dangerous for me here . . . and for you; for us all. We should have met out of town, not *here*. For God's sake, the place is crawling with Provos.'

'I know, so, but he insisted.'

The doorbell rang. Twice, then a third time. The signal meant the caller was alone, as planned. Liam nodded, left the sitting room and went to unlock the front door.

Liam was small-time. He gave low-grade intelligence on well-known figures in the Belfast Brigade of the IRA. Just their movements. Where they went. Who they met. Registration numbers. Snippets of conversation from people who knew them. Pub talk. For all that he got paid a hundred quid a week. Tax free. He was just eighteen and very small-time indeed, which was why Michael was his handler. They were both new recruits to the long war. But Liam said he'd got something big this time. Real big. He'd met someone with a message. So he'd set up the meeting and Michael had turned up feeling sick with fear. He was sitting on the edge of a synthetic leather sofa in a council house in the Ballymurphy district of West Belfast. The sitting room door opened and Liam ushered into the wan light a haggard man in a long dark overcoat, black shoes and trousers, a black hat and a black scarf. Removing his hat, the man said, 'How's your ma, Liam?'

'She's fine.'

'Her knees and ankles?'

'Swollen again.'

The visitor brought his dark eyes onto Michael. Addressing Liam, he said, 'This is your man?'

'Aye.'

'He's Army?'

'I am,' said Michael, his mouth dry, wanting to stamp some authority on his rising panic.

The man shrugged off his coat and unwound the scarf from his neck. A white collar under the soft chin showed him to be a priest. Liam's priest.

'Get yerself upstairs now and look after your mother. I'll call you when I'm done.'

Liam obeyed. The priest shut the door. He started speaking even before he'd turned around.

'It's my job to look after the living and the dying. Sometimes, I help them pass over. I put oil on their forehead . . . I rub it into the palms of their hands . . . I give them bread for the last time . . . we call it *viaticum* . . . which means "provision for the journey". The moment of parting, after giving the oil and the bread . . . it's always unforgettable.'

The priest sat on a shiny armchair near to Michael. He, too, sat on the edge of his seat, his arms wrapped around his overcoat and crumpled scarf. His hair was white. Thick black eyebrows bristled over his pale, lined face.

'Last week there came a knock to the door,' he said, looking at the ragged carpet. All the colour had gone. A loose weave of grey strands was all that remained. 'It was after eleven. I opened up, and there on the step was a man I'd never seen before. A broken nose face. He didn't even look at me, but I heard him well enough. "There's someone needs you, Father. You won't be long." He walked off, into the dark, and I followed. Didn't even get my overcoat. A car was waiting, engine running, a back door opened. The man didn't speak. He just drove me half a mile to a house that had been half burned out the month before. I knew the family that had moved out . . . they're decent folk.' The priest paused to moisten his lips. 'I went in, thinking I'd see one of the family, but there, at the end of the corridor, was a man in a denim jacket with a mask over his head. Roll-neck jumper. Corduroy trousers. He had a pistol in one hand. "Upstairs," he said. "He asked for you. Make it quick." Up I went and I stopped outside the bathroom . . . the floor was soaking wet, the bath full of discoloured water . . . and blood swimming round the taps. A short bulky man with thick arms appeared from one of the bedrooms and said, "Get on, will you. His time's up." He had a mask on, too . . . slits cut for the eyes and mouth. His shirt sleeves were rolled up and he was drying his hands on a filthy towel. There were red washing-up gloves hanging out of a pocket. "It took us three weeks to get a confession. You've got three minutes." I went into the room and there . . . I . . .' The priest dropped his head and his shoulders began to judder. He made a strange squealing noise and Michael shrank back into the sofa, the worn material squeaking loudly as he moved. Looking up, facing the drab wall, the priest said, 'I knew him . . . I'd known him from birth . . . I'd baptised him . . . and he was strapped arms behind his back to a wooden chair, dressed only in his underpants and socks. He couldn't lift his head. There was blood all over his chest and knees . . . and he was shining . . . shining all over because of the water. This voice from the mask said, "Three minutes and no heroics. I'm warning you. I'll shoot you as easily as I'm going to shoot him."'

Michael's mouth clacked for lack of spit. He was hot though the room was cold. The air was damp and his skin tingled with a sudden flush of sweat. The weak central light had no shade. There were no pictures on the walls. The gas fire didn't work.

'His name was Eugene . . . he was a father to four children,' said the priest. 'I had to kneel down in a pool of blood and water at his side. "It's all a mistake, Father," he said. "I'm no tout. But they think I am. They think I'm an informer. It's a mistake and I'm done for. This lot are the Nutting Squad. They're gonna shoot me in the head. They're going to put my head in a plastic bag . . ." I took his hand . . . and I was about to speak when he spat out some blood and whispered, "Listen to me . . ." I leaned near to his breath and closed my eyes.'

But Eugene's mind wasn't on sins and a final cleansing. He had a message. Before they blew his brains out, he was going to do something big . . . something that would change the future. He was going to send a message that could help bring the Troubles to an end.

'Eugene spoke quickly,' said the priest after a short, sickening pause. 'He said, "Ó Mórdha's going to Donegal. Next Wednesday. He'll be alone. Tell someone in British Intelligence . . . someone who deals with touts."'

Néall Ó Mórdha. Michael knew of him from intelligence briefings. He'd joined up in the forties. Veteran of the fifties. Founder member of the 'Provisionals' when they split from the 'Officials' in 1969. Part of Southern Command. On the Army Council. A hardliner. Aged fifty-eight. Married to Bláithín. Keeps a dog. Irish water spaniel.

The priest stared at Michael expectantly, moisture shining on his upper lip. 'Do you understand what I'm saying? Have you got the message?'

Michael hadn't . . . not quite; but he nodded. Only the priest wasn't to be fooled.

'You don't follow a damn thing, do you?' he said, despairing. 'You're as lost as the boy upstairs. I'm talking to a greenhorn . . .'

The priest let his head drop onto his chest. After an age of slow, measured breathing, he looked up, his eyes dark with knowledge and purpose.

'Eugene had always talked to me. Shared his doubts and regrets. I knew he was in the IRA. And I'd let him know my mind about political violence. Told him he couldn't come to communion as long as he carried a gun.'

And Eugene, in turn, had fought back, arguing the moral case for the armed struggle; that innocent people get killed in wars, even just ones. By default, the priest had come to learn a great deal about the Republican movement and its masked soldiers. He knew how the organisation was structured. He'd been given a glimpse of internal rivalries and the disputes over tactics.

'The IRA is run by a seven-man Army Council,' said the priest, as if Michael didn't know his left from his right. 'They decide if there's going to be a ceasefire. They could even stop the war.'

Michael nodded impatiently.

'The last time I'd spoken to Eugene, he'd told me there was a struggle at the heart of the IRA between those wanting to shoot the Brits out of Ireland and the growing feeling among some that the only way forward was Sinn Fein and democratic politics, that an electoral mandate for a united Ireland could reach further than the gun and the bomb.'

Where was the war going? This was the big question. In recent years the INLA had killed Airey Neave outside the House of Commons. The IRA had murdered eighteen soldiers at Warrenpoint. They'd assassinated Lord Mountbatten at Mullaghmore. Ten Provisionals had starved themselves to death in the Maze. And the British troops were still in the North. Thatcher wouldn't bow. The Saracens were still patrolling the housing estates. But there'd been a swing in a surprising new direction: following the hunger strike, Sinn Fein had emerged as a real force in local elections.

'This is only last year,' said the priest.

'Yes,' added Michael, asserting his authority. 'And they're still bombing London. Remember the summer? Hyde Park? Regent's Park? Nine soldiers dead. Three civilians killed. Fifty injured.'

'And Gerry Adams has just won a seat in Westminster,' replied the priest, presumably for Eugene. 'That's *national* politics with *international* significance. He's the MP for West Belfast. He's *my* MP.'

'Liam told me you had a message,' snapped Michael. 'Who cares if Ó Mórdha goes to Donegal?'

'You should.'

'Why?'

'Because he'll never give up the armed struggle. It's a religion to him. He's the one man on the Council who stands in the way of change. The others can be persuaded. Eugene was saying that the debate between the gun and the ballot box can be tilted in the right direction . . . and now is the time.'

Michael leaned forward and the seat covering squeaked again. The priest's head had dropped once more. He was holding his coat tight.

'What is the message?'

The priest spoke to his knotted hands. 'Ó Mórdha has a cottage in the hills. Few know the place even exists . . . Eugene was one of them. And he told me.' The priest rummaged into the coat on his knees, finally pulling out a sheet of folded paper from a pocket. His hand was shaking as he passed it to Michael. 'There's only one house in the valley . . . by a stream and two trees. I've written down the details . . . you'll find it easily enough on a map.'

Michael frowned and took the paper. 'Did Eugene say anything else?'

The priest looked up with the waxy stare of someone who's just killed a man.

'Eugene said, "Get Ó Mórdha, and you'll get a peace process. Let him go and the war will never end."'

The priest had done Eugene's bidding and an awful silence filled the room. It was as though they were both standing over the battered body of a tout. Looking into the space in front of the dead fire, the priest began mumbling confidentially. He'd heard the one confession in his life that he was meant to repeat. And it wasn't quite over. The priest was back in that wet, burned-out council house.

'A voice came from behind the mask. "Time's up." I reached into my pocket for the blessed oil . . . I always carry it with me, just in case . . . and I began to rub it into one of Eugene's broken hands. I did them both, watched by this man with the filthy towel hung on one shoulder, and then I anointed Eugene's forehead . . . and it was only when I stood up that I realised I hadn't brought my bag. I couldn't give him any bread for the journey . . . this man who'd never come to communion. You know, they dumped his body in an alleyway with an empty milk crate on his head. That was *their* message. Telling the kid who found him what'll happen if he grew up to become an informer.'

The floor creaked upstairs and Liam's mother called for help. He wasn't by her side. Michael knew at once: he was behind the door, as if to earn his £100. After a glance at the ceiling, the priest stood up, wrapped the scarf around his neck, pulled on his coat and settled his hat low on his head.

'And *I've* got a message, too,' he whispered. 'Let Liam go. Stop using him. He's only a boy. You've played on his vulnerability. You've made him feel important, full-size and useful. For once in his life he thinks he's not just another nobody. He's got a job and a wage.' The priest paused to study Michael's pale face. 'You're scared, aren't you? It's no fun sitting in a hovel knowing the IRA are on the other side of the front door. Well, I wanted you to feel that fear, to sweat a bit, because this is where Liam *lives*. Far from an armed compound in Lisburn. He doesn't even know when to shut up. He talks easily. Like he did when I pressed him hard about the money. Didn't want me to think he was a thief. Just give it some thought before you go home: if I can find out in five minutes that he's speaking to the Brits, how long will it take the Provos?'

Michael swung his legs off the bed. Wrapped in his overcoat like that priest, he walked to the bathroom to rinse his face. On turning around he thought again of Liam, as if the kid were kneeling on the floor, handing over the Browning. The boy had risked his life, knowing what the Nutting Squad had done to Eugene. He'd risked everything, trusting in Michael to do his stuff.

12

Anselm knocked on the door of a small bay-windowed house in the village of Long Melford, part of a row of seventeenth-century dwellings, distinguished by various shades of paint, but joined by tangled ivy and a gently undulating roof of auburn tiles. He'd decided to call unannounced mid-morning on the understanding that the unprepared witness was always more enlightening than the person who'd had time to edit and organise their thoughts. With best intentions, such people often left out the apparently trivial details that were, in fact, of critical importance.

'Hello?'

The woman was smiling – almost professionally. But the greeting was genuine. She wore loose jeans and a flowery shirt with the sleeves rolled up. Gardening gloves and a trowel revealed what she'd been doing moments before. Her grey-brown hair was simply cut and carelessly ruffled. She'd aged without lines to the mouth or eyes.

'I wonder if I might speak to Nigel Goodwin,' said Anselm.

'I'm afraid he won't be back for half an hour. Is there some problem? I'm his wife . . . we share everything.'

According to Olivia, this woman had accompanied her husband to Martlesham, only to swallow whatever she might have said. Anselm addressed her directly, as if she were the sole object of his visit. 'I don't want to cause you any distress but I'd like to talk about the death of Jennifer Henderson.'

The woman's sunny smile vanished instantly. One hand came

to her neck as if to fumble with a necklace that wasn't there.

'I've been asked to make discreet enquiries,' continued Anselm, reassuringly. 'I understand the police didn't take your husband's concerns seriously. I do. Along with yours. That's why I'm here. To listen rather than to speak.'

'I think you'd better come in,' she said, stepping to one side.

The sitting room was small and tidy. Prints of various cathedrals adorned the brightly painted walls. Three armchairs and a sofa hugged a round coffee table. Spread across the glass surface were a selection of books on gardening and an imposing volume on herbal medicine entitled *Heal Yourself.* It was a cheerful room for a cheerful couple. Sunshine streamed through mullioned windows. Taking a seat, Anselm explained his role as an investigator based at Larkwood, introducing Mr Robson as a colleague from his days at the Bar. He summarised the letter, observing that Detective Superintendent Manning had concluded that the anonymous author was Nigel Goodwin.

'Your husband is a doctor?' asked Anselm.

'Of a sort, yes.'

'He's given up practice?'

'No.' Sensing Anselm's misunderstanding, she added, 'He's a vicar. A doctor of systematic theology. Specialised in Karl Barth.'

'Ah.'

Anselm suddenly decided to say nothing further at all. And not simply because he'd never fully understood Barth's colossal *Dogmatics.* (Not a man for jokes, Barth, he'd thought.) It was, instead, a trick he'd learned from the Prior. Silence forces most people to speak. They begin with trivia and then, bit by bit, they start to reveal their deeper concerns. Helen Goodwin, proud of her husband, a partner in his ministry, kind and outgoing, had her own monumental thoughts. She was perched on the edge of her seat, glancing regularly at Anselm's habit, wanting to share them with someone likely to understand. The charged quiet became gradually prickly and then unbearably painful. As if climbing gingerly onto a window ledge, she said, carefully: 'Strange, really, that Nigel joined the Church and Michael went into the Army.'

She'd assumed knowledge of Jennifer's father. She wanted to talk about him as much as her husband. This quiet man who stood at the back of every photograph.

'Why?' prompted Mitch.

'Well, Nigel was the sporty one,' said Mrs Goodwin, her hands working as if she were warming a ball of clay. 'Played rugby for Suffolk. Climbed mountains. Jumped into rivers. He'd been in the cadets and loved the marching and the uniform and the chance to fire a real gun and scream his head off, whereas Michael was shy and retiring, hated any kind of confrontation. He was the peacemaker in the family. Always wanted to get people to sit down at a table and sort out their differences. Hated violence of any kind. Loved Evensong. You can imagine everyone's surprise when he announced he wanted to join the Royal Anglian Regiment. We thought he saw the Army as a kind of peace-keeping force . . . not a *fighting* force as such, if you see what I mean. We imagined he wanted to build bridges in the Third World. But he didn't build anything . . . he went to Northern Ireland instead.'

She made the statement as if it were charged with menace and meaning. She looked from Anselm to Mitch, her blue eyes inviting a reaction. None was given.

'He was there during the Troubles,' she explained, hopefully.

Still no response. After a moment's further uncertainty, she seemed to make the final leap: 'We don't know what happened while he was over there . . . but when he came back he was a completely different man.'

Mrs Goodwin's hands stopped moving. Having made this central disclosure – the significance of which was lost on Anselm – she appeared to relax, grateful to leave behind the habitual deference. She was used to milling around fêtes and fairs, listening to the entanglements in other people's lives, but now, for once, it was her chance to talk. Few wanted to know if the vicar's wife had had her own experience of hell.

'He ended up with the Intelligence Corps,' she said, and then abruptly changed tone. 'Look, I'm telling you this because I have my own theory about Jenny's death . . . but I can't tell you in front of my husband, and you won't understand why I think what I think unless you understand what happened to Michael after he came home from Belfast.'

Mrs Goodwin crouched forward. She knew her husband would be back soon. There wasn't much time.

'They were very close as brothers,' she said, quietly. 'Which makes what has happened all the more tragic.'

Always fighting, of course (she explained, smiling). As boys they pulled each other's hair out. But as they got older – Nigel was the elder by two years – their individual characters began to emerge (the quiet and withdrawn as against the loud and extrovert) and the sheer difference between their outlook and behaviour brought them together rather than pushed them apart. It was a principle of complementarity. The one needed the other. Michael would quieten Nigel down while Nigel would draw Michael out of his shell. A mutual friend once said that when Michael joined the Army he was following a path opened up by his brother. And vice versa. When Nigel began studies in theology, the way forward had already been illuminated by his quiet, reflective sibling. They chose their careers out of personal conviction, certainly, but in a strange way they were indebted to each other. They'd bound one another into their radically different futures . . . Michael was *involved* in Nigel's life of spiritual reflection and Nigel was *involved* in Michael's life of military action. No surprise, then, that Michael asked Nigel to be Jenny's godfather.

'At the time Nigel was studying at Oxford,' said Mrs Goodwin. 'Michael had only recently left Sandhurst and got married. He was a lieutenant with a young wife still training to be a vet in Edinburgh.'

'Emma?' supplied Anselm, securing a bond between them; showing that he was familiar with some of the family history.

'Exactly. She just plugged away at the books while Michael went to postings in Cyprus and Germany. After he was promoted to captain, Emma got a job in Sudbury, and he transferred to the Intelligence Corps. That's when he specifically asked if he could go to Belfast.'

'Why?'

Anselm was beginning to worry slightly. How this account of brothers in arms meshed with the death of Jennifer Henderson was beyond his imagination.

'He wanted to make a difference. He said there was a deep sickness in the society that needed healing. Ancient wounds in Irish history that were still wide open. He wanted to help close them.'

'Always the peacemaker,' ventured Anselm.

'Nigel's own words, when Michael told him. Michael said something had to be done to bring about *lasting* change, regardless of the risks. We're now convinced it's why he'd joined up in the first place . . . it had nothing to do with building bridges in Africa.'

'Why are you so sure?' appealed Anselm.

'Because, looking back, he went to Sandhurst the year after the pub bombings in Guildford and Birmingham. The carnage had spilled out of Northern Ireland onto the English mainland. And there were tell-tale remarks . . . He once said, "We caused the trouble over there, we've got to bring it to an end." We think he picked a terrible intractable problem on purpose . . . and did his best to help resolve it.'

Mrs Goodwin looked at her watch and Mitch, as if picking up a signal, pushed her narrative forward. 'You said he was different when he came home.'

'Yes. He'd been four years at Thiepval Barracks. Lisburn, south of Belfast. We'd seen him on leave, of course, but he never spoke of his work. All he'd say was that he now worked for a special unit. It was all hush–hush and dangerous. Emma was scared to bits . . . she told me not to say but it was called the FRU, the Force Research Unit. Whatever the dangers might have been, with us, back home, Michael was his usual quiet self. There was nothing untoward. And then, in December nineteen eighty-three, he came back . . . traumatised.'

'And he never spoke of what happened?' asked Anselm.

'Never. We knew that he was being treated by the Army doctors, but that was all we got from Emma. She knew nothing either . . . or if she knew, she wasn't going to tell us anything. All we could do was watch Michael, locked up, deep inside himself. And that's when his relationship with Nigel began to fall apart.'

Only it didn't quite tumble, bit by bit. Michael just turned his back on Nigel. He didn't talk to him any more. Didn't call. Didn't share his thoughts on politics. Didn't even stay in the same room as Nigel for longer than a few minutes. Always walked off to find something he didn't really need.

'It was as though he *blamed* Nigel for whatever had happened,' said Mrs Goodwin, trying to understand, even now, after all these years. 'He severed the bond with his brother. The door was shut. There was no handle. He simply wouldn't answer to the most gentle knock.'

'Returning to this trauma,' said Anselm. 'Didn't things improve as the treatment progressed?'

'No. Something final had happened, for Michael, in relation to Nigel. He couldn't even look at him any more. And as for the treatment, whatever it might have been, Emma as much as said the psychologists had given up . . . but then we saw something . . . miraculous. Michael's face gradually began to shine. There was a terrible vulnerability in his eyes . . . and they were wide open, but only to Jennifer.'

'How old was she at the time?' asked Mitch.

'Six or seven. She'd just started ballet with a Russian émigré in Stowmarket. Ex-Bolshoi and half crackers. Michael left the

Army and worked part-time for a company run by a friend from Sandhurst days. They imported woollen cloth from Italy and Michael managed the office and translated all the faxes and letters. He'd done A level. That filled up the mornings and two afternoons. Whenever he could he went sailing on his boat, always alone. The rest of the time he did the shopping and looked after Jennifer. But, you know, it was the *dance* that soothed Michael . . . made him feel better. He went to all her lessons, all her performances . . . watched her practise.'

'No words,' said Anselm. 'He didn't have to speak.'

'He just had to look . . . and he stared, at these beautiful, graceful movements.'

So much of ballet was about death, thought Anselm. Final flights of anguish. Harrowed eyes, heavily blacked with theatrical face-paint. The slightly opened mouths. The triumph of grace over brutality. All done through gestures, great and small. Michael had found a therapy that reached into his darkness without the pain of light.

'We saw this change in Michael,' said Mrs Goodwin, 'but somehow, it pushed him even further away from Nigel, and from me. Jennifer became his life, and there was no room left for anyone else but Emma . . . and she did nothing to bring the two brothers back together again. I don't blame her, but she seemed to accept Michael's very private decision . . . as if she understood why he'd turned away from Nigel. Michael who'd always been a peacemaker effectively smashed the family to pieces. Or Northern Ireland did. Very, very gradually, we stopped visiting *theirs*. They never came to *ours*. Nigel went to a parish in Truro and then Carlisle . . . Canterbury, Bristol . . . a mission station in Zimbabwe . . . by the time we came back to Long Melford, the distance between Michael and Nigel was immense. The only link between them was accidental . . . Emma and I stayed in contact by phone; she let me know how things were going.'

Mitch looked up and said, 'And what did Jennifer make of her absent godfather?'

'Well, she had no idea what had gone on. How could she? No one told her. So she presumed he was too busy looking after other people's families.' Mrs Goodwin smarted at the unfairness; the depth of misunderstanding. 'Children never *really* know what's happened inside their parents. Why they think what they think and do what they do. The turmoil. The old wounds. The damaged love. All the confusion that can never be put into words. For Jenny, there was no shattered family. Just an adoring mum and dad, a distant aunt and an uncle who couldn't care less . . . relatives you had to invite round when pushed . . . which is how we met Peter Henderson. Jenny insisted. And that day is—'

A key jangled on the pavement outside. A flash of anxiety and something like regret seized Mrs Goodwin's face. She quickly left the room, and closed the door behind her. Voices sounded in the corridor. After some hushed insistence, someone went upstairs, their feet stamping reluctant cooperation. Intuition told Anselm another door had, in fact, been closed. Mrs Goodwin wouldn't be explaining her theory of Jennifer Henderson's death. And not just because her husband had come home. It was written on her face. She'd felt the sudden and appalling defencelessness that comes with complete honesty. The realisation that you can't retract what you've said. She preferred by far the anonymity of listening to others in the church hall. It was safer. Open your mouth and people asked questions. Keep quiet, and you could think what the hell you liked and no one cared a hoot.

13

'Sherbet lemons,' said the old man, a twinkle in his eye. 'Two ounces.'

It was not a question. The capped vendor was certain. He'd spent a lifetime memorising the needs of his customers.

'You can read my mind,' said Michael, reaching behind his jacket. 'I can.'

The old man tipped the jar of sweets into a measuring dish on some metric scales, ignoring the red needle. He knew what two ounces looked like.

'Still got the old gyp?'

Michael didn't answer. Like a specialist in earthquakes consulting the Richter scale, he was quantifying the shake in his outstretched hand, asking himself if the tremors had reduced in severity. He smiled. There'd been some improvement. Deep down the tectonic plates were beginning to seize up.

'Do you want some fresh veg?' The old man had followed Michael to the door. 'I've got some sprouts in this morning.'

Michael examined them. 'Not if they come from Brussels.'

Taking off his cap, the old man sighed. 'We know each other, you and I.'

'We do.'

'Half a pound?'

'Just what I was thinking.'

'Funny, isn't it. I mean, with my wife, Christine, we've stopped talking to each other. No point in saying anything. We already know what's going on up top.' He tapped his head with a finger, not seeming to appreciate that the gesture was also code for 'bonkers'. 'Thirty-one years we've been married. We just sit there, happy as Larry, switching channels. I hold the remote control. She eats peanuts. I press the buttons. Hates her name. Says it's old-fashioned. You married?'

'Yes.'

'Children?'

'Yes.' Michael took the proffered brown paper bag holding the sprouts from Bramfield. 'We don't speak any more either.'

The vendor tilted his head slightly. He wasn't quite sure what Michael had meant.

*   *   *

After dropping the sprouts into a waste bin, Michael took the concrete stairs from the road down to the promenade facing Southwold Denes beach. Following the unforgettable route, he passed a string of huts and found the steps onto the sand. To the right, wooden groynes reached out into the sea like resolute black fingers. They had a fight on their hands. Longshore drift it was called . . . that action of the waves shifting sand along the coastline. The groynes arrested the process. Kept the beach in place as if they'd brought time to a standstill, made it splash back and forth in the palm of one's hand.

'It's all I want to do, Dad,' said Jenny, with the simple conviction of any other seventeen-year-old.

They'd come to Southwold in August. Madame Semiglázov, her teacher, had entered her star pupil for the Prix de Lausanne in January. If Jennifer won, she'd get a six-month scholarship to the Royal Ballet School in Covent Garden. Michael hadn't been able to work out why Jenny couldn't just take the train up to London and ask for an audition, but Semi-detached (as they called her) had her own strange ways of thinking. She didn't explain herself. You were expected to trust everything she said, no questions asked. And prior to the competition she'd insisted on 'Jzenni' taking regular short holidays. Emma had gone shopping and Michael and his daughter had taken the concrete stairs and the steps onto the beach. They'd sat with their backs to the sea wall, as Michael did now, the barrel of the Browning hurting the bones of his lower spine. The pain drifted away, pushed along by another wave of anguish.

'I only want to dance.'

Her hair was scraped off her face and tied in a knot at the back. On anyone else the style might have looked severe, but with Jennifer, it wasn't really a style. It was what she did when she got out of bed. Her elegance was completely natural. Her fine black eyebrows contracted, drawing together her long dark lashes.

'If I don't win, it's all been for nothing,' she said, gazing out to sea. 'I was never any good at school, never one of the clever ones, but I knew how *to move* . . . knew how to speak with my body. To put everything into the way I walk, stand, turn, run . . . and fly. I've learned how to fly . . .'

No matter what happens, it hasn't been for nothing. You've reached into me, saved me from drowning without even knowing what you were doing.

'. . . and if I can't fly high, very high, I don't want to fly at all.'

Michael said, very quietly, barely louder than the murmur of the surf, 'Next year, Nimblefoot, you'll leave home and move to London. You'll be a student at the Royal Ballet School.'

'How do you know? It's up to the judges in Lausanne.'

'Because you dance like a bird in a cage. They'll know you belong outside.'

'Oh Daddy.' She leaned into him as if it were cold. The sun was high, a few clouds were clumped and low. Striped beach partitions flapped in the breeze. Parents and grandparents stood close to the breakers, their feet bare, trousers rolled over the knees, skirts tucked into a belt. They were bent forward watching the children cry with ecstatic terror. The sea was immense and they were small. It was the great unknown and there were monsters out there – prehistoric things with tentacles and yellow fangs. Jenny said, 'If it wasn't for you, I'd never have got off the ground.'

'We've both learned to fly,' said Michael.

I've flown far away from what I've done. Can't even remember what he looked like. I used to try . . . as if I owed it to him . . . but he's gone. There's just a dark track in my mind and three closed gates.

'I'll dance for you, Dad,' said Jennifer, pulling away.

'No, Nimblefoot, you dance for yourself, and for all the people who can't do what you can do.'

The cage door is open, darling. I only ever watched. I've never locked you in. You're ready to go now. Fly, my little girl, fly.

'Let's go and wrong-foot that man in the sweet shop,' said Jenny, rising. She looked down at her father, her face dark against the bright sky. Her features were lost, like those of the farmer in Donegal. There was just a sharp outline and the sound of a smile in her voice. 'We haven't tricked him since I was a child.'

Michael stood up. The pain from the gun returned to the base of his spine. Jenny had moved towards one of the groynes in his memory, those barriers that keep everything that's precious within reach. Head down and forlorn, he hauled himself up the metal steps and concrete stairs, fleeing the weight of Jenny's unfulfilled expectations. She'd won the Gold Medal in Lausanne. And at the end of her scholarship at the Royal Ballet School she'd joined the Royal Ballet itself. But that didn't mean she'd always be able to fly. Neither of them had looked beyond the snow outside the Théâtre de Beaulieu in Lausanne. They'd given no thought to the brutally unexpected . . . the arrival of Peter Henderson, that later slip on a church hall stage and the bowel cancer. But who did? Actually, Néall Ó Mórdha did. He'd always been ready for a shock. And look what happened to him.

The vendor of sweets saw Michael coming from a hundred yards. He smiled. He was on familiar ground. He stepped inside his shop and had just brought down the jar of sherbet lemons when Michael swept into the shop, hand reaching towards the ache in his back.

'Wine gums,' he said.

The old man blinked and frowned. One hand pushed back the cap.

'Hundred grams,' added Michael.

Christine's husband recoiled slightly. Something had gone wrong. Life wasn't like this. Certain things were for sure. There was no room for doubt. He looked at Michael as if he'd unzipped his fair, English skin to reveal the beast within: a metric monster who'd trespassed upon his kingdom of hallowed certainties. He said, eyes bright with resistance, 'Have we met before?'

14

'I've read all about you,' said the Reverend Doctor Nigel Goodwin, looking at Anselm with interest, his hands thrust into the pockets of a creased white linen jacket. 'Remember, Helen? He was in the *Sunday Times*.'

'Sorry, it never registered.'

'But I read it out. The monk from Larkwood Priory – it's just up the road. Remember? Well, well, well . . . you weren't listening, were you?' The specialist in Karl Barth shook his head knowingly, his lively features charged with lenience. 'Talk to myself, half the time,' he confessed, turning towards Anselm. 'Sick of my sermons, I suppose.'

Sensing the muscular curiosity that comes from a man of the cloth faced with a confrère's celebrity, Anselm deftly avoided any discussion about past cases by producing the letter sent to Larkwood's Prior.

'I'll make some tea,' said Helen, finding an excuse (Anselm thought) to leave the room. She needed a breather. She needed to work out how to escape a storm of her own making. Anselm knew about Michael and Northern Ireland. He knew too much. And if Nigel got going about Jennifer, he might raise a wind, inadvertently, because he didn't know what his wife had been thinking for twenty years.

'And how about some of that magnificent fruit cake?' added her husband, merrily.

Doctor Goodwin was one of those challenging people who radiate energy with the smallest of gestures. He read with eyebrows raised, one foot quietly tapping the floor, his fine mouth following the shape of the words. Silver-framed glasses amplified the mood of concentration. Anselm could easily imagine the doctor, masked and determined, abseiling through a window of the Iranian Embassy, Heckler and Koch at the ready. Grappling with Barth in the quiet of the Bodleian seemed barely credible.

'I didn't write this,' he said, laying the letter on the table cluttered with books. 'But I could have done. Each and every word. I'm glad to know I'm not the only one who was troubled . . . deeply troubled by Jennifer's passing. And I'm relieved to learn that someone like yourself, someone who can operate outside conventional channels, is prepared to look into it. You're dealing with a closed universe. Finding a way into Peter's world is not going to be easy. Even I couldn't find a route, and I was Jenny's godfather. How can I help?'

Somehow he was staring vigorously at Anselm.

'In the first instance by telling me why you went to see Detective Superintendent Manning.'

'Because there's no one out there like you.' Doctor Goodwin was being strictly factual, not complimentary. 'I had an anxiety that I couldn't in conscience keep to myself. I'd seen Jenny on her birthday, the day she died, and despite . . . despite her terrible condition . . . she was in fine spirits . . . a bit drowsy but otherwise . . . *at peace*. It was inspiring. But then, suddenly, she was dead. She'd recently had tests and as far as I know everything was fine. I spoke to her doctor and I sensed a certain anxiety . . . a compassionate anxiety. He smoothed away my *imputations*. Said he'd examined the body and she'd died of bowel cancer. The condition had been advanced. Devouring. Urged me to treat myself as I'd treat a distressed parishioner . . . to tell them that "death is completely natural . . . that it comes at the *right time* . . . that it's we who *rebel* . . . that it's *we* who cling onto life long after it's time to let go".'

'What was the doctor's name?'

'Ingleby. Bryan Ingleby. He was a close friend of Peter's. More of a father figure.'

'Where was he based?'

'Needham Market.'

'He took over Jenny's care just after the accident.'

The sitting room door opened and Mrs Goodwin entered pushing a tea trolley on wheels. Everything was beautifully laid on a white embroidered cloth: fine china, biscuits and slices of the famous fruit cake. She busied herself, like Martha in the gospel, only there were no complaints etched onto her smooth face. Anselm was right: she didn't want to talk. She'd already chosen the better part: mute service, a role the merits of which the evangelists had singly failed to appreciate. Thinking of what she'd already revealed, Anselm said, innocently, 'I would be greatly helped if you could simply tell me the family story . . . from the moment Peter Henderson entered Jennifer's life' – the place in the narrative when, in fact, Mrs Goodwin had been compelled to leave off – 'because it seems to me that this is where the territory of motive begins. This is where we have to look. If Peter Henderson killed Jennifer, the rationale will be imprinted on a simple succession of facts . . . neutral from one perspective, but – I hope – revealing from another. In a case like this, one simply has to keep walking around the *facts* . . . like Cartier-Bresson before he took a photograph.'

The request snagged Mrs Goodwin. Perhaps she'd intended to slip out of the room to do the ironing. Instead she sat down, wondering – Anselm thought – how her husband would take up the tale. She looked worried.

'I'd been moving around a lot,' said Doctor Goodwin, stealing a cherry off the serving plate. 'Parish appointments the length of the country, so I'd drifted out of touch with Jennifer's family . . . my brother and Emma his wife. But we still shared a few important moments . . . and one of those was the day we all met Peter Henderson; a cold, unforgettable day in February.'

Doctor Goodwin edged forward as if to share a secret.

'We'd been invited to Sunday lunch. My brother Michael, he's a . . . quiet man. Conventional. An old-fashioned liberal. Shirt and tie decency. Never saw him without polished shoes. Loved Evensong . . . well, he used to . . . and then there's Emma: vaguely theatrical, a vet who might have been a stage actress. Very proper, occasionally racy. But always *correct*. Knew how to use a line of knives and forks. Went down a bomb at the mess dinners with her panache and wit. An ideal companion for Michael. And both of them devoted parents. Now, coming from that background, you'd have thought that Jenny would be drawn to some quiet type with a bit of unexpected colour . . . whereas Peter . . . well, he was a sort of roadside explosion.'

Arrived in jeans. Hadn't shaved. When Michael lit a cigarette, Peter said, soft spoken and reasonable, 'No offence, but they'll kill you. And possibly the rest of us if we hang around long enough.' He sat with an arm around Jenny. A handsome man: clean lines to the facial bones; balding early; black tufts above the ears.

'And Emma had made this beef Wellington,' said Doctor Goodwin. 'An immense fillet wrapped in pastry, and when she brought it in on a silver tray, Peter said, "I'm vegetarian." "I beg your pardon?" says Emma. "I'm sorry but all the evidence suggests that animals are as loving, societal and emotionally complex as we are. They have rights. And one of the more basic is not to be eaten." "I *told* you, Mum," says Jenny, absolutely mortified. "Sorry, darling, I must have forgotten." And then Peter says, as if to help out, "Emma, they're as sensitive as you are," which didn't go down very well, so he threw his hands in the air and said, "I'm sorry, but the practice of meat-eating is one of the most serious moral questions of our time . . . " And so that was the first subject for discussion . . . over the beef . . . all the while no one daring to refer to the elephant in the room.'

'Which was?' asked Anselm.

'His age,' interjected Mrs Goodwin.

'Peter was thirty-two and looked older,' resumed her husband, 'whereas Jenny was only nineteen and looked younger. She was still a girl . . . to me at least . . . and there she was, holding hands with a man who seemed old enough to be her father.'

'Thirteen years,' pressed Mrs Goodwin. 'That's a big age difference. Jenny was simply mesmerised by his confidence, flattered by his attention. A Cambridge don who appeared on telly had dedicated his latest book to her. Who could resist that?'

Me, thought Anselm. 'What was the subject?'

'Charles Stevenson. An American philosopher,' said Doctor Goodwin.

'Never heard of him.'

'Emotivist school. Held there could be intelligent disagreement over moral questions.'

'How refreshing.'

'And ironic, because emotions were running high. At least on the Goodwin side. Within a very short time it became clear that Peter was atheist, anti-monarchist and pacifist. Frankly, I was attracted to him. He was unnervingly honest. Said what he thought, in clear, dispassionate terms. Didn't seem to appreciate that a social situation might require tact over conviction. Or at least moderation of argument. You see . . . Emma had gone to enormous lengths to welcome him; she was standing there, holding the silver platter, and he didn't seem to realise that her generosity needed some kind of acknowledgement. He only saw the issue of meat-eating. In a way he was innocent.'

Perhaps he was annoyed, too, thought Anselm. Emma had forgotten Peter was vegetarian because she didn't take the underlying argument seriously; didn't consider his belief worth remembering. Wasn't that the greater insult? He tried Helen's cake and paused to think some more: it could not be fairly described, even tactfully, as magnificent.

'How did Michael react to this challenge to his universe?' asked Anselm. 'You mentioned dinners at the mess and I imagine—'

'Very observant,' congratulated Doctor Goodwin, stealing another cherry. 'My brother was in the Army. Royal Anglian

91

Regiment. Served overseas. Cyprus. Germany. So he was uncomfortable with the jeans and so on. But he swallowed all that. The problem came when Peter turned his attention onto Northern Ireland. And I don't mean the bravery of our boys in the fight against sectarian terror . . . I mean the scandal – his phrase – of collusion. British Intelligence feeding information about Republican targets to Loyalist murder gangs. The Army killing unarmed men before they could surrender. The whole "shoot to kill" controversy.'

'I'd have thought Peter Henderson might have found a way to justify measures of that kind,' said Anselm, dispassionately. 'You know, a greater good requiring the moral destruction of the man who, in other circumstances, wouldn't harm a fly. Doing a grave wrong to do a supreme right.'

'But he didn't,' said Doctor Goodwin. 'Peter's point was that without legislative safeguards, anything could happen on the ground. Executive actions had to be subject to independent judicial scrutiny. You'd have thought Michael would have agreed. He'd never have sanctioned *anyone* doing *anything* outside the law. As it is, he was blown from his seat.'

Anselm had let his eyes drift from the doctor to the dried-out cake, to Helen, the reluctant architect of the developing moment. She was rigid in her seat, one hand on each knee, her gaze burning holes in the carpet. They both knew that Nigel had given his roving work as the explanation for his distance from Michael, rather than it being a consequence of Michael's mysterious trauma. More particularly, Nigel had abbreviated Michael's CV, leaving out the posting to Belfast and the shift to intelligence work. And Anselm, tingling with prescience, now wondered if Michael's return to England – traumatised to such an extent that he'd left the armed forces to translate faxes from Italy – might just be linked to the subject into which Peter Henderson had stumbled: the scandal of collusion. That, at least, appeared to be Helen's belief. And probably her husband's, too. Why else had he left those two otherwise innocuous facts out of the reckoning? Husband and wife had finally got an insight into why Michael had come home shattered. Alone, it seemed, Helen had linked the Belfast experience to Jennifer's later death – another such moment, perhaps. She'd developed a murder theory in the dark that she couldn't share with the man she loved and served. She'd never told anyone.

'Blown from his seat?' queried Anselm.

'Sent flying.'

'By an argument?'

'No, insensitivity.' Doctor Goodwin stubbed some cake crumbs on the plate with his finger. 'Peter said that to shoot an unarmed terrorist as if he was a stray dog could be challenged on a number of grounds, but the most devastating and intellectually accessible was this: it was simply wrong . . . and it was then that Michael's chair went flying backwards. Bear in mind, the merits of Peter's argument had nothing to do with it. He was having a swing at Michael's *identity*. He knew damn well that Jenny's father had once been an Army man. The Canary Wharf bomb had gone off the week before, ending an eighteen-month ceasefire by the IRA . . . and here was Peter complaining about British atrocities in Northern Ireland. Michael couldn't take it. He stormed out of the room. I can still see Emma, smiling brightly, "Anyone for baked Alaska? Hot on the outside, cold in the middle." And Peter – imagine this – he didn't even flinch when the chair went back, any more than he'd flinched over the beef Wellington.'

Because he thought the issues were too important, mused Anselm. Poor Michael. Army pride to one side, he'd undergone every parent's living nightmare. His daughter had hitched herself to a man he could never embrace as a son. Even so, Anselm hadn't yet heard anything that warranted the description of a 'roadside explosion'. Peter was different, yes. But wasn't there something attractive about a man who couldn't restrain his honesty? A man who actually *had* some beliefs, held them strongly, and was prepared to upset everybody in order to defend them?

'Did Michael return to the room?' asked Anselm.

'Yes, he did. To apologise.' Doctor Goodwin's expressive face showed all the pain of that remembered humiliation. 'He made a stumbling speech about his regimental tie and becoming an old bore. And then he held out his hand . . . that was so typical of him. He had to shake on it.'

'And Peter took it?' asked Anselm.

'Oh yes. He even stood up. And that's when Peter dropped the bombshell that no one had seen coming . . . only there was no uproar afterwards. Just a stunned silence. He said, "Jenny's got something to tell you." He made it sound as if he was blurting out the good news to smooth over any embarrassment. Jenny glanced at her mother and then her father and then her mother again . . . but we all knew already. She put on this hopeful, anxious, breaking smile . . . and then she said it. "I'm pregnant."'

Abruptly Helen stood up, frowning and distressed. 'He'd staged the argument on purpose. Nigel doesn't agree' – she glared at her husband, ready to meet any fresh challenge – 'but I don't accept any of that *intellectual honesty* claptrap . . . his so-called "innocence". He knew damn well what he was doing. He'd had a good go at both Emma and Michael. He'd played us all into position so he could minimise any chance of reproach. He'd got a nineteen-year-old girl pregnant when he should have protected her, when all he'd had to do was take *precautions* . . . simple, adult *precautions*' – she glanced at Anselm as if he might not know what they were or, at worst, might entertain doctrinal objections of the more unyielding kind – 'and then, rather than take any responsibility, he staged a fight with her father over nothing and waited for Michael to apologise . . . for *Michael* to apologise to *him* . . .'

'Did the ploy work?' asked Anselm, doubting if it had, in fact, been a ploy; thinking that the shoot-to-kill issue might have been 'something' rather than 'nothing'.

'Of course not,' snapped Mrs Goodwin. 'Given the *fait accompli*, no one in that room would have rebuked him . . . we just kept our thoughts to ourselves, for Jenny's sake.'

'Even Michael?'

'Especially Michael. He made another speech. Shook his hand again. Accepted Peter into the family. And Peter just smiled as if he'd pulled off a military triumph.' Mrs Goodwin paused as if to gather in the prophetic significance of that remembered Sunday afternoon. 'Poor Jenny . . . she'd found someone wild and exciting and he was going to take her to a strange and foreign land. And in time, he did. And poor Michael, not knowing what would happen, bowed his head and served the coffee, laughing and nodding by turns at everything clever Peter had to say. He put himself under Peter's feet and that . . . that smooth-talking *bastard* just wiped clean his dirty trainers.'

Doctor Goodwin looked at his wife as if she'd come clean off the leash. He reached for one of her hands and squeezed her fingers tight. He wasn't reproving or annoyed. Just grateful, Anselm thought. She had a way with words. Said the sorts of things he could never say from the pulpit.

'How did we end up getting into all that?' he said, helplessly, all his energy gone.

'I don't know,' said Helen.

Yes, you do. Anselm nodded to himself. *It's because of me. I took your hint.*

Doctor Goodwin let her hand go and he turned to Anselm. 'I've more to say . . . about Peter and Jenny. I could do with some fresh air. Can I take you to where it all began and ended? There's something important about place, don't you agree?'

Anselm did. Gratified, Doctor Goodwin went to a bureau in the corner of the room. With quite extraordinary care, he took a letter from a drawer and transferred it to an inside jacket pocket.

'I'll stay here,' said Helen, pushing the tea trolley towards the door. 'I've lots of jobs to do in the garden.'

Of course you have, concluded Anselm. She had nothing else to add. In the end, despite getting cold feet, she'd done her bit for Jenny. With a little adroit nudging from Anselm, Nigel had completed Helen's story about Northern Ireland without Helen having to open her mouth. It had gone without a hitch, for Nigel hadn't quite known what he'd been saying – what the facts about Michael had meant to Helen. Anselm didn't fully grasp them either. But it was only a matter of time. He just needed to brood upon the meaning of the suppressed information. Taking her hand at the door, he almost said, 'Your secret's safe with me.' Instead he murmured, 'Thanks for the cake.'

She smiled. They both knew it was dried out; that it should never be called magnificent.

15

Evening light saturated the long pier at Southwold. The clouds above were soaked an angry crimson. Softer yellow smudges and faint purple streams ran into the watery blue of the sky. Michael stood alone on the silvered wooden planking, hands in his coat pockets. He was looking at the Water Clock.

The clock was an amusing scrap metal sculpture, tall like the grandfather kind, only twice the size and made up of different objects in a welded open casing. Beneath the round face at the top were two taps. They were open and the water tumbled into an old Victorian bath. In the bath lay two recumbent figures with short tubes sticking out of the sides of their mouths as if they were biting on cigarettes. On a platform beneath the bath were two other figures – boys, Michael thought – standing either side of a toilet basin. Near the ground, in a line like targets at a fair, was a row of tulips.

The Nutting Squad had used a bath on Eugene. By the time

he came up for air, he'd lost the will to resist. He'd told them what they wanted to know — what they already believed — even though it wasn't true. There was nothing he could say to persuade them he was innocent. They'd gathered evidence from people who knew him backwards. It all pointed in one direction. Upwards. They knew he was a tout. But they were wrong. Just like the trader in the shop.

Michael looked higher at the hands of the clock and higher still at the blood in the sky.

According to the *Belfast Telegraph*, to get at the inner man, to reach what he was *really* thinking, they'd broken Eugene's fingers and toes, burned holes in his muscles with cigarettes and placed a hot poker under his arms. Eventually, after a bath, he'd made a taped confession. They'd sent it to his wife as a kind of explanation.

Michael closed his eyes against the wet clouds. He almost heard Liam's tread on the weathered planking. The priest had gone and the informer had come back into the room.

'What will you do?'

Michael didn't reply.

'You'll stiff him, won't you?' Liam knew the argot.

Michael's stomach turned. The priest had done Eugene's bidding: a Brit who dealt with touts had been told a secret worth dying for. Néall Ó Mórdha was the stumbling block to any peace process. He would never abandon the armed struggle. He'd be alone in Donegal next week, Wednesday night.

'You'll have to rub him out,' murmured Liam, importantly, as if he knew about these things. 'He has to go down.'

A *priest* had set up a man to be killed.

Michael's mouth was dry, the spit on his lips crusting like a young scab. What else could the priest mean? What did he expect? That the Brits would frame Ó Mórdha? Engineer a charge on tax evasion to get him banged away for two years? What difference would that make? The man of God had come to Michael because

Eugene had told him to speak to someone who dealt with touts: the people who, according to IRA propaganda, organised the execution of unarmed volunteers.

'It doesn't work that way,' said Michael. 'There's nothing I can do.'

'What do you mean?'

'I fill in a CF, a contact form. Someone taps it into the computer. Someone else thinks and acts. And they won't be sending the SAS into Donegal.'

'You can't do nowt?'

'I said I'll fill in the form.'

'That's not enough.'

'It'll have to do. I'm on leave from tomorrow.'

'You heard what your man Eugene said. You can't just type it up. You can't just take a holiday, not now . . . look, I can help.'

Liam leaned back hard, shutting the door with his shoulders.

Michael appraised his first agent with dismay. Five foot ten. Eighteen years four months old. Thin. Brown greasy hair. Pasty complexion. Spots on the forehead. Black-framed glasses. Large brown eyes. Mouth sloping to one side. First contact: arrested for shoplifting. Charges dropped. Proposed to FRU by Special Branch.

'Do you hear what I'm saying?' whispered Liam. 'I can help.' The floor above creaked and Liam brushed the sound aside with an impatient, pasty hand. 'I'm no small fry.'

Michael dropped his head into his hands and the armchair squeaked as if stabbed. The priest had come and gone, a messenger who enjoyed the luxury of not having to act on what he'd said.

'I said I can help.'

Nigel . . . what do I do? Michael squeezed his eyes tight shut. *You were cut out for this, not me. You're the one who saw wars simply. What do I do? I've got a kid in front of me who wants to help me kill someone.*

A flash from a sermon came to Michael's mind. Nigel was in the pulpit at the Royal Memorial Chapel at Sandhurst, broad and strong, hands on the lectern. He'd been invited by the chaplain to address officer recruits destined for the Medical Corps. Michael had tagged along.

'Life is short, the crisis fleeting, experiment risky, decision difficult,' declared Nigel. He'd gone back to the *Aphorisms* of Hippocrates.

(Michael saw his brother's roving eyes.)

'Doctors – like soldiers – must respond, often quickly and with resolution. One day, you may find yourself alone in a fleeting crisis. The moment of hesitation will have passed and it will be your duty to act.'

For effect, Nigel let his gaze settle upon one individual – someone he'd judged timid and unsure.

'On that awful day, my friend, be calm. Stare the fast approach of death straight in the eye. Look at the sickness and the suffering. And then get on with it. Take the risk. Make the difficult decision. Save a life, if you can. Don't let hesitation slow you down. And afterwards, looking back on the crisis, you just might notice a Still, Small Voice – hidden at the time, but present in your anguish. You were never, in fact, alone.'

Michael dropped his hands and looked over at Liam; at his large, demanding eyes.

'What did you steal? Before you were pushed towards us lot?'

Liam's jaw dropped in astonishment.

'Eh?'

'Answer the bloody question.'

'Pork chops . . . a cabbage. A carton of Silk Cut . . . menthol.'

'What's wrong with your mother?'

'Nowt.'

'The swollen knees and ankles?'

'She's too fat.'

'She's in bed?'

'Couldn't be bothered to come downstairs. I said I can help. I'm no eejit.'

'Where's your father?'

'Never had one.'

Michael leaned forward and the armchair squealed. He was going to finish Liam's days as an informer right there and then but Liam barked.

'I'm holding guns for the IRA. Ammunition, too. And detonators. They trust me.'

Michael blinked at the nodding head.

'That's right. I've worked my way in. They think I'm small fry with a sick ma. An eejit.'

Michael's seat yelped.

'I keep the guns for two weeks at a time and then they move 'em. I've had a pistol and four rifles for a couple of days now I have. There's a Browning automatic under your chair. And a silencer behind the boiler. You can use 'em and put 'em back and no one'll know a thing. You can stiff the Army Council fella using one of their own tools. The ballistics will show the bullets came from a thing used by the IRA in other killings. No one'll think it was the Brits or the UDA or whoever. And yous lot can then feed the results to the IRA through me and they'll go crazy trying to find one of their own.'

Michael felt faint. The Army had sent him on a psychological training course to help him identify when an agent was slipping off the rails. Liam had developed none of the symptoms . . . but he'd obviously crashed through all the barriers without making a single noise. He'd acted outside the authority of his handler and he hadn't even broken a sweat.

'Father Doyle says as a people we're *in need*,' muttered Liam, adjusting his heavy glasses, his back still to the door. 'We can't get out of the cycle of violence and mayhem. Neighbours are killing neighbours. There's no end to the funerals. The grief. Well, thanks to your man there, Eugene, we can do something. You can't just fill in a bleedin' form and leave it to some other fella. Father Doyle brought you the message, so. Now it's over to you to do yer stuff.'

Stuff? Michael could no longer move: the cheap synthetic covering was silent. His first agent was out of control. Worse: Michael was sitting on an arms dump belonging to the Provisional IRA. The enormity of the situation crashed in upon him.

He'd been with the FRU six months. Liam had been recruited two months prior to that. They were both green though Liam was that smidgen longer in the tooth. But they'd been told some grade A1 intelligence with a fast-moving shelf life. Do your stuff? Liam – like Father Doyle – meant assassination. But that's not the way it worked. Sure the SAS took short cuts and he'd heard rumours of a Rat Hole, a place where top handlers managed top agents, cutting corners every now and then . . . but no one he could think of was going to authorise the killing of Néall Ó Mórdha next Wednesday. And yet, the Republican zealot was going to be there. It was a moment of opportunity. To tilt the balance against violence. Eugene had said so, just before they shot him.

'Are you going to answer me or what?'

Colonel Stauffenberg attempted to kill Hitler, thought Michael. He, too, was backed by a pastor . . . Bonhoeffer. If they'd succeeded, the war would have been cut short by a year. Thousands of lives would have been saved. If they'd killed him in 1939, there would have been no war, no holocaust.

'Well, are you even breathing?'

Michael let his eyes come into focus. He saw Liam's earnest face against the peeling wallpaper, his mouth half open. This petty thief was no backroom conspirator in the High Command. Father Doyle was no Bonhoeffer. *And I'm no hero.* Michael shuddered at the exalted grubbiness of his circumstances. The chair whined.

Nigel, what do I do?

Michael listened, still paralysed, aching to hear that Still, Small Voice.

At first he wasn't paying proper attention. But then, in complete horror, he started tracking Liam's words: his murderous advice, whispered just in case, for once, his mother had come downstairs and paused on her way to the kitchen.

'You have to be calm, you know. They say a man's life flashes before him just before he dies. Well, it's not true.' Liam came over and sat down in a chair by his handler. 'He sees the future he might have had. His eyes are full of wonder . . . you can see it, just before you kill him. It's the look of a newborn . . . and you can't hesitate. You turn out his light.'

Michael stood up as if the devil himself had slipped into Liam's skin. He stepped away, backing towards the dead gas fire.

'You'll have to practise,' promised Liam. 'Look into the eyes of someone you love. Try to . . .'

This wasn't Liam speaking. His voice had changed. His syntax had altered. This is what the kid had heard at some other door. He'd heard an old hand teaching a new recruit how to be a trigger man. The evil had entered Liam's lungs like Silk Cut, the poison and fumes stealing into his soul. He'd memorised the phrases, turning them over with the insight of a child learning Shakespeare.

Get Ó Mórdha, and you'll get a peace process, sputtered Eugene from the torture chamber in Ballymurphy. *Let him go and the war will just drag on.*

Liam was still speaking. He'd tipped up the armchair that Michael had been using. On his knees, he felt inside the frame for the 'tool'.

'You can't hesitate,' he said, bending lower, proudly repeating to Michael what he'd learned from the master. 'You move quickly. He has to go down . . . you do the job.'

Michael stared at the threadbare carpet, appalled at Liam's metamorphosis. The weave had once been soaked in colours. Where had they gone?

'There's no other way,' growled Liam, still kneeling, holding the gun by the barrel, offering the grip to Michael, his features blank and grey like the carpet. 'All the thinking's been done, hasn't it? If you want peace, you'll have to pull the trigger.'

In a kind of daze, Michael took the gun and asked for the silencer. Eyes narrowed as if he'd walked into a snowstorm, he told Liam there'd be no assassination and that they'd meet on Saturday of next week, when he'd return the weapon, modified with a tracking device in the handle. The rifles? Too big to hide. For the time being they would have to stay under Liam's mother's bed. His standing as an agent would be under review, along with the level of pay.

On reaching Thiepval, Michael sat down at his desk to fill in the CF but found himself staring at the page. His hand reached into his pocket and he took out the scrawled directions to a cottage in the Blue Stack Mountains. He watched his hand put it away again. He watched the other hand put the unmarked CF back in a drawer. All the while Liam's Browning was lodged at the base of his back, the silencer standing like a stick of Brighton rock in the overcoat pocket that hung on the door.

During the night Michael tossed and turned. At one point he sat bolt upright . . . he could have sworn he'd heard a voice. But there was no other sound save the distant rev of a Saracen and the soft tick of his bedside clock. Instantly, as if carrying on where he'd left off, he thought of Colonel Stauffenberg, but it was Nigel's words – the reference to Hippocrates – that came sharply to mind:

Take the risk. Make the difficult decision.

And then, mysteriously, he slept as if drugged.

By morning, when he woke, Michael wasn't sure he knew himself. He was strangely cold, deep in his bones. The barracks – the whole of Northern Ireland – seemed a little far off; not quite within arm's reach. Somehow he'd made a decision without articulating its content or implications. While shaving, he asked himself what lay at the forefront of his mind. It wasn't the Troubles and the need for a solution, and it wasn't the death of Eugene or his attempt to give it some clout. No, it was Liam Finnerty, spotty and callow. Michael wanted to change the direction of Irish history, so that people like Liam wouldn't be needed to pry on rebels, hide their guns and take pocket money from the ancient invader. Michael dried his face, unable to see any further than the actions necessary to fulfil his objective. After dressing in casuals, he set about his duty.

First, he called Emma, saying he wouldn't be coming home. Hush-hush. Then he put the Browning and silencer into his Billingham bag and took a train to Limerick in the Republic of Ireland, where he bought a jalopy for 450 punts, cash in hand, and left the gun in the boot. The next day, using his British passport, he flew from Shannon airport to Edinburgh, spent three nights in a hotel rehearsing his moves, and then came back again, re-entering the country on his Canadian passport. The whole back and forth was an expensive palaver. He wasn't covering his tracks, as such, because a careful look at the plane manifests would reveal his name. No, the shift in location and identity was an attempt to separate himself from what he was about to do: to make the difficult decision, he would go away as a peacemaker and come back as a killer. The ruse helped him assume the role he'd never dreamed would be the ineluctable consequence of his coming to Belfast. And so, while the British Army officer was on leave in Scotland, the Canadian assassin headed north in a rattling Fiesta.

The Water Clock struck the hour, and Michael snapped out of his remembered holiday. After a moment's clunking, the two figures in the bath sat up, spouting water from the pipes in their mouths. On the level below, the boys' metal trousers dropped and they started to pee, each of them missing the toilet pan. It was funny, only Michael thought he might collapse. He turned away, thinking of Eugene and Liam, a man and a boy, both of them touts. They'd both relied on Michael to take down Néall Ó Mórdha and cut short the long war.

16

Crossing the road, Anselm and Mitch turned as one to look at the upstairs window. A net curtain fell. The monk and the musician shared a glance, each confirming to the other his strong suspicion: Doctor Goodwin did need to take a breather, but only because he wanted to move the conversation away from the person upstairs.

'I came back to Long Melford a few months before Jenny died,' he said, as the Land Rover juddered into life. 'Early retirement. Zimbers hadn't been the easiest assignment. I wanted to write and I'd been asked to do some tutoring at Cambridge. Turn right.'

Doctor Goodwin had given no indication of where he was leading them. He restricted himself to simple directions.

'Straight on. We bought the house with family money before I was ordained. Stayed there in the holidays. Whenever I saw Jenny, I saw Peter and he never tired of asking me, when I left, how I squared a loving God with suffering. He was absolutely sincere, but I think, deep down, I, too, scandalised him, with my myths and incantations. I was a colluder . . . with ignorance. Stick to the A134.'

Anselm looked over the empty fields, meditating on collusion. It was a disagreeable word. *The Force Research Unit. Shoot-to-kill. Stray dogs.*

'I would have liked to discuss *faith* with him,' continued Doctor Goodwin. 'Not its content, but its function as a kind of daring commitment to what we don't fully understand, but I fear the very sight of me provoked him . . . to assert what he believed was true, as a man of reason and science. He didn't seem to appreciate that so much of science rests upon a faith in evolving explanations, a readiness to question all our certainties. The recognition of doubt as shared ground in the search for truth . . . well, it could have brought about a very *interesting* discussion, for both of us. As it is, he preferred to set up things I didn't believe and then knock them down.'

You provoked your brother, too, thought Anselm. *Michael had to turn away, even after Jenny's fall from grace. Why? Because he didn't like Evensong any more? Or was it guilt, roused by what you represent?*

'Helen can't forgive Peter,' acknowledged Doctor Goodwin, careful (for professional reasons) to dissociate his name from the declaration. 'She's tried but one can't escape history. There's been no gathering in of all that's happened. So the resentment lives on. And so it should. Because it's *honest.* It's the necessary precursor to any profound reconciliation. And, in our case, I doubt if that day will ever come to pass. He killed her, you know. We can't prove it, but she was murdered. He knows it and we know it. Bear to the right.'

Anselm leaned on the shuddering, grimy window, thinking of Helen. She didn't think it was Peter at all but she'd said nothing to disabuse Nigel. *I have my own theory about Jenny's death . . . but I can't tell you in front of my husband.*

'What about Michael?' asked Mitch, with a tap to the indicator. 'Is he sure, too?'

'I can't speak for him,' said Doctor Goodwin, perfunctorily. 'As I told you, my work had kept us apart. After Jenny's death he . . . he slipped further out of reach. I don't know what he thinks.'

'And Emma?'

'She felt as I did, as Helen did . . . because there was only one person who wasn't surprised by Jenny's sudden death.'

'Peter?'

'Exactly. It was as though he'd known she was dead before she died.'

Anselm put the counter-argument, intrigued to know how Doctor Goodwin would reply: 'But this is a man who'd argued for the importance of legislative safeguards. How could he come to kill a defenceless woman?'

'Because when he found himself in a concrete situation that he didn't like very much, his ideas gave out. High principles often collapse when they get in the way of a quiet life. And Jenny was the weight dragging him down. You'll understand what I mean once I've told you her story . . . and this is where it begins, Polstead.'

Doctor Goodwin opened the farm-style front gate bearing a plaque that read 'Morning Light'. He let Anselm and Mitch pass onto a gravel courtyard and then led them to an adjacent lawn and a neat arrangement of teak garden furniture. Ahead stood a thatched cottage, the clean lemon plaster pierced by white-framed windows of different sizes, randomly placed, it seemed, adding a capricious stroke to the builder's seventeenth-century construction.

'Jenny loved this place,' said Doctor Goodwin, eyeing the warm, grey thatch. 'She thought she had everything that was worthwhile and good . . . a home off a biscuit tin lid, a young son, a brilliant partner . . .'

Of course, there'd been no marriage. Church or civil. Peter — rightly — wouldn't take vows or enter a civil contract inconsistent with his beliefs. But right from the word go, he'd protected Jenny financially, placing all the main assets in her name. House, car, even the contents of the house. That was *his* avowal of trust and commitment. His only property rights were set out in Jenny's will.

'Till death us do part,' observed Mitch.

'Absolutely.' The doctor flicked a crisp, brown leaf off the table.

'The career in ballet,' invited Mitch. 'She just let it go?'

'Sometimes the big decisions make themselves.' Doctor Goodwin glanced at his questioner. 'Jenny had become a mother. Suddenly, without time to think or choose, she had this little boy in her hands. But make no mistake about this: even though she'd lived and breathed for dancing, she wanted this child and all he represented. And as the years went by, though she didn't dance, I got the impression she was *grateful*; thankful for this very different life that had come with the birth of her son. She'd been surprised by contentment.' Doctor Goodwin paused reflectively. 'And, I'm sorry to say, distress.'

According to Emma – who'd told Helen – problems began to surface between Peter and Jenny within a year of Timothy's birth. The age gap needn't have been an issue, of course, but it was. Jenny was still very young, still growing up; whereas Peter was settled, mature, and knew his mind. There was a profound imbalance of experience. They were not equals – and couldn't be. Before she could assert herself, Jenny had yet to catch up and become who she might be. But there was also the sheer intellectual disparity between them. Jenny wasn't especially interested in the French Eighteenth-Century Argument. Or the English one. She listened to Peter's valiant attempt to explain Kant's Categorical Imperative, but had to cut him short to change Timothy's nappy. Jenny had more important things to do. More pressing, at least.

'So Peter found other company.' The phrase was laden with meaning. 'At the same time his media career was taking off and he was very much in demand, very much appreciated, and very much at home . . . when away from home.'

Some women – Doctor Goodwin supposed – can tolerate the affairs of their partner. They can even be an agreed course of diversion. But Jenny wasn't like that; and parallel relationships, however fleeting, had never been canvassed as part of the balance of things. But this was the central problem: nothing had been canvassed or agreed. They'd been bound together by Timothy's birth and were now trying to learn about each other and find an agreed way forward.

'My view is that Peter simply lost sight of Jenny,' said Doctor Goodwin. 'He could no longer see the qualities that had once attracted him. She was no longer the thin, haunting beauty he'd met in a wine bar off Soho. He wasn't interested in playgroup gossip and the tensions that come with relationships determined by children. He bought a flat in London because of his media commitments. Couldn't make it home, especially if he was on *Newsnight*. In effect there was a separation, though it was never decided, never named, and was, I can assure you, the last thing Jenny wanted.'

'And what of Timothy?' asked Anselm.

'Well, there's a curious twist to the story. Because of Peter's absence, Timothy became very close to his mother. And she to him. They were . . . friends. And because of the strength of this bond, I don't think Timothy quite noticed that his father was busy elsewhere. If anything, he was proud of him . . . this man who was always on the radio and television with his face peering out of magazines and newspapers. The person who really lost out, of course, was Peter. He wasn't there for Timothy in those very early years. He didn't watch him slowly grow. He regrets that now, I suspect.'

For Michael and Emma, continued Doctor Goodwin, it was very difficult. They could only watch the years unfold. Emma was devastated. She saw Jenny lose her dancing career only to find herself alone while Peter stimulated some television producer's assistant in White City (her phrasing). She found fault with all he did, especially his parenting after the accident, which set her apart – strangely – from Jenny. For throughout her ordeal – this sustained rejection – Jenny remained steadfast . . . waiting for Peter to come home.

'And Michael?' asked Anselm, from afar, polishing his glasses on his scapular.

'He bottled it up. Silence was the price he paid for staying close to Jenny's hand. He moved quietly across the room, offering fresh coffee.'

Inwardly boiling, outwardly cold, thought Anselm. Baked Alaska the wrong way round.

They ambled down a lane flanked by trees coming presently to a church of flint. Sheep were grazing in distant fields. Scattered headstones leaned in various directions as if to resist the wind. One of them was upright, still strong. Purple tulips stood in a vase beneath an inscription:

Jennifer Goodwin
1977–2008
Dance, dance wherever you may be

The doctor's voice came very low. He was harrowed, as if he could see his god-daughter's upturned face: 'I was in Bristol at the time of the accident. I came to see her. And she just said, "God has left me." She was in bed staring down at her legs. There was going to be no cure for the lame. No miracle on the Sabbath. All I could do was listen.'

He reached inside his jacket pocket and he took out the precious envelope. Giving it to Anselm, he said: 'I went to Zimbabwe ten days later. I wrote to her every week and never got a reply. It was only after I came back to Long Melford that she put pen to paper. It's as though she was resuming the correspondence that had never taken place, referring back to my letters of encouragement. By this stage, she'd been diagnosed with bowel cancer. She'd been given a year to live. Five months had gone.'

Anselm removed the letter. Mitch came close so that he, too, might read Jennifer's message. The writing was small and elegant. There was no 'Dear Uncle Nigel'. She'd written directly from her concerns:

I cannot walk. I have cancer. I am going to die.

I've decided to stay at home.

I won't have all those tubes and medicines.

I won't have different nurses holding my hand.

I won't be on the agenda when the night shift go home and the day shift turn up.

I might be alone.

It could be painful.

I'll be very frightened. I'm frightened already.

I might hang around on the edge of living, held down by this body of mine that doesn't work.

Things couldn't be much worse.

You gave me the strength to write those words. You taught me not to be ashamed of saying that things are bad and awful, when they are. You said there's a liberty in all honesty. You said, by the same token, that I should never give up on surprises. Well, as the end nears, I thought we might talk about that.

Anselm slowly folded up the letter.

Taking it back, Doctor Goodwin took a step towards him and said, his voice shaking: 'I never found out what she wanted to say. The letter turned up the morning after she died. It had been written a couple of days earlier. When I saw her for the last time, on her birthday, she gave no clue about what she wanted to say. It was obviously going to be something very private. The fact is, she died that night. Seven months of projected life had vanished.'

A terrible dark clarity lay between Doctor Goodwin and Anselm. Mitch was standing apart now, head down. The family history was over and the doctor's energy was back, bristling with grief and confidence: 'After the accident, Peter lost everything he'd worked for, everything he'd enjoyed,' said Doctor Goodwin. 'He couldn't stay in London any more. He couldn't take that invitation to speak at the University of Milan. He wasn't free for

Have I Got News for You. In a way, his life ended. He was as stranded as Jenny, only he could still move about. He was trapped in the house staring at a future he hadn't chosen and didn't want. This is the critical turning point for everyone: what do you do, faced with the loss of what once gave meaning to your life? Do you accept it or do you hit out? What was Peter's response? Emma's letters to Zimbabwe told the story. He refused all help. Left his friends in London. Pushed Jenny's friends out of the picture. Slowly and carefully he narrowed down her world until it was just the two of them. He was planning to kill her.' Doctor Goodwin turned to Anselm. 'We didn't see what he was doing at the time. All we saw was Jenny in the sitting room, alone with Peter . . . where he could say and do what he liked.'

Anselm looked at the tulips by the grave. Their purple heads were drooping. 'Was there a gathering for Jenny's birthday?'

'Oh yes,' replied Doctor Goodwin, with feeling. 'Peter called a meeting beforehand. I couldn't make it. But Helen went. He said he wanted to give her a special night. They discussed how best to do it and everyone agreed to bring something. He'd got the family together so they could see her for one last time . . . that's what he was doing.'

'Who was present at the party?'

'Peter, Michael, Emma, Helen and myself . . . and Vincent Cooper, he dropped in and dropped out when no one else was there.'

Anselm made a querying look.

'A friend of Peter's. Introduced him to Jenny. Emma couldn't stand him.'

'Do you have his address?'

'No . . . but he manages a specialist garage in Newmarket. Classic cars.'

'Six people, then. And you're sure no one else came to see her?'

'Yes. I asked Timothy . . . very carefully.'

'Could you draw up a chronology for me?' asked Anselm, coldly.

'Leave aside the conclusion you've reached about Peter and simply put down who saw Jenny when. I want to know who spent time with her alone . . . even for a matter of minutes.'

Doctor Goodwin's expression showed he thought the exercise professional but pointless. He took out his diary and jotted down Larkwood's fax number.

'Ask yourself,' he said, with a click from the ballpoint pen. 'Why did Peter lose his head in Manchester? He found out what happens when you break the biggest convention of them all.'

As the Land Rover trundled out of Long Melford, Mitch said, 'The GP was something of a father figure.'

'Yes, I noted that, too.'

'So we see him next?'

'No.'

Doctor Ingleby had to be at the heart of the matter. He was close to Peter and he had treated Jenny. If anyone knew the truth, it was him. Which is why Anselm didn't want to meet him until he was better prepared; armed, hopefully with information that would help him crack open any shell of secrecy.

'Tomorrow we go to Newmarket,' he said. 'We go to the man who started the ball rolling between Jenny and Peter.'

Mitch said he'd trace the address and . . . but Anselm drifted away, towards the last written words of Jennifer Henderson. She seemed to be whispering from the grave, telling him again and again that she'd kept waiting for a surprise. She'd held on while her body gave out.

After Vespers that evening Anselm grabbed Larkwood's archivist by the elbow.

'Could you do some research for me?'

Bede seemed to increase in size and get redder.

'On what subject?'

'The Force Research Unit. A part of British Military Intelligence. Operated out of Northern Ireland during the Troubles.'

17

The sun rose cold and determined, bringing little assurance of any future warmth. Under its indifferent gaze, Michael walked out of Southwold. His mind blank, void of thought or memory, he came to the mouth of the River Blyth, where he mooched around the fishing boats and wooden buildings that sold the night's catch. Afterwards, he took the rowing boat ferry to Walberswick, the village where he'd urged Jenny to go back to dancing. He followed the dunes inland and arrived, finally, at the place where he'd stood with his daughter facing the vast expanse of shivering marshland and heath. He sucked a sherbet lemon. It was viciously sharp. His eyes watered and he could no longer see anything clearly. He almost felt Jenny's hand in his.

'You're a dancer,' said Michael. 'So dance.'

'I can't remember how.'

'Learn again.'

'You've forgotten what it took out of me, Dad. Remember Semi-detached wiping the sweat off my legs with a box full of tissues? The injuries . . . the swollen knees and ankles? I couldn't go through all that again.'

Michael turned to his daughter. Her lank hair was pulled tight off her face, as she used to wear it when practising her routines. But now the explanation was carelessness. She looked old, though she was still young. Twenty-nine. She'd lost the glow of expectation that had once made her run rather than walk. She'd been battling to find a foothold in Peter's world for too many years. Only they didn't talk about Peter. Or his interesting friends. Or the dalliances. They were both loyal.

'I daren't try,' she said, without returning her father's gaze. She was drinking in the loneliness of Tinker's Marshes. Birds darted just above the ragged stubble of reeds and winter grass.

'What have you to lose?'

'Height,' she laughed, ironically. 'I won't be able to get these hooves off the ground.'

'Then fly low, Jenny. You can still fly low.'

With money from her parents, Jenny opened a small dance school in Sudbury. 'School' was a somewhat grandiose term for the upstairs floor of an abandoned bus station. But the premises enjoyed a convenient location and the tuition on offer came from a winner of the Prix de Lausanne and one-time member of the Royal Ballet. A trickle of children became a respectable flow. Within three months, Jenny had made links with local schools and an amateur brass band. And then, by chance, Vincent Cooper came back into her life.

Cooper had been to the same school as Peter. He'd gone into modern dance and found regular work on the West End theatre circuit. Jenny had met him after a performance of *Cats* in a wine bar off Soho, the fateful and future introduction to Peter being born over a glass of Bordeaux. Going by those light-hearted remarks that disclose painful truths, it seemed that Cooper had been drawn to Jenny but had kept his distance because he was so much older, which had made Peter's sweeping entrance into Jenny's life all the more poignant. The man who would have protected Jenny had honourably stood back, unaware that by so doing, he'd left her exposed to the whims of a joyrider. Michael hadn't met Cooper often, but when he had done, he'd sensed guilt and loss in his eyes. But that was all in the past. Tired of city life, Cooper had quit London for Sudbury, finding work as a dance therapist with a mental health charity. In his spare time he'd restored other people's classic cars. But then he'd bumped into Jenny. He'd offered to help for nothing.

'You needn't turn up *every day*, Dad,' scolded Jenny, one Saturday morning.

Jenny glanced at Cooper who was limbering up in one of those leotards that had never been worn by anyone in the Royal Anglian Regiment, save predecessors in title during the war when Suffolk's sons were compelled to throw a cabaret in the absence of women.

'I'm fine now,' she added, sincerely, reaching for his hand and finding his little finger. 'You can go. I'm having lunch with Vincent . . .'

Michael didn't mind the gentle push. He ambled out of the old bus station as he'd once ambled out of Covent Garden. This was the role of the father . . . to usher his child from one room to the next, to help them make the great transitions, to be there, by their side, right to the end of each new departure.

'You're a good father,' said Emma, chiding. 'Me? I'd pour the coffee over Peter's head. And as for that Cooper, dear God, he's got a lot to answer for. He knew what Peter was like.'

'Don't be silly, darling,' replied Michael. 'No one is responsible for someone else . . . for what they do, for the choices they make, for what then happens. And he cares for Jenny. Always has done.'

'He should have warned her, then.'

Despite Jenny's growing independence, Michael still made fugitive visits to the school, but within minutes of his arrival, she nudged him away. She was up to something. He'd find out, she said. You're in for a surprise, he told himself. Once, when leaving, Semi-detached arrived, striding past him as if she was late for a meeting with one of the Romanovs, an heir to the lost crown.

'Nothing would surprise me,' said Emma, serving a Marks and Spencer chicken Kiev. 'I'm preparing myself for the worst.'

The worst happened three months later. Michael and Emma

were sitting in the front row, with Timothy sandwiched between them. Peter couldn't make it. He was playing to the gallery on *Question Time* and, no doubt, would afterwards be playing the field or having a Scotch with the presenter. Jenny had booked a church hall with a stage. The Sudbury Brass Band had been retained. Semi-detached stood in the wings, severe, demanding and proud. After the young dancers had shown what they'd learned, Jenny came onstage, cheeks flushed, hair drawn tightly back, her eyes dark-rimmed and blazing. Funnily enough, the overstated make-up stripped her bare of any defences. The brutal contrast in shade magnified her vulnerability, revealing Jenny for who she was behind the day-to-day endurance: someone sad; someone faithful.

'And now, a little surprise,' she said, voice wavering.

You'd have thought she was standing before the judges in Lausanne. Two minutes later, Jenny flew right off the platform into the trumpet section. The kids were stunned.

Michael wiped his cheeks. That sherbet lemon had really pricked his eyes. He'd lost his vision. But now everything was coming back into focus. He looked around at the river and marshland. There were old wooden row boats beached on the orange silt. The heath towards Squire's Hill was a cold, trembling green. The sky was vast with kinks of cloud like curled locks on the head of a sleeping child. The world, he thought, is a very beautiful place. But what madness had entered Jenny's mind? She'd returned to the dance that had won her the Gold Medal in the Théâtre de Beaulieu when she was seventeen years old. Semi-detached had helped, scaling down the choreography to bring most of the steps within reach. But not all. There'd been one – just one – that had sent Jenny into a spin.

'You danced for me,' whispered Michael, the shock fresh upon him. 'To thank me for helping you pass from one room to another . . . into the last room in the house; the quiet room with a door that opens onto the garden.'

18

On boarding the *Jelly Roll*, Anselm glanced instinctively at the noticeboard. All the photographs had been rearranged. They'd been in a line, but now they formed a circle. In the middle, like a hub, was a boy whom Anselm had never seen before.

'He's the explanation for everything,' said Mitch.

'Who's that?'

'Timothy Goodwin, Jennifer and Peter's son.'

'Where did you get the photograph from?'

'I took it.'

'When?'

'Yesterday.' Mitch had snapped him coming out of Nigel and Helen Goodwin's house in Long Melford. 'I wanted to know who'd been sent upstairs while we talked of murder, so I went back and waited.'

The doctor – followed discreetly by Mitch – had driven the youth to a charming house near Lavenham, a medieval building that leaned to one side as if it might fall over at any moment. Emma Goodwin had come to the door, smiling wide and woodenly.

'While his father's in prison, the lad's staying with his grandparents.'

So, thought Anselm, with sudden warmth, this is Timothy. Black hair, deliberately roughed up. No sadness or strain around the intelligent eyes and finely drawn mouth. No obvious vulnerability. You wouldn't know that his mother had died and his father was locked up in Hollesley Bay. A face that hides inner turmoil, concluded Anselm.

'He's the explanation,' repeated Mitch. 'He's the reason Emma defended her son-in-law – though, of course, we were wrong to assume that Jenny and Peter had married. Emma spoke up for him even though he'd reduced Michael to a dumb waiter holding a coffee pot, even though Peter had abandoned her only child and daughter. And Michael turned up, too, head down, doing his best. They swallowed their rage for Timothy's sake. They've swallowed their belief that their daughter was murdered, because they don't want their grandson to know that his father killed his mother.'

Anselm made a murmur of agreement. However, he was very much aware that a key element of this simple analysis was contested. One person, a subdued woman, saw things very differently. As much as she might detest Peter Henderson, she didn't accuse him of murder.

'What did you make of Helen's unfinished theory?' asked Anselm.

'She thinks Michael killed his own daughter. That's why she won't tell Nigel. And Nigel, who didn't tell us about Michael's breakdown, thinks his brother just might have done it, too, but he can't begin to say so to his wife. Maybe not even to himself. But he'll be damned if Michael takes the rap for killing Jennifer, when the person who really killed her, slowly squeezed the life out of her, even before she fell off that stage, even before the cancer set in, was Peter, the decent guy who'd kept absolutely no property for himself.' Mitch made a wry laugh. 'He's a good man, the doctor. He wants someone to pay for cutting short Jenny's life, before they could have that chat. But he knows – if his worst fears are true – that the law would condemn his brother, leaving Jenny's husband without a stain to his name. He knows that such a result would be unjust. He finds it ungodly. So, deep in the shadows of his mind – among the regret at losing his brother and the guilt at losing Jenny – he begins to see things *simply*. He closes his eyes to the *complications*. He cuts to the quick. He believes that Peter killed Jenny – because the chances are, he did – but he removes his doubts as a daring act of faith in Michael. He remembers the mediator of his childhood; and the man who'd do anything to bring about peace at home and abroad.'

This time Anselm was genuinely impressed by Mitch's thinking. There'd been no flights of fancy. Furthermore, Anselm – brooding among his bees – had come to an identical conclusion. Strange, really: the one member of the family whose photograph he did not possess now stood clearest in Anselm's mind. Listening to Helen and Nigel had summoned part of Michael's soul.

'He loved her, in a way, like no one else,' said Anselm, quietly. 'She'd been his salvation, though the girl probably didn't know it, didn't know that her grace and talent had reached into her father's secret crisis.'

'Which means that when Jenny stopped dancing, something must have stopped in Michael, too.' Mitch meant the beating of the heart. Long before Jenny's accident, Peter had brought the taste of dying to the young woman and, through her, to Michael. She'd stopped dancing; and he'd stopped healing. Neither of them had complained – Jenny out of love for Peter, and Michael out of love for Jenny. Which made subsequent events all the more unbearable. 'Michael must have been devastated to see her paralysed,' said Mitch. 'Devastated again to be told of the cancer. And what could be more devastating than to watch her being cared for by Peter.' Mitch turned away from the noticeboard and addressed Anselm directly. 'Helen knows all that . . . knows that father and daughter were bound together . . . so why does she think that Michael might have killed his own child?'

As if in answer Anselm pulled at Mitch's elbow. He wasn't going to be led astray by an enquiry into motive. People really did do strange things for the strangest of reasons.

'Let's talk to a man who repairs classic cars, shall we?'

*   *   *

Mitch parked the Land Rover near the centre of Newmarket. Emerging onto the High Street, he strode ahead, purposefully.

'Can I question this guy?' he asked, over his shoulder.

'Sure.'

At the Bar a QC often entrusts a minor witness to his junior counsel, so in giving his consent Anselm felt a sudden frisson of self-importance. It was the nearest he'd get to professional distinction. And Vincent Cooper wouldn't have *that much* to say . . .

Mitch strode on, leading the way, finally entering a narrow alley that opened onto a broad forecourt. Ahead, beneath a framed wooden sign – graceful gold lettering on a deep navy-blue background – stood the specialised business of Vincent Cooper: 'Vintage Automotive Services'.

The work bay was open and brightly lit. In centre stage, leaning into the gaping mouth of a sleek olive-green sports car, was a man in loose cotton trousers and a baggy white T-shirt. Like a surgeon on his rounds, he shone a lamp into a dark cavity tutting concern and mirthless know-how.

'Jaguar, E-Type,' said Mitch, nostalgically. 'Simply beautiful.'

The man hung the light on the bonnet and stepped away from the vehicle. His hair was straw blond, his eyes china blue. Oil stained his forehead. Wiping his hands on a rag, he glanced uncertainly at Anselm's habit.

'Elegance itself,' continued Mitch, admiringly. 'Yours?'

'Wish she was.'

The man looked powerful without being muscle-bound. His voice was rich and moist, like cake, his tone careless, reminding Anselm of a silk who'd been expelled from Eton. He'd worn the disgrace like a pink carnation.

'Nothing compares with her shape,' declared Mitch, one hand drawing the shape of the long bonnet with a reaching paw.

'No.'

'Thing is,' said Mitch, slipping his hands into his back pockets, 'she wasn't that good at taking corners. Not at speed. Something wrong with the design, there. Came off the road too easily.'

'Depends on your idea of beauty,' objected the mechanic. He roughed up his hair with a practised flourish. 'Depends on how you handle the wheel. You can't separate shape and movement . . . they complement each other. They make style and poise and grace.'

'You talk like a dancer.'

'I was, once . . .'

'Yes, I know.'

'Really?'

The man laughed as if preparing himself to receive a compliment – some accolade for a past performance – but then the moment of communion snapped because Mitch's voice turned rich and careless: 'Yes, but – no offence – we're not that interested in your career. We'd like to talk about Jennifer Henderson's.'

The man continued to wipe his hands on the rag, but his face was still.

'Yes, that's what I said, Vincent,' pursued Mitch, scratching the back of his head. 'The woman who once danced for a living. Like you. My friend here has received a letter saying she was murdered. We're not policemen. But we've still got questions. Questions for you, because you were there the night she died.'

Vincent Cooper kept wiping his hands, though the activity was, by now, quite without purpose. He stared at Mitch, unblinking.

'Sure, we can talk,' he managed, finally. 'Let me get my coat, okay?'

'Absolutely, I'll just admire the Jag. Always wanted one, but in the end, I went for something strong and sturdy, just in case I hit a rhino.'

Cooper retreated to a door at the end of his workshop, throwing the rag on the floor as he stepped out of view.

Anselm didn't know what to say. He looked at Mitch rather like Doctor Goodwin had looked at Helen. He, too, had come off the leash. After a few long, drawn-out moments Mitch checked his watch.

'Where is he?' asked Anselm.

'He's done a runner.'

'Where to?'

'Home, I'd imagine. We'll just give him another couple of minutes. Time to unearth whatever he's hidden away.'

'*You know where he lives?*'

'There's only one Vincent Cooper in the telephone book. I tailed him from home to work this morning, just to make sure. I'd like to get there just when he thinks he's safe and sound.'

Mitch walked briskly out of the garage. All the way back to the Land Rover he kept a few steps ahead of Anselm, a man who knew where he was going and what he was going to do when he got there.

19

Jenny was smiling to herself, toying with resistance, putting up a show. Go back to dancing? You must be crazy. But she'd listened to Michael. She'd given in. She'd found excitement and hope in her father's mumbled suggestion. The recollection of that timeless wavering was burned into Michael's soul. If he'd said nothing, Jenny might never have walked onstage again. There would have been no paralysis.

No one is responsible for someone else . . . for what they do, for the choices they make, for what then happens.

Michael had often said that to Emma, but it wasn't always true. Michael felt responsible for Jenny's fall. Because not so deep down, in the asking, he'd been thinking of himself, too. He'd wanted Jenny to dance again because from her first tentative steps, he'd been at her side . . . and being there had taken him far away from

Eugene and Liam and Ó Mórdha: the ugly universe of brutal, heartless movements. He'd found some grace in a graceless world and he wanted it back.

After taking the rowing boat ferry once more across the Blyth, Michael tramped towards Southwold. But he didn't hear the distant breathing of the sea. He didn't see the trembling heath and wetlands. He was driving a Ford Fiesta into the Blue Stack Mountains. It was the last place he wanted to be. But he had no choice. He was preparing himself to relive another moment heavy with responsibility – this time not for what he'd said, but for what he'd done.

Michael stopped the car at the side of the road about a mile from Ó Mórdha's cottage. He'd thought of driving closer but it was a clear night and the engine seemed eerily loud among so much silence. Once the quiet had returned to its overwhelming grandeur, Michael stepped outside. He looked up. The stars seemed to shout out their presence. The moon, reserved and full, stared down upon the butterwort and sundew. He listened and looked harder . . . there was no still, small voice up there. Just light. An unearthly watching light. Michael set off. The Browning was in his left jacket pocket, the silencer in the right.

There was no path, so Michael trotted through the flora, stepping on tufts of shadow as if they were stones across a deep, green sea. There were no sounds but the fall of his feet, the sigh of the grass and the suck of the bogland's moisture. He only stopped to rest when he saw a fine strand of blue smoke spiralling high into the night sky. He'd reached dry ground. Ahead lay the cottage, this side of a molten stream. A dull orange light described a small window. There were wooden fences, marking out the land for grazing. A path wound its way towards a string of three gates. Without thinking about his next move, Michael climbed the first and ran to the second, vaulting it in a single movement. He paused, listened and took out the Browning. On clearing the third, he withdrew the silencer and screwed it slowly onto the gun. Then, like an expected guest, he walked slowly to the farmhouse. Drawing close, he could hear the stream licking the turf and stones of its banks. The sound, hungry and insistent, drowned out his approach.

Oddly enough, Michael's meticulous preparations hadn't included what to do once he'd reached the door so, on impulse, he simply knocked and stood waiting while his heart pumped tension through his veins. Mechanically, his thumb released the safety catch above the pistol-grip. He spread his legs, pointing the weapon at chest height in expectation and a sort of screaming readiness.

Footsteps sounded in the hallway.

The handle turned.

The door creaked open and for an instant Michael thought he was going to vomit, but the bile didn't rise; it turned away, falling back.

Low-wattage light rolled over the hearth like a worn-out carpet.

And there was Ó Mórdha peering into the darkness, a hand shielding his eyes from the shocking power of the moon.

Time slowed. A dog was watching from the end of a musty corridor, alert and curious. A grandfather clock was ticking heavily like an old dripping tap. A tin kettle was rattling on a stove. During this absurd, drawn-out delay, Ó Mórdha's eyes got accustomed to the shift in light. He saw the gun. The man who wanted to blow the British out of Ireland was looking at the great reckoning, come a bit too soon.

'Can I help you?' he said, in a childlike voice – the words that had run through his mind before he'd opened the door.

For a brief second Michael's eyes met Ó Mórdha's: and he saw that look of the newborn passing like candlelight behind the wide pupils, flickering with hope and naked supplication.

'You're dead,' whispered Michael.

But just as Michael's finger began to squeeze the trigger, he heard a very quiet voice . . . very quiet indeed, sounding within himself, its insistence more terrible than the heavy tick of the clock and the moan of the kettle:

'Michael, Michael, Michael . . .'

It was a call . . . a voice in the night, as if to wake him . . . but from what? He didn't want to know.

BAM-BAM, BAM-BAM.

Michael was running as fast as he could, racing along the dirt path back to Southwold. He stumbled and tripped over his own feet. He moaned, chased by a dreadful presence inside himself.

He'd heard that voice again.

In passing through those three gates again, one after the other, Michael hadn't *simply* remembered what had happened in Donegal. He hadn't *simply* relived the sensations. He'd approached, in stages, the enormity of what he'd done, passing through the barriers that separated a man from brutality – upbringing, fellow feeling, the commandments. And, in so doing, he'd opened another kind of door . . . and from the other side, within the darkness of his mind, he'd heard that voice as if for the first time. It had been fresh and urgent and utterly of the moment, addressing him here and now, by the Suffolk marshes, speaking to him from the pit of a numbed soul. And – to his complete horror – he realised that there was more to come than just his name. He'd almost heard the first imploding word when, desperately, he'd pulled that curtain down once more, blocking out any other sound but the staggered report of the gun.

BAM-BAM, BAM-BAM.

Michael came to a halt. He was still terrified of what he might have heard. He looked around at the bare marshland, feeling sweat cool on his brow and itch upon his back. He felt hunted and exposed. There was no escape. The voice hadn't finished. It was going to say something else. If Michael persisted with his plan to kill Peter Henderson, then that voice was going to deliver its message.

Michael began to run again, stumbling once more in a panic.

Danny the shrink had said nothing about this kind of thing. He'd encouraged Michael to talk about the past, because the past was dead and it could no longer harm him. He'd never remotely suggested that the past was very much alive; that *it* might speak to *him*. That it was more dangerous now than ever before.

20

Anselm was forced to admit that the sensation was unpleasant. He felt like a junior to Mitch the QC.

Having walked silently to the front door of Vincent Cooper's home – an Edwardian terraced house near Newmarket railway station – Mitch took a key from his pocket, slipped it into the lock and gently pushed open the door. With caution and determination, he walked slowly down the corridor. Anselm, too late to make any protest at the conduct of his leader, shut the door and followed Mitch to the entrance of a back room. Cooper was on his knees by a hastily lit fire, prodding what appeared to be burning letters with a bold finger.

'I wouldn't bother, if I were you,' said Mitch. 'I've already read them.'

Cooper made a jolt and turned.

'What the—'

'I made copies,' interrupted Mitch, his tone all reassurance. 'Just in case. But carry on, if it makes you feel any better.'

Anselm was quite sure that wasn't true, but Cooper was utterly convinced. He rose in one perfect movement, his features drained of all emotion save fear.

'How the hell did you get in here?'

'I opened the front door.'

'Get out, now, or I call the police.'

'Ask for Detective Superintendent Manning. She thinks Jenny

died of bowel cancer. Maybe you'd like to tell her why she's wrong. Why you ran away from a monk and a layman. And why you made a fire.'

Cooper swallowed hard. He looked down at the grate and the soot on his hands.

Mitch entered the room, sauntering towards a bookcase to the right of the chimney breast. Volumes on dance, ballet and theatre gave way to a silver-framed photograph of Cooper and Peter flanking Jennifer, taken long, long ago. Mitch stared at the three of them. Two men and a woman. He had that look of reckless anticipation that preceded every improvisation.

'Did you sleep with her?'

Cooper's jaw tightened. 'No. We were just friends.'

Mitch angled the picture to the light.

'Why did you leave London?'

Cooper made no reply. Mitch continued.

'Why come to Sudbury of all places?'

No reply.

'Why leave town shortly after Jenny died?'

No reply.

'You were there. At Polstead.'

'I came and went before the others even arrived.'

Mitch seemed to speak to the photograph: 'You loved her, didn't you? Only Peter Henderson got there first. You knew things hadn't quite worked out and you came to Sudbury hoping to make up for lost time. Only time, once lost, can't be found again. You ended up killing her, didn't you?'

Cooper moved sideways with slow strides, his eyes fixed on Mitch. One arm reached out for a chair at a cluttered dining table. Slowly he pulled it back and sat down, nodding at the other side of the mess, the heap of books, the bills and unopened mail.

'I did nothing,' he said as Anselm and Mitch took their places. 'Only what Jenny asked of me. No more and no less.'

*   *   *

The emails started coming a month or so after Jenny had returned home from hospital – sometimes during the day, at others during the night, often more than once in the same hour.

'She asked me to kill her,' he said, addressing Anselm. 'Sent me a key to the back door. She wanted me to come during the night and end it all for her. Said Peter couldn't change a lightbulb. Said I was the only person she could trust. Only person who knows what it feels like to be a dancer who can't move her legs, can't feel them any more . . . to be attached to limbs that . . .' Cooper had drifted into quotation, revered territory. He stopped himself, spitting, contemptuously, 'You know what she said. You read them.'

Anselm's eyes moved onto Mitch, and he was quite sure that Mitch hadn't. But Mitch wasn't surprised in the least.

'I stopped replying to the emails and then I got the letters.' Cooper sat back, arms folded tight. 'Always the same thing. Please come and kill me. In the middle of the night, when she was asleep.'

Anselm spoke quietly, like Cooper at the outset of his story.

'Did you visit her?'

'Yes, course I did. And it was worse . . . said the same stuff, wanting me to push her under.'

Cooper's throat was enflamed. A bulging vein snaked along his neck. He seemed to swallow a stone, nodding his head to get it down.

'Why print off the emails?' asked Anselm. 'Why keep the letters?'

Cooper stared back in astonishment. 'What else could I do? She was saying to me what she couldn't say to anyone else . . . not even her father . . . I couldn't throw them away. This was *Jenny*, stripped naked. This was all that was left of her . . . she'd given herself to me. Those letters were all I had.'

'Then why set light to them today?' asked Anselm, again very low.

'Because your friend here thinks that in the end I went and did as I was asked.'

Cooper, too, had spoken softly, his voice charged with pain and injury.

'Well, what *did* you do?' Anselm glanced at the black curls of paper in the grate. 'You told us a few moments ago that you'd only done what Jenny asked.'

After about six months, the flow of emails and letters dried up, explained Cooper. Jenny never mentioned the subject again. She just lay there, not exactly peaceful but abstracted. Peter read her stories. They watched films together. Prior to Jenny's accident, Peter had pretty much ignored her . . . not maliciously . . . he just didn't see her; didn't recognise who she was. But afterwards – in the front room of the cottage where the bed had been placed by a window – he was like a nurse and friend, a sad man, devoted to this woman who kept saying sorry. Sorry for holding him down. And then, unexpectedly, an email went ping on Cooper's inbox. Jenny wanted to see him. She had a special favour to ask of him.

'As soon as I arrived, Peter left the room,' said Cooper, one hand easing the tightness in his throat. 'And then Jenny explained . . . she was sorry for having asked me to kill her – she was speaking completely calmly, as if suicide was the same thing as changing the sheets or doing the washing up. She said that it wasn't right to have asked me because it could never have been my job. The law wouldn't help, she said. And it wouldn't help Peter either. So they'd made a decision . . . a big decision, and I wasn't to tell anybody.'

Cooper glanced at Mitch and Anselm as if wondering who deserved the focus of his attention. He settled on Mitch, the accuser.

'They'd made an agreement that if things got so bad that Jenny couldn't take it any more, then Peter would help her to kill herself. Their doctor was a guy they could trust. No one would ever ask any questions.'

'When was this, in relation to the cancer?' asked Anselm, removing his glasses to blink at the mess in front of him.

'A few months before the diagnosis.'

'How many?'

'I don't know . . . three, four.'

Anselm spoke to himself, his eyes raised high. 'A long time after the paralysis.'

'Yes,' agreed Cooper, unthinkingly, not caring about dates or times. 'She was completely resolved. Relieved, even. Like someone who can hear a train coming on the Northern Line.'

'What did she ask you to do?' asked Mitch.

'Make an Exit Mask.'

'A what?' interjected Anselm, still brooding on the timings, still looking upwards.

'An Exit Mask. She'd researched it on the internet. She'd seen videos on YouTube showing you how to make one . . . and a demonstration by an Australian on how to use it. I looked, too, later. Couldn't believe my eyes. It was like *Blue Peter* for grown-ups . . . "Here's one I made earlier." Peter had printed off the assembly instructions and put some money in an envelope.'

In accordance with Jenny's wishes, Cooper had bought a helium gas cylinder from Amazon (designed to fill kids' balloons), some electrician's tape from B&Q, a roll of large freezer bags from Sainsbury's and a long rubber tube from a home brew centre.

'The idea is that you put a bag on your forehead, fill it with helium and then . . .'

Cooper looked helplessly at his two inquisitors. The anger had gone. He didn't look so strong any more.

'You made this thing?' asked Anselm, nonchalantly, restoring his glasses.

'What else could I do?'

'Refuse.'

'They'd have made it somehow. I just helped them do what they didn't *want* to do . . . not what they *couldn't* do. And anyway, Jenny wasn't committed to using it, just having it ready . . . a parachute, she called it.'

'Okay, having made the mask, what did you do with it?' asked Mitch.

'Just a moment,' interjected Anselm. 'Did Jenny say anything else about her motives for planning her suicide, apart from things getting too bad?'

'Yes,' nodded Cooper as if he'd left out something obvious and important. 'The son. Her boy. Timothy. She felt she had nothing to offer him any more. She didn't want him to watch her get frightened and struggle.'

'No,' said Anselm, ponderously.

'That's why she didn't want to go to Switzerland or Holland, where they pull the plug and it's all legal. She'd have to explain to Timothy why she had to end it all. She didn't want to . . . she couldn't. So I did as she asked.'

'Odd that, really, when you wouldn't do it before.'

'Because before she was depressed, whereas this time she'd thought it through, carefully. Like I told you: she was real calm. Completely sure of herself. All the thinking had been done.'

Anselm made a nod. 'So off you went to B&Q.'

When Cooper brought the completed Exit Mask to Jenny, she told him to leave it in a small potting shed at the end of the garden. The plan was this: if Jenny ever made the final decision to end her life, Peter would simply collect the mask and help Jenny to use it. Afterwards, he wasn't to worry about getting rid of the evidence. All he had to do was put it back in the shed. When Cooper heard that Jenny had died, he was to come the same day and collect the mask, tube and cylinder and dispose of them.

'She was protecting and helping Peter,' explained Cooper, pushing aside more of the mess, and leaning on the table. 'The doctor would look the other way, but if someone still had concerns they'd never find any evidence. The shed would be empty. Peter hadn't bought anything. No one in the home brew centre would remember his face. Amazon hadn't sent him any helium. It had all been kept simple, for him. He didn't have to make anything; he didn't have to dispose of anything. All he had to do was open that door on a plane that was losing height and falling to pieces in mid-air.'

Mitch then said, 'But she was being smart, too, in asking for your help.'

'Unless it was Peter's idea,' interjected Anselm, who'd reached the same conclusion on smartness.

'How?' snapped Cooper, resenting the hint of manipulation.

'You already knew what Jenny was thinking and why,' explained Mitch. 'If she'd suddenly died, you might have said something to the police. You'd wanted to keep her alive. So you'd have told them your suspicions. And that would have led to an investigation and maybe Peter's arrest. By involving you in the planning she tidied up those previous emails and letters.'

'Or Peter did.' Once again Anselm politely completed the diagram of due inference.

'Jenny didn't use me,' explained Cooper, wearily. 'She came to me because she knew I understood her. More than anyone. You name them . . . Peter, Emma, the doctor and, yes, even Michael, her father, *none* of them could even *begin* to understand her like *I* did, to understand what she felt like after her legs had been taken away from her. She didn't need to explain a damn thing to me. Not a thing.'

'Because you're a dancer?' offered Anselm.

'Because I'm a dancer.'

'Not now you're not,' threw in Mitch, dousing Cooper's emotion. 'You're a mechanic who fixes second-hand cars that run on four star. What did you do with the mask after Jenny died?'

Cooper appeared suddenly stunned.

'You kept it, didn't you?' whispered Mitch. 'Like the emails and letters, you couldn't get rid of anything that had come from her mind or hand. No wonder you couldn't throw away the bag that contained her last breath. Where is it, Vincent?'

A flush of grief and surrender changed Cooper's face. He stood up and left the room. A door opened and closed. Moments later he returned holding a white plastic carrier bag from Curry's. He laid it warily on the table among the detritus of his life offstage.

'You can't prove she used it,' he said, barely audible. 'You can't prove it killed her. Not now. You're too late. You can only prove that I made it.'

'Quite right, Mr Cooper,' agreed Anselm. He stood up and gingerly opened the carrier bag, gazing intently at the homemade suicide kit: a crumpled freezer bag for those tasty leftovers, an orange rubber pipe to siphon off the young beer and a small gas cylinder with a picture of balloons on the side. 'You're all as safe as houses.'

'A piece of advice, though, Vincent,' added Mitch. 'Don't hide your spares under a plant pot. You'll only invalidate your insurance.' With a wink, he tossed the front door key high over the table.

Cooper didn't move at first. He just glared at the thief who'd stolen Jenny's secrets. Then, without even blinking, he snatched the key from the air, his arm following the sharp and savage arc of a punch.

Anselm sat in the passenger seat of the Land Rover with the carrier bag on his lap, astounded by Mitch's performance. He'd sensed that Jenny's friend was disconsolate. He'd seen into a grieving man's vulnerability and then stunned him, brutally and without hesitation. It's what QCs did. It's why Anselm would never have made the grade. He looked at the plastic bag with distaste, wondering if the mask would fit Bede. For the time being he'd store it in the shed by his hives and later he'd—

'I think we ought to go to the club,' said Mitch, puncturing Anselm's meditation. 'I'd like to talk to you. On my patch.'

'When?'

'Tonight.'

Anselm looked aside. Mitch wasn't simply proposing a night

of merriment. Far from it, he was showing more purpose and determination, still very much a man who knew where he was going and what he was going to do when he got there.

21

Michael ran and ran. The wind brought the sound of the sea over the Denes. Heavy tufts of grass struggled against the grip of the sand. Seagulls swooped low, skimming the track ahead, their wings outstretched and long and still . . .

'She'll never walk again,' Emma said once more.

She'd murmured the phrase repeatedly ever since she and Michael had left the ward. Down the hospital corridors and stairs, she'd been speaking to herself, and then to Michael and then, it seemed, to God. She'd moved from recognition to shock and then complaint; from disbelief to anger and despair.

'She'll never walk again.'

All the consultants had agreed. They'd all come in with that quiet, careful tread, guiltily moving one foot in front of the other. They'd all spoken in that soft reassuring voice when they might as well have shouted out the shattering implications of their message. They'd all taken occasional refuge in technical language, trying to distance themselves from the meaning of their own words, to soften their impact on Jenny . . . wide-eyed Jenny, lying absolutely still, visibly crushed by the weight of their knowledge and certainty. Then, one by one, they'd walked out again.

'Why on earth did she go back to dancing?' pleaded Emma.

Michael gripped the steering wheel and kept his eyes on the rear lights ahead. It was raining hard. A misty spray obscured the camber of the road. Headlights appeared like dull moons. Emma knew very well that a return to the stage had been Michael's idea.

He'd told her. And now she wanted to be angry with him, only she knew that wouldn't be fair. But that left her rage and unhappiness internalised and without direction. It could only harm her. Without for one second minimising Jenny's situation, Michael realised that everybody was gravely injured now. That everyone was paralysed in some way, unable to move into the future.

'She'll never walk again.'

Emma spoke as if she hadn't said it before. They were silent for a while, appalled by the words. The tyres hissed upon the bitumen. The wipers flapped back and forth. The red lights flickered in the haze.

'Michael . . . did you hear what Jenny said?'

Emma didn't need to say any more. Michael knew what she was talking about. Jenny had grabbed her father by the arms and almost hauled herself upright, straining forward, bringing blood to swell her face and lips. The hospital bed had creaked and clanked.

'My life is over . . . I've nothing left . . . I can't move . . . I'll never take Timothy to school again. I'll never collect him . . . or put his meals upon the table. I'll never put him to bed, or get him up. I'll never go to him if he gets scared in the night. What can I show him about *life*? What can I teach him? What special message have I got for him . . . something to recite and remember me by . . . after I'm gone?'

Michael had said, 'No, no, no, no, no . . .' gently lowering her onto the bed. Choking and inadequate, he hadn't been able to reach her desolation. He'd had nothing *honest* to say. Jenny's head had turned to one side upon the pillow. Life and warmth had ebbed away from her fingers. In an awful parody of her legs, they'd seemed incapable of further movement. Her long black lashes had slowly closed and opened again, closed once more and opened again. She'd been staring at the rest of her life.

'The thing is . . . Jenny's right,' said Emma, her face averted to the misted window. 'Her life is over. What has she got to live for now? If she was an animal, I'd gently put her down. It would be the right thing to do.'

'But she's not,' whispered Michael. 'She's our girl.'

Emma just looked at the spray from the oncoming traffic. But her comment – brutal and sincere – worked like leaven between them. Everything that neither of them would ever dare to think or say foamed quietly in the darkness of their minds. It was true: no animal would ever be left to suffer *like that*. Emma always told a crying child that putting a whimpering pet to sleep was part of loving; that ending a life was sometimes the only way to be compassionate. But, paradoxically, those words of comfort just made Jenny's situation all the worse, for she was worth so much more than any wounded spaniel. And, being worth so much more, she would have to accept the suffering that comes with being human. She was entitled to a very different kind of compassion . . . only for the moment, in the aftermath, Michael didn't know what it was; and neither did Emma. They were driving home in the pouring rain, desperately asking themselves what could be done and what they might do. Neither of them dared to say what they were thinking . . . that the answer might be 'Nothing'.

'We'll find a way,' said Michael, through his teeth, refusing to give up. 'We'll help Jenny get to the other side of what's happened . . . somehow. We'll do whatever's necessary.'

Michael had found something honest to say, even though it didn't quite mean anything. But he'd expressed all his fervour and protest and love. This accident would not defeat his hope.

'Yes, you're right,' said Emma, reaching out and taking one of Michael's hands. She was crying now, hating herself for being angry with the man who'd only ever wanted the best for his daughter. 'We'll find a way and do what's necessary, regardless.'

Michael ran and ran while the gulls screamed high overhead, gliding across a cloudless sky. Emma had spoken about killing as a duty. She'd spoken of animals, but Michael, privately, had known all along that in certain circumstances, it could apply to a human being. He'd learned that lesson from Eugene, long before Jenny had fallen off the stage. Every so often the configuration of events called out for radical action – the type of action one would never dream of taking; but it was necessary, to resolve a crisis. Sometimes you had to think beyond the troubled voice of your conscience.

The wind brought the sound of the sea over the Denes and the thick grass struggled against the grip of the sand.

22

Mitch's club was situated in a long narrow cellar beneath a hairdresser's and, appropriately, an office belonging to an insurance company. The walls were red and the ceiling, supported by narrow iron pillars, was black. Small tables huddled side by side, cramped between the low stage at one end and the glittering bar at the other. Anselm had not walked down those basement stairs for years. The last time he'd paid at the door as a barrister; now he was a monk, who got in for free. Inside, nothing had changed. Not even the decor. It had, in fact, become suitably tatty. All that shone were the bottles and glasses and the instruments under the bright lights. It was going to be a good night. The place was crowded. A couple of sax players were knocking out Anselm's kind of tune.

'Never thought I'd see you here again,' said Mitch, smiling.

'Me neither.'

The Prior had approved of the outing because Anselm felt sure that Mitch had something to say about the missing £287,458.16; that his foray into truth-finding had already prompted a desire to confess. Anselm wasn't entirely surprised. After a couple of weeks all novices tend to break down and spill out the life story they've never told anyone before. It's part of the reconstruction process. And Anselm was ready to listen. They were sitting at Mitch's private table in a corner by the wall. He was leaning forward, confidentially.

'I know who wrote that letter to your Prior.'

'Do you?' replied Anselm, surprised. He'd expected a different kind of opener.

'Yes. Helen Goodwin.'

'Really? Why?'

'She claimed not to have remembered the article in the *Sunday Times*. Nigel had told her about it. It's memorable. You're memorable.'

Anselm shook his head. 'The letter blames Peter.'

'Yes, I know.' Mitch nodded. 'She set you on the path. She knew you'd go to the police. She knew Manning would tell you about Nigel's allegations. She knew you'd come to Long Melford. She was expecting you. Gambled you'd come when Nigel was out. Told you what she'd never write down . . . only Nigel came home and cut her short.'

'Blaming Peter was just a lure so she could hint it was Michael?'

'Yes.'

Anselm was impressed again. Mitch's improvisations were getting better.

'But that means the letter wasn't written by Peter Henderson's accomplice.'

'True.'

'Which would also mean that no one is setting out to kill him.'

Mitch thought for a long moment . . . and then smiled. Anselm had been right all along: it wasn't that type of case. But he didn't say so. He was thinking some more, watched expectantly by Anselm. The sax duo was playing 'Quiet Please', a Sidney Bechet curtain-raiser.

'So . . .' began Mitch, 'Helen says Jenny was killed by Michael and Cooper says Jenny was killed by Peter. Either way, it's a mercy killing and not a murder.'

Anselm understood now.

This was Mitch's concern. Not the theft.

This was why Mitch had tailed Vincent Cooper and questioned him with ruthless persistence, lying about the private letters he hadn't in fact known about. On reading Jenny's desperate note to Nigel the day before, Mitch had come to a few stark conclusions and he'd decided that Anselm should know them, because they had certain implications.

'If you proceed with this investigation,' he warned, 'you'll bring the house down on a family that's managed to build a fragile peace. No one needs to know what Jenny decided. It was her life . . . and we have to respect her choice.'

Anselm nudged his glasses. He was, of course, aware that assisted suicide was a substitute explanation for the allegation of murder. He'd been surprised that Mitch hadn't mentioned the matter upon leaving Nigel Goodwin. It had been an obvious inference to make. Rather than speak his mind, though, Mitch had charged after Vincent Cooper, evidently intending to bring the investigation to a sort of crisis point . . . between himself and Anselm.

An ambience of contentment had taken over the club. The sax players had stopped for a quick break and everyone was chatting and drinking, the hubbub creating an envelope of privacy around Anselm and Mitch. No one was listening to them. No one spotted their seriousness.

'We don't know what Jenny was going to say to Nigel,' said Anselm, quietly.

'We can guess. She'd lost hope. She was scared of dying. She'd given up on surprises. She wanted out.'

'Wrong, she wanted to speak to Nigel,' insisted Anselm. 'And she didn't . . . because someone killed her first.'

'With her consent.'

'How do you know?'

'Vincent Cooper said so.'

Anselm came closer to the table. They were eye to eye now.

'What if Peter made Jenny want to die? What if suicide was *his* solution to *her* problem? What if Jenny didn't have the wherewithal, intellectually and spiritually, to defend herself? What if Jenny was bullied into dying?'

'We'll never know.'

'What if Peter made it *look* as though Jenny had chosen death, when in fact she'd longed to live?'

'We'll never know.'

'What if this fragile peace rests upon the most serious of crimes?'

'Maybe it doesn't matter any more.'

'Well, I think it does.'

'Why?'

'Because if Jenny wanted to live then she was entitled to live. It was *her* life . . . a messy, broken, failing life, but it was *hers* and no one else's. If someone took it away, then Jenny was simply executed. No family can live with that kind of secret, not in the long run. Windows get broken in Manchester and children end up in hospital.'

The two sax players had threaded their way back to the stage, drinks in hand. They were smiling, enjoyed the friendly acclaim. Someone called out for 'After You've Gone'. The melody struck up and feet began to tap out the beat. It was a great song, one of Anselm's favourites; it turned him suddenly wistful and Mitch couldn't help but soften.

'It's the letter to your Prior, isn't it?'

'Absolutely. It's the stumbling block. The author spoke for Jenny. That's why we have to listen. It's why we have to keep going and find out what really happened.'

'Maybe they got it wrong . . . maybe they didn't know what she was really thinking and feeling, deep down inside.'

'And maybe they did.' Unable to stop himself, Anselm turned away from Mitch towards the stage, drawn by the delicious hint of melancholy in the refrain. 'Maybe they're the one person who knew the secrets of Jenny's heart . . . why else would they write to a monk rather than the police? It's their patch, isn't it?'

To loud clapping, Mitch raised his trumpet. The three musicians looked at each other, wondering what they might play. In the end, they took turns to choose, and Anselm had to smile because Mitch kept sending him messages through the song titles, warning him about the investigation. 'There's Going to Be the Devil to Pay' . . . 'You Won't Be Satisfied' . . . 'Don't Blame Me'. They were at ease again, speaking for the first time about the meaning of life and death; keeping well away from the deeper questions on bop, bebop and the avant-garde. At intervals a young woman with a pierced nose and tattooed fingers brought over bottled beer until, towards midnight, the club closed. The guests left. The musicians got paid. The bar staff went home. But Mitch remained, and so did Anselm. They sat at the corner table, sipping soda water, talking of their very different lives: Anselm of the monastery, Mitch of the club. They found common ground on the subject of oddballs, be they monks or musicians. There were only two truly sensible people left in the world, and they were both seated here in a deserted jazz club.

'It's not just the letter, is it?' asked Mitch. 'There's something else. Why are you so determined to look beyond the evidence of Vincent Cooper?'

Anselm was too tired to resist. 'Because I met her once.'

Mitch gave a slight start and Anselm nodded, ready to explain.

'I was filling in for a hospital chaplain. She was in for some routine tests. A nurse suggested I drop by. I did.'

'You met Peter?'

'No.'

Anselm hadn't stayed long because it was late. 'She told me she had cancer. What can you say?'

And Anselm, sipping his soda water, told Mitch how cancer had eaten into his mother's life and those of her husband and children. No one had been equipped to deal with the strain. The illness had shown up everybody's failings; placed them under pressure and helped them fail one another. There'd been a lot of confusion because no one had been prepared to accept the future. Anselm, however, had tried and been surprised.

'I was nine, very young, like Timothy. I didn't resist. Helped her go, if you like. We talked about life, how *good* it was, how each morning was *mysterious* and *wonderful* . . . but that now it was evening and the succession of days would come to an end. Because we were honest with each other, we survived. I was shattered and she was shattered. But she didn't try to hold onto life and I didn't ask her to stay. Each remaining moment became charged with meaning . . . there were even times of *ecstasy*, impossible to anticipate . . . they just came like a hot flush . . . which is why I feel for Timothy. We've both stood by a bed wondering what to make of death, wondering what to make of the confusion downstairs . . .'

Mitch was turning his glass in circles on a beer mat. He smiled sadness and gratitude for having been trusted. But there was a focus to his stare, something objective and dispassionate.

'You can't make this investigation into Jenny Henderson's death an attempt to reproduce your own history.' Mitch waited, letting his words sink in. 'You can't save this other family by . . . imposing your understanding of what it is to face a crisis. Maybe Jenny saw things differently to your mother. Maybe she wanted to help Timothy differently.'

Anselm sipped some water. He knew there was more to come; and he knew already what Mitch was going to say. The musician had come full circle, arriving at the point he'd wanted to make when suggesting they meet 'on his patch'.

'Anselm, I have to be honest. I think the investigation should stop right now. I'll stay on board for as long as I can. However . . . if Vincent Cooper's story is broadly confirmed, then I'm off. You're on your own. You see, I, too, feel for Timothy. I, too, have stood by a hospital bed. I, too, know about accidents. And I'm not going to destroy the peace that was achieved just because it rests upon a crime, committed because the law didn't recognise the scale of the predicament. I'm not going to help you make a criminal out of someone who did what you'd never dream of doing . . . just because you once discovered ecstasy when they'd only found despair.'

Mitch pulled into Larkwood just as the bell for Lauds was ringing. They'd been up all night. Curiously – perhaps because each had spoken their mind – they were very much at ease with one another, even though their working relationship was now tenuous. So when Anselm said he proposed to meet Doctor Ingleby alone, Mitch knew there was no cloaked rebuff. Handling Peter Henderson's alleged accomplice would be a delicate matter and two onto one could only be confrontational.

As Anselm got out of the Land Rover, Mitch said: 'There's just one thing that puzzles me about you.'

'Is that all?'

'You're reluctant to accept Cooper's evidence that Jenny wanted to die, even though we've got the Exit Mask . . . and yet you believe what he says about Peter . . . that he was involved in killing her. Why? Why not reject Cooper's story altogether? Why not drop Peter from the frame and forget the letter to your Prior? What about Michael?'

Anselm wrapped his cloak around his shoulders, considering the matter. It was a good point. There was, indeed, a glaring inconsistency in his position.

'Instinct, I suppose,' he replied, aware that his explanation was on the thin side. 'I just can't imagine a father killing his daughter. It's . . . unnatural. And anyway, he adored her. It's inconceivable.'

The thought remained with Anselm as he shuffled into his stall. The bells fell silent, leaving a deep echo to swim through the nave and over the fields, linking the Priory to the world with a fading call to rise from sleep. Into the emerging silence, Father Jerome's hesitant voice intoned the ancient words that greeted every dawn at Larkwood:

'Deus in adjutorium meum intende.'

O God, come to my aid. After the communal response, the rest was in English, but Anselm didn't get that far. He was no longer that which in days of old moved earth and heaven (to quote Tennyson). He'd lost his stamina. Before the short refrain was even complete, Anselm had dropped oars and fallen fast asleep.

23

Michael could feel the capped trader watch him with interest. The old man sidled from behind the counter, coming closer to see if he could believe his eyes. The customer was checking the sprouts; pressing them with a thumb to see if they were soft inside, like a ripe melon.

'They're all nice and firm,' he said, confidently.

'I can feel that,' replied Michael, sinking a nail into the skin.

How much can someone take before he tells you what you want to hear? Michael was thinking of Eugene. *How much pressure is necessary before a man begs you to kill him? Before he chooses death?*

'Did I tell you about my supplier in Bramfield?' asked the trader. 'He talks to 'em. Swears it makes a difference. Can't see the point.'

'Me neither.'

'They'll never answer back.'

'No, they won't.'

'And if they did, what would they say? "Please don't eat me." That would make life very complicated . . . for him, for me, for you. Best thing would be not to listen, but then you wouldn't feel right when you threw 'em in a pan of cold water. Turned the heat on.'

'You sure wouldn't.'

'Best thing is not to think about it. What you don't know can't harm you. Of course, if you *do* think about it, a sprout *looks* like a brain, a very small one, but that's as far as it goes. You can talk till the cows come home and it won't understand a thing. Mind you, it just shows you how important appearances can be. My Christine, she can't eat 'em. Can you guess why?'

'They look like brains.'

'Exactly. Can't shove her fork in without saying "Ouch".'

Michael picked two sprouts and dropped them in a brown paper bag.

'The IRA didn't like them either,' he said, in a far-away voice.

'What?'

'Brussels sprouts.'

The old man took off his tweedy cap and wiped his brow, thinking hard.

'The Irish Republican Army hated sprouts?'

'Yes.'

'What . . . the whole lot of 'em? All those bombers and gunmen?'

'Without exception.'

The old trader slapped his thigh with his cap, knitting his brows in consternation. Christine had *nothing* in common with Irish terrorists. She was from Cardiff. So a sprout having the appearance of a brain had nothing to do with it. Then he had a flash of English imperial insight: the Irish . . . they weren't that clever.

'Because they thought sprouts might talk back?' he suggested, not too sure of himself.

Michael moved along the trestle to a crate of large green cabbages. He glanced back at the old man, pitying his confusion, charmed and wounded by his simplicity.

'I think we're beginning to understand one another, you and I,' said Michael, envying his innocence. '"Brussels sprouts" was rhyming slang for "touts". Informers. People who fed intelligence to the British Security Services. When the IRA caught them they weren't very nice about it. Tied them up and told them to talk. If they confessed, they were shot; if they kept quiet, they were tortured to death. Not much of a choice.'

'That's what I call hot water.'

'No, cold, actually.'

Michael handed the cabbage to the trader, along with the two sprouts in the paper bag.

'In fairness, sometimes they made an exception. They'd let someone go . . . a kid for example. But you'd need a pretty convincing story. How much for the veg?'

The old man's face showed his fresh bewilderment at his customer's latest bout of mysterious words and strange choices; the growing enigma of a man he'd thought to be one of the remaining Few: a simple Englishman.

'Anything for the back?'

'No thanks.' Michael paused. 'You won't be seeing me again.'

'You're off?'

'Yes.'

'Where to?'

'The continent.'

The old man nodded as if he should have known all along.

'The cabbage is forty-five pence,' he said. 'As for the sprouts, you can 'ave 'em.'

Michael put the vegetables in the boot of his Citroën and then took the A12 towards Ipswich, crossing the River Orwell south of the city. He then made for Pin Mill, the riverside hamlet where Arthur Ransome had situated *We Didn't Mean to Go to Sea* and where Jenny had calmly asked Michael to kill her. Having parked the car by a pub, he went to the exact spot where the conversation had taken place: an isolated grassy bank overlooking the salty, winding river. Then, as now, the tide was out. The Orwell had withdrawn. A group of barges with brick-red sails, all huddled together, had been lowered onto the soft bed of ochre sand. Ragged sheets of green algae lay around them like skins, sloughed off by some strange sea creature. Michael listened to the breeze: Jenny was speaking again.

'Seeing them there, tied together, ropes hanging in the sand . . . makes you wonder if the tide will ever come back.' She was pointing at the barges, sitting in her wheelchair. 'Or will they stay like that, waiting, waiting, waiting, sinking slowly into the sand, slowly falling apart.'

'The tide will come in, Jenny,' said Michael, eyes squeezed tight shut.

He was sitting on the grass beside his daughter in the shade of wide oaks and slender alders. They'd come for a jaunt after a follow-up consultation at the hospital, six weeks after Jenny had returned to Polstead.

'And when it does, they will float again,' said Jenny. 'They will rise slowly off the sand. They'll drop their sails, catch the wind and sail out to sea, away from the wrecks and rusting—'

'The tide comes in,' interrupted Michael. 'It always comes in.'

'But not for me, Daddy. Not for me. Because I can't move.'

Michael ground his teeth, screaming inside his exploding mind.

'Even if I ever felt better again, wanted to smile again, I'm still stranded. And so is everyone around me. None of the barges with their big sails can head off anywhere without having to head back here again. Someone always has to stay behind, moored to me.'

'I'll stay, my darling.'

'I know, Dad. You're always there. But it's not enough. You're not enough. I'm sorry, but you're not. I want to go out to sea again, on my own. That's what it is to be alive, to feel alive and love living. It's to be free, moving in and out with the tide.'

They were both crying – the most awful, calm, brutally simple tears. Michael's hand reached out for Jenny's and when she took it, he realised, with shame and self-hatred, that it was she who was keeping him afloat and not the other way around. She was by his side in this moment of unbearable anguish. He was going under and Jenny was holding tight, leaning over the edge of her wheelchair.

'Dad, do you remember when I was a child, I sometimes tied my laces too tight?'

Michael sniffed and nodded.

'I couldn't undo the knots and my feet were swollen?'

'Yes, I remember.'

'You'd carefully pull the laces apart?'

'Yes, by a basin of cold water. And when you were free, you'd stick both feet in and sigh.'

'That's right. It felt lovely, really lovely. A relief.'

Jenny looked down at Michael from her chair, black hair held loose in a bun, her strong black eyebrows arched with a curious knowing. She had a slightly tilted smile.

'Would you do it now?'

Michael frowned. He didn't want to say what had almost tripped off the end of his tongue – 'But you can't feel anything' – so he deepened his frown as if this unsettling exchange were some parlour game of wits and illusion.

'I don't mean here, this minute. But some time when I'm not looking.'

'Darling, I'm just not following you.' He shifted around onto his knees.

'Untie the knots, Daddy. Let me go. No one will miss me.'

Michael gazed into his daughter's slightly open mouth, not believing that he'd heard such words, words that had entered the pulp of his soul with the heat of a radiant poker.

'No, no, no, Jenny, no, no, you can't think like that . . . ever, never, not now, not tomorrow, not—'

'Daddy, I'm trapped in here' – she touched her legs as if they didn't belong to her – 'like I was trapped in those shoes. Take them off, like you used to; let me feel that cool, refreshing water. Let me walk away.'

She nodded at Michael as if she were reassuring a frightened child just before she turned out the bedroom light. Then she moved her serene face towards the family of boats. It was as though parent and child had made some sort of pact, only Michael hadn't had his full say. Which was how it was meant to be. He *had* no say. None at all. Nor did Emma, or Peter. Or Nigel and Helen. Not even Timothy. This was about Jenny's life. Her independent, sovereign existence. All at once, his heart seemed to tear open and a hole appeared, vanishing into some darkness of unimaginable dread: if he didn't do what Jenny was asking, then someone else might. Out of a love and kindness seen to be greater than his own.

The rigging and cables rattled against the tall masts. Small triangular flags fluttered. The sea wind was bringing home the tide.

On the way back to Southwold, Michael purchased a box of toothpicks from a corner shop, surprising the girl on the counter when he asked for a plastic bag. Half an hour later he bought an old armchair from a second-hand furniture dealer whose shabby goods had spilled onto the pavement. After a lot of manoeuvring, he managed to fit the chair in the back of the car, on top of the tarpaulin, the cabbage and the sprouts. The garrulous dealer gave Michael some string because, try as they might, they couldn't quite shut the boot.

24

Securing an appointment with Doctor Bryan Ingleby was easier and quicker than Anselm expected. The mention of Jennifer Henderson's death no doubt accelerated matters because after a long, freezing pause, the general practitioner proposed they meet the following day when he would be visiting the Grove, a hospice in Leiston. He suggested they convene at the nearby abbey ruin – a place where they were likely to be afforded both seclusion and privacy. That arrangement in hand, Anselm put down the phone and settled his gaze upon the expectant Sylvester.

'How's it going, then?' said the old man, with a conspiratorial grimace.

'What?'

'You know.'

'I don't.'

'You do.'

The Nightwatchman beckoned Anselm closer with a bony finger.

'I'm the only monk in Larkwood who knows how to load, fire and clean a Lee Enfield .303,' he confessed, his frail white hair almost standing on end with menace. 'The kickback's a real shock first time round. Almost knocked my shoulder out of joint. But you get used to it. You have to *lean* into the bang. Left foot forward, head down and *lean—*'

'It's not that kind of case, Lantern Bearer,' said Anselm, in a calming voice. 'But if I need armed protection, I'll come to you.'

'I know about knives, too.'

'I know.'

'And hand to hand.'

'Like I said, it's not that sort of investigation.' Anselm regarded the man fondly. If he'd ever fired a .303, it was in his imagination; the knives and hand to hand had been boy's stuff under canvas. 'The battle is in the mind, Leaping Wolf,' he said. 'The dangers are in the shadows. Among what people think or might have thought. Whether the light should be shone towards the darker corners.'

Larkwood's Doorkeeper sniffed.

'Doesn't sound much fun.'

'It isn't.'

'Well, remember what Baden-Powell used to say:"Be prepared." Anything can happen. And it usually does. Especially to the unwary.'

Anselm made a low bow of obeisance and shambled off, heading along the West Walk side of the cloister. Reaching the end, he tugged open the arched Processional Door that led to the church. Entering the cool of the nave, he breathed in the scent of wax and fading incense.

'Be prepared,' he said, dryly.

It wasn't a bad motto. Pulling up his cowl, Anselm slid onto a bench.

He hadn't been prepared. Either for Mitch's warning or his ultimatum. The jazzman seemed to speak again, this time out of the vast silence.

What if Jenny chose to die . . . why should you expose the fact and expose the man who helped her? Think of the son, Timothy. Does he need to know? And even if she was murdered, pushed under before the cancer took her to pieces, does it matter any more? What's the point of finding out? Because life's sacred? Because someone always has to pay if a rule gets broken, regardless of the circumstances?

These were Mitch's questions and Anselm would have to reply at some point. But it wasn't now. His approach was to find out the facts first and then appraise the implications afterwards. Mitch was operating the wrong way round: working backwards from what he *feared*; he didn't want *to know* the facts. But those very facts, never presented to the court, had put Peter Henderson behind bars. They couldn't be ignored, even if Mitch thought it best to look the other way.

'Help me.'

Anselm listened to the quiet echo of his voice in the empty nave.

'Help me find out who killed Jennifer Henderson.'

The smell of beeswax was warming. Incense lingered from the

night before. Colours of evening streamed through the stained glass, sending paths of red and blue light along the shining flagstones.

'Help me find out what happened and why.'

Jenny had wanted to talk with the pastor in the family, a man whose job it was to speak out for hope in the worst of situations. She'd died before she could open her mouth.

'*Exauce-moi.*'

Anselm often slipped into French if he wasn't sure he'd been heard. His voice was so quiet it barely sounded outside his cowl. He closed his eyes and took a slow, deep breath.

A door opened and shut.

Someone tiptoed up the nave. A heavy presence sat down beside Anselm. A man coughed secretively.

'The Force Research Unit,' came a dark whisper. 'Shady outfit according to some of my sources. Pay attention. It's complicated.'

Anselm let his head fall back in disbelief. He looked at the horizontal beams, great wooden arms extended across the benches far below. He'd asked for help and it had come in the form of Bede. He should've been prepared.

'Undercover work in Northern Ireland was carried out by the SAS, 14 Intelligence Company and the FRU. The first two were controlled by the Royal Ulster Constabulary. But not the FRU. Got it?'

Bede waited for Anselm to react. Getting nothing, he came slightly closer.

'The FRU worked outside the normal structure of command. Minimal operational control. Few restrictions. Underhand and under the carpet, some might say. They handled informers. Mainly from within the Republican community. Recruited people to infiltrate the IRA itself. To keep one step ahead of the bombers. Only it gets a bit murky. D'ye hear or what?'

'I do, Bede.'

'Pull your cowl down, then.'

Anselm obliged and turned to face the wrath of the archivist.

'Do you know what their motto was, these handlers?'

'I don't.'

'"Fishers of Men". Matthew chapter four, verse nineteen.'

'"Come follow me and I will make you . . ."' cited Anselm, quietly.

'That's the one. The weight of opinion, scholarly and otherwise, is that some of these fishermen got carried away in the eighties. Sacrificed one agent to save another. Set up killings.'

'Authorised assassinations?'

'Well, once you're inured to violence and killing, you can see the logic of it in a grubby war, can't you?' Bede dried his top lip with a quick swipe from a habit sleeve. 'If the Army would shoot a certain bloke if they caught him armed on the street – because they know he's already shot one of ours and will shoot another as soon as he gets the chance – then why not skip past the rules of engagement every once in a while? Why wait until he's tooled up? The IRA did just that, all the time. No hanging around on their side of the fence. I'm not saying I agree, I'm simply telling you how some minds in the FRU must have been working. Seems a few handlers passed on information to interested parties, knowing the details would be used to organise an ambush . . . end someone's life. All it took was a leaked address, a location and a time. After that the fishermen sat back and let some other crew chuck their nets overboard.'

Bede stared at Anselm, trying to see past his mask of cold concentration.

'It's all part of the madness of killing for a cause,' he continued, giving his voice a driving whisper. 'If one group intends to kill the other anyway, then why not give 'em a helping hand if it suits your own purposes? Saves time, money and manpower.'

Anselm didn't respond.

'What do I think?' said Bede, as if in reply. 'I think well-meaning people got sucked away from a simple understanding of right and wrong. Thought the rules didn't match the situation on the ground, so they dumped 'em. Believed they could act outside of the law for the sake of a greater good. I think the fishermen forgot that one day the lion would lie down with the lamb and that the sheep would be separated from the goats' – for a split second Bede faltered, like Noah wondering what the hell he was going to do with all the animals, but then he got back to the Role of Man – 'which, I imagine, is where you come in. It's judgement day, isn't it? You're the Terminator.'

Bede waited for Anselm to confirm his suspicions, but Anselm looked ahead, thinking of the broken man with his head lowered in all the photographs. This, then, was Helen's theory that she couldn't bring to Nigel: his brother, the Army man, shattered by his FRU experience in Belfast, had killed his own daughter. How could he have done such a thing? Because he'd done it before. He'd crossed the line once already. He'd been involved in killing for the greater good twenty-five years earlier. Faced with Jenny's final crisis, what had he done, this man who knew how to make impossible decisions?

'Does that help?' ventured Bede, crouching forward, sending a rush of blood to inflate his round, conspiring face.

'A great deal, thank you.' Anselm was remote, following Vincent Cooper's ghost into the blurred area between the red and blue.

'You're investigating collusion?' asked Bede, as if he promised not to tell.

'Yes,' muttered Anselm.

'Well, you'd better be careful,' murmured the archivist. 'I've done the reading and I'll put the books outside your cell. The people who were involved in that old game are still capable of anything. Wouldn't think twice of setting up another ambush if they thought it would tilt things in their direction. You might need to start checking under your car. An "up and under", that's what they called them. A bomb in a Tupperware with a magnet.

Under the car and *up* into the seat well. Should have been called and "under and up". That's how they got Airey Neave.'

Anselm returned to himself, blinking at the shadows.

'I'll be fine, Bede. It's not that kind of case.'

Part Three

The Diary of Timothy Henderson

~

14th July

My mum's gone but I still have my memories.

My first is sitting in a pushchair in the rain. Rather than buy something, my mum had made this cover out of an old jacket and some wire. In the middle she'd cut a big hole and sewn in a plastic window. There was a blanket over my legs and I felt like I was driving a car. I was all warm and dry but she was out in the rain. I've thought about this loads of times but it was only last week that I realised while I was nice and dry she was getting wet.

Another is getting into trouble. I was walking in the middle of the road. She went mad and shouted that I could have got killed and then I started crying because I realised if I died I'd never see her again. Mum told me that two minutes later I was in the middle of the road again.

I don't remember much of my dad. Just crawling around his feet when he was sitting in the armchair. That's what he was. A pair of shoes, the bottom of some trousers and a big open newspaper.

21st July

There are too many of them, these memories. My dad was working all the time whereas my mum was just there like the house and the trees. When I got up in the morning she was there. When I came home from school she was there. When I woke up at night she's the one who came if I got scared. We were friends. I told her everything. That's why I'm blocked up now because I find it hard to say to anyone else what I used to say to her.

28th July

I never saw my mum as a dancer even though she'd won a prize in Switzerland. She showed me photos and everything but I still didn't think it was her. Then one day I asked her to do *Swan Lake* in the sitting room. She said no and laughed but I pushed her into it. All she did was lift her arms and look across the room in a sort of miserable way but I was completely gobsmacked. She'd totally changed. I can't describe it. She looked like she was floating on water. She looked beautiful. My mum wasn't the same after that. She wanted to dance again.

4th August

Granddad thinks it was his idea but Mum opened the dancing school because of me. We talked about it every night. She was worried I'd mind, because she wouldn't be around as much as before. But I told her to do it. I wanted to see her floating again.

11th August

Victor Cooper moved to Sudbury and offered to help out. He said he'd had enough of London. He was very friendly but I didn't trust him. He was trying to fill the space left by my dad. He said I should try dancing and I told him I wasn't Billy Elliot. I didn't like the way he did anything my mum asked.

21st August

My mum kept saying sorry that she was going to the school in the evenings. Same for Saturday. But I didn't mind. She was full of ideas for the future. And then she broke her spine. I don't remember exactly what happened even though I was there. All I can see now is my mum in the sitting room before she went back to dancing, with her arms lifted up, pretending to be upset.

25

Anselm ambled among the bold remains of fourteenth-century dressed stone and flint flushwork, passing through an arch into what was once the south transept of the monastic church at Leiston. Standing there, hands behind his back, examining a crumbling clerestory window, was a tall man in a long dark green overcoat. Anselm came alongside.

'This enchanting place was founded by the Lord Chief Justice of England,' said Doctor Ingleby, after a glance at Anselm's habit. 'Happier days, I suspect, when law and theology went hand in hand. When medicine played beneath their vaulting majesty, guided by the precepts of each.'

Doctor Ingleby gave Anselm a melancholy smile. He was in his early seventies. Both gentle eyes were like late moons, with a soft waning light. His collar was up, his neck protected by a bright-yellow scarf.

'I love this kind of spot,' he confessed. 'They're the vestige of something good that speaks to me, a hunger and yearning for the great answers, the pillars reaching up to the sky. Traces left on the ground of former certainties. There's a comfort in all that. I find humility in what's left of the attempt.'

They were quiet, looking at the remains of a high window:

stone clinging together in the shape of a narrow arch. There'd once been a row of them, running the length of the nave and around each transept. Light had fallen in shafts upon the bowed heads. Anselm wondered if the doctor had very subtly just laid out his understanding of the territory they were about to enter: the complex area of medical practice and the law in a changing world.

'I've been asked to look at Jenny's death,' said Anselm, finally. 'I won't hide anything from you. I've spoken to Nigel and Helen and I've spoken to Vincent Cooper. Would you tell me about Peter and Jenny and their time together?' He paused and then said, 'Peter is in a prison. And I don't mean behind bars. Would you help me free him?'

Doctor Ingleby didn't reply. At the mention of Peter's name, the light in his eyes went out.

Anselm was impressed. He'd questioned many people faced with very serious charges and most of them betrayed clear signs of discomfort. But Doctor Ingleby did not belong among them. He must have known that Anselm intended to accuse him – very respectfully – of conspiracy to murder and falsifying a certificate of death, and yet he concealed his feelings to perfection. Almost. Years of handling bad news had taught him how to hide his emotions, but there was a tell-tale tremor in his voice.

'I met Peter many years ago at University Campus Suffolk,' said Doctor Ingleby. 'He was giving a lecture on end-of-life issues. It's a complex subject. We both thought it important to ask the philosophical questions that arise when medical science enters unexplored territory. In fact, to ask the questions well in advance, before the technology gets us there. This is the challenge of the modern age, wouldn't you say, Father? Magellan's days are finally over. We know the world is round and what lies at the end of certain rivers. Now the voyage of discovery is . . . intellectual, ethical. We've entered a new, forbidding country.'

He broke off, looking at Anselm to see if he was on board.

'The right-to-die debate is one of the more compelling,' he continued, 'because our ability to keep someone alive puts into the question the nature of the life we would preserve – its content and quality – set against the death we would at all costs avoid. I forget the exact point Peter raised that night . . . I think it was something to the effect that patients must have new *choices* . . . as sophisticated and far-reaching as doctors had new *obligations*. I really can't recall, save that Peter and I didn't quite agree. We had a most urbane and stimulating argument. It made us friends . . . and in time close friends.'

His voice seemed to dry out. He'd spoken airily, as if to warn Anselm, subtly, that he might be out of his depth, all the more so if he pined for the days of empire when God and the Lord Chief Justice had double-checked any prescriptions emanating from the dispensary. But then the doctor had been ambushed by feeling. It had come out when he'd said Peter's name. Gathering himself back together, he took up his thread: 'Needless to say, like any explorers on a quest of importance, we have our quarrels . . . about which route to take, whether to turn back or press on. There's no other way. How else do you cross the Antarctic without a map?'

Very slowly, if at all, thought Anselm. But he moved matters on: 'You became Jenny's doctor.'

'Yes. Their previous GP had retired just before Jenny's accident. Her replacement was newly qualified. Jenny wanted someone . . . older.'

'And wiser?'

'Possibly. She didn't say. If she had done, I'd have directed her elsewhere. Most of all, she wanted a friend.'

The faint tremble in Doctor Ingleby's voice had gone. He'd found his feet now that the narrative was in his control.

'There was very little I could do,' he said, analytically. 'Hers was not a medical problem, not truly. Physically and psychologically, she was . . . reduced. Reduced to what we all are, if you take away what we might call essential capacities. She was clearly depressed.'

'Suicidal?' suggested Anselm.

'At one point. But she was a very brave girl. To the point of foolishness. She didn't want medication and it might have helped, at least in the short term. But she wanted to see all the pain through to the other side, unaided, a great dancer once more, transcending the heat in her mind and body.'

'What, then, could be done, medically?'

'Nothing. So I paid regular visits. Talked. In time, her mood lifted. It's a pity her uncle Nigel was so far away. He might have helped.'

They'd walked out of the church, finding, eventually, the former cloister. It was now a grassed square. A broad band of shadow fell from a reduced refectory wall.

'I began to come more frequently,' said Doctor Ingleby, gazing around at the neat lawn. 'And at a very specific moment, for no apparent reason, she changed. I was astonished to find that she was all at once . . . at peace. Profoundly at peace. The cancer diagnosis came in shortly afterwards but it didn't seem to have any appreciable effect. She was already deeply' – the doctor looked to the ground as if he might find the right word lying in the grass – 'reconciled . . . and that preceding reconciliation overwhelmed the power of the later illness, what it would do and where it would lead. It was almost as if she was one step ahead and couldn't be caught.'

Was that a hint? thought Anselm. Are you trying to tell me that Jenny had made a choice, forbidden by the law, and that the choice had set her free? That he knew the Exit Mask was in a garden shed?

'How did Peter manage?' asked Anselm, heading off towards the Chapter Room, the place of big decisions.

'Heroically,' came Doctor Ingleby's voice from behind. 'He was devoted to her. From the moment she fell off that stage, he was there, at her side.'

'No, he wasn't,' observed Anselm. 'He was on *Question Time*.'

Anselm had spoken like he'd done in the Old Bailey. Instinct had taken over. The repressed barrister had wanted to pique the witness to get behind his self-control.

'That's cheap, I'm afraid,' said Doctor Ingleby.

He'd overtaken Anselm and stood between him and the broken entrance to the room where monks had listened to the wise teaching of their abbot. 'Yes, his relationship with Jenny had been strained. They were very different people struggling to keep hold of the happy ground where they'd met. But they found it eventually. I don't know how, but they did. I saw them together, right up to the day Jenny died. You didn't.'

Anselm remained firm. Sometimes you had to push a witness.

'But prior to the fall,' he observed, reluctantly, 'he was more in London than Polstead. And on Jenny's big night, her modest return to the public eye, he was on *Question Time*.'

Anselm wasn't criticising Peter; he wanted to know if the doctor knew how Peter had reacted to the inner crisis that had engulfed him: the loss of his vibrant public life; and whether he'd considered – even in a kind of madness – a radical solution to his predicament.

'That is *exactly* what Emma would have said,' replied Doctor Ingleby, his injury giving way to a kind of tired recognition. 'She never gave Peter a chance, not even after he'd changed. A man can change, can't he?'

'Yes.'

'He can turn around completely without being condemned for who he once was?'

'Well, yes . . . but that's part of the old country, isn't it?' Anselm gave the shrug of the slightly lost. 'I wasn't too sure we brought it with us when we crossed over into the land of forbidding opportunity.'

The doctor half-smiled. 'We didn't leave *everything* behind.'

'Did Peter?'

'I'm not sure I take your meaning.'

'I'm wondering if he found a new way to deal with terminal cancer.'

Doctor Ingleby was taller than Anselm and he looked down at him with the stillness of a man checking an X-ray. He waited a very long while, and then, suddenly, he relaxed.

'I think you and Peter would get on rather well. You're not that different. He, too, says outrageous things that he doesn't quite mean. His heart is never on his sleeve, always in a back pocket, and usually of trousers he's not wearing. I'm assuming yours is in a side chapel at Larkwood.'

Doctor Ingleby had, of course, completely ignored Anselm's accusation against Peter and, by implication, the charge against himself: that he'd covered up this unspecified 'new way' with a false death certificate. His voice had remained steady. Was this because he believed that, regardless of anything Anselm might say, Vincent Cooper had destroyed the Exit Mask? Was this the calming factor?

'Could you tell me about Emma?' asked Anselm, changing tack. He'd detected a certain antipathy to the woman who hadn't given Peter a chance.

'If Peter's heart was sometimes out of sight, Emma's was lost . . . and she never found it again. Never went looking. She never got over the greater crisis.'

'Jenny's accident?'

'No, Peter's arrival into the family.'

Emma had never accepted him, never accepted his place in Jenny's life. That was her tragedy. Only Michael respected her decisions. When Doctor Ingleby had met them together, as a couple, he'd even wondered if she resented her own husband – his place in Jenny's life, his importance and closeness. She'd liked to have been the great figure of salvation in her daughter's life, and she wasn't. *Nobody* was. Nobody could be. Michael understood that, which brought him even closer, whereas Emma . . . Emma was left excluded by her own longing. She'd resented Nigel, too, because even though he was far away, he'd represented spiritual support, the voice of God even . . . the possibility of some transcendent response to Jenny's suffering.

'She even resented me, I think,' said Doctor Ingleby. 'My place as a health professional. She once remarked that a human being was the one animal she wasn't allowed to treat. She'd liked to have been there at Jenny's side giving her the tetanus injection, but she couldn't. Jenny had far more than a cut to the knee. Her condition was beyond us both. Beyond everyone. And Emma found herself empty-handed and furthest away, miles behind the vicar in Zimbabwe.'

But what a performer she was, thought Anselm. Because poor Doctor Goodwin had no idea that his sister-in-law couldn't stand him any more than his brother. Neither did Helen. She'd been on the phone to Emma for years bridging the gap, as women so often do when men fall out like boys. It had generated a kind of rarefied intimacy based on the mutual recognition that they were keeping the family together. And all the while, Emma had been seething.

Baked Alaska. Hot on the outside and cold in the middle.

They'd reached the crumbling doorway. Ahead, like a section of wall fallen flat on the ground, lay a slab of shadow covering half the Chapter House. They both lingered in the afternoon light of the cloister, and then Anselm stepped forward over a vanished threshold. Instantly he felt the cold.

'This is the room of teaching and decision, is it not?' asked Doctor Ingleby, entering and taking a position where a bench would have stood.

'Yes,' replied Anselm. 'It's a place where everyone has the right to speak honestly without fear of condemnation, without fear of being quoted afterwards, without pressure to conform to the will of the majority.'

Doctor Ingleby seemed to like that. He smiled, his half-moon eyes dwelling on Anselm as if he were the abbot of these revered ruins.

'Tell me, then, why it is you accuse me with silence? What is it that you dare not say?'

Anselm shivered slightly. He felt the gaze of a multitude, but they were very much alone.

'I have received a letter which suggests that Peter may have killed Jenny.'

The doctor seemed to jot down the point on a mental pad.

'I have spoken to someone who manufactured an Exit Mask at Jenny's request.'

More impassive noting.

'This person tells me Peter and Jenny considered you to be a doctor they could trust. Someone who would look the other way. A part of the plan. Perhaps Peter misunderstood you during that friendly argument over end-of-life issues . . . the stuff you can't remember about new choices and new obligations.'

A nod of acknowledgement, as if the point was already taken.

'The facts, then, suggest assisted suicide,' concluded Anselm. 'The letter, however, indicates otherwise. I'm told that certain members of the family agree. They remain silent to protect Timothy.'

Doctor Ingleby seemed to put his pen away and flip shut the pad. Anselm couldn't gauge his reaction to anything he'd said. The earlier vulnerability had been completely effaced. This – thought Anselm – is the resolve of someone who wants to put out a blaze, and fast. The building was on fire and lives were at stake. And he, Doctor Ingleby, had spent a lifetime saving them.

'Let this case go, Father,' he said, gruffly, as if braving the smoke. 'People will get hurt, and they needn't. And there's no need. Jenny died of bowel cancer. I should know. I signed the certificate of death.'

The doctor made a slight bow as if the Chapter meeting were over and then walked slowly away, entering the sunlight to step over a low wall robbed of stone. After a moment, Anselm turned and ran towards the entrance of the abbey. He arrived just in time to spot the doctor's departing car: a royal-blue Sunbeam Singer Chamois, one of the few classic cars that had ever made an impression upon him.

26

Michael pulled over to the side of the narrow lane. There, at the end of a winding track, protected by trees and a wild, high hedge, stood a ramshackle cottage. The thatch was green and dirty brown, the old straw rotting in the damp morning air. Windows were cracked or boarded over. A white enamel sink lay in a field as if it had been shot trying to run away. A couple of crows pecked the ground, their yellow beaks stealing the scattered seed. The horizon was bare, save for more hedges and more trees.

'This'll do,' said Michael. 'This is my valley in the Blue Stack Mountains. This is the way to Morning Light; the only way.'

He drove down the track, parked and unchained a gate with wire for hinges. The front door to the property was secured with a padlock. Using the car's jack, Michael smashed it clean off the frame and stepped inside. The dark and damp crawled all over him like germs in a grave. A faint wan light leaked into the room through holes in a ragged curtain. The place was sodden with forgotten voices, lives spent in earnest, not knowing that this is how their world of cares would end. As Michael's eyes got accustomed to the dark, he gradually perceived an uneven tiled floor, pitted plaster walls, a metal bucket, pieces of blackened wood, wallpaper hanging like blown streamers, a dank, empty grate.

Within five minutes, Michael had prepared the room. He'd placed the armchair by the fireplace, replicating the position of Peter's worn lounger in Polstead, the comfortable cushioned seat in which he'd read those heavy books, warming his toes, throwing an occasional glace towards Jenny in her bed by the window. He never sat anywhere else. Michael could almost see him, legs crossed and thinking hard. Twelve steps from an imagined fuse box.

'Yes, this will do,' said Michael, sitting down.

'Timothy, would you come here please?'

Michael sat in Peter's chair to give himself the authority he didn't possess in the Henderson household. He'd just brought Jenny back from Pin Mill on the day she'd asked him to untie her laces once and for all. En route, he'd paused to buy a hardback diary. It was in a paper bag on his knees.

'You and I must help each other,' he said.

'How, Granddad?'

'By being strong.'

Timothy sat on a stool by the fire. Like many ten-year-olds, he seemed so much younger. He certainly wasn't ready to deal with his mother's sudden incapacity. His father's almost drunken disorientation.

'We have to work together, you and I,' said Michael. 'We have to bring something good out of this.'

The boy didn't look convinced. The boy appraised his grandfather with the disturbing percipience of the young who see life for what it is without yet being frightened. His hair was black and expensively dishevelled – a 'look' recommended by the stylist because it meant you didn't have to comb your hair in the morning. He wore a red T-shirt. His eyes were dark and emotional like his mother's; his expressions mentally calculating like his father.

'Something good,' repeated Michael.

'Is that possible?'

For a brief moment, Michael remembered Jenny at Timothy's

age, lying in bed one night. She'd been frightened about something, and he'd said, 'I'll always look after you,' and she'd replied, unblinking and with perfect composure, 'No, you won't.' She'd grown to forget the exchange, but back then, on the cusp of growing up, she'd appreciated, as we all must, that we step into the world alone and will leave it in a like manner. That there are experiences in between that lie beyond the protection of those who love us, who would happily die to save our life. Timothy was appraising Michael now as Jenny had done then: with a kind of dark knowledge that the parent had forgotten or was hiding away.

'Yes, it is possible,' replied Michael, firmly.

There was much to say that he could not say, but that he believed, passionately: that Jenny's accident was a shattering experience but that, in time, another kind of life could be built on the other side of disappointment, however crushing. That other people had been there and found peace. Making that point would have to wait, as much for Timothy as Jenny. For the moment Michael wanted to put in place some basic ground rules for the future that had opened out for them all.

He took the boy's hands in his and said, 'You must lead an absolutely normal life. Do the things you would have done if your mother hadn't fallen off that stage.'

'Wasn't paralysed.'

'Yes. Paralysed. She feels stranded, unable to move, a boat stuck in the harbour' – Michael saw the phrase in Timothy's mind: 'Because she is' – 'and the last thing she wants is for you to feel tied to the house, tied to the room . . . *obliged* . . . obliged to be there, to be sad, to limit your own life. You set her free to cope as best she can if she sees that you are free. Climb trees. Phone your friends. Get annoyed because you have to go to bed. Ask to stay up late. She can be happy at least to see you happy. She can begin to find a new normality, if you are normal.'

Timothy nodded, but he didn't speak. His expression said he didn't climb trees. He had a PlayStation.

'And you can help your father, too,' urged Michael, feeling out of step and lagging behind. 'Help him manage. Do some of the things he has to do before he gets round to them. Things he doesn't want to do. Think one step ahead of him. He'll see the clean dishes and be grateful.'

Timothy nodded again. He was in the scouts. He understood about a good deed a day.

'And finally,' said Michael, feeling strangely desperate, fearing he wasn't reaching the boy, 'I've got a present for you.'

Timothy frowned his curiosity. 'What is it?'

Michael took the diary out of the paper bag and said, gently, 'If ever you're confused and unhappy, come talk to me, but if you can't, put your feelings down on paper. Otherwise they'll get blocked like leaves in the drain. No one will ever read what you write. It'll help in the long run.'

Timothy took the book, unable to hide his disappointment. He'd expected something with a lot of RAM. And Michael knew at once that the boy wasn't going to use it; that just as he was too young for the crisis, he was too young to be properly helped. He was going to have to live it out for now, and deal with the consequences later. Michael made one last-ditch attempt to help his grandson.

'Don't bottle up your anger.'

'I'm not angry.'

'Okay, fine . . . but if ever you find yourself boiling up, go break the garage window . . . the one that's already cracked.'

Danny Carpenter had said just that: *Michael, thumping cushions is recommended, but frankly, I'm not convinced. Get a hammer and smash some glass. It's a fantastic experience. Then come and tell me what you feel.* Michael hadn't broken anything. He'd plumped up the cushions instead. Kept everything neat and tidy.

'Granddad,' began Timothy, 'can I go now?'

'Of course.'

I did the same thing, thought Michael with a stab of remembered distress. I asked could I go. Danny had watched him leave, powerless to reach inside another man. He never did learn about that trail in the Blue Stack Mountains and the blood spilled at the end of it.

Timothy was at the door, the diary under one arm. He turned round to look at his granddad and waved, his young face full of sudden emotion and warmth. He was a deep boy; a good boy; a boy whose feelings burst out like sunshine in winter. A boy of endless surprises. Michael waved back . . . they'd understood each other. When it came to making sense of boats sinking into sand, they were both secret travellers.

Michael breathed in the damp, tasting the spores of decay. His faith in a better life on the other side of disappointment had been dashed. Jenny had struggled. She'd done her best. She'd waited for the tide to come in . . . but cancer had come instead. *Cancer*. Hadn't she suffered enough? Didn't she deserve some kind of response for her faith? Some reply that surpassed her monumental fidelity? Not *cancer*. Not another desperate crisis. Not a *final* crisis without a solution. Jenny had simply closed her eyes and smiled . . . she'd said a kind of tide had come in after all, and the words had broken Michael's heart. He couldn't bear it. He couldn't bear to see his broken girl accept more suffering.

But that was Jenny's passage through life. Things could be different for Timothy.

Soon, he'd be installed permanently in Lavenham. He would be leading a normal life – as normal as possible in the circumstances. He would leave behind the time of grief and confusion. His mother's struggle and death. His father's window-breaking and neglect. The embarrassment at school. The pity in the street. Michael would then be able to take the youth gently in hand. Tenderly guide him towards the life he might have had, if only . . . if only so much had been otherwise, beginning on that fateful

Friday evening when Peter Henderson had bought Jenny a glass of Entre-Deux-Mers in a Soho wine bar. But first there had to be violence. The necessary calculated brutality that only Néall Ó Mórdha could fully understand.

Michael went outside and opened the boot of his car. Taking a couple of toothpicks, he transpierced each sprout and fixed them like eyes to the round face of the cabbage. Then, carefully, he lowered the head into the plastic bag. Back inside the cottage, he used another toothpick to attach the handles of the bag to the top rear of the armchair, leaving the target lolling on the headrest. He then retrieved the Citroën instruction manual from the glove box – in lieu of the book that Emma had bought for Peter – and placed it on the armrest. The title, he was sure, would absolutely fascinate him. Standing at the door, Michael let a narrow shaft of Sunday light fall across the stinking room. Caught, like a night animal asleep, Peter lay in his comfy chair, his green, bulging eyes closed over by a plastic skin.

This was the Killing House. The SAS had something similar in Hereford. A purpose-built training centre where the shoot-to-kill boys could go through the motions of close-quarters battle training.

27

Anselm stopped in his tracks, frowned and retraced his steps. He'd just closed the outside door to the kitchens – taking a short cut to the river and his route to Mitch's wherry – when he'd noticed a brother monk on his knees by Larkwood's flagging Fiat. It was Brother Wilfred, the community's retiring Guestmaster. Finding human contact a bit of a trial, the Prior had put him in charge of meeting people, organising their stay and generally extending the warm welcome of the Gilbertines. Wilf had become, to his astonishment, a screaming success. Anselm walked over to his side.

'She won't start?' he asked, obviously.

'I haven't tried.'

Anselm persevered.

'Wilf, the thing operates with a key. Stick it in the ignition and give it a turn.'

'Not until I know it's safe.'

Anselm sighed. This was one of those thorny subjects: the nature of intercessory prayer – asking for help in the light of what we had to do first. There was a minimum, surely? And even then, with all due respect to God's knowledge of the internal combustion engine, wasn't this a matter for the likes of Vincent Cooper?

'Wilf, give me the key.'

The Guestmaster bowed low, peering under the passenger seat well. Coming to his feet, he looked around nervously.

'Bede told me not to say anything,' he murmured. 'He says you're raking over some old coals. That we all need to be careful. The whole community's at risk. Because of you.'

'What in God's name are you talking about?'

'Bede just taps his nose. Reckons the Prior might have picked the wrong man for the job.' Wilf, always nervous and vaguely guilty, even when other people were at fault, writhed at breaking a confidence. 'Reckons you're a bit naive. Can't see the dangers.'

'What dangers?'

'Bede just taps his nose. But he told me to check for a lunchbox under the car. He knows an *awful* lot of strange things, Anselm. I thought he was all gob and high blood pressure, but he knows how to make a bomb. He says you take a small tube and fill it with mercury . . . it's called a tilt switch. Won't tell me the rest, but he says when you drive on a gradient the liquid flows to the other end of the tube and completes an electric circuit which detonates a fuse and then . . . bang. You're up there with Father Herbert who survived Passchendaele.'

Anselm snatched the keys, started the engine and drove the Fiat back and forth, pressing the accelerator and flinging the gears as if his foot were on Bede's head and his hand tearing at one of his arms. The car thoroughly rocked, he left the door open and ushered Wilf towards the driver's seat.

'It's not that kind of case, Wilf,' he panted, aping patience. 'No one's at risk. The old coals are cinders in the grate. Bede's still smarting from the fact he never rose higher than junior librarian and van driver for a rural outreach project that dished up books like meals-on-wheels to the housebound. It was a good, important job, but he wanted more. He's forever searching out new levels of importance. Tell him from me that he better check under his bed. I learned a lot of bad stuff at the Bar. Things you can't find out in books.'

'Sorry, Anselm,' mumbled Wilf, looking sheepish. 'I suppose it's me that's naive.'

'No, Wilf, you're simply trusting. And you can trust me. No one is in any kind of danger.'

Mitch had toasted crumpets and lathered them with butter and honey — Larkwood honey, Anselm's honey. They ate quietly for a while, Mitch waiting for a report on the meeting with Doctor Ingleby.

'He'd agreed to meet me because he wanted to find out how much I knew,' said Anselm, at last. 'He gave me Peter's side of the story without reservation, as if to counter whatever I might have heard from Nigel and Helen. He was, at times, strangely clinical, as if he were detached, when he plainly isn't. He cares for Peter. At the mention of his name, these curtains in his eyes just closed. He's hiding something, out of affection. He's frightened. Such is my guess.' Anselm reached for a crumpet wondering whether to be slightly offended that Mitch had said nothing about the honey, its exceptional texture and subtle flavour. He waited a moment, and then gave up: 'He seemed to give me a warning, too. Hinted that I might be out of step with my time; told me that I should leave matters well alone; that people might get hurt.'

'Sounds like a familiar message,' said Mitch, archly. 'And it suggests he *knew* about the pact and was *sure* that it had brought Jenny peace of mind. Which is why he'd been prepared to endorse it.'

Anselm agreed. 'He came to Leiston very sure of himself. But that's not how he went away.'

'What do you mean?'

'The letter,' replied Anselm, as if laying down an ace. 'It really disturbed him. Because it points to murder rather than suicide. He hadn't expected that and it left him a very worried man.'

Mitch threw his napkin on the table.

'That damned letter,' he exclaimed, as if a rash had come back. 'Why is it so bloody important?'

'Because the author speaks for Jenny,' replied Anselm, simply. 'And because they came to me rather than anyone else, expecting me to fight tooth and nail, in the face of the evidence. As you once did. Twice did.'

Mitch was stumped. Exasperated, he walked over to the noticeboard.

'We've got to find them,' he mumbled. 'We've got to find out why they'll write what they think but won't speak out . . . it's got to be one of this lot' – he was examining the photographs. After a moment his finger tapped the face of Emma Goodwin – 'What about Jenny's mother?'

On first considering her features Anselm had seen more of a choreographer than a vet. An artist who carefully organised other people's movements, not someone who castrated cats and put dogs to sleep. He'd then abandoned his own insight.

'She's supported him without fail,' said Mitch. 'She's gone the extra mile . . . and in doing all that she was deceiving Peter. Telling him she and Michael were behind him all the way. What if she wants him accused . . . but not by her? Or Michael? What if she wants someone else to expose him, so that she can move in and pick up the pieces of Timothy's life?'

Anselm studied the sympathetic smile, drawn by her natural grace. This was a website photo. Bring your animals to me, she was saying. I'll tend their wounds with loving care.

'Doctor Ingleby thinks she resented everyone,' he said, thoughtfully. 'Peter, Helen, Nigel, Ingleby himself . . . even Michael.'

'Why?' asked Mitch very interested.

'Because she felt displaced in Jenny's suffering,' recalled Anselm. 'She'd liked to have been the bringer of deliverance in her daughter's life but she'd ballsed up by loving wrongly. She was the wrong kind of doctor, too. Found herself on the far end of the settee with the cushion slipping off. She's full of bitterness while everyone thinks she's the cheeky joker at the party . . . according to Doctor Ingleby.'

Mitch turned around.

'She's your author, Anselm,' he said, confidently. 'She hasn't even told her husband. She's already got Timothy in her own home. She wants to keep him there. Save the boy when she couldn't save his mother. She can't put his father down with a quick injection, but she sure as hell can get him banged away. She hopes to break the link between Timothy and his father. She wants you to do it for her.'

Mitch reached over to the coat stand and shrugged on his sheepskin jacket.

'Why not tell Michael?' asked Anselm, surprised again by Mitch's peculiar improvisations. 'Why not write together, even anonymously?'

'Because she's moving him around like a pawn on the board.' Mitch tugged at a scarf. 'Michael served the coffee to keep the peace. He's kept quiet about his daughter's death for the same reason. Someone's raking up the leaves at Polstead while Peter's in prison. Did you see the neat lawns? I bet you it's him, swallowing his rage. Keeping things tidy, while Emma . . . Emma wants one hell of a mess. She's waiting for you to accuse him of murder. C'mon. It's time to let her read her own words.'

Mitch drove past the Spinning Mule and along the lane that led to the main road. Well back from the quiet junction, he slowed. A white net curtain was raised in a small, charming gate house, a cottage that had once belonged to the wool merchant by the Lark. A woman's aged, smiling face was pressed to the glass. A thin hand waved and Mitch returned the gesture, striking his horn for added effect. He was in high spirits. Within the hour Emma would be exposed and the significance of the letter would be shattered. At the junction, Anselm spoke.

'Turn right please.'

'Her surgery's to the left. Sudbury.'

'I know. But I want to go to a village near the sea.'

'Which one?'

'Hollesley. There's a prison nearby.'

'What? Now . . . before you've found out if Emma is trying to use you?'

'Yes, because Peter Henderson is expecting me today and I don't want to disappoint him.'

Mitch pushed the gear lever into neutral and slumped back. 'What else did Doctor Ingleby say?'

'Nothing,' replied Anselm. 'But after he left me, I wondered where he might go if I was to think the worst of him. So I drove to Hollesley Bay prison on the coast. And, sure enough, there in the car park was the doctor's Singer Chamois.' Anselm reached over and pressed the right indicator down. 'A prisoner has to book a visit in advance. But the doctor just turned up and used his influence. Whatever he had to say couldn't wait. He had to bend a rule. And do you know what? He drove there in a classic car that made me think of Vincent Cooper. They're all in this together, Mitch. Now, Peter's had the weekend to think over what he wants to say and I'm ready to listen. As for Emma, she can wait. I don't want to be harsh, but she's had years to handle this crisis sensibly and sensitively. Fact is, she got cold feet.'

28

Michael tiptoed around the Killing House towards the rear door. That, too, had been padlocked but the bolt housing had been detached earlier that morning, to recreate the garden entrance back in Polstead. Leaning against the outside wall, he withdrew the Browning from behind his belt at the base of his back. With one hand he removed the silencer from his pocket. Slowly, quietly, head against the crack of the door, listening, he screwed the silencer onto the pistol. With his thumb he knocked off the safety catch. Arm cocked, the gun pointing upwards, he gently opened the door. He walked two steps to the imagined fuse box with the clip door. Going through the motions, his left hand slicing the air, he flicked up the trip switch, cutting the electricity to the house that Jenny had loved, the ideal home in which she'd hoped to die. Michael was already in darkness. There were twelve steps to the centre of the sitting room and the chair where Peter read his books on right and wrong.

'Just think of Jenny,' came Emma's torn voice from Lavenham on the day he'd left for Holland.

'I will.'

'Keep her face in mind.'

'Yes.'

'She deserves to see him when . . . when you put him down.'

'I know.'

'She deserved someone much better. She deserved a happier life. She deserved the dancing career that she'd dreamed about and lost.'

Michael's eyes had already adjusted to the loss of the light. There was no time to lose. Like anyone else plunged into sudden darkness, Peter would freeze for a moment. He would have the alert confusion of a man waiting for the light to come back on . . . as inexplicably as it had abruptly gone out. Michael had already counted to four . . .

You can't hesitate. You turn out his light.

Liam had listened at the door to an IRA veteran breaking in a new recruit. He'd learned what had to be done to advance a cause, once you'd accepted that violence was necessary. He'd shared the unpalatable truth with Michael; and Michael had listened for the sake of Eugene. A few days later he'd looked Néall Ó Mórdha in the eye. He'd never forgotten the moment. It had given him a glimpse of eternity. Which is why, this time, Michael had planned to cut the power. He didn't want to see Peter's raised face and the light of false hope. Ultimately, it was distracting. He'd tried to step around the memory of Ó Mórdha by rehearsing with the trader in Southwold but in the end he couldn't face the man down. His childlike incomprehension, so like Ó Mórdha's, had kept a lingering tremor in Michael's hand; and it had to go.

. . . five, six . . .

'People bring dogs to the surgery,' explained Emma, close to his ear. 'They've bitten someone and I put them down, quickly and painlessly. I have to. Because they might bite again. The thing has to go down. And, you know, when it's lying there on the table, no longer dangerous, it looks peaceful; simply asleep. Grateful that it's all over.'

. . . seven, eight . . .

The memories were rushing through Michael's mind faster than he was moving down the corridor; their sound and texture ahead and behind, giving a push, drawing him on.

'Peter is not a good man, Michael,' murmured Emma, crushing Michael's hands in hers.

'I know.'

'Before they locked him up he was mouthing off on the radio about morality.'

'Darling, I remember.'

'He went to prison for the wrong reason.'

. . . nine, ten. Michael was in the sitting room now, driven by the voices of an Irish gunman and an English vet, people who knew a thing or two about killing. He raised the Browning, striding towards the shape in the chair. He imagined Peter, book in hand, frozen by confusion.

. . . eleven . . .

'He never cared for her.' Emma was angling her head, coming closer to Michael. 'And yet he got all the sympathy and praise.'

Twelve.

'If you want peace,' whispered Liam, 'you'll have to pull the trigger.'

BAM-BAM.

Michael had heard a mingling of detonations and screaming in his mind. But most important of all, against his fearful expectation, there'd been no hint of a still, small voice with something new to say. Not a whimper. Not a cough. Not a stutter. Which was a relief . . . as much as a strangely disappointing revelation. For such, in the end, was human conscience. When faced with the extreme crises that will haunt a man for the rest of his life, it had nothing to say, other than repeat his name.

What, then, had happened on the marshes by the Denes? Why had Michael felt the terrifying immanence of a fresh message? He'd got worked up, that's all. With the memory of Jenny still vivid to his mind and the gulls screeching overhead, his imagination had got carried away. There was nothing else to it. That voice in his soul had simply been a distraction. A temptation for a coward who fears what has to be done. With daring and contempt, Michael put himself back in front of Néall Ó Mórdha. He stared provocatively at the candlelight flickering behind the black, wide pupils.

Michael, Michael, Michael.

Three times, like the three gates. Michael waited and then he laughed. There was nothing more to come.

BAM–BAM.

Forgetting the Donegal operation, Michael unhooked a mouldering curtain from a rusted nail. Light splashed into the dirty room. Standing over the chair, he checked the target. Dissatisfied, he began an appraisal of the operation.

His hands had been still. There'd been no wavering. Good.

He'd only hit Peter once, though, ripping a trough through the top right-hand side of the head. Not good.

What had gone wrong?

He'd been distracted by those voices. They'd come to help, but in the end they'd got in the way, making him a fraction too rushed, a hair too keen, a breath too angry. Now that his conscience was out of the way, he had to deal with these others.

'I need to think of nothing and no one,' said Michael, quietly. 'Not about Peter or what he did. Not about Jenny. Or Eugene or Liam. I must bring the quiet of nothing. The quiet that doesn't listen any more. The silence of death itself; so I can bring death.'

There were eight rounds left: one up the spout and seven ready to go. Michael retraced his steps, counting down from twelve. At the door to the sitting room of the Killing House he turned around. Peter was no longer in the chair. All he could see was a torn plastic bag holding a split cabbage and two sprouts. He felt nothing.

29

Anselm was familiar with HM Prison Hollesley Bay. He'd been there in his other life. Originally a training college for those intending to emigrate throughout the empire it had, after a spell as a labour colony for London's unemployed, become a borstal and then a prison complex for Category D men and young offenders, counting Brendan Behan and Jeffrey Archer among its more distinguished alumni. Peter Henderson, being a Cambridge don, had brought a sort of silk trim to the club's standard gown of ignominy. The opportunities of the old world had slowly given way to the problems of the new.

A word with the governor secured not only a visit at short notice but Peter Henderson's temporary release. He would, after all, be freed in two days anyway.

'You'll have to wait an hour or so,' explained the governor. 'He's giving a literacy class.'

The delay presented Anselm with a last-minute opportunity to reflect. Turning to Mitch, he said, 'Bring him to Shingle Street please.'

Anselm walked onto the deserted beach of smooth pebbles. He'd passed a sign saying:

'Shingle Street is Special. Only you can keep it that way'

And another which made the often ignored link between the special and the dangerous:

'WARNING. Strong Currents. Unsuitable for Bathing'

The sky was completely swept of cloud. A misty pale blue swung down to the cold, slate grey of the sea and a thin string of houses, closed up for the season. The beach itself was wide and long with vegetation sprouting here and there among the shingle. It looked more like scrubland or desert. A place for Clint Eastwood to appear bringing rough justice. The terrain of *Unforgiven*. But the wind was wet and cold. This was Suffolk. No one was going to kick a door down, swear and send the damned flying from their chairs. Shivering, Anselm thrust his hands into his habit pockets. There were two competing narratives about the death of Jenny Henderson. Only one of them could be right.

As a matter of logic – thought Anselm – Jenny Henderson could simply have been brutally murdered. Peter Henderson might have snapped under the strain of caring. He might have got drunk and lost his head. He might have wanted his life back in London sooner rather than later. All manner of scenarios presented themselves. And Anselm excluded them all. Just as he'd now excluded the possibility that Peter Henderson had faked his kindness after the accident. Such vistas were inconsistent with what he'd learned about Peter Henderson's character. And it was unlikely that Doctor Ingleby would have agreed to conceal any such conduct. The most compelling picture – which Anselm took very seriously – was that Peter Henderson had effectively forced Jenny to consent to her own dying through a seductive but ultimately sinister compassion. Why? Because he thought it was for the best.

It would be very easy to do. All it would take was honesty when no one else was around. The weighed-down look. The tired voice. The anxiety for Timothy. Troubled glances. Always trying one's best. Strained fussing. False cheerfulness. A sigh in the kitchen. They would all add up to an incredible weight that would easily crush the spirit of an already crushed woman. Peter Henderson could have built up that weight, without even realising what he was doing. Or through wilful blindness. Or by hardening himself to what was happening . . . because he thought it was right.

For Jenny.

For Timothy.

And, yes, for himself.

And if his conscience began to speak, then he'd have shut it out or turned the other way: this can be done. Anselm had seen it many times, in good men and bad. And everyone else, those watching, will have seen his genuine kindness; because it was genuine. He was helping her down a very difficult road. His compassion couldn't have been deeper.

In those circumstances – in effect pressure – Jenny could easily have *wanted* to end her life. Vincent Cooper had evoked the most damning and terrible scene . . . Peter being kind, and Jenny constantly saying sorry. So she'd made a choice. And afterwards – this was Anselm's fear – Peter had done nothing to dissuade her. He'd given her his *support*. He'd backed *her* wishes. And by so doing he'd nudged her towards a calm that no one had properly understood. It was the calm of surrender. And having surrendered, it would have been very difficult for Jenny to tell Peter she wasn't so sure . . . that she'd even changed her mind. To the extent that if she did . . . if she tried . . . even Peter Henderson wouldn't have listened. Because bowel cancer when you're paralysed isn't very nice. Not for the patient. Not for those watching. The momentum towards a controlled, quick and merciful death was under way and he wouldn't want to consider the alternative . . . the undignified, drawn-out suffering, watched by a boy who still loved Spiderman. Had he used the Exit Mask? Not if Jenny didn't ask for it. Not if she was lingering a bit too long through lack of courage. Perhaps Peter Henderson had found another way when Jenny wasn't looking. Perhaps Doctor Ingleby had helped him.

Anselm reached down and picked up a fistful of stones. He walked to the edge of the sea and threw them one after the other at a chain of surf. In the distance, towards the mouth of the River Ore, he could see shingle banks breaking the surface of the water: a menace for boats rather than bathers.

There was – he thought, with a sigh – a second narrative. It was the simplest. The weight of evidence leaned heavily in its direction. And it was this: Jenny had, in fact, freely consented to her own death. Peter had helped her. Doctor Ingleby had smoothed over the legal wrinkle – judged a wrinkle by their shared convictions (Jenny's included) set against the extremely distressing nature of Jenny's medical condition. And if one item of evidence was needed to support this second narrative, surely it was Jenny's last testament to Nigel: her seeming avowal that she'd lost hope in any late surprises.

These, then, were the two differing interpretations of Jenny's death. And Anselm had little difficulty opting for the first. Because – more significant than any letter, be it to Larkwood's Prior or Nigel Goodwin – Peter Henderson had thrown a brick at his own reflection.

The downside of manipulating someone – consciously or otherwise – is that once you've finally got what you want, you're left feeling ill at ease. At least right-thinking people are. Because ultimately the manipulator would like the weaker party to *want* what they'd been forced to accept. To prefer the film on ITV as opposed to the documentary on BBC2. Nudge someone into taking their own life and you don't feel uneasy, you feel awful. Take their life yourself, just in case they get cold feet, and, in time, you'll feel not only awful but utterly devastated. And, in time – two years to be exact – Peter Henderson had broken down, crushed by a weight of his own making. Had Jenny chosen her death freely – the second narrative – Peter Henderson would have simply suffered from grief: deep grief. But not guilt. And it was guilt that had launched that brick.

And it was this guilt that gave Anselm his opportunity. Peter Henderson's secret battle with his conscience was his one weakness. Deep down he wanted to make a confession.

Footsteps sounded on the beach. The shingle churned quietly with each slow tread. Anselm turned, reminding himself that Peter Henderson was a special and dangerous man.

'Well, if it isn't the Monk who Left it All for a Life of Crime,' said the scholar, quoting the *Sunday Times*. 'I always wanted to meet you.'

30

After another two-shot rehearsal, striking the cabbage each time, Michael left the Killing House and drove to the Queen's Head in Bramfield (the village where the farmer talked to his fruit and veg). He'd been here twice before with Emma. The first time was eighteen months after Jenny's accident. They'd ordered a rare breed of beef, roasted to perfection. Michael now tapped the menu in exactly the same place. In due course, the same meal appeared on the table. He began to eat, pondering over Emma's anxiety as it roused his own.

'Peter's not looking after Timothy properly,' she said, prodding the beef. 'Never has done, and I don't mean the laundry.'

'What do you mean?'

'There are no . . . no *guidelines*. No rules. Or not enough of them.' She quaffed some wine, desperately. 'Lets him do what he wants. Watches what he wants, reads what he wants. The boy's not old enough to make his own mind up. The other day he was reading the *Kama Sutra* for God's sake. There were *pictures*, darling. And it doesn't end there. He's got a copy of the Koran. And *Mein Kampf.* Of course, he hasn't read the damn thing but he really shouldn't be filling his head with that kind of Nazi nonsense. It's the same with films. Peter *completely* ignores the wisdom of the censor. Eighteens all over the place and he's only *eleven*. Has a DVD-thingy in his room. Found him watching some *American* film in the middle of the afternoon about a boxing chap who can't understand the Trinity and a Catholic priest who uses the F-word all the time – second-generation Irish, I'd imagine – and this chap finally sneaks into a hospital and kills a brain-damaged woman. Almost a cabbage. Wires and tubes all over the place. Now, I ask you, is that really *appropriate* for Timothy?'

'No.'

'We have to do more, Michael. We have to make sure Timothy gets a decent chance in life. Take him out of the wrong books and films. Take him . . . sky-diving.'

'I don't know how.'

'Rugby, then. Get him into a club. He needs something physical to get rid of all that energy. Have you noticed? He can't keep still. Wiggles all the time. Jenny was *never* like that.'

'No, she just changed her clothes every five minutes. It's normal, darling. It's his age. I used to roll all over the floor with Nigel. Tried to punch his lights out.'

The mention of his brother's name stumped Michael. He stared at his plate, knife and fork suspended in time. Nigel was in Africa. But even if his brother had been eating beef at the adjacent table he couldn't have been further away. Michael couldn't face him any more, not after . . . Donegal. He couldn't bear to see his eyes and feel that relentless energy. Couldn't stand anywhere near him without recalling the homily he'd given to the medics at Sandhurst . . . that meditation on crisis, risk and decision; that meditation on the Still, Small Voice. When Michael had stumbled into his own crisis, he'd listened hard, almost on his knees, heart open, hands joined . . . around the pistol grip of a Browning automatic. He'd heard his name three times—

'Any parental control?' asked Emma, stabbing the beef. 'No. None. Timothy goes wherever he likes on the internet. Clicks this, clicks that. Talks to people in China. Just like I'm doing now. Michael? Hello. Are you listening?'

'Absolutely, darling.'

'Something has to be done.' Emma leaned back, exhausted,

peering at Michael over the top of her wineglass. 'We have to think of Timothy. Jenny can't . . . she's got enough on her plate.'

Michael paid the bill and stepped outside into the afternoon sunshine. Puffs of cloud seemed to be snagged in the nearby trees. A breeze tugged at the branches but the fluff wouldn't let go. Tiny birds pecked at the floss and then exploded across the blue sky, scared by Michael's approach. Following the memory of Emma's voice, he walked to St Andrew's, the local church with a thatched roof. She'd brought him here after they'd lunched a second time in Bramfield, this time on lamb. That had been a mere three months ago. Peter had just been sent to Hollesley Bay. Timothy was now fourteen.

'I want to show you something,' Emma had said.

Her tone had changed. Ever since Jenny's death the flash had gone. There was no zip, no fast outrage or hasty opinions. No daft outbursts, like the sky-diving proposal. She was harrowed by the loss. Her confidence shaky. There was a bluntness where she'd once been soft. At times she was shrill.

'Isn't it moving?' murmured Emma.

'Completely.'

Michael's voice had fragmented. They'd entered the cool nave and ambled to the chancel, watched, it seemed, by the grotesque carved headstops, sad and angry faces among the riot of vaulting. Emma was pointing at a memorial: a life-size woman lying on her bed, her infant daughter in her arms. Above the two reclining marble figures, as if on a shelf, his whole posture turned away, knelt a man, the husband and father, his hands joined in prayer.

'Sir Arthur Coke can't look upon what he's lost,' said Emma, touching the dead mother and child with a steady hand. 'Childbirth took away their lives. He was the Lord Chief Justice of the realm. A very powerful man. There was nothing he could do. There'd been no crime.'

Emma moved away, her hand catching Michael's sleeve.

'Let me show you something else.'

She led him to a black ledger stone with ornate white lettering. She began to read the inscription, her voice echoing among the arches and scowling faces: 'After the fatigues of a married life, borne by her with incredible patience . . .' – Emma skipped the details that didn't speak to her purpose – '. . . an apoplectick dart touch't the most vital part of her brain; she must have fallen directly to the ground (as one thunder-strook) if she had not been catch't and supported by her intended husband. Of which invisible bruise, after a struggle for above sixty hours, with that grand enemy to life (but the certain and merciful friend to helpless old age), with terrible convulsions, plaintive groans, or stupefying sleep, without recovery of her speech or senses, she dyed on ye 12th day of September in the year of our lord seventeen thirty-seven . . .' Emma paused, allowing Michael's attention to fall on the citation from the Book of Revelation. 'Behold, I come as a thief.'

Michael felt the weight of Emma's hand. She was still holding onto his sleeve. They didn't speak. Each of them was thinking of Jenny and the dart to her nervous system, and Peter who'd not been there to catch her. They thought of Jenny's groans over many years and the enemy of life who'd come too soon.

'Peter is the thief,' declared Emma.

Michael turned aside, like Sir Arthur on his shelf.

'He stole her future,' continued Emma, remorselessly. 'She was only nineteen. She wanted to dance. She wanted to fly.'

It was true. So true. She'd longed to soar above ordinary life. One of the headstops caught Michael's gaze. It looked like Peter. Deformed, of course, like one of those cartoons sketched at the beach, but it was him all right, in stone. The face looking down on him had the same high hairline, the same ears, the same dominating eyes.

'Michael,' said Emma – she, too, had found the scowling effigy at the base of the arch; she, too, was staring back, as if returning a challenge – 'you've never told me what happened in Belfast and you don't have to. I know what's in the camera bag and I know what's wrapped in the duster.'

Michael blinked suddenly as if grit had entered his eye.

'Whatever happened,' she said, her hand dropping off Michael's sleeve and onto his cold skin, 'I know you thought about it first, and very carefully. Whatever you might have done, I know you did it for the best. Because you are a good and honourable man. A man not frightened to make difficult decisions. A man not afraid to practise what his brother Nigel preaches.'

She was squeezing his fingers tightly, crushing them onto his wedding ring.

'It's a question of right and wrong now,' she said, with whispering inevitability. 'It's a question of what ought to be done. We're a messed-up family, Michael. I wish we weren't but we are. I'd like things to have been different. But there's a limit to what we can accept. And it is not right that a boy live under the same roof as the man who never loved his mother. It's . . . *unnatural*. Something has to be done. You can't look in the opposite direction for ever. You've got to get off your knees, come down off your pedestal and look at the future.'

Emma suddenly let the matter drop. Not even waiting for a reply, she stormed out of the church as if they'd had a blazing row, her hard shoes punching the stone flooring.

Michael found her at the cylindrical bell tower, an unusual construction in that it stood independent of the church itself. Ancient gravestones leaned right and left like a congregation of simple folk flummoxed by a difficult sermon. The dead had come out in droves to learn what the preacher was really getting at. Emma was chewing her bottom lip. Her face was stained with tears. She was shivering, though her hand had felt hot.

'If you can do it for your country, you can do it for your grandson.'

*   *   *

That had been the end of the matter. Michael and Emma had planned Peter's assassination in a church. It was as unreal as Father Doyle setting up Néall Ó Mórdha . . . only the Northern Ireland situation had turned out to be slightly different in the end. There'd been that last-minute hitch. Which was why, this time, Michael wanted to be absolutely sure of his ground: well rehearsed to handle the nerves; well prepared to handle any lingering doubts. He drove away from Bramfield along tight lanes, between amber trees and beneath a sky that had been written upon with lines of fading chalk. The world really was a paradise, if it wasn't for the snags on the ground.

'Behold, I come as a thief,' he said. 'The certain and merciful friend.'

31

Anselm was shocked. The unshaven man in the grey overcoat, collar turned up, appeared to have been ravaged by alcohol and years of sleeping outdoors in winter. It was the only comparison Anselm could make. He'd seen the ragged figures of shattered humanity limping around Waterloo and Blackfriars and Peter Henderson had found a place in their number. His brown eyes were deep and bleeding. The bags of dark blue skin beneath the lids seemed to have been stretched by the weight of sleepless nights. The black hair was all that remained of the well-known commentator and intellectual. It was still tangled and professorial, evidence of someone who always woke up thinking and dragged a hand over his head with intellectual dismay.

'I read of you with interest, Father,' he said, holding out his hand. 'The line that struck me most came towards the end. It was a summary of your work. Of what you do that makes you different:

". . . justice had been done in places beyond the reach of the law". That is quite an achievement.'

Anselm took the firm grip with a cautious nod of acknowledgement. Peter Henderson didn't appear to be joking. He was too broken for levity, even at his own expense. His voice was strangely dark, as if his larynx had been soaked in Carlsberg Special Brew. Not the sound Anselm had heard on the radio and television. The man had been radically changed.

'The author says you're more interested in mercy than justice,' continued Peter Henderson, with a note of query. He'd started walking along the beach, drawing Anselm after him. Mitch kept a short distance behind as if he were a guard outside a mobile confessional. 'When I put the paper down, I wondered if you'd ever considered that certain . . . intricate situations . . . require neither mercy nor justice. Just a blind eye. Not because it's expedient. But because neither mercy nor justice can reach the true depths of what actually happened. When all we can do is turn away and look in the other direction.'

'Yes, I have considered the possibility,' replied Anselm, judiciously. 'And I'm inclined to think that turning away is the first step towards barbarism. Because it would be the ultimate concession that we cannot regulate human affairs.'

'Perhaps we can't.'

'We have to give it our best shot.'

'Suppose there is no best shot?'

'Then our worst will have to do. Because the most intricate situation of them all is protecting the weak against the strong. We can't give up on that one. It's what makes us civilised.'

Peter Henderson blinked as if Anselm were Jack Bauer making one of those monstrous threats: he'd kill your own child if you didn't tell him who'd stolen the nuclear rods. He had a gun in his hand and he was screaming in the daring thinker's ear. Peter Henderson spoke quietly as if his life depended on his reply.

'What's wrong with a little barbarism?'

'Sorry?'

He'd made it sound like salt, necessary in small quantities but dangerous for your health if you weren't careful. He developed his theme with a subdued insistence: 'Barbarism. What's the problem . . . if it's contained? Understood as a narrow area without the usual standards, but hedged in by commandments . . . all the golden rules that more or less work to order? Isn't it . . . humble to accept that we can't pin Right or Wrong on the back of *every* event? That certain decisions and actions simply . . . happen, because of the circumstances? By turning away, we're just accepting that this is one of those situations best left to those who thought and acted for the best.'

Anselm came to a halt. Mitch kept back. The monk and the scholar faced each other. There was no doubting it: Peter Henderson was like a man on the rack, pleading for Anselm to stop pulling on the levers.

'I agree,' said Anselm, trying to see into the great man's troubled mind. Peter Henderson was asking him to drop the matter. He'd made an intellectual plea and was waiting now for Anselm's final answer. 'It would be nice for all of us if we could have a little area in our lives that belonged just to us, where moral systems and the law would leave us alone. But that's not possible. Take away the rules from intricate situations and – for reasons I don't quite understand – you end up with violence. An "up and under". And other quieter acts of domestic terrorism.'

Peter Henderson's unshaven chin sank to his chest, his profile hidden now by the upturned collar. They moved off once more, their feet sinking into the shingle as the sea made a sigh. All the others have failed, Anselm reminded himself. None had made him crack. Peter Henderson had been questioned by every kind of interrogator. Save a monk. Speak like one, then, thought Anselm, wondering what a monk would say.

'You know, Peter,' he began, 'when people look in the wrong

direction, they tend to walk into a lamppost. Or a bread shop window. The psychologist said that, I'm sure.'

'She did.'

'And I'm sure she urged you to look in the right direction. To face yourself. Well, I agree with you. I think she's wrong. She doesn't understand the intricacies of the situation.'

Peter Henderson kept his head lowered, his shoulders hunched. The breeze off the sea had a sharp nip; it brought salt to the lips.

'For now, I think you should avoid both mirrors and windows,' advised Anselm. 'Anything that brings you up front against your own reflection. I suggest you look slightly downwards . . . about the angle you've got now. That way you wouldn't see yourself at all. All you'd see is Timothy.'

Peter Henderson wavered and came to a stop once more. He averted his gaze inland, over the low, bare horizon. The breeze roughed his hair.

'You cracked in Manchester,' said Anselm, quietly; so quietly the soft collapse of the sea seemed loud. 'You cracked because of the noise inside in your mind. Speaking as a monk who broadly left the clamour of the world behind, I can guarantee you that this inner noise . . . this awful, accusing uproar . . . is not going to go away. I'm not giving you advice; I'm simply telling you what I learned after I'd made a run for it. You can shut your ears for only so long. You can try living outside rather than inside. You can try arguing back. But ultimately, there will come another moment of crisis. Because, in truth, this is not an argument you can win. It's about *listening* to what you do not want to hear. It's about *recognising* what you already know to be true.'

Peter Henderson spoke with his back to Anselm.

'You won't stop, will you?'

'No, Peter, I won't.'

'Why?'

'Because if you look away from yourself, you'll see Timothy. He needs you healed, not broken.'

Peter Henderson started walking towards four upturned rowing boats. They'd been laid on the beach in front of a white cottage. Rough grass had crept along the stony beach like so many hands wanting to pull them back onto dry land.

'Do you know the story of Captain Oates?' began Peter Henderson.

He'd sat down on one of the boats, a blue fibreglass thing. Something modern out of a mould. Anselm had followed and joined him. They were looking ahead along the shingle, the sea to the left, the empty house to the right. Mitch remained standing to one side, hands deep in his sheepskin pockets. Peter Henderson was unnervingly still, like a man who'd found resolution in the face of disaster. A man who knew he was going to die and might as well speak up. Bauer was going to pull the trigger anyway.

'The story goes he went out into the snowstorm. All he'd said was "I am just going outside and may be some time." He was choosing death so that the others might live. But the situation was a little bit more complicated than that. We're always told about the old war wound and the frostbite to his feet. But what of his hands? Could he still use them . . . for an intricate task like opening the toggles on the tent door?'

Peter Henderson narrowed his eyes and licked his lips.

'I think someone helped Captain Oates stand up. I think someone else opened the flap to let him out and then closed it again after he'd gone. Maybe they all helped. They'd have worked quickly, too, because of the blizzard. Do we condemn the man who gave a helping hand? No. The man who took his gloves off to fiddle with the toggles on the flap? No. Was Captain Oates any less heroic? No. Why? Because the rules weren't crafted for a crisis in the Antarctic.'

Anselm nodded ponderously and then said, 'Yes, they were, if someone twisted his arm and gave him a shove. Which, of course, they didn't.'

Peter Henderson laughed bitterly.

'You really won't give up, will you?'

'No.'

Peter Henderson came laboriously to his feet. Somehow the gesture made Anselm a subordinate. He was expected to remain seated like a student attending a tutorial.

'I brought Jenny's mask when she asked for it,' he confessed, evenly. 'I fitted the bag onto her forehead. I turned on the gas. We said goodbye. When she knitted her fingers, I pulled it down . . . she didn't want to do that part. She couldn't.'

Anselm glared at the dark shape against the windswept sky.

'Leave Vincent Cooper out of the reckoning,' ordered Peter Henderson, harshly. 'We'll say I made the mask. And as for Bryan, Doctor Ingleby, he was like a father to Jenny. He knew nothing about the plan or her intentions, not towards the end. He thought she was fine. She wasn't. I turned to him because I thought he might understand Jenny's situation . . . and respect her choices. But then the cancer came. That changed everything. When Bryan arrived . . . afterwards . . . he just assumed the illness had taken Jenny away. If you've got any doubts, just let them go. Not everyone has to die on the homeward journey. Let these two survive the storm, will you? They were brave enough to risk everything for someone else.'

Peter Henderson walked briskly away, towards Mitch and then, abruptly, he came back, aggression in his crunching stride, his arms swinging wide.

'I don't want you talking to Timothy, do you understand?'

'Okay.'

'You leave him alone. This is a family matter.'

'Sure.'

'Speak to Nigel,' he growled. 'And let Nigel speak to Timothy. And when that's done, go to the police. A detective inspector can speak to Jenny's parents. Nothing would give them greater pleasure.'

Peter Henderson strode over to Mitch.

'C'mon. Take me back,' he said. 'I've got another class waiting. They don't understand a damned thing either.'

Anselm remained seated on the upturned boat, drawing with his foot on the beach. Meaningless shapes, doodling. An attempt to make sense of the panic that had settled upon his mind. Peter Henderson had made a full and frank confession. But there was something amiss. The voluntary element. It was as though he'd been battered with an iron bar and finally spilled out what he thought the monk had wanted to hear.

32

Michael drove south to the coastal village of Aldeburgh. This was the next place on his list – the special locations charged with memories of Jenny, Emma and now Timothy. Places where important conversations had occurred. So important that Michael wanted to revisit each setting to evoke once more the full impact of what had transpired there. He was following them in order, adding up the significance like a man counting beads on an abacus. The result would be the death of Peter Henderson. And of all the exchanges that had made him sure – if confirmation was needed – that Peter had to die, it was the brief and sickening discussion that had taken place two weeks after Michael had seen the marble body of Elizabeth Coke and her daughter.

'Granddad, you once told me to speak to you if I was confused,' said Timothy just as they stepped onto the shingle between Aldeburgh and Thorpeness. 'Why did my dad throw a brick at that boy?'

The words whirled into Michael's mind like a sandstorm. It was the gritty question that wouldn't go away. The court had raised it, the national and local press had raised it, the neighbours had raised it. It had been joked about on *Top Gear* and *Have I*

Got News for You. Timothy's dad had been on the front cover of *Private Eye*, a bubble over his head saying, 'Don't answer back'. The family tragedy had been played out so publicly that ordinary sensibilities had been left behind. But what disturbed Michael now, on the beach, was that he'd already answered Timothy's question. He'd told him his father hadn't thrown a brick at anyone. He'd snapped, that's all. His feelings about Jenny had got blocked in a drain. But Timothy wasn't satisfied. He'd asked the question again because he was looking for a different answer. He was growing up.

'He didn't know what he was doing,' said Michael, loyally. What else could he say? Instinctively – and before he could stop himself – he went on the offensive. 'He bottled up his grief . . . is that really so confusing?'

'Yes.'

'Why, Timothy?'

'Because he told me Mum's death was a release,' he replied, edgily. 'He told me she'd been spared a long drawn-out illness. You agreed. So did Grandma. She said that Mum had slipped out of the back door. So what's there to bottle up? Why explode? It's like he was hiding something. Like he felt guilty . . . like he had a secret and—'

'Enough.'

Michael had barked. His breathing was out of control. He stammered an apology, reaching for Timothy's arm, pulling him closer.

'Talking about your mother's death is difficult for me, too,' he said, more quietly, wanting to harness his confusion and subdue the fire in his grandson. The boy's face was bloodless. He stood hunched in a blue woollen mariner's coat, a present from Brittany. His features, once so soft and enquiring, were hard with the anger he'd once denied was there.

'I can assure you, your father doesn't feel guilty,' insisted Michael, still reeling at the shock of Timothy's declaration. 'It's only grief

. . . you can be relieved that someone didn't suffer and still mourn their passing. No one ever *wants* anyone to die.'

Timothy's lips made a minute contraction and Michael felt that slight pressure in the throat that warns a traveller to reach for the paper bag. He'd felt the same thing in Donegal, just as the farm door opened . . . and when he'd got back to Belfast and Father Doyle had barged in with an old tape recorder and made him listen to Liam's trembling voice. But he couldn't bend over here and be sick while his grandson pondered over his father's strange behaviour, wondering if guilt and secrecy were part of the explanation.

'My dad wants to say something to me but he can't,' went on Timothy.

'What do you mean?' asked Michael, foolishly, scared instantly of the answer.

'I could be wrong, but I think he's all bottled up because of me.'

'Why?'

'I don't know. That's why I'm asking you.'

Timothy was inscrutable. But there was something about his questioning that was artificial. He was feeling his way, wanting his grandfather to reveal what he knew . . . as if he might be part of any guilt or secret. Michael cleared his throat. 'You're probably mistaken. He's had a great deal on his mind and—'

'No, I'm not,' pressed Timothy. 'Ever since Mum died he's looked at me as if he's let me down. It's like there's too much to say and he doesn't know where to start. That he feels sorry for me. For two years he's been sort of . . . hesitant with me . . . I can tell, he's wanted to say something. Then he threw that brick in Manchester.'

Michael didn't know if he could control the nausea that stirred in his guts. By his very public collapse, Peter had smudged the consolation they'd all given to Timothy – that Jenny had simply slipped out of the back door. Emma had landed on the phrase to calm his tears, but now the boy was dry-eyed and determined. He was sure that his father wanted to reveal something . . . a secret that was linked to guilt. This was horrific. Timothy was on the very edge of discovering that his mother's death wasn't . . . simple.

Peter never knew where to draw the line. It was as though Emma had dropped between them, flapping on the beach like one of the gulls hunting for scraps. *He doesn't understand that he's just a child. Treats him like an adult. Gives him choices when he should tell him what to do. The poor boy is growing up too fast. He can't carry the weight of responsibility.*

Emma had been talking about choosing films. The gamut between Universal and Eighteen. But this was far more serious. Peter wanted to talk to Timothy. He'd been holding himself back, but in his heart he wanted to sit down and have it all out, man to man.

'Why did my dad throw that brick?'

Timothy had asked the question as if he were giving Michael a second chance. At some point he was going to ask his father again, too. And this time he wouldn't be accepting 'Grief' as the answer. Would Peter tell him the truth? Would he put that burden on a boy's shoulders, thinking he's old enough to understand?

'I don't know,' said Michael, helplessly.

Would Peter go that far? Could he stop himself, now that Timothy had learned persistence? He'd already begun to question why Michael never saw Nigel, why Emma avoided Peter, why Helen moved around between them. He was systematically dismantling the myths upon which his childhood had been constructed. And, rest assured, he was going to keep asking his father the question that had never been satisfactorily answered. Faced with the pressure and prescience of youth, would Peter collapse . . . liked he'd collapsed in Manchester? Would he quietly tell Timothy that his mother had been killed? Would he tell him how it had been done and by whom?

They'd reached a sculpture on the shoreline. A gigantic steel scallop shell. It stood on the glistening shingle like an open fan, something dropped by the sea because it was too damn heavy to drag off the beach. Timothy stood behind the raised casing, shielding himself from the wind. He was still hunched, hands in his pockets. His black hair was still tangled, fashionably. His face was still pale, his eyes cold. But the clever boy who'd once flashed emotion at his grandfather had gone. He viewed his grandfather from afar and said:

'Why do you keep two passports?'

Michael was totally thrown. There was no connection to the previous discussion. The boy's mind had dodged from right to left and Michael had been left off balance.

'My father was a Canadian who settled in England,' explained Michael, uneasily, smiling false calm. 'He made sure his children obtained dual nationality just in case we ever wanted to live or work in Vancouver. I've kept the two passports ever since . . . it means I can always choose the shortest queue whenever I pass through a foreign border.'

Timothy made an unbelieving shrug, but he said nothing. He simply looked at his grandfather, his face stiff and cold, his brown eyes drained of colour, the whites bright like snow. And then, very slowly, and painfully, Michael understood. Years ago, when this whole tragedy had begun, after the accident, Michael had urged Timothy to speak to him. To share his anger and confusion. And his grandson had never taken him up on the offer, until now. And Michael had let him down. They both knew that the brick-throwing had a secret meaning, only Michael refused to tell him what it might be. He'd dished up the same old myth. And in so doing Michael had failed him . . . on the first and only occasion that Timothy had sought help; help to understand the pain in his family.

So why ask about the passport?

Because Timothy was clever. He asked questions to which he

already knew the answers. He was saying, 'You're not who you say you are. There are two of you. One of them isn't real. The other is hiding something, like my father, with my father.' The unspoken condemnation cut into Michael's fast-beating heart. They'd once been companions making sense of boats sinking into the sand. Two secret travellers who didn't need to say everything in order to be understood. But that time had gone. The sun had set on the convenience of silence.

'Granddad,' said Timothy a third time. 'Why did my father throw a brick at that kid in Manchester?'

'Because he's got a secret,' replied Michael, man to man. 'He has something to say to you.'

'Thanks, Granddad,' said Timothy, his suspicions confirmed; and he stepped forward out of the shell and into the wind. He had the frightened, wonderstruck appearance of the newborn.

They walked south, finally reaching some artificial boulders and old wooden groynes. The area had once been a bustling fishing port called Slaughden. The original village had completely vanished, claimed by the minute workings of the sea. A whole community – their lives and houses and memories – had been slowly undercut and gradually washed away. All that remained now was Slaughden Quay at the mouth of the Alde, where Michael kept *Margot*. Struggling along the steep shingle, they talked of Timothy's schooling as if there'd been no discussion about Peter's behaviour. They were side by side, helping each other over the slippery defences.

If you can do it for your country, whispered the wind off the sea, *you can do it for your grandson.*

Michael walked again to the great shell on the beach, this time alone, this time carrying a gun. In the evening light the shingle was brown with particles of blue, purple and red. It was as though he was treading upon elemental matter. Michael had, at last, come right down to the nitty-gritty. Peter Henderson had to die if only because, in the long run, he couldn't keep quiet. He couldn't keep his own secret. Looking up at the lip of the scallop shell, Michael read out loud the phrase from Britten's *Peter Grimes* that had been pierced through the steel, to be seen against the sky:

"'I hear those voices that will not be drowned.'"

Michael thrust his hands deep into his overcoat pockets and set off once more for the black groynes and grey boulders of Slaughden. He was going to silence Peter Henderson in two days' time. He'd head out to sea in the dark with *Margot*, dispose of the body and then head back to the quayside. Timothy would finally learn what his father had wanted to say – that he couldn't live without his mother. It had been grief after all, and the business in Manchester was nothing as compared to what happened upon Peter's release from prison . . . the house burned to the ground followed by a mysterious disappearance. In time, helped by Emma and Michael, Timothy would come to understand why Peter had vanished, probably to take his own life. Leaves had got blocked in the drain, more than anyone could have realised. There'd been guilt in there, too, for how he'd treated Jenny. These would be the sincere, adult conversations for which Timothy was now pining. They'd bind them all close together and that would be the end.

The very end.

The insistent voices would at last fall silent – even Liam's, the softest, most enduring and haunting of them all, last heard following the bang of a spoon against the bottom of a pan. The Nutting Squad had taped his confession and then shoved the recording through his mother's letterbox.

On the way to Southwold, Michael purchased a heavy-duty stapler.

33

'Did you get your confession?' Mitch asked, wrenching a gear.

'Yes.'

They were quiet, as though each of them were stunned by the sudden end to the investigation. After a mile or so, Mitch said: 'He told you . . . what he did . . . how and why?'

Mitch's hesitation demonstrated how difficult the conversation must have been. How brutal. His tone asked if it had been really necessary.

'Yes, he told me everything,' replied Anselm.

He was looking out over the low flat fields, thinking quietly to himself. They were moving away from the strange magic of the sea – that sense of open space, no boundaries, just air and water: an uncomplicated vista. After a few more miles, Mitch spoke again:

'Was this Jenny's decision? He did what she asked?'

Trees and hedges divided the pasture, imposing order on the land. Marking out ownership and responsibility.

'So he says,' murmured Anselm, eyeing the neat hedgerows.

Mitch sighed and Anselm knew he was appraising another landscape: the anticipated fallout: arrest, public reaction, private pandemonium. The Hendersons weren't best equipped to manage all that. Mitch cleared his throat. For some reason he accelerated.

'Are you going to hand him over?'

Anselm thought for a very long while.

'No.'

Mitch absorbed the reply but wanted to check for any misconstruction:

'You're not going to call the police?'

'No, I'm not.'

'Are you sure?'

'Completely.'

'He goes home to get on with his life?'

'Yes.'

The change in Mitch was instantaneous. Anselm hadn't quite noticed but his assistant's shoulders had been slightly raised. There'd been a taut quality to his arms and hands. But now he relaxed and, involuntarily, he dropped some speed. All at once, the friendliness re-established in the club seemed to warm them once more. Mitch's word of caution to Anselm had sunk in – this is what Mitch was thinking, making occasional glances at the enigmatic monk. Anselm had seen beyond his family history and opened his mind to a foreign kind of wisdom. Mitch's voice was nuanced with sympathy and admiration:

'Can I ask why?'

'Absolutely.' Anselm turned from the increasingly built-up fields. There were houses and fences and tended gardens; roads and lanes and narrow tracks. 'Because I don't believe him.'

Mitch took some time to process the information. The tension didn't return to his body and he didn't accelerate. He made a kind of knowing, melancholy laugh. The 'I should have known' kind.

'You don't accept his confession?'

'No.'

'Why not?'

'Gut instinct. I've spent most of my life listening to people tell me what they've done and what they haven't done, and Peter Henderson wasn't very convincing.'

'So,' concluded Mitch, 'the investigation goes on?'

'Yes, it most certainly does.'

There was nothing more to be said. But Anselm was very aware that the atmosphere between himself and Mitch had changed radically. The musician had given an ultimatum. He'd said if Vincent Cooper's story was broadly confirmed, then he was off. And that confirmation had come to pass, far sooner than either of them had expected. In an attempt to bridge the gap that had opened between them, Anselm shared some of his thoughts – the conclusions he'd reached on that lonely beach after Peter Henderson had walked away.

'He didn't kill her, Mitch.'

That was the first, critical point, but there was no rejoinder.

'And she didn't die of cancer. Peter knows that, which is why he confessed. Now think it through: if Peter had *agreed* to kill her and *didn't*, then someone else must have done it . . .'

Mitch stayed in the slow lane, listening dutifully.

'. . . and unless that someone else was part of some other agreement, which is unlikely, then there's only one conclusion: Jenny was murdered.'

'Then why the hell would Peter confess to something he didn't do?'

'To protect the killer.'

Because whoever killed Jenny was a part of the family. There were no other candidates. Peter – ravaged and tortured by what he knew – was prepared to take responsibility because he believed that his confession to a mercy killing was far more preferable to the exposure of the truth. It was the lesser of two evils. Faced with Anselm's determination, Peter had seized the initiative, intending to shut down the inquiry. He didn't want Timothy to know how his mother had died and who had killed her. In those circumstances, the only way to protect the boy was to protect the killer.

'So who is responsible?' asked Mitch. 'Michael?'

'No, I can't accept that.' Anselm hadn't even examined the possibility with any seriousness. There was no point. 'Michael wouldn't kill his own daughter. Helen Goodwin is simply wrong. No offence, but the idea belongs in the same bracket as yours, about someone planning to kill Peter Henderson. It's sheer imagination.'

'And that leaves who? Emma? Helen? Ingleby?'

He made the suggestions sound ridiculous so Anselm returned his thoughtful gaze to the passing fields. It was an argument to no good purpose. They let the subject drop, not speaking at all until Mitch drove under the plum trees at Larkwood.

'The investigation goes on, then?'

'It must,' replied Anselm.

Mitch cut the engine. A light rain had begun to fall. Very gradually, the purple leaves and distant hills lost their clear lines, the colours smudged into the late-afternoon light.

'I tried to warn you, Anselm,' said Mitch, with regret. 'I don't want to be involved any more. Me, I accept Peter Henderson's confession. And even if I didn't, I don't think anyone murdered Jenny − in the sense of killed her against her will. If it wasn't Peter, then it was someone who loved her. They'd faced the one fact that you can't face − that sometimes life is hopeless. That too often there are no last-minute surprises. This is the real world, Anselm. A world without miracles. No redemption in this life. Someone did what had to be done.' He turned the key and the motor grumbled. 'Your mother was one of the lucky ones; and so were you. Just let these people go . . . it's biblical, isn't it?'

Anselm stepped out into the rain, blinking as the rain touched his glasses.

'It is, Mitch. But so is "Thou shalt not kill".'

Anselm leaned back into the Land Rover aware that this was the sudden end of his great project of mutual rehabilitation. He wanted to say thanks for the music, the argument and the beer. And those sausages, too. Instead he ventured: 'And so is "Thou shalt not steal". Will you tell me what you did with the money?'

Mitch appraised Anselm as if he'd never quite seen beyond

the end of his nose. 'Steal?' he replied, remotely. 'You'd never understand.'

Anselm ran head down to the Priory's main entrance, pushing open the door and coming to a halt in front of Sylvester's outpost. He dried his glasses on his scapular and then appraised the old man. He was glowering back as if Anselm had an awful lot to answer for.

'There's a rumour going round,' he said, accusingly.

'Really?'

'Yes.'

'About what?'

'The young 'uns.'

The 'young 'uns' were, in fact, grown men. Anselm smiled, wearily. It was soothing to enter the Nightwatchman's world from time to time. Particularly when he felt misunderstood or saddened by the seemingly unavoidable breakages in human relationships.

'Which ones?'

'Benedict and Jerome. They're up to no good apparently.'

'What's the word on the camp trail?'

'That they're trying to make a bomb in Saint Hildegard's.'

'A bomb?'

'Yes. Out of altar wine, fertiliser and an old tractor battery.' Sylvester shook his bony head, his eyes large in their hollowed sockets. 'Bede reckons they wouldn't have got the idea if you hadn't been dabbling in terrorism. Me? I say this is what happens when things change.'

'What things?'

'Traditions, Anselm,' he revealed, mysteriously. 'The old rules.'

'What old rules?'

'Sign language.' Sylvester nodded at Anselm's incomprehension as if he would brook no opposition. 'That's right, sign language. We should never have got rid of it. It narrowed down what you could talk about and how much you could say. Those boys wouldn't be making a bomb as we speak if all they could do was twiddle a few fingers. They wouldn't take the risk of misunderstanding one another.'

Anselm was dumbfounded. First, no one was making an improvised explosive device. Someone was pulling the Lantern Bearer's leg. And second, no one in those good old days had violated the rule of silence more than Sylvester. The Prior of the day had been compelled to banish him to the shore of Our Lady's Lake to learn the values of submission and silence. Even then, the story went that Larkwood's scout had just sat down and talked to himself.

'Anyway,' said the old man, 'this came for you.' And, as if using that revered system of signals, he pointed with solemn deliberation at a sheet of paper on his desk. 'It's from a doctor. Have you got a temperature?'

'No, Flying Eagle, I'm fine.'

Anselm picked up the faxed letter. It was from Nigel Goodwin. Anselm had completely forgotten his request. Standing by Jenny's grave, he'd asked the doctor to leave aside the conclusion he'd reached about Peter Henderson's guilt and simply put down on paper who'd seen Jenny on the night of her death. He'd been interested to know who saw her alone, if only for a few minutes. Coming from anyone else the level of detail laid out would have been extraordinary, but Nigel Goodwin had spent his intellectual life in the world of Karl Barth. No unit of information was too small to merit exclusion. In the hands of many a reader, the chronology would have been overwhelming. But not in Anselm's. Which was not to flatter himself. It was just that years of cribbing from guidebooks for idiots had given him an eye for the telling, decisive particular. And there, at the bottom of the page, was a late visit to Polstead, after everyone had gone home. Anselm read the name in quiet disbelief. He'd given no consideration to the individual whatsoever.

34

Michael waited until dusk before he went back to the Killing House. During this, his last rehearsal, he wanted to replicate the light conditions. He parked the car and walked a few hundred yards to the cottage, thinking all the while of the lanes around Polstead. He waited near the sitting room window, checking his watch until the right level of obscurity had fallen upon the chair, the bag and the book. As soon as he was sure that sufficient light remained to provide an outline of bulk, he noted the hour and set off for the imagined fuse box.

He took out the gun and screwed on the silencer.

He quietly opened the back door.

He flicked the imaginary trip switch.

He strode swiftly, counting.

At twelve, two hands extended, legs apart, he fired.

BAM-BAM.

Michael's hands hadn't shaken at all. The voices had been far away, like a home crowd excluded from an away match. They'd chanted the old songs loyally, each ignoring the other, making a swell of combined noise to send Michael on his way. This time the target had been struck once above the left eye and once just below the nose. The plastic bag had been ripped open with a hopeless flap of resistance. The sprouts had simply vanished.

Michael was ready. His reconstruction was almost complete.

Danny Carpenter had been right: handle the burning emotions

and the heat will go out of them. Keep them buried and they'll stay scorching hot. Michael felt as if he'd finally discovered and completed the right kind of therapy: he'd revisited the past with a view to *repeating* the action that had caused the mental injury in the first place. Danny couldn't have thought of that. And he couldn't be blamed for proposing a tape recording of bells in Tibet. Or for recommending controlled violence – the exhilaration of causing damage to property. Because Danny didn't know what had happened in Donegal. And if he had done, he certainly wouldn't have counselled replication. No, as far as the Army was concerned, Michael had simply shown that he lacked the nerve for frontline intelligence work. Even Emma didn't know what had transpired, though she knew it had been hush-hush. The brutal fact beyond everyone's appreciation was this: there *was* no therapy. None had been devised for Michael's particular situation. So he'd had to manage on his own and muddle through, never imagining that one day the purging of his guilt would come so very close to vengeance: the killing of Peter Henderson. Only it wasn't revenge at all. It was an act of mercy for the benefit of the innocent, that they might live without . . . troubles.

Michael was ready. Though he could never be restored – Northern Ireland had seen to that – he was ready to make amends. Able, at last, to take the final steps.

Like a council worker sent to clean out a squat, Michael tidied up the Killing House. Within fifteen minutes the Citroën instruction manual was back in the glove box and the chair had been smashed to pieces, the chunks of wood and padding thrown on top of the plastic bag in the boot of his car. Back inside for one last check, he picked up some shreds of plastic, flaps of green matter and a couple of toothpicks. He then secured the premises, reattaching the padlock housing to the front and back doors with new screws bought from a hardware store. On the way to Southwold he tossed all the rubbish into a skip at the side of the road. All in all, it had been just like raking leaves at Polstead.

222

Yes, Michael was ready.

Ready to press PLAY on Father Doyle's tape recorder.

On the passenger seat, covered by his overcoat, lay the Browning automatic, potent symbol of the last of all steps open to those who know that something has to be done. Four rounds remained, one up the spout and three ready to go.

Part Four

The Diary of Timothy Henderson

~

28th August

How could someone who moved so beautifully not be able to walk again? When Mum came home I just watched her from far away, unbelieving. She just didn't budge. She couldn't. She was in a bed by the window in the sitting room. I watched her from the door, from the corridor, from the garden and she was always still. I tried to cry but I couldn't. Part of me couldn't move either. I wanted to give her my legs. I wanted to have an accident as well and bring my bed downstairs.

5th September

Suddenly my dad was there. I'd seen him mostly on television or heard him on the radio. My mum used to put him on and say, 'That's your dad.' But he dropped all that. He was in the house. He watched my mum, too. From the door, the corridor and the garden, and I was watching him, though he'd no idea. He cried a lot. He'd put his head in his hands and pull at his hair. But with Mum he was completely different, never showing her what he felt. He read her stories and poems and he put films on. He called out to her a lot. It was like he just wanted to say her name.

12th September

I feel bad writing this. But it's true. I was sort of angry with my mum. Because we didn't speak to each other much any more. We didn't have any of our chats. I know what it was, she felt guilty for being paralysed. She felt she shouldn't be there, reminding me all the time that she wasn't like all the other mums. But that's not what made me angry the most. What got to me was that she spoke to my dad. He was there all the time at her side and I was sort of in the way. I felt left out so I'd listen to them from the landing.

19th September

This isn't working. I'm putting down all these memories but I don't feel any better. I feel bad again. Bad because I couldn't make my mum understand how much I loved her. She was all wrong, thinking that she had to be like the others. I wanted her in any condition, moving or not. I don't think she ever realised that nothing had changed for me, except that she couldn't look me in the eye any more. That really did me in. It still does. It made me want to die.

35

After a fitful and feverish sleep Anselm mumbled his way through Lauds, not quite reading the words on his psalter but staring at the imprint in his mind of Nigel Goodwin's chronology. Forsaking breakfast, Anselm snatched the keys for Larkwood's Fiat, neglecting to fill in the register that recorded who'd gone where and at what time and when the car was likely to be back in the garage. Within minutes he was breaking the speed limit on the road to

Newmarket. The trip seemed curiously well timed. On the day that Peter Henderson was released from prison, Anselm had set off to confront the person who'd probably killed his disabled partner.

A more careful examination of Nigel Goodwin's chronology disclosed two points of substance, though only the second really counted. First, everyone except Helen had enjoyed a moment of privacy with Jenny on the night she died. Each had asked to see her alone – which, in the circumstances, was normal, because Jenny couldn't move, so time with her alone had to be organised. Doctor Ingleby had carried out a short medical examination. The others had been with her for a matter of minutes, no more, save Peter who was, of course, resident. But – second – the last visitor to see Jenny alive was not a member of the family but an old and disappointed friend. He'd come back after everyone had left. Peter had let him in and he'd then spoken to Jenny for a long while . . . until she'd fallen asleep.

Anselm slowed down and released his grip on the wheel. He wanted to find his calm and review, yet again, the surrounding now significant details.

Logically speaking, *anyone* could have done *something* to Jenny earlier in the evening. Michael, Emma, Helen, Doctor Ingleby, Peter . . . they all could have had merciful plans known only to themselves. But that was all fantasy. Ridiculous. They could have hardly acted in concert or by coincidence. And remember Occam: keep things simple. And the last person to see Jenny *awake* was Vincent Cooper . . . a man who'd told Mitch that he'd come and gone before the others had even arrived. A man who'd failed to say that he'd come back.

A man, therefore, who'd lied.

Anselm parked in Newmarket and went straight to the narrow alley that led to the specialised business of Vincent Cooper: 'Vintage Automotive Services'. Stepping onto the cold and empty forecourt, however, Anselm came to a troubled halt. The work bay shutters were down. Propped against the inside of a window was a large red sign belonging to Keegan's Estate Agents (Commercial Division) which announced: FOR SALE.

With a growing certainty that he'd found his man, Anselm walked briskly towards the railway station and the street of Edwardian homes that had caught Vincent Cooper's eye. He'd left Sudbury and bought himself a nice terraced house after Jenny had died. And now it was on the market again. Anselm paused at the gate by Keegan's blue (Residential Division) placard. The windows were like dull slate. All the curtains were drawn. Anselm knocked on the door without conviction, recognising that the place had already been abandoned.

'Where've you gone, Vincent?' asked Anselm, kindly.

He didn't want to condemn him. He didn't want to chase him around Suffolk. He just wanted to talk to him. Help him recognise that Peter probably couldn't keep the secret much longer. The breakdown in Manchester, if it meant anything, proved that Peter Henderson's conscience was very much alive and well. This tragic story couldn't remain buried much longer.

'You killed her and then you told Peter what you'd done,' said Anselm, staring up at the box room window. 'You didn't like the freezer bag and the rubber pipe and the gas bottle. I don't blame you. There's not much dignity in that . . . not what you'd want for someone you loved.'

Anselm turned away and ambled down the empty street, visualising what had happened next. Vincent had stepped away from the body. He'd called to Peter. He'd explained what he'd done. Maybe they'd cried together. But then Vincent had left because at this point, however shaken Peter might have been, there was a structure in place to be followed once Jenny had been helped to die. Friends and family were involved. A call was made to Doctor Ingleby. He'd come to the house. He'd examined the body. He'd spoken to Peter. He'd signed the death certificate.

Anselm pulled out of the car park, barely noticing the markings on the road, the oncoming traffic or the signs and lights. He now understood the reason for Peter's confession.

Vincent had killed Jenny knowing that Peter couldn't bring himself to do it. He'd 'helped her to die' because, like he'd said, as a dancer he'd had a unique appreciation of Jenny's psyche. Anselm saw him once more, leaning over the cluttered table, his eyes haemorrhaging a dark knowledge.

You name them . . . Peter, Emma, the doctor and, yes, even Michael, her father, none of them could even begin to understand her like I did, to understand what she felt like after her legs had been taken away from her. She didn't need to explain a damn thing to me. Not a thing.

But killing her, out of love, had cost Vincent Cooper everything. That's why he'd left Sudbury. That's why he'd left dancing altogether. He'd had to try and start his life all over again. And Peter, recognising the huge cost, had now decided to shield him from the cold scrutiny of the law. His old friend – the friend he'd displaced – had paid enough.

'Where have you gone, Vincent?' murmured Anselm. 'I need to talk to you. And you need to talk to me.'

Back at Larkwood, Anselm went to the calefactory and called Keegan's Estate Agents. Unfortunately (said Linda) the person responsible for both files – Trevor – was out and wouldn't be back until six. So Anselm went to Saint Hildegard's to check on Benedict and Jerome who were, in fact, trying to manufacture an improvised explosive device (a modest banger). But since (*inter alia*) the fertiliser lacked an essential ingredient – ammonium nitrate – Anselm left them to it. At the appointed hour, and once more in the calefactory, Anselm tried again.

Trevor was very helpful, but he couldn't be charmed into disclosing the present location of the vendor. In answer to direct questions he said, no, the client would not attend any visit to the house or the business, yes, a quick sale was hoped for, and yes (to that end), an offer well below the asking price would be considered. Then came the one surprising aside: the vendor was sick of England and was heading off to the sun. Somewhere in Spain. Both sales would be handled through his appointed agent.

'Which is me,' said Trevor, with a hint of his influence and sway. He turned persuasive: 'As to the asking price on the Edwardian bijou: frankly, between our good selves, I think if you came in at—'

Anselm put the phone down.

'You haven't gone yet, Vincent,' he said, quietly. 'And I'm going to find you.'

Anselm had never quite understood how his mind worked. He often failed to see the obvious. Lying in bed, listening to 'Sailing By', he'd suddenly recognise what had been plain all along, the insight appearing in his mind out of nowhere and prompted by nothing. It was a phenomenon he found more maddening than humbling. And it happened now, without the benefit of darkness and music. Stepping from the calefactory into the cloister, he suddenly stalled, staring ahead at the sunlight falling in the Garth. He felt sick.

'Nigel's chronology was based on information obtained from Timothy . . . Nigel had spoken to him very carefully . . . wanting to know who'd been with Jennifer on the night she died.'

Anselm blinked at the sharp green moss, bright with yesterday's rainwater.

'Which means that Timothy saw Vincent Cooper when he came back.'

And if he'd seen the late return, he'd seen everything else. Because he'd seen Vincent Cooper leave. The boy had probably seen or heard the conversation between Vincent and Peter. He'd probably seen or heard the call to Doctor Ingleby, along with his arrival and all that had transpired when it had been disclosed that Jenny was now dead.

'Dear God,' whispered Anselm. 'I asked you for help, but I didn't ask for this. I've stumbled onto the one secret observer . . .

Timothy Henderson witnessed the killing of his mother. And he's said nothing . . . to protect every single person in his family.'

The young boy had accepted his father's whispered explanation that cancer had taken his mother away sooner than expected. He'd cried, no doubt, listening to all the other stuff about a quick and merciful end. And all the while he'd known the truth. He'd buried it . . . for the sake of Michael and Emma and Nigel and Helen. And his father. For the sake of family peace. For the sake of cutting back on everyone's quota of anguish. He'd let them swallow Peter's story, not knowing that none of them believed him.

'You can't carry that weight, Timothy,' mumbled Anselm. 'It will destroy you.'

Anselm went in rapid search of the Prior. He found him alone in the nave, sitting at a bench near the back as if he were a casual visitor rather than the Superior. That was his way. He shunned all the trappings of Office. He listened to Anselm's explanation without interrupting, showing only his pained reactions.

'I don't know what to do,' admitted Anselm, his voice echoing softly. 'I'm stunned . . . my mind is frozen.'

The Prior closed his eyes. This was another of his ways. You got the impression you were no longer quite alone. After a peculiarly deep silence, he opened them.

'Talk to Nigel Goodwin,' he said. 'He's already questioned the poor boy and the boy will have sensed his purpose. If anyone should sit down and help Timothy go beyond what he's been able to reveal so far, then it's Nigel. This is his responsibility, not yours. He's the one who's received the boy's partial trust, not you. It would be quite wrong for you to question him, however delicately, if you were relying on what he'd disclosed to Nigel.'

Anselm quickly left the church and was heading towards the plum trees when he heard heavy feet stirring up the gravel behind him.

'You have the keys to the Fiat? The *comm-u-nal* car?'

Bede, softly panting, drew out the qualifier as if Anselm needed a firm reminder. The archivist stood legs apart, a plump hand on each hip.

'I do,' confessed Anselm.

'You're meant to put them back on the hook.'

'I'm sorry, I forgot.'

'And you didn't fill in the register.'

'I'm sorry, I was rushed.'

'There are rules, Anselm. You can't just forget them and run. They make the world go round. They stop an archivist killing a beekeeper.'

Anselm studied Bede with something like awe. He'd made it all sound so simple.

36

The mullioned windows of the cottage at Long Melford seemed to stare back at Anselm after he'd rung the bell. A figure moved behind the glass and, after a long delay, the door opened. There, on the hearth, was neither Doctor Goodwin nor his wife, but a boy Anselm had only ever seen in a photograph, excluding (of course) the fleeting glimpse at the upstairs window. Timothy Henderson spoke first:

'They're not in.'

Anselm began to introduce himself, stammering his surprise, but Timothy interrupted him.

'I know who you are. I read the article in the *Sunday Times*. You're a monk.'

'Yes.' Anselm was pleased the boy had opted for the primary designation.

'And a detective.'

'I prefer "puzzled explorer lost in the fog of human doubt and confusion",' corrected Anselm.

'That's a bit long.'

'It is. But it's true.'

Timothy flashed a sunny smile, its appearance so bright and unexpected that it bowled Anselm clean over. 'Do you want to come in?' he said. 'They'll be back any minute.'

Timothy was fourteen now (Anselm reminded himself). He'd been twelve when he'd lost his mother. His brown eyes still had their boyish simplicity, but the voice was breaking and his movements were slightly awkward. Adolescence made his body twitch with a kind of static electricity. Even his hair had been scrambled by the voltage. He'd gone into the kitchen, like a proper host, offering tea and something to eat. Anselm sat down, noting the *Sunday Times* folded on the coffee table. The bureau in the corner was open. Beside a pad of paper and a pile of envelopes was a diary, closed upon a biro. It had 'T.H.' scrawled all over the cover. Timothy had been writing when Anselm had rung the bell . . .

'My aunt makes this fruit cake,' said Timothy, entering the room. He'd balanced a plate on the top of each mug. On each plate was a slice of Nigel's favourite nibble. 'She's been making it for years . . . since she married my uncle.'

Anselm helped Timothy by carefully taking the plates off the mugs. When they were both seated, Timothy continued his story.

'And it's always the same . . . dried out . . . sometimes burned . . . but never, ever moist. Isn't that weird?'

Anselm agreed, watching the boy's bright, brown eyes. What am I to say? he thought, anxiously. You are a witness to murder. I can't talk about cake.

'And do you know something else? My uncle – actually he's not my uncle, he's my *great uncle* – he always says it's magnificent. Marvellous. Awe-inspiring. And it isn't. What do you think?'

Anselm said it was rather dry.

'Exactly,' said Timothy, precisely. 'It's obvious. But my uncle can't say it. Even though it is true, he can't bring himself to tell my aunt that this thing she's been bringing out of the oven for forty years is awful. And that he hates it. He's made it something kind to say the opposite. Which is a bit odd, wouldn't you say?'

Anselm said he would. The boy was on the edge of his seat, his crumpled jeans with washed-out white patches on the knees. His white trainers were new, with the laces left untied and shoved down the insides, between the shoe and the sock. The sleeves of his brown woollen jumper had been pushed up to the elbows.

'He doesn't speak to his brother,' said Timothy, clipping the words. 'But my aunt speaks to his wife. Yet, they never speak together, all four of them. That's weird, too.'

Anselm agreed.

'My grandparents don't speak much to my father. And neither do my great aunt and great uncle. And from what I've heard, they didn't talk much to my mother, either. So this is my family: my dad is sitting in a chair, sort of, and no one talks to him. And the people who aren't talking to him aren't talking to each other, except for my aunt and my grandma who only speak on the phone. Which is very weird.'

Anselm nodded. *And you have done your best to stop things getting worse. You've accepted a dreadful burden so as to keep your family from falling even further apart.*

'But the weirdest part of all this, is that they're all talking to me.' He started eating his great aunt's cake hungrily. 'Or they try to, but . . . the thing is . . . they don't tell me the truth. It's as though they thought it might bite them. Or me, I suppose. You see, my uncle Nigel – and I really like him – he seems to think he's doing Aunt Helen a favour. As if her life was worth living because he says her cake is divine. Worse, I suppose . . . she thinks her life's important because of the cake. Why not tell her it's really bad? Why not say it's dried out *again* because she's always doing two things at once? Why not throw it in the bin and kick the oven? If my uncle did that just for once in his life instead of patting her on the head . . . well, maybe Aunt Helen would get a life. Get one for herself, not him. Do you know she's got a degree in botany? And all she's ever done is make herbal tea for my mother. She knows *everything* about plants, what you can eat and what you can't. In the Middle Ages she'd have been a witch.'

Anselm ate some of Helen's cake. It was dry, lacking heart. He kept his eyes on Timothy who wasn't expecting or wanting Anselm's contribution . . . not just yet. This very clever boy was sick of listening. He wanted to be heard. But Anselm's skin tingled with apprehension. He felt with uncomfortable certainty that Timothy was testing him. Playing with him, even. He was going somewhere with this voluntary narrative of family dysfunction. He was angry and curiously out of control. Seeming to enjoy himself while being unhappy. Anselm had seen this many times before, but in hardened criminals and usually the violent: they'd had too much to talk about. Too much to say. They'd been buried in unmanaged feeling. But he'd never seen it in a boy. But, then again, he'd never met a child who'd witnessed a murder.

'Why doesn't my grandfather tell his brother what went wrong in his life?' asked the boy.

'I don't know.'

'Why doesn't my grandfather try and sort things out with my father?'

'I don't know.'

'Why doesn't my grandmother give him a chance?'

'I don't know.' Anselm brought the angry assault to a close. 'I *really* don't know.'

Timothy finished his cake, put the plate on the table and reached for his mug of tea. He slouched, involuntarily, looking at Anselm with that back of the classroom detachment. One of the bright lads who'd begun to see through everything around them and were giving cynicism a go. Only there was something advanced about this fourteen-year-old. He wasn't acting to see what things felt like . . . he was already there, and he didn't like what his eyes were telling him. He didn't like the world very much or the people in it. They were all rather disappointing. Monks included. Even the one lost in the fog and claiming not to know.

'I thought you'd be different,' said Timothy, one foot pressing up and down, as if he were smashing a bass drum. 'Just a little bit, but still different. And you're not. There's a lot of problems in my family and you know why.'

'I don't.'

'Yes, you do.'

'No, I don't.'

In truth, Anselm was being evasive. He knew about the shadow from Northern Ireland. He knew about Peter Henderson's impact on the Goodwins. He knew about the suspicions harboured in this very house. But it wasn't his place to bring these elements into the open . . . at least not yet.

Timothy put a finger in his mouth to pick loose a hardened current or cherry. As if giving Anselm a second chance, he said:

'Okay, why did my dad throw a brick at the boy in Manchester?'

He looked at Anselm from suddenly tortured eyes – the anguish appearing as swiftly and dramatically as the sunlit smile. The vast distance between the two emotions, suffering and jubilation, had been crossed with the snap of a finger and thumb. The boy needed help. He'd just stepped over a vast, yawning hole of complex, knotted feeling as if it wasn't there. All he had were these two intense reactions, one light, one dark. If he was to be balanced and healthy, he needed the immense grading in between. Otherwise he'd love without depth and hate without remission. He'd hurt himself and others, only he wouldn't feel much . . . except exhilaration and despair. He'd seek simpler feelings through excess alcohol and senseless sex, telling himself that he was living life to the full; that this was rock 'n' roll. He'd end up with cuts to his face – they always did. He'd end up crying without knowing why. Which – given his intelligence – he'd turn into some kind of

existential symptom because life was absurd and then he'd go the
route of many people who want radical answers but don't always
want to study the primary sources: he'd say that God was dead
and Nietzsche and Sartre had said it all.

Could things get any worse? The last words would go to the
French and the Germans.

Seeing Timothy's sheer . . . *impoverishment*, the confusion and
the bile, Anselm was simultaneously convinced that the true story
behind the killing of Jennifer Henderson had to be told. That
Peter Henderson's desperate attempt to protect his son from the
truth was profoundly misinformed. Something had to be done
. . . something had to be done.

'I said, why did my dad throw that brick?' repeated Timothy.
'You're a detective. You've been asking lots of questions. You must
have found something out by now.'

After a moment Anselm said, 'I'm sorry, Timothy, I wasn't honest
before. I do know why there are problems between your father
and grandparents, and why there are problems between your
grandparents and your aunt and uncle. But I don't know for sure.
I didn't answer your questions because it's not always appropriate
to be brutally honest with people you've only known for ten
minutes and when their aunt and uncle are due back in seconds.
Sometimes telling the truth – and I can see that is what you like,
want and admire – requires *time*. Planning. Cooperation from all
the people involved. Your questions are too deep and important
to be answered off the cuff – even honestly. I think you appreciate
that, but I can see you're sick of being messed around. In the
present instance, however, I also think you know the answers to
your own questions. You want to embarrass *me*, because you can't
embarrass *them* . . . because one of the strange things about being
kept in the dark is that you get to like it after a while. It makes
you *powerful*. Because you know far more than *they* could ever
begin to guess. They feed you the party line and think they've
got you on board whereas, in fact . . . you are watching them;

knowing what you know. And that is one good feeling among all the bad. Am I right?'

Timothy seemed not to move. He was suspended between light and dark, happiness and misery and – Anselm sensed – doubt and certainty. Doubt about whether he should reply; certainty about what he'd say if he did. Finally, coming to his feet, he snatched the *Sunday Times* off the table. In almost the same action, he quickly rolled it up and then smacked it against an open palm, hovering between the coffee table and the chair as if he were trapped. There was no room to manoeuvre; he couldn't pace back and forth; all he could do was shuffle on the spot.

'These people who lie all the time,' he blurted out. 'They say he killed my mother. Not to me, of course, and probably not to each other. They've all got their reasons to blame him. So they say he's a broken man. Did you know that?'

Anselm made no admissions. He watched the boy's erratic feet movements.

'They *tell* me it's grief but they *think* he feels guilty,' said Timothy, whacking the *Sunday Times* against his hand. 'Well, I know he's unhappy and I know he's got nothing to be guilty about.'

Anselm looked at the white knuckles.

'It's why you're here' – Timothy slowed his arm motion as if the rolled newspaper were a piece of wood; he tapped his hand lightly, glaring at the Monk who'd Left it All for a Life of Crime – 'it's why you came to see my aunt and uncle. You've got a theory. Are you going to tell me what it is?'

'No, Timothy, I am not,' replied Anselm, very calmly. 'Because I do not have a theory. I've had several and they've all turned out to be wrong.' Imprudently, he added, 'How about you? Do you have one?'

'No.'

'I'm surprised.'

'Why?'

'Well, like I said, you don't behave like someone who's *really* in the dark or lost in the fog . . . you remind me of your father. You both know something you don't want to talk about.'

This was the moment of enquiry that should have been left to Nigel, but what could Anselm do? The Prior always said that the truth reveals itself in the concrete circumstances of our lives. You have to respond, as if to a voice. And this moment of opening mutual sincerity could not be slowed, postponed or avoided. It was happening. Timothy was sitting down. He'd thrown the newspaper on the floor. His voice, no longer splintering high and low with adolescence, became quiet and even.

'They buy me books to make me laugh. They suggest I climb trees. Sky-dive. Would you believe that? Learn some tricks. They talk to me as if they were scared I might speak. And they're right there, only they don't know why they should be worried. They haven't got a clue what I might say.'

'Because they think you're in the dark.'

Timothy nodded, one arm massaging the muscle of the other, his nails leaving white scratch lines on his skin. 'They tell me all these lies when I could tell them I know the truth. And I look at them all, one by one, and I keep thinking . . .'

Anselm couldn't help but frown slightly. Timothy was crouching forward, feet bobbing, hands rubbing his forearms.

'Thinking about what, Timothy?' asked Anselm, quietly.

'About the night my mother died. I was there. I know it wasn't cancer.'

Anselm held his plate still as if a bird had landed on the rim.

'I know she was killed,' said Timothy.

Anselm didn't even nod.

'It's not what you think . . . it wasn't one person, not *really* . . . it was a team thing.'

A team. Anselm felt the blood slow in his veins.

'Friends and family . . . you know, acting together.'

Peter, Michael, Emma, Helen, Cooper, Ingleby? It simply wasn't possible . . . unless this was some incredible attempt to share responsibility. To share the strain, equally. Had there been another, wider agreement . . . unknown to Jenny? Decided upon during the planning of her final party? They'd had a meeting; everyone had decided to bring something.

'I know how it was done,' said Timothy, seeing Anselm's disbelief. 'I was there . . .'

37

Michael took the call in his room at the Southcliff Guest House. He'd sat there waiting all day. Immobile, as if he'd been asleep; alert, as if he'd been waiting for Liam to knock on the door. At intervals he'd let his eyes scan the three photographs of Jenny: child, girl and woman. She was healthy in all of them. It was as though there'd been no fall. No illness. He was looking at the woman, the dancer, as he listened and spoke.

'He's back home,' said Emma. 'And he likes the book.'

'Good. Did you make the fire?'

'Yes.'

'There's kerosene in the shed?'

'Yes.'

'He called Timothy?'

'Told him everything's going to change for the better. "For you and for me."' Emma breathed so much tension into the receiver it almost burned Michael's ear. 'Bring Jenny with you.'

'I will.'

Michael put the phone down.

It had been decided weeks back that Timothy wouldn't go home immediately. That way his routine and schooling wouldn't be disrupted and Peter would have time to settle down in Polstead. With Timothy away from home on the night of his father's release, Michael was free to . . . do his stuff.

So everything was now in place.

After killing Peter, Michael would wrap the body in the tarpaulin, fold the edges over and fix them down with the stapler. He'd take the body to the Citroën using the wheelbarrow by the back door. He'd then set fire to the house with the kerosene . . . a wild act of vandalism, destroying all trace of Peter's life and Jenny's death. Nothing of their time together would remain. Within an hour, Michael would be on the lonely quay at Slaughden, hauling Peter onto *Margot*. After dumping him far out to sea, beyond the tug of the tide, Michael would drive to Harwich, cross to the Hoek as a Canadian, head north to Harlingen and come home as a Briton in a Volvo hatchback. He'd leave the gunman exiled on the continent, never to return to England. That whole other persona, the ruined FRU man who'd made the difficult decisions, would simply evaporate, like mist off a window. The police would come to Morning Light and find Peter's second act of uncontrollable violence and self-destruction: the razing of his own home. But they wouldn't find Peter. Peter, like the mist, will have simply disappeared, leaving behind words that now made sense: 'Everything's going to change for the better. For you and for me.'

The room was completely silent.

Michael found himself listening . . . listening to his own heartbeat.

It pumped gently . . . soft-hard, soft-hard, soft-hard . . .

How did I come to this? he thought, with a sudden last-minute gasp from his soul. And for one grisly moment, Michael thought he was going to hear a still, small voice. But he turned away, taking his mind to the last time he'd seen his daughter. She, too, had a voice . . . and it had been still and small . . .

There was to be a party at Morning Light on Jenny's birthday. It had been Peter's idea. After a long, tense discussion, it had been decided that everyone was to bring something. So Michael made two lemon drizzle cakes: a small one for Jenny and a big one for everyone else. When Emma came home, they set off, arriving at Polstead just after Nigel and Helen.

'What's that?' asked Emma, lightly, pointing at a small paper bag in Helen's hand.

'Herb tea. My own. Jenny loves it.'

Nobody else did. Her hands were trembling. Michael noticed that kind of thing.

'And you?' ventured Nigel, rocking on his heels, hands in his pockets.

'Cake,' said Michael, simply. 'Lemon drizzle.'

'Ah, that's the business,' enthused Nigel. 'Lots of tang. But, if I'm honest, you can't taste the sponge, can you?'

He really had *no idea*. The distance between them was vast.

'It's the lemon that counts,' replied Michael. 'Jenny loves the lemon.'

They all looked at each other, frozen, except for Nigel, bobbing back and forth.

'Well, let's get going, then,' sang Emma, smiling brightly. 'We're here for a party, aren't we?'

They all trooped inside, hale and hearty, greeting Peter woodenly, embracing Jenny warmly, and roughing up Timothy's hair. Poor boy, he'd no idea either. Thankfully, Peter put on some music to fill the void.

'Let me see her on my own for a moment,' said Michael, with weak entreaty. 'I'd just like to have a . . .'

'You don't have to explain yourself, darling,' said Emma, bright and stiff. 'I'll put the kettle on.'

Michael tiptoed into the sitting room. A wood fire rustled with contentment. The lights were low. He simply followed suit, coming quietly to the chair by the bed near the darkened window.

'Happy birthday, darling,' said Michael.

Jenny was smiling, looking at her father with affection. A deep affection. The affection of travellers on the road.

'I made this for you,' he said, quietly.

'Oh thanks, Dad.'

'It's the nearest I could get to a lemon drop.'

She took the cake and bit it, wincing suddenly at the tang. 'That's what I call sharp.'

Michael nodded. She loved the taste; always had done; ever since she was a child.

'Don't try and persuade me to go back to hospital,' said Jenny in a forestalling voice. 'I've had the last tests and now I'm home. I want to stay here, surrounded by what I know and those I love . . . I don't want to be visited.'

Michael nodded again, unhappily. Why wasn't there a medicine? He'd pottered about the garden all afternoon handling plant food and fertiliser. Chemicals that kept plants alive. And he'd thought it awful: there's nothing for Jenny.

The fire murmured.

'Dad,' said Jenny, quietly, finishing the cake. 'Will you call me Nimblefoot again?'

'What?' He reached for her hand, but Jenny didn't need any of that understated support, those many gestures of understanding that had taken the place of words and tears. She almost seemed to push him away, but then took his hand, as if asserting herself.

'You haven't used that name since the accident,' she said, smiling again, a tone of reproach in her voice. 'We both know why. It would make us both sad. But every time you've spoken to me, I've expected to hear it . . . and it never came. Only now' – her smile seemed to spill over from her mouth, lighting up her face, like one of Timothy's sudden flashes of feeling . . . only Jenny's wasn't a rush of emotion, it was *deep*, something more than a sentiment or sensation. She seemed profoundly *contented* – 'only now, I want to hear the name again. Because it's me. It's me in relation to you. Say it, please . . . now.'

Involuntarily, Michael cast an eye over his daughter, taking in the prostrate figure covered by blankets, her toes raising two small mountains at the base of the bed.

'Nimblefoot,' he said.

'Again.'

'Nimblefoot,' stammered Michael, feeling emotion wrench his throat, the throat that had been wrenched so often that he was staggered he could still feel anything at all; stunned that the grip to his neck always felt like an awful, new experience. 'Happy birthday, Nimblefoot.'

'Thanks, Dad,' replied Jenny. She was nodding, as if to remove doubts he hadn't expressed. 'From now on, you think of me as Nimblefoot . . . like in the old days.'

Michael held his daughter's hand in both of his, struck by an alarming, foreign wonder. 'Why, Nimblefoot . . . why?'

'Because the tide has come in.'

Michael blinked uncertainly, remembering the stranded boats on the Orwell at Pin Mill. The red sails. The ropes drooping towards the ochre sand. The green rumpled sheets of algae. *You asked me to untie your laces . . . to let you go . . .*

'You said the tide always comes in,' repeated Jenny, 'and it has done. The tide, at last, has come in.'

Emma's heels echoed on the tiling outside the kitchen.

'How's my birthday girl?' she sang, an ache in her voice. And before Jenny could reply, Emma pulled up a chair, talking ten to the dozen about a male Rottweiler with a urinary tract problem. She'd carried out a radical surgical procedure corresponding to a sex change. His many problems were over. Before the story was out, Bryan arrived with his old leather doctor's bag that he never opened. Except this time he did, pulling out some party poppers. After a quick medical examination, they all trooped back into the room and everyone stood around the bed, all of them firing the multi-coloured streamers over Jenny's blinking, radiant face. It was like a send-off. Folk yelling and waving from the quayside after the champagne had been smashed on the prow. Michael watched her from afar, as if he'd walked to the end of a lonely pier. He ate a slice of cake slowly, his eyes smarting from the bite of zest and syrup. They welled up with a deep and secret relief: the tide had come in. At long last, the tide had come in for his girl.

Helen had eventually made a herb tea for Jenny and she sipped it appreciatively, though Michael was convinced that she – like everyone else – hated the stuff, and would have preferred to pour it down the sink. An hour or so later, Nigel and Helen left, followed by Doctor Ingleby.

'I'll speak to Jenny on my own, now,' said Emma. Her eyes were heavy with summoned cheer, the sparkle she'd once brought to the officers' mess.

'I'll wait outside,' replied Michael.

He kissed Jenny on the forehead and then went outside and looked up at the stars. But he saw the sandy mouth of a river. A wind was blowing life into the red sails. The ropes were lifting on the tide.

Michael packed, paid his bill and set off for Polstead. The Browning and silencer were in the glove box, the Billingham camera bag in the boot, along with the tarpaulin and the stapler. On the passenger seat, fitted with new batteries, lay Father Doyle's tape recorder.

When Michael had first come to Southwold he'd learned pretty quickly that if he was to shoot Peter, he would have to follow Jenny's story all the way from her accident to the night of her death. It was the only way to summon the anger he felt at Peter for his treatment of Jenny, throughout her life. No party could make up for what she'd lost.

That painful journey was now complete.

Similarly, if he was actually to pull the trigger with a steady hand, he'd realised that he'd have to go back to Belfast and the interrogation of Eugene; he'd have to cross the border and face everything that he'd never told Danny Carpenter, the joiner who put people back together. That second journey was almost over. He was almost there.

It was time to press PLAY. Time to hear the clang of a spoon on a pot or a pan.

38

Night was falling fast. Anselm drove slowly, his mind blank and heavy, like saturated blotting paper, incapable of holding another thought or idea. When the door had opened at Long Melford, he'd been trapped by a suspicion that he couldn't reveal. Now he'd been empowered. In this most difficult of cases, he'd been given strength by a child.

'Timothy,' Anselm had said, a warm hand on each of the boy's shoulders. 'Leave this with me, do you understand?'

He'd nodded.

'I'm familiar with this kind of thing.' Anselm had smiled confidence. 'I know what to do and what to say. I know when and I know how. There is a right time.'

A nod.

'When Aunt Helen and Uncle Nigel get back, tell them I called, but I think it would be best if you kept our conversation between ourselves. Remember what I said about handling the truth? That sometimes it requires cooperation? Well, that is how I'm going to move forward. I'm going to speak to the ones who don't like truth as much as you do.'

Anselm parked in a lay-by just outside Lavenham. Set back well off the road stood a medieval house, leaning dramatically to one side. Outside lighting revealed white window frames, grey timber supports and plaster washed a deep, salmon pink. The front door, a sequence of bolted planks, stood buckled within arched shoulders that held up a covered entrance. Anselm knocked hard, his heart beating violently. More so than in any case he'd ever handled at the Bar, when he'd *really* known what to do and say – along with the when and how.

'Terribly sorry, but we're Anglican,' said Emma Goodwin, looking down as if to check whether Anselm was holding a collection plate. 'Haven't got a *penny* on me.'

'I'm not here to talk about ways to God,' said Anselm. 'Oddly enough, that's not my strong suit. Neither is the cost. I'm here to speak about your daughter.'

Emma Goodwin frowned, one hand rising to grasp the join on her white blouse.

'I know who you are,' she said, paling. 'You're that monk . . . the detective.'

'I'm something else, actually. But may I come in? I think we need to talk.'

Emma Goodwin didn't offer tea or cake. She brought Anselm into the kitchen, drawing back a chair at a long table, and then walked to the far end of the room. Spot lighting from between the beams lit the polished distance between them. She stood with her back to the sink, arms folded. You are guilty, thought Anselm, instantly. This is what the first-timers did when they'd been banged away on remand – the ones who fancied their chances in court. They rarely sat at the table in the prison visiting wing. They got up and walked as far away as possible, talking to their advocate from a safe distance, as if he might smell the lack of moral hygiene. A light directly over Emma Goodwin's head cast a shadow beneath her brows, hiding her eyes, blacking out the sockets. Her mouth was slightly open. She looked terrified and terrifying. Anselm sat at the proffered chair. He didn't speak immediately because he was waiting for Michael to arrive. When he didn't come, Anselm said:

'If at all possible, Mrs Goodwin, I'd like to talk to your husband as well.'

'He's not here.'

'Will he be back?'

'No.' She'd snapped the word as if it were a lid on a box. She continued, as if to explain what she was hiding: 'Not today, anyway. A few days off. A holiday.'

Anselm thought for a moment, calibrating his mind to the incongruity. A holiday? On the day Peter was released? When Timothy would need his family around him. When—

'Why are you here?' Emma Goodwin's voice was abruptly shrill. She wanted him to go – just like the first-timers when told they didn't have a cat's chance in hell. 'What do you want?'

Anselm knitted his fingers and leaned his arms on the table. In a friendly, don't-worry voice, he said, 'May I call you Emma?'

'What on earth for?'

'So we can talk about Jenny,' replied Anselm. 'It might be easier if we're on first-name terms.'

Anselm stared compassionately at the figure by the sink. She was hunched, clutching her arms as if she were totally naked.

'Mrs Goodwin,' began Anselm, cautiously. 'Is there anything you'd like to tell me?'

'Absolutely not. Never. Ever. Are you finished now? I think it's time you went.'

Anselm stood up and shuffled to the door, head down, like he did when he was brooding in the cloister. When he'd stepped outside, beneath the beamed portico, he turned around, driven by an impulse he could not contain: a certitude that now was the time to be mercilessly direct.

'Mrs Goodwin,' he said, talking to the cowering woman at the entrance to the kitchen. 'I know how Jenny was killed.'

Anselm had skipped all the preliminary stages required before such a brutal declaration could be uttered. He'd made a number of assumptions about Mrs Goodwin's character – that she was as intellectual as she was emotional; that she was skilled at ending conversations she didn't want, using mock hysteria, if need be, to fend off the dull-witted; that she wasn't scared of a crown court judge or reporters or a monk who'd appeared once in the *Sunday Times*. That she was an inconsolable mother. Anselm's ruthless announcement brought them both back into the kitchen, Anselm to a chair, and Mrs Goodwin standing far off, arms folded by the sink.

'You know?' she asked, after fumbling for a cigarette.

'I do.'

She struggled with a box of matches and lit up, swinging her head away as the fumes burned her eyes. After a pause, she breathed in deeply, and then appeared ready to faint, her mouth dropping open as the blue smoke burst out of her lungs.

'I said I know, Mrs Goodwin,' asserted Anselm, evenly. 'I'm not guessing. I'm not adding up bits of evidence. I'm here to talk about the truth you're hiding.'

Mrs Goodwin's features began to work. Her nerves were out of control.

'Your husband isn't here,' said Anselm, as if that might give her some reassurance. 'You can speak freely. I'm not here to condemn you, or him. Or anyone else.'

Their eyes met along the length of the room. After holding Anselm's mild stare for as long as she could, Mrs Goodwin looked askance, drawing smoke through the stub so fiercely that her cheeks became hollow. She glanced back, with a flash of confusion and defiance.

'You can't prove anything.'

'I can. And I might. But I would prefer your cooperation.' Suddenly, Anselm thought of the ill-timed holiday. He coughed lightly – a bad habit picked up in the Old Bailey when he'd sensed blood.

'Where is your husband, Mrs Goodwin?'

'None of your damned business.'

'I would like to talk to him, too.'

'He's abroad.'

'*Abroad?*'

'Yes.'

'Where?'

'Holland.'

'Whereabouts?'

'Harlingen.'

Anselm appraised the desperate, dejected woman. How was he going to help her? How to persuade her to stop this very serious fooling around?

'Where is Timothy?'

'You've no right to barge in here. You're a trespasser. You're a—'

'Mrs Goodwin, I'm very much on your side. Where is Timothy?'

'Upstairs.'

'Really?'

'Yes. Asleep.'

'Would you wake him?'

'No.'

'Of course you won't. Because he's at Nigel and Helen's.'

Mrs Goodwin dropped the cigarette on the floor as if she'd burned her fingers. A hand came to her mouth. Instinct controlled Anselm's response. He sensed something more alarming than a hidden truth.

'Now, let's forget about Harlingen,' he suggested, kindly, feeling his heart stab against his chest. 'Where is your husband?'

Mrs Goodwin began to shake. She dropped her arms to her side, her whole body shivering as if she'd been pulled out of the freezer. She was gabbling quietly and shaking her head. Anselm rose slowly and approached her very gradually, one hand moving from chair to chair, coming closer as he spoke. A blue thread of smoke spiralled from the floor.

'I know the burden you carry,' he said, apologetically. 'Put it down, now. It's far too heavy. Let me help shift the weight.'

He'd reached the end of the table. Mrs Goodwin was mouthing

sounds, her oval face drained of blood, her eye sockets hideously blue as if she'd been beaten.

'Let me talk to your husband,' he murmured, holding out his hand as if to show he meant no harm.

Mrs Goodwin replied so quietly that Anselm didn't hear. He came a step closer, leaning his head to one side. He could smell her perfume and her stale, naked terror. His foot crushed the tiny smouldering stub.

'Speak up,' he whispered.

'It's too late.'

'It's never too late.'

'He's going to die.'

'Who is?'

'Peter.'

'When?'

'Now . . . tonight.'

Anselm raised a darkened eye.

'What do you mean?'

'He's got a gun.'

'Who has?'

'I can't contact him, he's on the road . . .'

Mrs Goodwin didn't finish her sentence. She was blinking erratically, her eyes glazed with complicity. Slowly, she reached for the packet of cigarettes. Unseeing, she placed the filter between her lips and felt for the box of matches. Anselm didn't even hear the strike of phosphorus along the sandpaper. He was outside, running down the dark lane to the car parked in a lay-by.

39

Michael drove slowly along the shadowed lanes, the hedges black against the allure of darkness. The day was over. People were heading home. Heading back to their families. An unremarkable routine, played out everywhere, today and tomorrow, just like yesterday. Everyone did it. Except some. They never return. They disappear. Sometimes they vanish without trace. Others, they turn up in the back of beyond. Like Liam. They'd taken him to South Armagh where the IRA had a dedicated interrogation centre. A cow shed. They'd have stabbed him with a needle in Belfast and he'd have woken up in the middle of nowhere. A farm with prison cells. Quiet, rolling hills. Animals tearing at the bleak fields. They did that when the security people thought the tout had a lot of explaining to do. They wanted to take their time and get to the bottom of things. There'd been no point really. As Father Doyle had prophesied, Liam sang like a canary as soon as he'd smelled the cow dung and silage. The big lads hadn't even had to string him up. They'd known from experience when a tout had told them everything. He'd still been a kid, caught with his trousers down.

Michael's right hand felt for the machine. Bile rose like mercury in a thermometer. He pressed PLAY . . .

Michael had been back in Belfast a week when the phone rang to say there was a priest at the front gate. He'd got a message for Michael. After the operation in Donegal, Michael didn't fly back

244

to Edinburgh. Abandoning the palaver of shifting identities, he'd driven straight back to Belfast, torched the jalopy a mile from his barracks, and walked back to base with the Billingham bag slung over his shoulder. Looking pale and ill, he'd told his colonel that it served him right for trying to have a quiet drink in Scotland. Liam had not turned up for the meeting on Saturday as planned. And now, the following Wednesday, Father Doyle was at the gate.

Michael brought the priest to an interview room. It was bare save for a table and two chairs. The walls were green. The windows glazed and covered with heavy wire netting.

'What did you do after I left you?' commanded the priest, sitting down. He placed a tape recorder in the middle of the table. 'What did you do about Ó Mórdha? I've heard nothing on the news.'

'And you won't.'

The haggard priest was large and imposing, a black brooding presence, with arms folded. He wasn't like Nigel, cultivated, articulate and ready to spar with words. He was a bruiser who delivered bread for the journey.

'What have you done?'

Michael resented the direct question. But there was something remorseless about those dark eyes. He seemed to be staring through a grille as if they were both in the dark.

'Nothing.'

'Really?'

'Yes.'

The priest's hand strayed to the tape recorder.

'You didn't arrest him?'

Michael folded his arms, feeling cramped. It was as though the walls had moved in to squeeze his shoulders. The central light was glaring but Michael narrowed his eyes as if to penetrate the gloom.

'No.'

'Why not?'

Michael wiped his mouth. His understanding of things was realigning. He'd thought the priest had expected an . . . executive action. The removal of Ó Mórdha. He'd thought Father Doyle had gone down Eugene's road, for the sake of long-term peace, and brought a message to Michael. And Michael had taken the same route to Donegal, thinking this priest was just another pilgrim on the road, resigned to a difficult journey. But he wasn't. Michael had misunderstood him; thought he'd seen into the priest's tortured mind. But he hadn't. Father Doyle's thick finger had come to rest on PLAY.

'Did you know that Liam was holding guns?'

'Yes.'

'And what did you do?'

Michael didn't answer so the priest took it for another 'Nothing'.

'Well, they came back while you were on holiday.'

'Who?'

'The IRA. They came for their guns sooner than expected.' The priest's eyes were burning with a strange white heat. 'One of them was missing. A Browning automatic. Fourteen rounds. And a silencer. Do you know where they are?'

Michael seemed to feel the heavy wire netting against his skin, pressing hard as the walls continued to advance inwards, bringing more darkness. The burly, ragged priest read the silence as a 'No'.

'Well, that's fine, so,' soothed Father Doyle. 'Because, thankfully, Liam did. And he told 'em what they wanted to know.'

The unkempt priest, still in his hat, coat and scarf – all a shabby black, save for the snip of white plastic at the neck – leaned forward, pressing his finger heavily on the PLAY button.

'Listen for yourself.'

The tape whirred for a few seconds. Someone walked away from the microphone. Seconds later there was a 'ding' . . . the strike of a spoon on the base of a pan . . . the signal for Liam to start talking; to repeat what he'd told them since he'd come to Armagh.

'I'm . . . err . . . Liam Finnerty and I make this confession freely.' He gave his address as if he were watching a clerk fill in a form. 'I've been workin' for British Intelligence since last November, eight months. They approached me, like, after I'd been nicked for shoplifting. I told 'em to run 'n' jump but they follerred me around for weeks. Kept pullin' me in. Said they could make the theft charge go away and help me ma. Offered me a few quid for the meter. That was that, like.'

Michael listened, head down, feeling the immense presence of Father Doyle. He was staring at him from an inner conflagration of rage and distress.

Liam had an extraordinary memory. He told them everything. He handed back every scrap of information he'd stolen for the Brits. It was all humdrum. Names and car registration numbers. Who knew whom. The building blocks of sound intelligence. Then, after two months (confessed Liam), he'd got a new handler. A man called 'Frank'. A jock from Dundee. Michael shuddered, listening to the flow of invention. The physical description, the strong accent, the mannerisms. The invented conversations, the apparent slip-ups by the handler that revealed telling personal details. But Liam made no reference to Michael. Michael was safe. The IRA's intelligence units would never track him down. They could just look for Frank, who only existed in Liam's terrified mind. Shortly he came to the guns. The heart of the matter.

'I never told him,' pleaded Liam. 'If I 'ad a done, he'd a taken the rifles, wouldn't he? Thing is, I wanted to fire a gun for real. See what it felt like. So I just borrowed it and went out on me own to have a go. But I didn't get the chance because I came across a patrol and I panicked and chucked the thing in a bin.'

Liam gave the exact location. And the number painted on the lid. And the time of day. He'd picked half an hour before the rubbish trucks lurched down the streets, stopping and starting. The boy was utterly convincing.

'I'm sorry for what I've done,' breathed Liam in a monotone.

'A tout's a tout. I know. I just want to go home. See me ma. An' tell Frank to leave us alone.'

Father Doyle pressed STOP. Just as deliberately, he pressed REWIND as if Michael might want to listen again. The tape whirred, spinning backwards while Michael watched the spools turn, thinking of Liam's boyish features. The eruption of adolescence hadn't gone yet. He was still awkward. Still a dreamer. Impressionable. The Nutting Squad would have let him go.

'He's dead,' said Father Doyle.

Michael looked up.

'Didn't you know? Hasn't the paperwork filtered through?'

Michael shoved back his chair, stepping away from the low hum of the machine. He found himself retreating to the far wall, not daring to meet the priest's accusing gaze.

'I warned you,' said the priest, banging the table with his white knuckles. 'I told you what would happen.'

Bang.

'I said let the boy go.'

Bang.

'I said you'd played on his vulnerability.'

Bang.

'And now . . . now there's going to be another funeral in Belfast. There'll be a handful at the side of the grave, no more. And if his mother, poor woman, ever comes downstairs afterwards, people will turn the other way. All that . . . for what? Nothing? You did *nothing*?'

Father Doyle tapped the table lightly a few times and then stood up as if he'd heard enough.

'You're no different to them,' he said at the door. 'The sooner you get your backside off this island the better.'

The priest had gone. The tape was whirring faster and faster, the sound rising to a crescendo until, finally, there was a soft, slow click. A report came through later that afternoon. Liam had been found naked by the side of a quiet country lane in South Armagh.

His hands had been tied behind his back with brown tape and his head had been covered with a black bin liner. He'd been shot from behind with a high-velocity rifle. There'd been no signs of torture on the body. The next day, his mother told the *Belfast Telegraph* he'd always wanted to be a train driver.

Michael's breakdown probably started at the moment he picked up the tape recorder. It was as heavy as a dead body. He stopped speaking, eating and caring for himself. He neglected his work. His colonel, recognising a certain fragility of character, transferred him back to Templar Barracks in Ashford, Kent. There, while sitting in the small garden of Repton Manor staring at an old oak tree, he was approached by a nice guy, a major, who introduced himself as Danny Carpenter. 'I'm a sort of joiner,' he joked. 'I help put the tongue back into the groove. No nails or glue. Fancy a beer?'

Michael's career with the Intelligence Corps had come to an end. After a mere six months. For the appraisal writers, he'd been a diligent operative better suited to desk work. Analysis, not action. Danny tried all sorts to bring the planks of Michael's life back into line, only once asking a direct question, when all else had failed.

'What did you do, Michael?'

And Michael had gazed at the ancient oak tree, once used to hang so-called witches while Cromwell brought the scourge to Ireland.

'I did nothing,' he'd murmured, enigmatically. 'Absolutely nothing.'

Michael pressed REWIND.

The tape began its trip home, whirring softly. Michael looked at the hand that would hold the gun. There was a very faint dying tremor. Journey's end was in sight. All he had to do was cross the border in his mind and walk to a cottage lit by a summer moon, sneaking between the mauve shadows of ling and bell heather.

He'd told Danny that he'd done nothing. That wasn't true. He'd made the biggest mistake of his life.

40

Anselm seemed to park, pull the handbrake and snatch the keys from the ignition in one fierce movement. He ran across the gravel towards Morning Light. Opening the door without so much as a knock or a call, he strode down a corridor and into the sitting room, fearing that he may be too late, spilling out a command with as much relief as panic:

'Peter, you have to leave at once.'

Peter Henderson was standing near an armchair by a fire, half-moon glasses on the end of his nose and a book in one hand. He was about to remonstrate when Anselm spoke again.

'Trust me, you must get away from here.'

Peter Henderson had shaved. He looked smart in loose jeans and a baggy woollen jumper. His face remained a field of devastation – deep ruts in the skin and shadows like potholes on his sunken cheeks. He stepped back, and sat down again, saying, 'Still charging around things you don't fully understand, I see.'

He nodded towards a facing chair as if it were time to go over that very confused essay on Charles Stevenson.

'Peter, I know how Jenny was killed,' said Anselm, pointing anxiously towards the door.

'My confession wasn't sufficiently compelling?'

'No.'

'Why not?'

'Because I found a witness.'

Peter Henderson slowly closed the book and placed it on the armrest. He seemed to have died.

'You must leave now,' said Anselm. 'Instantly.'

'Why?' His voice was low and dark, shocked and spare.

'Let me take control of what is happening, Peter,' replied Anselm. 'Let *me* handle *this* crisis. For once in your life, don't ask so many questions. Accept that sometimes you have to wait for an answer. And that time is not now. So please, leave at once.'

Anselm wanted Peter Henderson safe out of the building because he wanted to be alone when Michael Goodwin arrived. He wanted to speak to him: this quiet man of so many secrets. But Peter Henderson wasn't moving. He sat like a punctured life-sized doll, sagging to one side.

'Leave now,' ordered Anselm.

'No,' he said, as with a last breath. 'I'm going nowhere until you explain yourself.'

Anselm strode forward.

'Okay, have it your way,' he said. 'Michael intends to kill you tonight.'

The smile vanished.

'That's right, Peter. No *Moral Maze*. No wondering which way to turn. He's armed. He's resolved. He trained with the SAS. He's on his way here. Now get out. Go to Larkwood. Ask for Wilf. Speak to no one. Wait.'

For a while Anselm paced around the room as if he might get somewhere in bringing matters to a close. It was almost dark outside and the fire's reflection flickered on the crooked windows. As he turned to the grate, Anselm's eye caught the title of the book Peter had been reading, an intrepid study by Geoffrey Bannon: *Killing, Ethics and the Law*. Sitting down in the armchair, Anselm opened the book randomly. His gaze instantly fell on a passage that made him smile. To illustrate a point, the author had imagined an atheist tormented by a stutter with his foot trapped in a hatch on the sinking *Titanic*.

41

Michael parked in the lane that ran to Morning Light. Very slowly, he opened the door. Minutes later, he was walking calmly towards Jennifer's cottage as if it were that farm in the Blue Stack Mountains. He reached the gate and quietly lifted the latch. To avoid the crunch of gravel he stepped on the lawn he'd raked ten days earlier and moved swiftly around the building towards the back door. A light was on in the sitting room, shining softly through pale green curtains. The rest of the house was in darkness. Peter, hopefully, was by the fire enjoying a good book. Something to make him think.

It had been like this in Donegal. Only the light had been stronger from a bright moon. He'd crossed three gates, not one. He'd moved on tiptoe towards a silver strand of light, a rippling stream on the far side of Néall Ó Mórdha's bolthole. He'd seen smoke like a thread from a needle, dangling from the stars into a squat chimney.

There was smoke rising now from the fire by Peter's armchair.

Standing by the wheelbarrow near the back door, Michael placed his thumb on the latch and quietly opened the door . . .

In Donegal, he'd opted for a knock. It had been a last-minute decision, a strange nervousness, as if he needed Ó Mórdha's permission to kill him. A surviving decency that had tracked him from Edinburgh where he'd left his better half.

He'd heard footsteps fall soft upon the wooden floor inside.

He'd seen the handle turn.

The door had creaked open all the way as Ó Mórdha peered into the darkness, a hand shielding his eyes from the shocking power of the moon.

Michael stepped into Morning Light. The gun, with silencer attached, was in his hand. His finger was on the trigger. The safety catch was off. He was in the kitchen. After a few seconds he walked with slow, silent steps to the fuse cupboard and tugged open the door. There was a slight thunk. Michael listened intently. A page turned.

Ó Mórdha's eyes had got accustomed, too. Michael should have fired before then, but time had slowed as if it were concrete passing through a sieve. Michael had stood, legs apart, arms extended, the Browning absolutely still in his hands. There'd been a low light in the hall. A dog had watched from the end of a musty corridor. A grandfather clock had ticked. The kettle had rattled on a stove. Michael had noted all these details even before the expression on Ó Mórdha's face had been able to change from curiosity to terror. Finally, the IRA commander had seen the gun.

'Can I help you?' he'd said, in that child-like voice.

For a brief second their eyes had met; and Michael had seen a flicker of naked supplication. He'd come to put it out.

'You're dead,' he'd explained.

But just as Michael had squeezed the trigger, he'd heard a very quiet voice within himself . . . very quiet indeed: 'Michael, Michael, Michael . . .' and he'd fired a millisecond later, to drown out whatever might come next.

BAM-BAM, BAM-BAM.

Only Michael had closed his eyes. On opening them he'd seen Ó Mórdha standing to one side, looking down the corridor, aghast. There, by an open bedroom door, lay man's best friend. Michael had shot the dog. It hadn't even barked back.

'What the—'

Michael had turned and run. Under the light of the moon he'd scaled three gates, tripped and fallen twice and had finally stumbled into the driver's seat of his car. He'd never forgotten Ó Mórdha's look of astonishment, any more than he'd forgotten the sound of Liam's confession. Eugene and Liam had both taken a bullet so that Michael could remove Néall Ó Mórdha from the Army Council and tilt the balance in favour of peace. And he'd shot a pedigree dog. A man and a boy had died so that he could put down an Irish water spaniel.

Throughout the years that followed his return to civilian life, Michael had watched the unfolding of history with horror. One atrocity followed the other: the Brighton bomb that nearly wiped out the British Cabinet, the mortar attack on Newry police station, the Remembrance Day bombing in Enniskillen . . . the 'spectaculars' didn't end. And behind them all, Michael saw the dumbfounded face of Néall Ó Mórdha looking at his dog. Michael had missed his chance – his obligation – to act decisively. Of course, he wasn't so simple-minded to think that killing Ó Mórdha would have prevented the Brighton attack, all the way to Canary Wharf and beyond. But he couldn't escape the nagging doubt that it might have brought forward the peace process, if only by a year, six months even, and that would have been lives saved. Innocent lives. People who'd done nothing wrong except get out of bed and go to the wrong shopping centre. It would have given some purpose to Eugene's secret confession and Liam's later silence. Those two meaningless deaths and the vague, long list of casualties that might have been prevented lay on Michael's conscience . . . something Nigel would never understand. They accused him now, every time he saw Ó Mórdha on the television. He'd come round to the idea of peace eventually: once it was clear that the long war would never be won.

Michael reached out and put a finger on the trip switch below the fuse box.

Another page turned. Peter cleared his throat.

But there's been another presence throughout the years. The echo of that voice. The echo of his own name. Beyond all thought and feeling, choice or argument, this sound had remained strangely insistent, uncomfortably present . . . only Michael had refused to acknowledge it was there; refused to open the ear of his heart. And when he'd tried, tentatively, on his long journey here, to Polstead, he'd heard absolutely nothing. So this was where his past and future came together: the failure in Northern Ireland would be redeemed now. He was going to kill Peter, not because he'd done a great wrong − this was not about vengeance − but to make a difference for everyone else's tomorrow.

Michael breathed in slowly. There was no panic. No shake to the hand. There were four rounds in the Browning: one up the spout and three ready to go.

Michael flicked up the switch. Then he was off. Counting the cost: one, two, three, four . . .

42

The problem was this: the atheist with his foot caught in the hatch − Albert − was shot by Ernest because he, Ernest, couldn't imagine a worse way to go than drowning. And Albert was in one hell of a flap. What Ernest didn't know was that Albert (terrified by the gun) would have preferred to drown, but he couldn't get the words out. What neither of them could have known was that, first, Albert's foot would have come free an instant later. But, second, irony of ironies, when they'd finally got near a lifeboat, Albert would have met his end anyway, injured horribly by the whip of a snapped cable, dying in agony before the ship could sink and let him drown. Now, if Albert and Ernest could have shared a cocktail afterwards and talked things through amicably, Albert would have said he'd have preferred the bullet after all. And *thank God* he had a stutter. So, in the end, everyone was happy.

Except the author.

According to Professor Bannon, Albert's preferences were—

Suddenly, the lights went out.

There'd been a click from down the corridor but that sound was overtaken by the stamp of feet sweeping forward. Anselm rose in a panic, dropping the book to the floor. Soft light from the fire picked out some objects in the room. A clock ticked against the wall – he hadn't noticed the mark of time until now, when it was about to be halted, once and for all – and he could hear the thumping dread of his heart.

Oh God, I'm finished, he thought, numbed.

Each second slowed, opening up space for one last-ditch reflection, something charged with high meaning and importance. In the popular imagination, Anselm was meant to see his life pass before his eyes – his infancy, parents, loved ones, a kite in the wind – but something else came to the fore . . . a man with a flushed, perspiring face. He appeared like an overweight angel to insulate Anselm from the banality of what was about to happen.

It was Bede. He'd come to say, 'I told you so.'

It was that kind of case after all.

A dark shape appeared at the mouth of the corridor. Anselm tried to call out but his voice jammed. His final deliberation came like a weak sigh:

'*God . . . I'm not ready.*'

Anselm had always imagined that death might be like falling under a general anaesthetic: giving in to the sudden, overwhelming pull of darkness . . . followed by a burst of light and the great answer to the great question: had the fifties jazz revival reached heaven?

There was no such tug from below. No trumpet blast. Just an enormous crash and then it was all over.

Part Five

The Diary of Timothy Henderson

~

26th September

I'm not going to write about the cancer. I'm going to write instead what my mum said about it. And then this diary is finished. Because what Mum said is why I'm all blocked up. I'm hoping that once I've got it down, I'll be able to forget and get on with things like I used to. Everything I've written so far was just a way of avoiding the subject. But I've sort of arrived here now, and I want to say it.

On the night my mum died we had a party. After everyone had gone my dad was doing the washing up. I sat with my mum. And it was like the old days. It was just me and her and I could tell she was really happy that it was just us two. We talked about school and then she made a speech. She'd been planning it and she was really serious. This is what she said:

> There are many people who think I lost a lot when I gave up dancing. And I did. But I got you. And they don't realise how much I'd rather have been with you than on the stage in London with my name in lights. We've had each other, haven't we?

I said we'd had a great time. That I'd never forget that pushchair with the plastic hood when she got wet and I stayed dry. And then she said:

You know, Tim, there was a time when I thought my life was over, because I couldn't move and I knew I'd never take you to school again or make your meals or put you to bed. You must have felt it because I wasn't very happy. Well, I want you to know that I am now. I'm contented. I'm not worried about the cancer, honestly. I'm still your mum and between now and when I go there's a lot we can talk about. We can help one another understand what it is to live and die. We can travel the journey together. Shall we do that?

And I said, 'Yes.' And she started crying and so did I because I didn't want her to leave me. And then she said:

This cancer will get me, Tim, but I've had a good life. And that's thanks to you.

I went to bed and I couldn't sleep. I kept thinking about what my mum had said. It had upset me. I didn't like to see her tears.

A monk came to the house when I was wondering if I should go on and say what happened. I'd stopped writing for half an hour and then he rang on the bell and I've told him everything. He said he'd sort it all out. He'd speak to everyone.

43

Anselm's life had been saved by an anecdote and a song.

Mitch had found himself thinking about the Red Barn Murder of 1827. A young girl had gone off with a charlatan. The stepmother, however, had dreamed that the girl had been murdered, her subconscious going so far as to identify the location of the body.

Dreaming about the truth was all very fine – thought Mitch – but he'd have arrested that very exact dreamer. She had some questions to answer. Which had brought Emma Goodwin to mind. The woman whom he believed had written to Larkwood's Prior, supporting Peter Henderson in public while planning his demise in private, her eyes fixed upon the grandson. Mitch had seen her on the evening news standing outside Hollesley Bay prison earlier that morning. She'd made another appearance before the cameras, seeking privacy and compassion for Peter. The sound of her measured words had worked away at Mitch's imagination, finally nudging him offstage halfway through a sax solo on 'After You've Gone'.

I'll speak to her myself, he'd thought, driving over to Emma Goodwin's. An hysterical interview had followed that sent Mitch straight to the back door of Morning Light, where he'd seen a man reaching into a fuse box. Mitch had rushed through the open door, felling Michael just as he'd lunged into the sitting room. The one bullet that had been fired had gone through the ceiling. When the lights finally came on he saw the man who'd hidden from the cameras: the man he'd longed to meet. He was leaning with his head against the wall, sobbing like a child.

'I'll keep the gun, Michael,' Anselm said at the kitchen table, after sharing a pot of sweet tea in silence.

'I'm sorry,' he replied, hopelessly.

'I'll make more tea.'

'I'm so very sorry.'

They spoke in snatches well into the night, until Michael snapped – it happened very easily, like the breaking of a wafer – and he began, without prompting from Anselm, to describe the route he'd taken from Belfast to Polstead: the unforgettable landmarks of his past. The conversation that had never happened with an Army psychologist took place with a monk.

'I'd never even met this Eugene,' said Michael, staring to one side. 'But he knew he was going to die. In those last few minutes before they shot him, he tried to give some meaning to his life. He paid the heaviest price known to a Republican . . . he became a tout . . . so that one of the hardliners could be removed. Eugene's dying would have meant something, the shame on his family would have been given some purpose, if, by his death, he'd managed to do something good.'

The clock ticked softly like a dripping tap.

'But I *knew* Liam,' whispered Michael. 'I knew the boy. He was *my* agent. I was *responsible* for him. He trusted me to do what he couldn't do because he was just a kid. Born and raised in Belfast. He'd never be in a position to pull a lever and shift the points. But I was. And I was *his* chance to change the world of riots and funerals. And he died, too, because he thought he'd found some meaning in it all, through me . . .'

Two men had placed their deaths in Michael's hands, expecting him to make something good out of the horrendous manner of their dying. They'd each known what was coming. They'd each fallen on their knees, heads bagged, believing that, yes, even this will be worthwhile.

'I failed them,' said Michael, simply.

Anselm thought it prudent not to argue. But he also sensed a momentum to Michael's reflection.

'I've felt responsible all my life because they died in the hope that I'd do my part, and I didn't. When I came back to England I tried not to think about what had happened. Because if I did, I'd have to find something to say to these two ghosts. Explain why their bodies had been dumped with all the others, on the heap of senseless loss and misery. I closed my eyes but they wouldn't go away . . . they were there all the time, accusing me.'

The grandfather clock thunked softly, the pendulum swinging right and left as if it didn't know which way to go.

'I couldn't talk to the Army psychologist,' said Michael, raising his tortured gaze to Anselm. 'How could he ever understand? He wanted me to go back to the beginning and take him through each step of the crisis and my collapse. He wanted to help me but he couldn't . . . no one could . . .'

'Except Jenny,' murmured Anselm.

'Yes,' replied Michael, moved and stung at the sound of her name. 'Only Jenny.'

Anselm made a nod of understanding. 'She brought you the grace that we all come to long for . . . once we realise that we've lost it for ever.'

Michael gaped at Anselm. 'Yes, Father, she did. She gave me some hope. Through Jenny, I actually *learned* to *close* my mind . . . seal off what I couldn't bear to remember. It wasn't difficult; all I had to do was look at her.'

Anselm sighed a compassionate 'Yes'. This man had found a kind of salvation based on distraction: he'd looked away from the bad and kept his eyes on something good. She can't have known the scale of her importance. But then she was struck down before Michael's eyes. And then, having been struck down once, she was struck down again. He'd learned that partial salvation can only ever be temporary. He'd lost the one barrier of grace between himself and the memory of those voices urging him to kill for a transcendent cause. Voices that told him sometimes you have to break the rules; sometimes you have to do things you'd never, ever dream of doing. For the sake of something good. They'd spoken with the appalling authority of the damned.

'Michael,' began Anselm, tentatively, laying his hands on the table. He was reaching over to the slumped figure on the other side of the table. 'I have no comprehension of what you have experienced, endured and lost. But I can't help wondering . . . was it ever your duty to give meaning to someone else's life, to their death, to the suffering in between? Isn't this the quietest of roads . . . travelled only by the person who must live, suffer and die? Aren't we each on our own road?'

And – thought Anselm, sadly – wasn't Jenny on hers?

Michael turned aside again, hunched and preoccupied, as if he didn't want to hear what Anselm had said. He began talking almost to himself. 'I don't understand what happened . . . but tonight, as I came into the room, I knew what I was going to do, and why; I'd thought it all out and gone through all the steps, but just as I raised the gun, I . . .'

His voice dried suddenly. Michael stared ahead, a man desperate to make sense of an experience that had overtaken him. He blinked, almost in time with the soft thump of the clock, the relentless drip of time.

'Go home, Michael,' said Anselm. 'Get some rest. But we'll have to talk again . . . about that lonely road and where it sometimes ends. I can't spare you next time; no one can.'

Anselm and Mitch walked in the dark along a quiet lane that led to the church in Polstead. They could hardly see each other. The previous day's rain had left cloud behind, obscuring the moon and stars. There were no night lights to guide them. The monk and the musician tracked the other by the sound of their footsteps, by their breathing.

'Thank you,' said Anselm. 'You saved my life.'

'I did.'

There was relief in his voice.

'And you were right,' continued Anselm. 'Someone *was* planning to kill Peter Henderson.'

'They were.'

'It was, after all, that kind of case.'

'It was.'

Anselm took a more global perspective: 'We've not seen eye to eye from the beginning.'

'We haven't.'

'You saw an assisted suicide, I saw a murder. You even wondered if it mattered.'

'I still do.'

'I don't. Because I look to the law. Whereas you, in certain circumstances, will look the other way.'

'That's right.'

'But we were united on one point, Mitch. We both wanted to protect Timothy. You wanted to preserve his ignorance. I wanted to harness his father's conscience. These were important questions, about law, choice and the need to know. None of them mattered. We both got it wrong.'

'Why?'

'Because Timothy had already lost his future and his past. At least the ones he might have had, and that we would have wanted to protect. He's going to have to find a new way of looking back and looking forward.'

'Why?'

Mitch had slowed, dropping away from Anselm's side. They came to a halt, looking at each other in the darkness. Black trees, bunched and tangled, towered on one side of the lane. On the other, a field lay open, allowing the night to breathe.

'He was there, Mitch. He listened in secret and he watched them all struggle with illness. He knows exactly how his mother died. He's known all along.'

The silence made a soft beat like the grandfather clock in the room where Jenny had died.

'But he was only twelve,' murmured Mitch, as if age were a natural protection against harm, against the terrible things one might see. The idea was simply too awful.

'Tell them all to come to Larkwood,' said Anselm, under his breath. 'Except Peter. He's already there. So that's Michael, Emma, Nigel, Helen and Doctor Ingleby. This afternoon. Two o'clock. It's time for the Henderson family to talk together as they've never talked before.'

'What are you going to do?'

'Ask that truth be given a chance. This is their moment. This is their chance to gather in all the pain and misunderstanding that's never been faced before; gather it in and decide, together, how they're going to build a very different future.'

44

Having left Mitch to track down Vincent Cooper, Anselm prepared the Old Mill for the gathering of the Henderson and Goodwin families. The threshing area, with its jammed grinding mechanism by the wall, was (he thought) an appropriate location. He placed a round table and seven chairs in the centre of the room. He built a fire. He thought of Schiller: 'It is wise to disclose what cannot be concealed.'

By 2.15 p.m. everyone was present: Michael, in a navy-blue blazer, head lowered; Emma, bolt upright, still wearing her long black coat; Nigel, in a rumpled white jacket; Helen, in what seemed like borrowed clothes; Doctor Ingleby, in a tweed suit, his chair furthest away from the table; and finally Peter, in jeans, his hollowed eyes resting on the fire.

'Normally, I'm diffident in these situations,' began Anselm. 'I think families need to decide for themselves how and when to resolve their differences. But since I nearly got shot last night, I thought I might take a more direct approach. You have all run out of time. This is the moment of decision. My guess, Peter, is that everybody has something to say to you. In those circumstances, I strongly suggest you get your defence in first.'

'I mistreated her,' said Peter Henderson.

The room was eerily still.

'She was so very young, when we met. So innocent. I was so much older. Without her simplicity. She—'

'You took her life away before she had it,' shouted Emma. 'You never valued who she was, and what she wanted to do with her life, you never cared, you were so damned full of yourself and what you were going to do next.' She gagged abruptly as if she'd tried to breathe under water. Her eyes were bright and dark with agonised resentment. 'Why?' she managed. 'Why?'

Emma couldn't say any more for the moment. There was too much to hurl in accusation. It was all pressed into that one word. A trembling hand covered her mouth as if she might disgorge the ocean of poisoned feeling that had never been expressed.

'Because I was blind, Emma,' said Peter Henderson. 'In every sense.'

'You could have loved her,' exclaimed Emma, uncomprehending. 'You could have made her happy. You'd have been happy.'

Peter Henderson tried to reply, knowing that words would fail. 'Things changed, Emma, too late, but they changed. And I loved her, like you would have always wanted, and more, because only I could know what I'd thrown away. I've wanted to tell you this since she died, but I know you'd never have believed me.'

'But what of Timothy?' murmured Emma, agreeing and choking. 'He *needed* you. You left him to grow up without any guidance. You weren't there.'

'But I'm here now.' Abject and reduced, Peter Henderson had little else to say. 'I'm going to be there in his future. I lost out, too. I don't want to lose any more.'

There was a long pause. And everyone realised that in this one short exchange, fifteen years of resentment and recrimination had been disclosed. All anyone could do was repeat themselves. It didn't seem possible. It had taken two minutes. A shocked silence filled the space of all the arguments that had never happened.

'What changed, Peter?' asked Anselm, quietly. 'When did you discover Jenny?'

'After the accident,' he replied, just as quietly. 'From the moment I walked into the hospital. And I didn't only see her, I heard everything she'd ever said in the past, everything I'd never listened to . . . and it was like a great roar in my head. An awful noise

267

. . . and yet her voice was barely audible, just asking me to spend some time with her. And now it was too late.'

Jenny was saying something very different now. She wanted to die. She wanted to be swept up fast off the floor of Timothy's life . . . and Peter's. She wanted out. She felt like she'd already gone, that nothing of value remained, just some excess baggage that hadn't been squeezed through the closing doors of dying.

'I wanted her to say to me what she'd once said,' murmured Peter Henderson, tears breaking out. 'That *we* mattered. I wanted to go back to where we'd once been . . . only I hadn't been present . . . I'd been somewhere else. I wanted her to see that I'd come home . . . but she was blind to me. I wanted her to speak again . . . about *us* . . . only she wasn't saying it any more; she was saying something very different, and I couldn't bear to listen.'

Michael's head lay on his chest as if he'd been shot. Emma was the same. They were like bodies propped up for inspection. Helen was staring to one side. Doctor Ingleby was leaning forward, his face lined with a sort of paternal unease. Nigel was trying to meet Peter Henderson's gaze, but the philosopher wasn't entirely present. He was with Jenny again, when he'd found her ten years too late.

'Because she couldn't move . . . because she'd lost *so* much . . . she thought she had no value – for me, for Timothy, for anyone . . . but especially herself. Whereas, from where I stood, it was the opposite . . . the complete opposite. It was only when she'd lost everything that I saw her for who she was, simply and cleanly. She was just . . . there. Irreducibly there. Present. Alive. Herself. Without the distraction of talent or gifts. I know this is a strange thing to say – a travesty of what she endured and where she found herself – but, for me, it was as though she'd lost nothing. And I just wanted to be with her.'

Jenny's desire to die did not ebb away. Her mood swung in a circle, certainly, from desperation round to calm deliberation, but the central axis, the still centre, was a chosen death. That is what she wanted. She was unable to listen to Peter, just as Peter had once been unable to listen to her: she wasn't remotely interested in his declaration that she mattered, profoundly. How could she? There was nothing left of her.

'Tell us about the conversation,' said Anselm, remorselessly.

Peter Henderson had the bewildered look of a man overtaken by a storm; accusing himself because he hadn't checked the forecast before stepping outside.

'Jenny became deathly calm,' he said. 'There was no communication between us. Nothing I said or did reached her, until I said I'd . . . help. Then, for once, she looked at me differently. She looked at me with hope.'

'The conversation, Peter,' nudged Anselm, firmly. 'What did she say? What did you say?'

Peter Henderson had been examining his hands darkly as if they'd held something he shouldn't have dropped. He raised his eyes to Michael and Emma who, in a dreadful representation of the waking dead, looked up as one.

The conversation had taken place in the middle of the night, three months before the cancer diagnosis.

It was blustery outside and a kitchen window, left open by accident, was banging against its frame. Peter came downstairs to close it. Jenny was awake. He sat by the bed in the darkness, listening to the whistling in the trees. During a lull – one of those strange moments of absolute silence during a squall – Jenny said:

'Peter, I'm not scared to go.'

'Don't talk like that.'

'This is my life, Peter. I've taken a long look at what it's worth. I've waited for some kind of surprise, something to change how I understand my situation, but nothing has come. How could it? I can't wait for hope; I have to go find it. Will you help me? Just this once?'

Peter couldn't answer. He nodded meaninglessly.

'I'm fine for now,' said Jenny, 'but if things get worse, I just want to slip away, quickly and quietly . . . after a party. Do you understand?'

Peter nodded again.

'I'd like champagne. I'd like to see Tim and Mum and Dad and Nigel and Helen and Bryan. And then, when everyone's gone, I want you to help me go.'

'I can't, Jenny, I can't,' murmured Peter.

'I'll help you to help me. We'll help one another.'

'No, Jenny, I'm sorry, but I can't.' Peter stood up, leaning over the bed in the dark, feeling Jenny's warm breath. 'I don't want you to go, my love, I want you to stay.'

'Your job is to help Timothy understand that I'm not leaving him,' she whispered, loudly. 'That I've already gone. That I've found peace for everyone.'

Anselm stood up slowly.

The action drew to a close the remembered night. He walked over to the hearth and threw a log onto the fire. Looking down at the wood and the flames, he asked Peter Henderson to explain what had happened over the next few weeks – how he'd contacted Vincent Cooper who'd overseen the fabrication of the Exit Mask; how he'd given Jenny a sort of freedom of movement, not questioning where she wanted to go or why. How he'd accepted a passive role so as to restore her autonomy. Returning to the table, Anselm said:

'What was the effect of this agreement to cooperate with one another?'

'She changed.'

'How?'

'She became more calm.'

'Did she speak of the mask?'

'Never.'

'She never discussed using it with you?'

'No. It was as if . . . having made it, she forgot about it.'

'And, as between yourselves?'

A pause followed that quietly spoken question.

'We began to get closer . . . like never before . . . in a way that couldn't have happened before . . . because we'd made a momentous decision together . . . and now we were on the other side of it. We were in a new land.'

'Side by side?'

'Yes.'

'How was that possible, given your previous . . . treatment of her?'

'I don't know.'

'Yes, Peter, you do. Tell us. It's important.'

Peter Henderson looked at his hands again. 'Because I'd heard her, and she'd heard me, and because of that . . . we were . . . *present* to one another. It took time for us both to realise it, but once we'd sorted out the manner of her dying, we gradually noticed that we'd found one another, found what we both thought we'd lost. I loved her; she loved me. It was as simple as that. She knew it, and I knew it. The paralysis couldn't change this discovery . . . nothing could. It was mysterious . . .'

Emma Goodwin's eyes were wide and vacant, as if the shutters had been pulled down. Michael had reached for her hand. Helen was watching Michael as if he might speak. Nigel held his head in his hands, elbows on the table. Doctor Ingleby listened from a strange distance.

'What was the effect of the cancer diagnosis on you?' asked Anselm, pertinently.

'I couldn't believe it,' replied Peter Henderson. 'I'd come home at last and now she was definitely going . . . whether she chose to or not. There was nothing either of us could do, except submit to what was happening.'

'And for Jenny?'

'She was frightened. She said things couldn't be worse.'

'Did Jenny talk about ending her life?'

'No.'

'Did you refer to the mask?'

'Never. I abhorred the thing. It stood between me and Jenny . . . against what was happening between us.'

Anselm removed his glasses to clean them. Rubbing one of the lenses on his scapular, he said, ponderously, like a man casting his mind back to a turning in the road, 'Jenny was frightened, you said. Did she stay that way?'

'Yes.'

'Was she depressed?'

'Sometimes.'

'Would that complete her mental picture . . . fear and despair?'

'No.'

'What would you add?'

Peter Henderson began kneading a brow as if he wanted to completely rearrange the shape of his face.

'She was composed. Right alongside the fear. As the weeks went by, it was as though the illness had become detached from her, running parallel to who she was. Sometimes . . . she seemed to look at it from afar . . . as if it couldn't harm her. She was at peace.'

'What do you mean?'

Michael had spoken. He'd taken his hand back from Emma and was staring over the table in confusion.

'I don't know, Michael. Honestly, I don't fully understand what happened. But it was as though the certainty of death had brought some kind of light into her life. You, me – if we're lucky – we see to the end of the street; Jenny . . . she saw *everything*. She saw the whole road. No obstacles ahead, no distractions to the side. She knew where she was going and it removed most of the anxieties that claw at the rest of us. She said she could still enjoy a sherbet lemon.'

'A what?' whispered Michael in disbelief.

'A sherbet lemon.'

Anselm had finished cleaning his glasses, but he'd kept them in his hand as if preferring a slightly blurred view of the table and the people around it. He said: 'Of course, there's no way of knowing what anyone is really thinking, is there? Illness is a very private thing. As private as choosing death.'

It wasn't really a question, so Peter Henderson didn't reply but as if pushed over the edge his voice dropped a register, cracking hard in his throat. 'I just wanted to go back to the wine bar where I'd first met her. I just wanted to run things differently. And I was just grateful for what was left, now, between us. Time together became invaluable. I pushed everyone away . . . it was like we'd met for the first time.'

No one seemed to be breathing. Anselm's heart was in his mouth. He settled his glasses on his nose and said, 'The truth of Jenny's final year alive is this: she chose to end her life' – he looked around the table – 'but she never took the most important step. She never asked anyone to get that mask. On her birthday there was a party. For once everyone was together in one room. You all came and went . . . except for Vincent Cooper who came back because he'd forgotten his wallet. But Jenny died that night. And this is where the complications—'

'We all know she was killed.'

Nigel Goodwin spoke to the ground. He spoke for the young woman who'd written him a letter, a cry from the heart.

'Someone took her life. Someone thought they could—'

'Do you want to know who it was?' exclaimed Helen at last, looking around the table at the harrowed, watching faces. Throughout the entire meeting she'd angled her head to one side, but now she'd turned on everyone, flushed with authority. 'Well, I can tell you.'

Nigel raised bloodshot eyes to his brother, shaking his head, knowing he couldn't stop Helen once she got going. She was off the leash again. Her features were contorted with a suppressed certainty that had been swallowed for the common good and which she would now spill all over the floor. 'It was . . . it was . . .'

'Timothy.'

The silence following Emma's abrupt declaration acted like a vacuum sucking in the horror of those who'd always known and those who couldn't believe what they'd heard. She'd used her cheery winter voice, the voice that dealt with difficult situations, only this time there was no baked Alaska on the table.

45

The truth, at last, was out. The contaminating history of resentment and disappointment had been surpassed, an incredible fact which dramatically reduced the importance of the family's troubles, for any amount of adult conflict was as nothing compared to the moral and legal crisis which now fell to be resolved: a twelve-year-old boy had murdered his mother, thinking he was doing her a favour.

'I knew and yet I didn't know,' muttered Peter Henderson.

Unable to sleep, he'd come downstairs in the middle of the night and found that Jenny wasn't breathing. He knew she was dead. And he knew it couldn't be the cancer, not yet, and he couldn't think any further; wouldn't allow himself to think of Timothy, the only other person in the house.

'I called Bryan and when he came, I knew for sure it wasn't the cancer.' Peter looked over at his friend's fallen face. 'You were shocked, like me; and I know you thought I'd done something to cut short the disease. I couldn't tell you what I feared. I couldn't even tell myself.'

And so he'd prepared Timothy's breakfast the next morning after the body had been taken away. Frosties. A boiled egg with soldiers. He'd watched his son eat slowly, reading all the signs of numbed responsibility, translating them into sadness, shock and distress. Humanising what had happened. Trying to keep the future vaguely normal.

'Timothy had heard the conversation,' interposed Emma, taking a packet of Pall Mall from her bag. She was rigid in her chair, commanding, ready to field any questions. 'He'd heard the same banging window. He'd come downstairs and listened from the corridor to his mother talking to his father. He'd heard her say that she'd like to go if things got worse.' She shuffled out a cigarette. 'And they did. She got cancer. He'd heard her say she wanted a party . . . champagne . . . and he'd heard Peter say he just couldn't do it . . .'

She broke off to strike the match.

'I told him to help his father,' mumbled Michael. 'I told him to do the things he didn't want to do . . . I meant the dishes . . .'

Emma resumed control, blowing smoke through the corner of her mouth. She was the only one who'd got used to the unthinkable. 'His father threw a brick at a child. Timothy wondered why. Wouldn't let the matter drop, no matter what I said. To get away from it all, I took him for a ride on the London Eye. Just as we got to the top, he started whispering in my ear. We'd gone up into the sky on a great big wheel . . . by the time we'd come down to earth I'd found out my grandson had smothered my daughter. He'd come downstairs with his Spiderman pillow and placed it over her face, counted slowly to twenty and then gone back to bed. Not much you can say to that.'

He'd only done what his father couldn't do. He'd known about some wretched mask that no one wanted to use. He'd seen himself as joining a secret team. A *team*. He'd been the one who'd done the difficult bit. He hadn't been on his own, not really.

'Not much you can say to that, either.'

But Emma had had to find something. She'd told Timothy never to mention it again. She'd assured him – 'Well, what else could I say?' – that he'd helped his mother when no one else had been willing or able. Told him she did something similar every day to cats and dogs; that we were far kinder to animals than humans. She'd bought him a large waffle covered with Nutella and ice cream.

'I told him it was our secret,' said Emma. She paused to produce a small ashtray from her handbag and placed it on the edge of the table. 'We've never spoken of it since.'

It struck Anselm at this point that Emma Goodwin had really drawn the short straw. She'd longed to be a figure of salvation in Jennifer's life and, that desire denied, she'd found herself the confidante of her killer. She'd had to absorb the shock and work out her next move before the London Eye had reached ground level, where everyone had clambered out to get on with their lives. She'd had barely any time to think. No wonder she'd bought a waffle. But she'd stuck to her guns. She'd opted for secrecy and then devoted herself to living out the implications of the decision. As if following Anselm's thought, she said:

'And we need never speak of it in the future, if Peter will just pull himself together.' She spoke as if she were in the officers' mess, adjudicating over an unfortunate punch-up between an aspiring lieutenant and a brigadier. 'Timothy was doing just fine until his father threw that brick.'

'Emma, the boy has committed a murder,' said Nigel, in a drugged whisper.

'Oh wake up, Nigel,' snapped Emma. 'She was *my* daughter. I know what Timothy did. But you have to face facts. We all have to. Jenny would have died anyway within another six months. She went quickly. She was spared the cancer. It's not an agreeable way to go. I've seen it. Animals are no different to us in that regard. Frankly, there's something to be grateful for and now the boy needs *our* support and not *your* condemnation.'

'But, Emma—'

'Nigel, you weren't there.' Emma was imperial in her disdain. 'You were preaching "My yoke is easy, my burden is light" in

Chitungwiza. I'm the one who's had to carry the weight of Timothy's secret. I'm the one who's had to work out what to do. I'm the one who's taken all the responsibility. Now it's your turn' – she was speaking to everyone now – 'you can all drop your mawkish sensibilities and give me some help.'

You really have hardened yourself, thought Anselm, from deep within himself. He was observing her, not minding that she'd seized control of the meeting. You made a decision to protect Timothy from what he'd done and you've never once drifted off course. When Peter began to crack you tried to help him with every fibre in your being – not because you cared for him, but because his collapse threatened to expose Timothy. In hurling that brick, Peter Henderson was accusing his son. He had to be stopped. So you planned to kill him. You used your husband's love and his troubled past. Even now you can't see what you've done and what is happening . . . that harm is following upon harm. That your decision was a fatal one.

'What's to be done?' asked Helen, frightened and confused.

'We have to do something,' added Nigel.

Emma regarded them with monumental scorn. She eyed Peter and then Doctor Ingleby as if challenging them to make an equally trite contribution. But everyone was stunned, like deserters caught by a searchlight. Only Emma was used to the glare. She appraised Anselm harshly, challenge in her eyes.

'I suppose you'd like to beat all the swords into ploughshares?' she mused, as if the idea was as far-fetched as a light burden. She leaned forward to stub out her cigarette. 'You're off with the birds. Burying the hatchet . . . now you're talking. It falls short of reconciliation but it works. I've been doing it for years.'

'Emma, stop this,' pleaded Nigel, no longer quite recognising his sister-in-law. 'We all have to—'

'Shut up and listen,' she said, smiling bitterly, as if she were back in the London Eye. 'There's a decision to be made. There are only two solutions. You all have to make a choice. There are risks each way. It would be best if we can all agree to go in the same direction. Share the danger. Share the responsibility. Agreed?'

She didn't need an answer. She shook a box of matches to check if she had any left, her roving eyes querying the level of courage and determination. Nodding more contempt, she knocked out a Pall Mall and lit up.

'The first road is the widest, the easiest to take and it leads directly to hell,' she said, leaning back, head held high. 'It means going to the police station and explaining in a hushed voice exactly what happened . . . what is it, two years ago? It means sitting down with social workers dressed in black jeans and lawyers who want to be paid upfront – everything that Peter found so humiliating and exhausting and demeaning – and then going into some courtroom where a bewildered Solomon does his best to weigh up the mess that's landed on the bench, wishing – I may be wrong, of course – that he hadn't got out of bed that morning. Because this is no ordinary case. He's going to sentence the boy for matricide. Compassionately, mind you, and he won't allow the papers to print any names, given the boy's tender years, but our Timothy will still come home with a criminal record stamped, "Murderer". Everyone will know it was him that the papers were talking about. All the pundits will use "Boy G" as a tragic example of something gone wrong in our society or the legal system or God knows what, and "Boy G" will have to sit there listening or reading or watching, taking his medication and hoping his psychologist knows some good tricks on how to deal with exposure. He'll end up with an entry in Wikipedia as the boy who'd committed an accidental mercy killing. Do you seriously expect Timothy to survive that ordeal?'

No one answered.

'Because this is the route proposed by . . .' – Emma didn't quite know how to designate Anselm. She was enraged with him: for his interference; for what he represented; for his distance from the trauma in her life and that of her family – '. . . by this stranger who never knew Jenny. This idealist, detached from the messy circumstances of our lives.'

Anselm gave no visible reaction to Emma's charge. He was waiting to hear the alternative course of action, watching Emma pull aggressively on her cigarette. She was about to make her bid for burying the hatchet.

'There is a second road,' she said, quietly and firmly. Her tone and manner had subtly changed. She was back to the role of advocate rather than prosecutor. This was the elegant, persuasive woman who'd appealed to the heart and mind of Judge Moreland. She was desperate to win the argument. 'And this road is narrow and difficult and few would take it. But it leads to something like peace. Most important of all: we're the ones who'll have to survive an ordeal, not Timothy.' Emma smiled pain and certainty at the confusion around her. 'What do we do? I'll tell you . . . nothing. We do absolutely nothing. We come together. We bury our differences and we support a boy who made a decision far harder than ours. We help him carry his burden. Make it lighter. Because it's ours, too. We're all part of the circumstances that led him to think it could ever be a good thing to take someone's life. When he crossed over that line he brought us all with him.'

'What do you expect us to do?' asked Nigel, uneasily. 'Buy more waffles?'

'Yes, Nigel. Lots of them. With different toppings. Because a waffle is ordinary life. That's what Timothy needs. He's troubled by what he's done. He'll always have nagging doubts, but we'll show him by our constancy that no one condemns him; that his secret is a family secret; that he acted for us all; that the past is dead in the past; and that he has a life to lead, now and in the future.'

'Emma, you're asking us all to be complicit in the covering up of a crime.' Nigel Goodwin used a worried, collective voice, summoning everyone together, including Anselm. 'You're wanting us to follow where you've gone.'

'That's right, Nigel, I am. That's the ordeal you have to accept. It's the price you pay for having failed to shape your godson's conscience. We're all guilty of that one. Which is why I can't and won't turn around. To be honest, none of you have any real choice but to come my way. Any more than I had a choice when I'd got out of the London Eye . . . when I found myself standing where you're standing now.'

Emma tapped ash into the ashtray, waiting for any further comments or questions.

'It's criminal,' mouthed Helen, guiltily, but not quite objecting.

'So what?' replied Emma, smartly. 'It's the lesser of two evils. You understand that, don't you, Nigel?'

Anselm had an acute sense of people stepping ever so slightly away from him. The atmosphere of indecision was palpable. They were all standing at a divide in the road. It was time to choose a future for Timothy. Neither was perfect. Both involved difficulty. One was wide open to problems, the other narrowed them down. Emma stood up as if to lead the way. With one last push, she said:

'There really is nothing much to think about.' She shouldered her red leather handbag. 'If you don't come with me, then it will be your responsibility to take Timothy to the police. You will have to sit with him while a detective calls social services. You'll have to explain why the road to hell is paved with good intentions.'

Emma picked up her ashtray and emptied it on the fire. Without waiting for Michael, she left the threshing room. After a moment, he stood up, head down, and followed the strong scent of his wife's perfume. With an embarrassed cough, Nigel pushed back his chair, helping Helen fuss to her feet. Leaning towards Anselm, he whispered, pastor to pastor, that he'd have to give the matter some careful consideration and that, well, the *issues* weren't entirely . . . Anselm didn't catch the rest. Shortly they'd gone. Peter Henderson was next.

'I tried to warn you,' he said, walking away. 'I told you that pinning "Right" and "Wrong" onto events wasn't that easy. That maybe, once in a while, we should just not bother trying. Out of humility. But you wouldn't listen. Now you've fallen into the same pit as me . . . along with Emma and Nigel and Helen.' On reaching the doorway he turned around. 'Don't try and climb out, will you? Sit tight and feel bad, for all our sakes.'

Only Doctor Ingleby was left. He sat, legs crossed, in no apparent hurry to go.

'Well, that was a disaster,' said Anselm at length.

'Yes, it was.'

Anselm blinked uncertainly. He wanted a word with Schiller.

'You may not have made a ploughshare,' observed the doctor, after a suitable pause. 'But you managed something verging on the miraculous. You've got the Henderson and Goodwin families talking honestly to one another. It's the beginning. I wonder what will happen next.'

Anselm made a slight, puzzled start. Doctor Ingleby had spoken as if he knew the answer already.

46

Over the following week, Anselm found himself in a state of near paralysis. Each day he'd waited for the phone to ring – for Sylvester to struggle with the list of extensions and buttons and flashing lights – hoping that the Goodwins and Peter Henderson had gathered privately and decided to take what Emma had called the wide road to hell. But no call had come. They'd left Anselm to make his own decision. And, in truth, he didn't know what to do. The aim of the meeting had been to secure the cooperation of the entire family before involving Olivia Manning. And none had been forthcoming, which placed Anselm as the outsider threatening to wreck their chosen fragile peace. Left alone and shuffling in the cloister, Anselm inevitably had to examine whether the Wikipedia route was, in fact, the road to a lasting, deeper reconciliation; whether it was morally necessary, regardless of the views of the main actors; whether the claims of the law could ever be laid quietly to one side. The questions were of fundamental importance because it was a basic tenet of Anselm's thinking that (generally speaking) half-truths lead to half-measures – of peace, fulfilment, happiness and so on – which, showing up what is lacking, produce the lingering taste of disappointment, while acceptance of the truth in its entirety leads (in time) to the full portion, simply prepared. The relationship was exponential. There were, of course, exceptions to the rule. The trick – the very difficult trick – was picking which truths to leave in the cupboard. As a rule of thumb, murder wasn't one of them.

The primordial question that troubled Anselm, however, was this: can a twelve-year-old kill someone and just turn the page? Bolstered by understanding adults and the confidence that he'd fulfilled his mother's deepest wish, could he get on with an ordinary life? Or was there some primitive need to render a public account? If so – and Anselm thought there was – Emma's attempt to share her grandson's burden in secret was profoundly misguided. More. In the long run it wouldn't work. So, from one perspective, Anselm was sure about what he ought to do.

Nonetheless, he couldn't make the move. He couldn't pick up the phone to Olivia Manning. His mind sent the signal but his hand wouldn't react. He couldn't even open his mouth and confide in the Prior, though a brief conversation had taken place after a Chapter meeting.

'Are you all right?'

'The danger has passed. Truly.'

The Prior had searched Anselm's face.

'Do we need to chat about this?'

'We do, but not just yet.'

Anselm didn't want to 'go to the end of his concerns' – to use the Prior's customary phrase – because that would involve revealing the conspiracy to murder Peter Henderson, a development that would almost certainly compel the Prior to call Olivia Manning himself, an outcome that Anselm wanted to postpone if not avoid entirely. An inquiry into Michael's attempt to shoot Peter would lead ineluctably to Anselm's presence in Polstead and his investigation into Jennifer Henderson's death. Which would flush out Timothy's secret. And while such an upshot was consistent with Anselm's desire to ventilate the truth in its entirety, it would have been obtained without the consent or cooperation of the two families at the heart of the conflict – elements that were necessary for any future reconciliation. As Doctor Ingleby had remarked, they were, for once, talking to one another. Astonishingly, despite the Browning and all it represented, there was a faint chance of lasting compromise . . . which would be blown the moment Olivia Manning walked through the door. And among the many things that Timothy didn't need to know just yet was the fact that his grandparents had tried to kill his father. That was one for the cupboard.

'Come to me when you're ready,' the Prior had said.

'I will.'

'And the greater question?'

He'd meant the investigation.

'I'm contemplating havoc and wondering how to avoid it.'

The conversation had almost ended there because the Prior had scurried off a few steps but then he'd suddenly stopped and scurried back.

'Everyone's talking about homemade bombs,' he'd said, as if the Vatican had issued a controversial encyclical. 'My thoughts are these: an unstable compound is going to blow up anyway. At which point, you might as well get on with it: trigger the blast and face the consequences.'

With that piece of advice, he'd scurried off again.

Anselm had gone to see Mitch. They'd sipped beer on deck.

They'd spoken of Vincent Cooper, the melancholy man who'd lost the woman he loved and found himself involved – he'd thought – in her killing. There'd been nothing to run away from.

'I take it you didn't find him,' said Anselm.

'No.'

'You left the message with the estate agents?'

'Yes.'

The message being that he needn't sell his property or leave the country since 'matters had been resolved'.

'How resolved?' Mitch had asked, opening another beer. He'd waited a week and he was still none the wiser.

Anselm had hesitated, and then said, 'Timothy killed his mother. The family want to keep it quiet. They've left me to decide what I do with what I know.'

Mitch had dropped the beer cap on the deck. Together they'd watched it roll off like a penny, teeter and fall.

'What are you going to do?' Mitch had said, an age later, showing Anselm he was immeasurably glad that the decision wasn't his to make; that playing second fiddle had distinct advantages.

'Have another beer.'

'And then what?'

Anselm had to make his choice. Timothy was demonstrably sharp-minded and angry, and Anselm couldn't imagine him accepting changed toppings on the waffle for much longer. He needed professional help. He had a conscience. And whatever the state of its development, exposing what Timothy had done as a 'compassionate error' – to put it mildly – would actually bring about the shaping element that Emma had complained was missing. Or would it destroy him?

'And then what?' Anselm had repeated, confounded. 'I wait.'

'What for?'

'God knows. It's a Gilbertine thing. When you're in a hole you just sit tight and wait for a light to come on.'

*   *   *

When despondent, Anselm sought distraction with Larkwood's Doorkeeper, the erstwhile leader of Peewee Patrol. Simply being in his presence was enough to place anxiety at a distance. Things fell into perspective even though he might say nothing to ease a troubled mind.

'Hail, Leaping Wolf,' said Anselm.

'What's up with you?'

'I'm under siege.'

The old scout pointed to a chair at the side of his desk. He'd lost his belt again, because a length of electric cable had been tied around his waist. A tartan blanket lay across his bony legs, his heavily booted feet sticking out as if they belonged to a Jarrow marcher.

'Baden-Powell lasted two hundred and seventeen days,' he sighed.

It didn't seem possible. While others might draw comfort from the storm on Lake Galilee, the Watchman turned to the Siege of Mafeking.

'He was outnumbered,' observed Sylvester. 'But he didn't give up. He'd just been promoted, like you. I shook his hand, you know. At Olympia. He told me the Boers were—'

'Sylvester,' interjected Anselm, despairing, 'what would you do if you were on the trail to Mafeking with an important message about peace, and you hadn't lost your way, but you were beginning to doubt where you were going?'

There was a small pause while Leaping Wolf placed himself among the Legion of Frontiersmen. The heat seemed to beat down on his bare head. He was grimacing pluck and determination.

'I'd find a friendly Zulu.'

'A Zulu?'

'Yes. Someone not involved in the fight but who knew the way. Someone who'd been there before.'

Another pause followed this somewhat novel suggestion – Baden-Powell was unlikely to have many friends among the Zulus – and then Anselm said, 'Would you pass me the phone?'

Blinking at his sudden return to rural England, and probably disorientated by Anselm's slightly agitated manner, Sylvester hooked his walking stick around one of the receivers and dragged it across the table.

'Thanks, Arrow of Light,' murmured Anselm. 'You deserve a medal with clasp and bar.'

Anselm rang the nearest person he knew to a friendly Zulu in the Henderson–Goodwin War. Oddly enough, the friend had already tried to call Larkwood but the message hadn't got through. Siege conditions, joked Anselm. They agreed to meet in what remained of the Chapter House of Leiston Abbey. The room set aside for big decisions. 'A place where everyone has the right to speak honestly without fear of condemnation, without fear of being quoted afterwards, and without pressure to conform to the will of the majority.' It was the Zulu's idea. He'd remembered Anselm's description word for word.

47

Doctor Ingleby had brought a collapsible picnic table, two folding chairs and a wicker hamper. He'd placed the table in the centre of the Chapter House and laid it with a cloth, plates, glasses, cutlery and a bottle of claret. He'd procured a quiche, tinned corn and potato salad. Still in his long green coat, he rose to greet Anselm, as if he were welcoming the monk into his home. They were quite alone. The sky was overcast so the shadows on the lawn were barely noticeable. From where Anselm was sitting he could see the ruins of the south transept and the Lady Chapel. The air was perfectly still.

'I don't think you and I have been entirely honest with each other,' said Doctor Ingleby, with his melancholy smile, pouring

Anselm a glass of wine. 'So I thought we might have another conversation. And what better meeting place than here, beneath the sky where men once spoke without fear.'

The doctor urged Anselm to help himself. He produced salt and pepper from his pockets, details he'd almost forgotten about.

'We both know things that we've kept to ourselves,' he said, laying them down. 'We both held our tongues while Peter and Emma did the talking. Shall we speak plainly? If either of us is to decide what to do – freely and without pressure to conform – then I think we need to . . . open our hearts to one another.'

Anselm nodded cautiously. While appreciating that Doctor Ingleby had signed a false death certificate, Anselm hadn't considered where that now left the doctor. He, too, had a decision to make. Did he inform the police or not? The wide and narrow roads lay before him. Timothy's fate was in his hands as much as it was in Anselm's.

'May I propose one condition?' asked Doctor Ingleby.

'Which is?'

'We promise never to repeat what the other has said.'

'Unless you confess to a crime.'

'Agreed. And I'll make one further exception. In the days to come, should you wish, you can speak to your Prior. He is, I imagine, a kind of father.'

Anselm was surprised by the unusual concession. It moved him, too.

'Who begins?'

'I will,' volunteered Doctor Ingleby, magnanimously. 'I'm under the moonshadow.'

Doctor Ingleby had been diagnosed just after Jenny. Cigarettes during the sixties, cigars through the seventies, and a pipe starting in the eighties, right up until the X-ray found shadows on his lungs. He'd been an occasional user, in fact, the shift in method reflecting his advancing years and a romantic idea of style and burgeoning gravitas. Happily the initial treatment, though aggressive, had bought back time.

'But that was later, of course,' said Doctor Ingleby. 'When Peter asked me to look after Jenny, I was still tugging on my pipe.'

In fact, he'd been wafting matches over a bowl of rich tobacco from the Dordogne while Peter had been explaining his reasons for seeking help.

'I'm not entirely naive,' he said. 'Peter had already told me that Jenny was suicidal so it rather begged the question as to why he'd come to me. One of the side-effects of desperation is that you lose tact. You can't conceal what you're thinking because all the internal walls are falling down. I knew what Peter was thinking. I ought to have been insulted but I've come to tolerate being misunderstood.'

'So why accept?'

'To protect Jenny.'

Knowing Peter's moral beliefs, his intellectual bravery, and bearing in mind Jenny's extreme condition, Doctor Ingleby feared they might embark upon some ill-judged enterprise. Not everyone wants to take their life when the lights go out on life. Some people find a way. And it takes time and endurance. He'd known many patients who'd been surprised to find that the dark tunnel had an end. That they could look out from their condition upon a sunlit garden once more. So Doctor Ingleby had agreed to come to Polstead, intending to monitor this particular patient very carefully indeed.

'Everything Peter recollected was true,' confirmed the doctor, tasting his wine. 'Jenny's depression receded and she became, in part, resigned. Calmer' – he laughed affectionately, placing his glass back on the table – 'and more honest. She didn't want to exploit any presumed flexibility in my principles, so she asked me outright . . . poetically.'

'Asked what?'

Doctor Ingleby recalled the words as if he were citing Wordsworth on daffodils. 'She said: "Given a choice, I'd like to wander along and suddenly stumble upon death . . . without planning or mental preparation . . . simply turn a corner and then die, as if I'd found a flower in a forest." She wasn't at ease with that dreadful mask. She knew Peter could never use it. She looked at me for a very long time as if saying, "Could you arrange that for me?" because we both knew that she wouldn't be wandering anywhere. That she had no choices left and would never stumble again.'

In keeping with the 'poetic' nature of the request, Doctor Ingleby had made no reply. He'd smoothed his understanding into the skin of her hand. Long years of medical practice had taught him to say only what was necessary. She'd taken consolation in his silence because he'd not gone the route of so many others: explaining that her life had immense value; that depression had shifting shades; that light could come as unexpectedly as a flower in the forest.

'The conversation changed our relationship,' said Doctor Ingleby. 'There was a new warmth. Peter had tried to shuffle me into position, which showed how little he understood my approach to death and dying, whereas Jenny – unknown to him – had simply made an honest appeal, respecting that I'm a doctor subject to professional guidelines and the law; and that I, too, had a right to make a choice rather than be ambushed by circumstances. She never raised the matter again.'

And he watched her slowly change. He saw her reach for Peter's hand. He saw them talking quietly, like old, worn companions, no longer troubled by shyness, the fear of rejection or the quick misunderstandings that plague every opening romance.

'When the cancer diagnosis came through, she was shaken of course, initially, but Peter is right. Over time there was no profound change in her mood. In the depths, she was astonishingly calm. Unlike me.'

For Doctor Ingleby had just made his own visit to the oncologist. He'd seen the shadow on the X-rays. He'd thought wistfully about the cigarettes, the cigars and the pipe. He'd loved his pipe. Bought a tremendous hand-carved thing from a shop in Ettal, a pretty Bavarian village where his wife had been born. He'd finally found a way of enjoying tobacco and all along the damned stuff had set out to kill him.

'It was Jenny who helped me,' he said, laughing. 'Said the remainder of my life had immense value and that moods change like the weather. Our eyes met and I thought of those flowers around the corner.'

In fact, Doctor Ingleby's prognosis was the opposite to that of Jenny. It turned out there was some hope. He felt lucky. He even felt oddly guilty: it just wasn't fair. Jenny had never touched the weed in her life, not even as a curious adolescent. She'd been hounding her father for years, but he wouldn't listen. He was still smoking. And now even her mother had started – hating it but persevering anyway with dogged resolution. But it was Jenny who'd got the rogue cells, not them; and not Doctor Ingleby. Jenny who'd already been robbed of so much.

'Life is not fair, Father.'

Anselm agreed.

'And the wicked prosper,' he added. There was something in the Psalms about that. 'I don't have any answers, save to say that discovering peace of mind has nothing to do with finding out why.'

Doctor Ingleby raised his glass. He'd liked that one. But he had a sort of troubled rejoinder:

'Perhaps it doesn't, but do you know, ever since Jenny died, I've been asking myself: how did she do it? How did she discover peace of mind in the worst of all circumstances?'

His soft, moon-shaped eyes were gentle and far seeing. He didn't expect Anselm to reply because he hadn't quite finished:

'I appreciate you may not like this, that it might wound your sense of the sacred, but from my point of view – speaking as someone who was there as a friend and doctor – I'd say it's

290

because she'd organised her own way of dying. She felt in control, even if she wasn't. It's what makes the outcome bearable for Peter . . . and Michael . . . and all the others. It helps us all accept a little more easily what Timothy has done . . . it mitigates his responsibility. Doesn't that make it easier for you?'

The doctor paused, giving Anselm his chance to contribute, but he didn't take it. As if to fill the hiatus, the cloud began to break. Sunlight appeared like fire without flame eating away at the edge of torn paper. Patches of blue appeared. The shadows along the walls took a sudden depth. Doctor Ingleby touched the bottle and Anselm made a nod.

'I listened with admiration to how you led Peter through Jenny's final months,' said Doctor Ingleby, pursuing his argument, pouring slowly. 'But the more I listened the more I thought, He's hiding something. You were at pains to show that Jenny *might not* have chosen death . . . even though everything said by Peter demonstrated that the choice *had been made* – her peace of mind, her resignation to the cancer, her stable mood. For some reason you won't let the fire go out. Am I right?'

'Yes, you are.'

'Why, Father? Is it the burning bush? Your reverence for life?'

He'd made it sound like a species threatened with extinction at the hands of lawless hunters. There was regret in his voice, and pity. Raising his glass, Anselm stared into the deep red wine.

'Yes . . . and a reverence for death, and how we get there.'

48

It was Anselm's turn to be honest. Until this moment, he'd not been free to say what he knew. As in his days at the Bar, he couldn't refer to anything he'd discovered until it was a matter of public knowledge. And even then, he could only go so far. But

Peter — and indeed Doctor Ingleby — had now repeated the substance of Jenny's testimony with one or two critical omissions — elements unknown to everyone (it seemed) save Anselm and, perhaps, Peter. Now was the time for Anselm to speak. To a large extent his secret explained his paralysis.

'I'd been sent to fill the chaplain's shoes at Ipswich Hospital,' said Anselm. 'Just for a week. One of the nurses asked if I'd see a young woman who was paralysed and suffering from terminal cancer. She'd come in for some routine tests and her father had asked if someone wise could persuade her to remain in hospital rather than go home.'

Doctor Ingleby meshed his fingers, leaning them on the edge of the table. A very light breeze flicked the edges of the cloth.

'I did my best, but I didn't put my heart into it,' confessed Anselm. 'My mother had died of cancer. She'd decided to stay at home, too. It was what the French call a "strong" time — for her and for me. We both learned a great deal in those final weeks . . . about how to live and how to die . . . so I understood Jenny's longing. I rather think my experience did the opposite to what Michael intended . . . I all but sent her home with a blessing.'

The mutual understanding opened a sort of door between Jenny and Anselm. No sooner had Anselm finished speaking when she blurted out a request. Would Anselm keep a secret? She had something shocking and surprising to say. The room was dark save for a small bedside lamp, bent low to reduce the glare. There were tulips in a vase. The door was ajar. It was quite silent save for the sporadic chat of a nurse pushing a trolley of medicines along the corridor outside.

'She told me about her relationship with Peter, her early exile from his life, and Timothy, whom she'd lost after the fall . . . everything . . . through to the hopeless agreement with Peter, the clumsy mask and her conversation with you.' Anselm broke off. 'She admired you enormously. She found you compassionate and wise.'

Doctor Ingleby received the compliments with a nod of gentle rebuff. His eyes were creased with foreboding.

'This is three days before she died,' he calculated.

'Yes,' replied Anselm.

Anselm had listened to Peter's testimony, finding it knitted hand in glove with what Jennifer had said to him. Same for her account of Doctor Ingleby's earlier disclosure about finding flowers in a forest. But there was one vital difference. Jennifer had said something to Anselm that she hadn't said to anyone else.

'She was more transparent with me, I think, than she was with Peter,' ventured Anselm. 'It happens. Sometimes it's easier to open your heart to a stranger. But what Peter doesn't know is that his opening out towards her, his coming home, had a very gradual effect on how Jenny viewed her condition and – latterly – the approach of cancer.'

She wanted to be with him, Anselm explained, as if it couldn't get any more simple or silly than that. She'd begun to experience a strange kind of *romance*, even though she couldn't move; even though her cells were breaking down. A belligerent will to live had begun to rise out of her decision to die. Doctor Ingleby nodded. He'd seen the same thing. But Anselm stalled. His eyes drifted to the ruins opposite. Light played upon the broken walls, picking out dimples in the stone. Most of the dressed masonry had been hauled away. It took a trained eye to know what had once been there; its proportions, the majesty of art through simple lines soaring high into the sky. In a peculiar way, nothing had been lost. He blinked and fell quiet, hearing Jenny's voice again as she spoke in the half-light.

'A while ago, if you'd asked me if I was ready to die, I'd have said, "Yes". If it was allowed, I'd have filled in the forms and taken the tablet, if there was one. And I'd have done it because I thought it was *better* that way. Better for *everyone*. They're all *waiting* for me to go. They're all frightened to live normally until I've gone, as if it was tactless to be happy among the dying. No one can live as they ought and might. I thought I could set them all free. Give each of them a further seven months of ordinary life.'

'What about this will to live, Jenny?' asked Anselm.

'I was prepared to let it go . . . after all, look how much time I've got left . . . look at how reduced I am. What would it matter? What's the value of what I'd be throwing away? What would I be losing?'

Anselm was meant to say "Nothing" or "Not much" but he simply watched her from his shadow, unnerved by the terrible stillness of her body. The limbs that wouldn't move. The torso rising and falling with each slow respiration. It was like a strange shell, inhabited but abandoned at one and the same. She was in bed, slightly elevated, her face caught by a fugitive light. A kind of mischief played upon her lips.

'But now?' prompted Anselm.

'Now?' she replied. 'I want my life. I was ready to die before but now I *want my life*. I know that in one way it's broken, disappointing, limited, worthless, empty and insignificant . . . but it's *mine*. It's all I've got. I'm still me. And I know it will soon become messy and painful and frightening, but I still want it. I want to live what I've got . . . do you understand? It's as valuable to me now as it ever was. I'm still . . . *full* of something . . . and it can be exhilarating, despairing, violent and peaceful – every state you can think of – and I just want to keep hold of it . . . for as long as possible.'

She was pleading with Anselm as if she required a licence from some credit-rating authority to prove that her final months were worth clinging onto, in themselves for what they were, and not for what they might be worth to anyone else.

'I do understand,' replied Anselm, crushed and humbled, because he didn't know. He didn't know what it was like to be utterly stripped down so that all that remained was something essential and intangible: the brute fact of existence, known through an infinite shading of mood, thought and feeling.

'Why have you changed your mind, Jenny?' he asked, after a while.

'In part because of Peter; in part because of you.'

'Me?' Anselm was astounded. He'd just sat there and listened.

'What you said about your mother wanting to stay at home. How you learned together about living and dying.' She appraised him gratefully. 'I'm a mother, too. Whatever I've lost along the way, I'm still a mother. I've forgotten who I was to my son. I've not helped him at all . . . but you made me think that I could still be *someone* for him. That the little I've got could still be shared. I'm *desperate* to see him.'

Anselm sipped some wine, noting Doctor Ingleby's unease.

Coming away from Polstead to the hospital had been a little like going to a monastery (Jenny had said). It was the first time she'd been away for any length of time. And, short though her stay had been, she'd viewed her life differently, she'd found other certainties. She'd even met a monk and got a fresh perspective on parenting. Before leaving the next morning, she'd handed him a letter. It's for my uncle, she'd explained. He's a vicar and I've ignored him because I was angry and didn't have anything to say, but now I do; would you post it please? And – if at all possible – could you smuggle yourself into my family? Are you allowed? I'll invite you. No one understands one another; there's a lot of resentment, pretence and disappointment. We need someone to begin pulling us back together. An outsider. You see, my partner's a sort of soft-spoken Jack Bauer . . . have you seen *24*? Well, there's this counter-terrorist unit . . .

'A week later, I called up to check how she was doing,' said Anselm. 'A boy answered the phone. It was Timothy. And he told me very simply that unfortunately his mother was dead. I was instantly suspicious.'

After reflecting for several days, Anselm became convinced that something terrible had happened. Cancer was, of course, the most obvious explanation, but Anselm couldn't forget Jenny's *drive*, her hopes and plans for the next few months. Her conviction. Her desperation to see Timothy. Not knowing any of the family history, and only knowing Peter Henderson's reputation as a bold thinker, Anselm's tentative assessment was that Peter Henderson had been luring Jenny into accepting her own voluntary death; that Jenny had come home and told him of her change of heart; and that he'd overruled her somehow . . . the precise mechanism being covered up by a doctor who'd agreed to conceal an assisted suicide. Precisely why Peter Henderson would want to kill a woman who only had seven months to live had left Anselm bewildered. But that didn't remove the stark reality that Jenny was dead and the starker question that it raised: had she been murdered?

There was, of course, nothing Anselm could do. The cause of death had been properly certified by a medical practitioner. He was left – on the face of things – with a completely unfounded misgiving. And it wasn't until an article appeared in the *Sunday Times* two years later drawing attention to Anselm as an offbeat investigator that someone wrote to Larkwood's Prior on Jenny's behalf.

'As soon as I met Peter Henderson, I knew he hadn't killed her,' said Anselm. 'I realised I'd misread the signs. But at least I knew that she hadn't died of cancer. I began to think about Michael and Emma, alone or in concert, loving parents driven to an extreme measure by an extreme misunderstanding. I never contemplated for one moment that Jenny's killer was the boy she'd gone home to help with the little she had left in the bank; the boy who needed a handle onto living and dying; the boy who still doesn't know that his mother changed her mind.'

Timothy wasn't alone. Jenny hadn't had time to tell Doctor Ingleby. She hadn't had time to talk to her uncle about surprises. She hadn't had time to start smuggling Anselm into the family chaos. She hadn't even begun to share her thoughts with Timothy.

'Like you, I've always felt strangely guilty, though I had better cause,' said Anselm, narrowing his gaze. Much of the cloud had drawn back. Afternoon sunshine had grown strong, removing the dimples from the ruined walls. The stone was bright and hard on the eye. 'In a way, I sent Jenny to her death. I know it's irrational. But if she'd stayed in hospital, none of this would have happened. And now I'm poised to demolish the family she asked me to help rebuild. The irony has left me dumbstruck.'

Doctor Ingleby ate quietly and thoughtfully. When his plate was quite clean, he laid down his knife and fork in the careful manner of a man who'd just completed a complex surgical procedure. He wiped his mouth on a paper serviette and said, 'I filled in the certificate of death. I did so knowing that what I wrote was false. I knew it wasn't cancer. I'm at the very centre of this tragedy. I won't keep that kind of secret on my conscience.'

Doctor Ingleby reached inside his green overcoat and withdrew an envelope from a pocket. Handing it to Anselm he said, 'This is my confession. Take it to the police. It's your right, after all you've done for Jenny. It's also your duty. After that, be at peace. I'm the one who must walk alone down the long wide road, not you.'

The meal and the conversation were over. The monk and the doctor packed up the hamper, folded down the table and snapped shut the canvas chairs. They didn't speak again until they'd reached Doctor Ingleby's Sunbeam Singer Chamois.

'Goodbye, Father,' he said, holding out his hand. 'Give me the rest of today to sort out my affairs, will you? I don't want the police to come and find my flowerbeds in a mess. There'll be pictures in the paper and I'd like everything to be in order.' He sighed, leaning on the car door. 'I've spent over forty years in medical practice . . . in the surgery . . . at patients' houses . . . at the hospice. And do you know, after all that, what's best and true of me lies in a garden shed. Odd, isn't it?'

49

On the way to Martlesham Anselm and Mitch were silent. In effect they were delivering the bomb that would blow apart the Henderson and Goodwin families, their myths and best intentions. Anselm had feared the responsibility of this moment and now he was simply a messenger.

'I didn't expect to see you so soon,' said Olivia, when Anselm entered her office.

'Me neither.'

'You've solved your case?'

'No, I've come with a letter.'

'Another?'

'This one, I imagine, is the last.'

Olivia opened the envelope with the nail of her thumb and withdrew Dr Ingleby's confession. She read it quietly showing no emotion.

'What's a moonshadow?' she asked, looking up.

'Cancer.'

She reached for a black overcoat. 'I think I'd better ask him a few questions.'

Doctor Ingleby lived off the Barking Road, south of Needham Market. His house was modern and small. Ribbed mauve tiling with skylights capped walls that framed an abundance of glass. He was evidently a man who liked the light. Huge windows looked onto a large garden of shrubs and flowers enclosed by a high, trimmed hedge. To one side lay a tended vegetable patch, neatly banked and furrowed with sections covered over by sheets of black plastic. Like Anselm, the doctor had prepared for winter. Muffled voices from inside the house drifted over the lawns and gravel driveway . . . music . . . something operatic. A window was open. Reaching the front door, Olivia pressed a white buzzer.

No reply.

She pressed again.

Still no reply. Just two voices, a man's and a woman's, rising slowly like a great wave.

Olivia tried the door and found it wasn't locked. She pushed it open with a long, steady finger . . .

The hallway was covered with a rich cherry-red carpet, the deep pile running right up the stairs to a small landing. Though it was mid-morning, the lights were on. A large painting of two majestic elephants dominated one wall.

'Doctor Ingleby?'

Olivia had called out but there was no response. The wave of song was opening out, arching towards the shore. The picture buzzed lightly against the wall.

'It's the end of *Norma*,' said Olivia, her features hard and enquiring. 'Callas, Corelli and Zaccaria . . .'

She walked slowly down the corridor into the sitting room, emerging with a shake of the head. Same for the kitchen. They stood at the base of the stairs, looking up towards the empty landing and the source of the music.

'It's the final scene,' explained Olivia in a monotone. She raised her voice – 'Doctor Ingleby.'

Her tone had been insistent. Anselm called out, too, following Olivia up the stairs as the music grew louder. He traced the voices to a door, pushed it open and found Doctor Ingleby's study. Framed cartoons of doctor jokes. Laden shelves from floor to ceiling – journals, textbooks, novels and papers leaning right and left to make a vast herringbone. Cardboard boxes instead of filing cabinets. A tidy roll-top desk and a cup of unfinished cocoa. A carved pipe on a stand. Several burned matches in a stone ashtray. Framed photographs of the doctor and a woman. An ergonomic chair. A CD player on a side table. A rich, heavy smell that could only be called brown.

The great wave of song rose high and then, with a sort of devastating delight, collapsed into silence . . . and then Callas was on her own . . . *Deh! Non volerli vittime del mio fatale errore* . . . the song had begun again. Doctor Ingleby had switched on the REPEAT button. The music would go on for ever.

Turning around, Anselm saw Olivia, serious and knowing. She stepped back into the corridor and Anselm followed her to the bathroom. He didn't enter. He kept his distance one step behind Mitch. All he could see was Doctor Ingleby's serene, bloodless face. He was lying in the bath, his white flesh in shocking contrast to the crimson water.

An ambulance was called. The forensic people came. Police tape was strung across the entrance to the property and the house. There'd be an investigation to rule out foul play. And it would be thorough. By the time they'd finished, the detectives would know more about Doctor Ingleby than anyone else. For the time being, all they had was a statement from the nearest neighbour attracted to the scene by the sudden activity next door. Doctor Ingleby had spent the afternoon on his knees in the garden. Raking. Weeding. Cutting back. Jobs for late summer and spring . . . not autumn.

'What were they singing about?' asked Anselm.

'She's asking forgiveness for having betrayed the gods, crying for her children . . . sacrificing her life to save the man she loves.'

'What did the first line mean?'

'Don't let them be victims of my fatal error.'

They were standing some distance from the house by a blue gardening shed. The door was yellow and the windows were blocked by drawn yellow curtains. From afar they could hear the crackle of radios and the crunch of gravel underfoot. This is where the music ended. Olivia handed Doctor Ingleby's letter to Anselm. He read it holding the paper with trembling hands.

> I've been under the moonshadow now for two years.
>
> It's growing stronger and stronger. I walk along these lanes under its strange revealing light. Nothing looks the same any more. Everything is painfully beautiful. Many would stay and look for as long as they can, but I'm ready to close my eyes. I've seen enough. I've made a choice.
>
> I've been involved in such choosing only once before in my life. A patient who couldn't act for herself turned to me for help. I listened. She wanted death to come as a surprise, like finding a flower in a forest.
>
> Jennifer Henderson died from an injection of insulin administered between the toes during a medical examination. She felt nothing and was not aware of what I was doing.
>
> I acted alone and without the unwitting assistance or knowledge of anyone. I make this known now because I understand that doubts have arisen in the family over the manner of her dying.
>
> To those who cannot understand Jenny's decision or my actions I ask them to at least remember her autonomy and my acceptance of all responsibility.

Anselm raised his eyes. An aeroplane was drawing a faint, silent line across the blue sky. There wasn't a cloud in sight.

'Well,' said Olivia, not quite from on high, but like a senior officer might regard a junior colleague. 'We now know that Jennifer Henderson didn't die of cancer. Nigel was right all along. So was your correspondent. So were you, because I'm sure you followed a hunch. And now the family knows it was suicide.'

There was a very faint tone of enquiry in Olivia's voice. Not quite, 'Are you sure it was worth it?' so much as 'Wasn't it easier for the family to accept beforehand?' She couldn't utter the question, of course, because a crime had been uncovered. She was as troubled as Anselm by the tension at the heart of any investigation – will the outcome lead to necessary closure or will it open worse, unforeseen distress? – but she evidently couldn't help wondering if life would be a lot easier all round if certain stones in the garden had been left unturned.

'Hopefully, Peter Henderson can start afresh,' said Anselm, as if giving Olivia his justification. 'No one's accusing him any more.'

Mitch drove Anselm back to Larkwood. Norma's final plea kept ringing in Anselm's ears. He saw the homely study. He saw the face in the bath. He saw the chalk line being drawn across the sky.

'You did the right thing,' Mitch said, fervently, unsure that Anselm was listening. 'If you'd thrown that letter away, the letter to your Prior, Peter Henderson would be dead now. You saved his life. You brought the family to the negotiating table and they walked out as one. Even though they were heading for a cover-up, they know what it feels like to be on the same side for once. It's a start. Who knows where that might lead?'

Doctor Ingleby had asked exactly the same question. He'd sat throughout Emma's crystal-clear presentation of the wide road and the narrow road and he'd said nothing. Both roads led to a kind of hell, in fact, because each of them resulted from Timothy's shocking action; his shocking implementation of what his father simply couldn't do. The doctor had smiled at Anselm, knowing the answer to his own question.

'Look at what this means,' urged Mitch, slowing down, looking more at Anselm than the road. 'It means that Timothy didn't kill his mother. It means the weight he's been carrying since his mother's death has *gone*. It means the weight carried by Emma since his confession has *gone*. It means the weight she was asking everyone to share has *gone*. It means Peter Henderson doesn't have to lift another brick. The crisis facing that family has completely *disappeared*. They can look back and say *it wasn't even there*. It's all been a colossal *misunderstanding*. All they're left with now is the usual knockabout stuff – you know, attempted murder, mutual detestation, unremitting hostility to what the other person thinks and stands for . . . they're just your average middle-class family from the Home Counties.'

Anselm didn't laugh. He was meditating on Doctor Ingleby's letter. According to his confession, he'd killed Jenny believing that he was fulfilling an explicit request from a patient to her clinician. But he'd said *nothing* of the sort when Emma disclosed Timothy's secret. He'd just sat there, watching and listening. He could have explained, there and then, that Jenny was already dead when Timothy had entered the room . . . but he hadn't done. He'd gone home to reflect. He'd made no such admission to Anselm in the Chapter Room, where, a week later, they'd met to speak honestly and without fear of condemnation. On the contrary, far from disclosing his role in an assisted suicide, he'd made a very different confession: that he'd become Jenny's doctor so as to *protect* her – from Peter and from herself. And yet, even as he poured the wine – with some ceremony – Doctor Ingleby had *already* decided to cut open his wrists. Why? Because of the moonshadow? Absolutely not. Anselm was in no doubt: nothing could have prompted Doctor Ingleby to take his life – at this particular moment – save for what he'd heard in the threshing room: that Timothy had killed his mother.

'Anselm, this is *good news*,' urged Mitch, pulling into a lay-by. 'You solved a case where there was no crime, no suspect and no evidence. You went out into the dark without a torch. And you've come back after giving Timothy a completely different future – the one that his grandparents were prepared to kill for . . . and you landed that in the bag at the cost of the truth. What's wrong with that?'

Anselm reached over and pressed the indicator down, signalling that they'd better get back on the road. In his mind he listened to Callas, Corelli and Zaccaria sing desperately about forgiveness and sacrifice. But Anselm was deeply troubled. He doubted the letter. Had Doctor Ingleby in fact killed Jenny? Or had he entrusted Anselm with a secret narrative: the meaning to the song.

50

Anselm listened with stunned dismay.

A telephone call had eventually come from a representative of the Henderson and Goodwin families. They'd been informed of Doctor Ingleby's letter. Collectively, and with unanimity, they'd agreed that Nigel should contact Anselm. Would he speak to Timothy and explain that he hadn't, in fact, killed his mother? The illusion of responsibility would have to be dispelled delicately, ideally by an outsider, someone not involved in the tangled family history. And who better than Anselm, a concerned party who already commanded Timothy's complete confidence?

'Yes,' replied Anselm, barely hearing his own voice.

'Thank you.'

'With one proviso. You agree to meet me with Michael.'

'He won't agree.'

'Then make him.'

Arrangements were made and Anselm put the telephone down.

In a daze he ambled out of the monastery to a bench that faced the old abbey ruin. Sylvester couldn't help with this one. The Boer War held no parallels. He was on his own.

And he was mildly indignant. He was, after all, the contemptible swords into ploughshares man. Now that the moral crisis had miraculously disappeared, they could wheel him in like Francis of Assisi so he could talk to the birds. There was one ironic consolation: Jenny's last wish had been fulfilled. Anselm was now at the heart of her family, his mission to bring peace and reconciliation where there had previously been war and resentment. But even that well of comfort was poisoned. He was to begin his intervention with Timothy. And he would tell him without equivocation that Doctor Ingleby had killed his mother. Only, he wasn't sure.

'May I propose one condition?' asked Doctor Ingleby.

'Which is?'

'We promise never to repeat what the other has said.'

'Unless you confess to a crime.'

'Agreed . . .'

And Doctor Ingleby had confessed to no crime. He could have done. The confession had been in his pocket the whole time. There was no reason for him to hide what he later claimed to have done. Anselm gazed over towards all that remained of the old abbey, built in the thirteen hundreds: tall arches, empty windows onto the sky; night stairs from a vanished dorter; moss, lichen and vermilion creepers swaying gently in the wind. The crisis – in terms of finding out the truth – had peaked not passed. For while the letter may have brought peace of mind to Jenny's family, it had left Anselm tormented. Doctor Ingleby had said one thing and he'd written another. He'd left Anselm with a haunting ambiguity.

Anselm brought Timothy to his circle of beehives, introducing each by its saint's name, shortly digressing into the anxious question of commerce: what to do with the honey. So far he'd put the stuff in pots, made *swedgers* – 'Glaswegian for "a sweet"' – and he was now planning a devastating spiced mead, something to challenge Larkwood's legendary cider. Then, reaching his pew, they sat down.

Where to begin?

Given his concerns, Anselm had decided to approach matters with the precise sensitivity of the lawyer and not the scruples of the monk. He would construe the *meaning* of Doctor Ingleby's letter rather than assert – and thus adopt – its *implications*.

'You understand that Doctor Ingleby has died?'

'Yes.'

Timothy was dressed in jeans and a red jumper. Black ruffled hair moved in the slight breeze. He sat angled towards Anselm, vaguely apprehensive, but pleasantly so. Someone had told him the monk had a surprise for him.

'He took his own life.'

'Yes, my dad told me. He had cancer.'

It was chilly, but not uncomfortably so. After the lazy warmth of autumn that slight nip to the air brought the promise of crisp mornings, frost, a lively fire in the evening; the comforting dark of winter.

'Yes, he did,' confirmed Anselm, not wanting to believe that this was, in Timothy's short life, his second experience of suicide. The boy thought both of them were related to choice in the face of illness. In fact, one of them was murder; the other was almost certainly not what it seemed.

'He wrote a letter, explaining himself.'

Timothy nodded. Anselm paused.

'He admits to having taken another life, once before; did you know that?'

'No.'

He was a burdened boy. His voice flat and his speech dutiful. He ought to have been troubled by his appearance and preoccupied with the striking girl who routinely ignored him, not by this – the inescapable weight that comes with an irreversible decision; the greatest decision that any human being can make. Two years ago he'd acted with the terrifyingly simple moral outlook of a twelve-year-old submerged in a catastrophe. He'd seen no grey. No reason to hesitate. He'd known what he believed his mother had wanted. But since then, without necessarily knowing why, he'd grown ill at ease. Begun to feel some nausea. And, slowly, it had grown; like a signal from a tumour. He'd seen his grandmother crushed by his secret. He'd seen his father's endless troubled glances over breakfast before hurling a brick at a boy just like him. He'd begun to question himself . . . unable to understand why this inner voice was both insistent and troubled. He'd been left adrift and anguished. All he'd learned was that the certainties of a twelve-year-old's universe aren't that robust.

'He took another life?' he repeated, lamely.

'Whose?'

'Your mother's.'

The breeze returned to tousle the boy's hair some more. '*My mum's?*'

'Your mum's.'

Timothy's wide, deep eyes began to swim. He couldn't process the implications. Two years of his life – everything he'd ever thought and felt about his mother's death – had suddenly disappeared. The sense of guilt distilled from his father's and grandmother's strained behaviour had evaporated.

'It wasn't me?'

'That's what the letter means, Timothy.'

'I didn't do it?'

'Doctor Ingleby has left no room for doubt.'

And Anselm, in a low and measured voice, spelled out the implications of the text, because Doctor Ingleby's words left no room for misunderstanding: by the time Timothy entered that room, his mother had already picked her flower and gone.

Timothy stood up, pushing both hands into his already tangled hair. He walked around the hives, raking his feet through the long grass. He muttered to himself and then came to a restive halt in front of Anselm.

'It wasn't me?' he asked again.

'That is what the letter means.'

Timothy threw his head back, unable to believe the news. He was no longer an exile. His father would look at him differently; his grandmother would stop buying him sweets and cakes and ice cream, all the confectionery she could think of to sweeten his soured world.

'Not me?' He was almost laughing.

Anselm made a gesture of surprised agreement. And then he spoke for Doctor Ingleby. It was part of the meaning of the letter. 'Timothy, you can move away from the sitting room now; you don't have to trouble yourself any more for what you thought you'd done.'

If this was Doctor Ingleby's message, it had been delivered. But despite Timothy's evident relief, Anselm felt ill at ease. He believed in the liberating power of the truth, not merciful fictions, and he didn't know, in his heart, which of the two was now at work. There was no time to brood. Timothy was approaching him, hands working and suppliant.

'Can I tell you what happened?' he asked, unsure of himself but driven now to make a clean breast of everything. 'I've never told anyone before and I'd like you to understand . . . to understand why I did it . . . even though I didn't do it . . .'

Anselm pointed to the space on the bench at his side, moving his arm slowly, to introduce some calm; to communicate his readiness to hear anything.

'All the time Mum lay there, unable to move, I couldn't forget what she'd said,' explained Timothy with remembered distress. 'That she wanted to go if things got worse. And I couldn't forget my dad, how upset he was, holding onto her hand, saying "no" when Mum was begging him to say "yes".'

Anselm could picture the scene. This is who Jenny once was; not who she became.

'And when she got cancer I knew she was frightened and worried and she actually said to my dad, "Things can't get worse", and he couldn't reply because she was right, wasn't she?'

Anselm made an ambiguous gesture, a tilt of the head, something to give him comfort.

'And I remembered what my mum had said, that she'd want to go without realising it, after a party . . .'

Another gesture.

'And that night . . . the night of my mum's birthday . . . we had a chat, me and my mum.'

This Anselm did not know. His eyes flickered. What had Jenny said? If Doctor Ingleby's confession was false, her son had killed her shortly afterwards. Instinctively, he moved along the bench, closer to Timothy, bringing a hushed confidentiality between them. Anselm sensed the darkened room, a low light, the silence from the garden and the distant fields.

'She told me that despite everything, she was contented, but I knew it wasn't true.'

But she was, Timothy.

'She told me that she wasn't worried about the cancer, and I knew that wasn't true either.'

It was the truth, Timothy.

'She said that before she died we could talk together and understand what it is to live, but I knew she'd already found her answer, but that she could never tell me.'

Anselm made no gesture. This was Jenny's plea to salvage what was left of her life. Her son hadn't believed her. Anselm gazed upon Timothy with horrified pity.

'She asked me could we travel a journey together . . . but I knew she didn't want to do it. She was being brave for me so that I wouldn't feel upset.'

No, Timothy. You're wrong.

'I knew she was accepting the cancer because she had no choice . . . because my dad couldn't do what she'd asked. And I understand why, because it's not very nice, but . . . I'd heard her ask him . . . I'd seen her pulling at his hand and crying . . .'

Timothy became very quiet. He turned away from Anselm and

began to look around, as if noticing his surroundings for the first time: the murmuring hives, the surrounding aspens, the white crosses of dead monks, leaning among the trees like strange markers for those lost in the woods.

'She told me that she'd had a good life,' said Timothy, his voice subdued and strained. He coughed to ease his throat but then he just let the tears go – fresh tears that no one had ever seen, because no one would have understood his distress . . . his tortured belief that she didn't mean it. He'd had to keep them back. 'My mum's last words to me were that she'd had a good life . . . and all because of me.'

Again he was quiet and then he suddenly turned to face Anselm. His stained face was curiously alight, shining; his wide eyes deep and vulnerable.

'I did it because I loved her,' he murmured, wanting desperately to be understood. He was speaking from a very dark place in his memory. No one had ever joined him there before. 'I only did it because I loved my mum . . . except' – and he gazed at Anselm with a sad and sunny wonder – 'it wasn't me, was it? I didn't end her life after all.'

They reached the car park and Anselm saw Peter Henderson peering into the plum trees as if checking for any remaining fruit. There was none. It had all fallen in late summer. He turned to Anselm, with a grateful smile. He'd begun growing a beard. It was silvery, in striking contrast to his black hair. He seemed younger. He was changing his appearance for the new world that had opened out in front of him. He was a different man. Old wine in a new skin.

'I want to thank you for your persistence,' said Peter Henderson.

Timothy, a packet of swedgers in his hand, had clambered into an olive-green E-Type Jaguar. The classic car that Anselm had seen in the work bay of Vintage Automotive Services. Peter

Henderson had got his wheels back. He'd spoken to Vincent Cooper.

'Except for Michael and I, we're all talking,' he said, scratching one cheek in amazement. 'We're telling each other how angry we are. It's good. I can imagine that one day there'll be different, warmer conversations. We're all learning.'

Anselm hoped so, and he nodded to show his confidence.

'I wasn't there for Timothy's childhood,' said Peter Henderson, suddenly, as if they were back on Shingle Street when he'd made a false confession. 'But I'm going to be there for the youth and the man. I'm going to guide him. Teach him. Lead him. Walk by his side. This is possible because of you.'

This was the new Peter Henderson: he was reduced, accessible and humble. Anselm couldn't imagine him being rude on the *Moral Maze*. He liked him. The nation would, too. But as the sleek Jaguar pulled away, Anselm made a private vow.

At some point in the future, when the waters were calm, he'd tell Peter Henderson that Jenny had changed her mind. It was the truth given to Anselm by Jenny and it couldn't be buried. Peter Henderson was a grown man; a skilled and nuanced thinker. He shouldn't live in ignorance, not of the most vital truth in his personal history. It was necessary that he be told. How else was he to learn that Jenny had been transformed not by a planned death but because of his love for her? She'd wanted him to know this; it had been her last gift to him.

And then it would be for Peter Henderson to work out the implications of what had happened on the night Jenny died. How his dear friend Bryan had made a merciful mistake, but a mistake nonetheless. And then he would have to make the most significant decision of them all: whether to tell Timothy. Timothy, who once thought that he'd killed his mother.

And – Anselm was quite sure – he would make the disclosure. Because after a troubled past contaminated by merciful lies and merciful fictions, he'd want his son, now grown, to know the unmerciful truth. He'd want him to understand that killing is always complicated; that people's preferences about dying complicate matters even more.

Later that evening Anselm stood patiently by the window in his cell watching the entrance to the Priory. Presently a car arrived. The driver alighted, looked around and then took a track into the darkening trees. Shortly afterwards, another vehicle pulled up. The driver followed the same winding path. Anselm came away from the sill. Opening a drawer, he retrieved the Browning and silencer. He looked at it for a while, finger on the trigger, testing its weight. The thing had nearly killed him. Leaving his cell, he paused in the corridor to lodge the gun behind his belt. It was only on lifting his eyes that he saw the archivist, aghast at the end of the corridor. Ignoring Bede's open mouth, Anselm nipped past him and went quickly outside.

51

Anselm went to the agreed meeting place: Our Lady's Lake. Michael and Nigel Goodwin were waiting for him, standing far apart like strangers trapped on Holy Island, each of them caught short by the shocking speed of the tide. They were looking in opposite directions, not daring to consider the space between them.

The water was a troubled mirror of the fading sky. There was no cloud, save a gash of red above the treetops. Centrally placed, surrounded by water, was a statue on a platform of rock. A woman's arms were lowered, her hands open. Anselm came between the two men and faced the expanse of coloured water. Michael, hunched and broken, came to his right; Nigel, confused and remote, came to his left.

The family were talking, apparently, mused Anselm. The anger was coming out, at last. But it wasn't anger that kept these two men at a distance. It was their understanding of conscience, heard or not heard, understood or mistaken. It was Michael's incomprehensible actions and Nigel's separation from the obligation to act. They were honourable men separated by experience. And that was the key, thought Anselm, looking at the carved figure on the rock. Nigel, who'd have sailed through that window of the Iranian Embassy without a second thought, had turned to the refinement of thinking; while Michael, like Barth himself, had been obliged to make certain decisions; he'd had to take his beliefs on bridge-building to their proper terminus, only he'd got lost. He'd needed his brother's compassion and guidance. Instead he'd turned away, distracted by an unimaginable uproar.

'Michael, you are a good man,' said Anselm. 'You are a moral man. A civilised man. And you nearly killed me. Speak to your brother. Tell him about the confusion of voices and how you lost your own. Talk to him about the still, small voice; what you heard, what you did and what you wish you had done. Look back on that regret in the light of what you nearly did to Peter Henderson. There's a truth in there waiting to be found.'

Michael Goodwin had had the opportunity to reflect since Anselm had last seen him, sharing a pot of tea in the kitchen at Morning Light. Then, in the aftermath of what he'd nearly done, he'd been confused, unable to understand an experience that had overtaken him in the short distance between the door and the sitting room.

'I still don't know what happened,' he said, speaking more to Anselm than Nigel. He wasn't ready yet to take his brother all the way back to that Belfast tenement. To speak of Eugene and Liam and Father Doyle. He first had to share this overwhelming insight that had crashed upon him.

'Twice in my life, I've heard a sort of voice,' said Michael, eyes strained as if he were swimming under water. 'Inside my head. It

313

called out my name. On both occasions I didn't want to know what it was going to say. The first time I closed my eyes and fired, the second I ran away like hell. Each time it was like an ambush. Afterwards, when I *did* try and listen, there was nothing . . . absolutely nothing . . . so I thought this voice of mine, this sound in my head, was just my imagination, a fantasy. And then . . .'

Michael fell quiet.

Anselm waited. Nigel looked at his brother, hands joined with distressed understanding.

'And then . . . in Jenny's house . . . I followed the same route I'd taken in Donegal. I was doing it again, following the same pattern, intending to do what I wished I'd done the first time around: silence someone whose death would solve so many problems' – he paused, squinting at the slash of orange, bright now, above the jagged black treeline – 'but as I set off down the corridor, I heard myself again' – Michael suddenly looked at Anselm as if he were haunted – 'it was my voice, talking to me: "Michael, Michael, Michael . . ." and this time I couldn't stop myself listening and it simply said what I'd always known to be true but had run away from, for the sake of Eugene and Liam and all the misery I'd seen in Belfast. It said, "This is wrong" . . . that's all, very, very quietly, just as I raised the gun. And I knew it was true . . . that it was wrong now and it had been wrong then but I couldn't stop myself. And, you know, it was Peter who once tried to tell me. And I hadn't been able to listen.'

Michael had finished: he was staring at the dying light with eyes that ached for the simple days of rough and tumble on the lawn. And this – thought Anselm – is why you could reach Timothy after his mother's accident: you recognised his early exile from pranks and silly laughter. The days when lemon drops simply tasted bitter.

'Mike, speak to me.'

It was Nigel, hoarse and demanding. It was the older brother, arriving home to find his little brother devastated by the mess on the floor: broken heirlooms; breakages their parents would never forgive. There'd been an accident.

'Tell me what happened.'

'I can't, Nigel.'

'Tell me about Eugene and Liam, please.'

'I can't.'

'I'll understand.'

'I just can't. I'm—'

'You can,' interposed Anselm. He turned to Michael. 'You told me. And now try and turn to your family. At Larkwood we call it an "opening of the heart". It is very painful. But it's the only way to build relationships with depth.'

Michael pulled his eyes away from the sky and stared at the shimmering water; but he didn't speak.

'We'll go to Harlingen together,' said Nigel, more ordering than suggesting. 'We'll take your car back and stay there for a while. As long as it takes.'

'And when you return,' said Anselm to Nigel, after a long pause, a pause that expressed Michael's consent, 'talk to Peter. Maybe you could help him understand your brother's desperation, how he could be driven, out of love, disappointment and despair, to a kind of madness. Peter is a changed man. Perhaps now's the time, at last, to have that "intelligent disagreement over moral questions". If you can build a bridge to him, then in time maybe everyone else might be able to cross over . . . even Emma.'

Ordinarily Anselm would not have been so liberal with his advice. He felt impertinent. But Jenny had asked him to try. And this was his one brief chance.

'There's one last thing,' said Anselm.

He put his hand beneath his scapular and slowly pulled out the Browning.

Michael turned his whole body to one side, not wanting to

315

see the dreadful thing, not wanting to be harrowed again by the memory of Liam's young face, his outstretched hand and all the confusion that followed.

Anselm was about to hurl it in the lake, when Nigel grabbed his arm. He took the gun, walked past Anselm and put his arm around his brother's shoulders.

'Mike, take it.'

'I can't, I can't.' Michael's voice was strangled and sobbing.

'You can, Mike, here, take it for the last time.'

Michael shook his head, his shoulders heaving in a chilling upsurge of grief and regret.

'Do you want me to do it for you?' asked Nigel, quietly. 'I'll throw it, if you like, but you've got to watch at least.'

Michael nodded and turned to the sparkling water, still under his brother's arm. After a still, charged moment, Nigel tossed the pistol high in the air. It span, black against the sky, turning and turning until, with a short swallowing sound, it vanished for ever.

52

Anselm could not forget Doctor Ingleby. He wanted to know the answer to the conundrum: where did the truth lie? With the spoken word, uttered in the ruins of Leiston Abbey, or in the letter written before he'd even got there? The first had been given to Anselm in secret; the second publicly, for the world.

It was an important question.

A vital question.

Because if Doctor Ingleby didn't kill Jenny, then it was Timothy. And if it was Timothy, then it begged the question as to why Doctor Ingleby would assume responsibility. Either way, one of them had committed murder.

Reflecting upon the matter during Lauds, Mass, Vespers,

Compline and 'Sailing By', Anselm found himself drawn repeatedly back to the meal he'd shared with Doctor Ingleby in the former Chapter House. With each recollection, the eating and drinking assumed an increasingly ritual aspect, something to which Anselm had been blind at the time. What had seemed to be an admittedly peculiar picnic became something of a ceremony whose full meaning was known to Doctor Ingleby alone. Driven to understand its significance, and hoping to clear the ambiguity between word and text, Anselm contacted Olivia; and she put him onto Pat Randall, one of the detectives charged with examining the circumstances of the doctor's death. She even gave him access to the house outside Needham Market. An interesting if puzzling picture had begun to emerge for the investigating officer.

Doctor Bryan Sheldon Ingleby qualified as a general practitioner in 1968, starting his career at a practice in St John's Wood, London. On his way to work he'd stumbled on the Beatles preparing to cross Abbey Road – the iconic shot, with Paul McCartney walking barefoot, holding a cigarette in one hand. Doctor Ingleby had held Paul's shoes and socks, giving him a light just before the Fab Four had walked onto the zebra crossing. John Lennon had wanted him in the picture, leading the way, but for some daft reason Doctor Ingleby had said no. He'd instinctively recoiled from the limelight, and in so doing had lost his place in history. Doctor Ingleby had recounted the story to everyone the police had contacted.

As it happened, the young Bryan was more of an opera fan. He'd already married the much younger Maxine, a German, who worked in management at Covent Garden. There was some talk among the detectives as to whether Maxine or her husband had ever met Jenny Goodwin while she was based with the Royal Ballet. There was no evidence either way, save that for six months Jenny, Maxine and Bryan had milled about the same building. Perhaps they'd crossed each other in a corridor. It was a tantalising possibility.

At around the time that Jenny had met Peter, Maxine had disclosed to Bryan that she'd been seeing a colleague. Someone well known to him. A close friend, actually. For well over twenty years he'd argued with Bryan about the merits of Sutherland over Callas, Bryan not spotting that Maxine was carrying out a vaguely similar exercise about the men who shared her emotional life. In the fallout Bryan had let Maxine's lawyers come up with a settlement and, wanting a quick resolution, he'd signed the papers not caring if he'd been taken to the cleaners or not. All he'd wanted was enough capital to buy a small property in rural Suffolk. They'd been childless. And this had been a great pain for him. Maxine had said no. Told him all they needed was each other.

Motoring towards his own retirement he'd taken over a sole practice in Needham Market. Very quickly his reputation grew. At the time of his death, he had 732 registered patients, many travelling significant distances to see him. All of them knew the Abbey Road story. All said he was like a father to their children. He'd worked for years at the Grove Hospice in Leiston, soon becoming a vigorous and dedicated trustee. By his last will and testament all his assets had gone to the hospice, subject to a proviso that if declined, the RSPCA would become the sole and absolute beneficiary. He'd given his net worth to life, be they human or animal. Tributes had poured into the local press. Opinion was divided upon what he had done.

Only, of course – thought Anselm – he might not have done it.

Detective Inspector Randall had been to see the General Medical Council. Doctor Ingleby's record was clean. Not a single complaint. No investigations, procedures, warnings or disciplinary action of any kind. Nothing. He'd written a number of articles in the *Lancet* on palliative care and end-of-life issues, and while he'd raised pressing questions about intervention and patient choice (with frequent references to Magellan), there'd been no evidence that Bryan Ingleby was a man who would support or oppose assisted suicide, be it inside a possible law or outside existing legislation. Nothing to explain why he might have cooperated with Jennifer Henderson (in the terms set out in his letter).

'Mystifying,' said Anselm, quietly, in the conference room at Martlesham.

'You can say that again.' DI Randall went to get more coffee. Back at the table, he ate another biscuit, crunching it with a surprising level of aggression. 'He was a really organised bloke, everything in its place, all the boxes ticked, never late for a tax return and yet we couldn't find any record for the insulin – coming in or going out. There's none missing. Which doesn't add up to much, because he could have got it from . . .'

Anselm nodded, reaching for the milk, but he'd drifted off, involuntarily. He'd seen Doctor Ingleby – Bryan now – raising his glass of wine in the Chapter House. He'd seen the mystery in his eyes.

Where was the truth, Bryan? On your lips or on the paper?

After a sandwich from the canteen, DI Randall drove Anselm to the house off the Barking Road. He stayed outside, keen to smoke. Technically he'd given up the week before but he'd found a packet in the glove box that morning. Waste not, and all that. He'd smoke the lot, one after the other.

Anselm clipped the door shut behind him. The house was chilly now and silent. All the atmospheric warmth had gone, even from the cherry-red carpet. The painting of the elephants, once rousing, seemed banal, a predictable tribute to an endangered species. The life in the building had seeped away. Anselm went straight to the study. He pressed PLAY, turned the volume down and sat on the chair facing the roll-top desk. Callas began quietly:

'Deh! Non volerli vittime del mio fatale errore . . .'

Anselm listened, gazing around the room. He opened a drawer and shut it again. He reached for the pipe but then thought better of it.

'What am I doing here?' he said, quietly. 'What do I hope to find?'

Only the truth. I want to understand our meal together. Because afterwards you made me your messenger.

Just then, a movement caught his eye. DI Randall had struck a match in the garden. As he looked through the window, Anselm's eyes fell upon the blue shed with the yellow door and the windows blocked by drawn yellow curtains. Bryan had spent his last afternoon out there, doing spring's work in autumn. All of a sudden Anselm was standing by a royal-blue Sunbeam Singer Chamois and he heard, once again, that bemused voice:

'I've spent almost forty years in medical practice . . . in the surgery . . . at patients' houses . . . at the hospice. And do you know, after all that, what's best and true of me lies in a garden shed. Odd, isn't it?'

The shed door was unlocked.

Inside, Anselm saw a rake, a hoe, a spade, bags of compost – everything you'd expect – neatly organised for the coming season. But what gripped his attention was the chair – one of the collapsible canvas chairs that Bryan had brought to Leiston Abbey. The other was leaning against the back wall beside the table. A sheaf of papers and a pencil had been left on the seat. Picking them up, Anselm sat down and began reading by the light of the open door.

Bryan had been reading various oaths, ancient and modern, written to frame the ethical standards that govern medical practice. He'd compiled them into a bundle and stapled it together. Certain phrases had been marked with the pencil.

The first text was the ancient Hippocratic Oath, considered by Anselm on the day he'd begun his investigation, convinced that Jennifer Henderson had been murdered. Bryan had underlined: 'I will give no deadly drug to any, though it be asked of me . . .'

Anselm turned the page.

This was the Prayer of Maimonides. Bryan had isolated one

sentence: 'Thou hast chosen me to watch over the life and health of thy creatures.'

Next came the World Medical Association Declaration of Geneva, as revised in May 2006. Bryan had marked 'I solemnly pledge to consecrate my life to the service of humanity' and, lower down, 'I will maintain the utmost respect for human life.'

Anselm turned to the last page, the Oath of Lasagna, written in 1964. Bryan had underlined a short paragraph: 'Most especially must I tread with care in matters of life and death; this awesome responsibility must be faced with great humbleness and awareness of my own frailty. Above all, I must not play God.'

Anselm rose and opened the yellow curtains. Sunlight spilled into the cosy room, brightening the tools neatly lined along one wall, the bags of nourishing compost and a few clay tubs. He looked over to the house and thought: So this is the answer to the riddle. After forty years of medical practice, you brought the best of yourself over here. You left it on a chair for me to find.

'It is your oath. Your sacred oath. And you did not break it.'

DI Randall was lighting another cigarette.

'You told me the truth and you gave everyone else a fiction.'

So what did that mean, thought Anselm, stepping outside, thumbs hooked into his belt.

It meant a great deal.

It meant that Timothy had murdered his mother. He'd never know it, of course, but that was the truth about her last night. Jenny had told him her hopes and expectations and he hadn't believed her. He'd come downstairs with his Spiderman pillow and done what he thought was best. Now, because of Doctor Ingleby's confession, Timothy would think, at best, that a doctor had ended his mother's life; at worst, if his father initiated him into the unpleasant world of big truths, he'd think that the doctor had made a mistake. But the awful distance between the two was something that would never directly concern Timothy . . . he'd had a close shave, there.

It meant that Bryan Ingleby's reputation would be tarnished

for some and destroyed for others – people he'd admired and served. In a way, that didn't count. What mattered most was that Bryan would be remembered for having done something he would never do; for believing what he did not in fact believe; for having crossed the line between compassion and mercy outside the law; for having played God.

There were other, practical consequences that Bryan would have found distressing, too. The Grange Hospice would censure him in strong terms – terms he might have drafted himself, in other circumstances. And they would almost certainly decline his bequest. But he'd prepared for that eventuality: there was nothing else he could do. So the animals would benefit.

'So why did you shoulder the cost, Bryan? Why take the responsibility?'

Anselm turned from the covered vegetable patch, where he'd halted, to look back at the little hut that held the oldest and most revered oaths known to civilisation.

'You did it for Timothy,' said Anselm. 'You saved him from a lifetime's complications. You made him your patient when there was no doctor who could help him, of mind or body. With that paternal smile of yours, you picked up the consequences of Peter and Jenny's grappling, their frightened attempt to deal with paralysis and terminal illness. You chose death to give a second chance to the grandson you'd never had.'

It was Abbey Road all over again. The world would see a very different picture indeed.

53

On the day that Anselm had nearly been shot the Prior had asked him if he wanted to have a chat about things. He was referring, in fact, to a Gilbertine tradition. The practice had trickled over from France as *une ouverture du cœur*, literally an 'opening of the heart', but the Larkwood community, seeking a brief translation, came to call it 'a chat'. At the time of the Prior's suggestion, Anselm had said no. The time has to be right – a moment arrived at by a kind of inner gestation – and he hadn't felt ready. But he did now; now that he understood the meaning of Bryan Ingleby's death. And so, having first thrown the Exit Mask in the bin as a preliminary to his own catharsis, Anselm arranged to meet the Prior for a walk through the woods, along a track that climbed up the nearest thing in Suffolk to a mountain.

In certain respects it was a very important meeting. Not least because it followed the conclusion of Anselm's first case since the Prior had released him from the cloister to bring Larkwood's flickering light into the market place. Not least, also, because the Prior himself would have to make a fairly significant decision if the case itself was to be laid quietly to rest.

As soon as Anselm and the Prior left the open air and entered the seclusion of the woods, Anselm began to lay out the history of the Henderson and Goodwin families. He spoke methodically and without commentary. When he'd finished, he went straight to the heart of his concerns. Perhaps it was that brief foray into the world of Professor Bannon, but the law in relation to killing was high on Anselm's agenda.

'When I last saw Mitch, he argued that there should be a law for Jenny's kind of situation. That if she'd been allowed to take her own life, then her tragedy and that of Timothy would never have happened. There'd have been a system with fail-safes. She'd have filled in all the forms. Doctors would have assessed her state of mind. There'd have been a private interview. And there would have been no room for confusion. But the matter doesn't end there. It begins.'

The Prior gave a nod, his glasses catching the green light that filtered through the trees.

'Because Mitch's law, in other circumstances, would allow a less caring family to manoeuvre someone into accepting a death that they didn't want, and no one would ever know.'

The same forms would be filled in. The same doctors would give the same opinions. And the private interview would yield nothing to contradict any previously stated intentions. There'd be no confusion. And someone's life would end, wrongly.

'Vulnerable people could be subjected to a kind of moral terrorism . . . urged to die for a good cause. And Mitch's law would not be able to protect them . . . because, in truth, we can't investigate a person's consent. We can't penetrate the full mystery of someone else's mind. And that's the nub.'

Which brought Anselm back to his starting point. How could Jenny have been protected?

The answer was devastatingly simple. It was moral education. The careful nurturing of conscience by principle and prohibition.

'The real problem was Timothy's moral outlook. There was no hinterland of ifs and buts. He'd seen nothing wrong with what he'd done.'

He'd only begun to glimpse the gravity of his action once his grandmother had turned frosty; once his father had thrown a brick through a window. Wouldn't a commandment or two have helped? Even if they were only viewed as ancient wisdom, literature from a nomadic people trying to cross the desert? He'd needed *something*. All at once a hot, corpulent presence entered Anselm's mind, and he was compelled to pay tribute to its sagacity.

'I wonder if Bede understood the heart of the problem. He said that dreadful things happen when people lose a simple sense of right and wrong. Or, I might add, if they never had it in the first place.'

The Prior, until now silent but attentive – his function to listen not speak – felt compelled to raise a concern.

'Speaking of Bede,' he said, confidentially. 'I'm worried about him.'

'Why?'

'He's losing his grip on reality. He swears blind he saw you with a pistol and silencer. All I could say was that at least we wouldn't hear anything.'

Anselm cleared his throat. 'We have a decision to make; or perhaps you do.'

This was a delicate matter and one of the reasons for the walk in the woods.

On entering the foothills (about a mile back), the Prior had learned that Michael and Emma Goodwin were guilty of conspiracy to murder Peter Henderson; that Michael Goodwin was also guilty of attempting to murder a monk, along with Néall Ó Mórdha, now a prominent Sinn Fein activist; and that there were unquestionably other, miscellaneous offences (like the unlawful killing of a dog) which would, in time, find themselves onto any indictment should the details ever be reported to Olivia Manning. The question was whether to say nothing. For the sake of . . . peace. Timothy's peace. A family's peace.

'Where is the gun?' asked the Prior, after a long pause.

He appreciated its significance: forensically and symbolically.

'Decommissioned.'

'Permanently?'

'Beyond reach.'

'We'll not try and get it back, then.'

Like detective superintendents and generals, priors can make swift, controversial decisions. The matter was closed.

They walked on, getting steadily higher, the monastery sinking into the valley below. But Anselm picked up the subject, because he'd been moved by Michael Goodwin's struggle to do what was right. The young Army officer had tried to square his conscience with the demands of extreme circumstances; he'd thought the voices of the dead – brutalised, unforgettable voices – were more important than his own. The situation was in direct contrast to that of Timothy. Far from lacking a moral sense, he'd been a man of acute sensibility.

'He went to Belfast a man of peace but he became a terrorist,' said Anselm. 'He tried to kill someone without the moral protection of the law. He was desperate, because he'd heard and seen desperate things. He felt he had to do something drastic, because the circumstances were drastic. And so he stepped over the line . . . to cut short the suffering. But the only way he could pull the trigger was to ignore the same voice that would have stopped Timothy reaching for his pillow. The quiet voice of contradiction. And it's only because he'd run away from himself that he could ever have entertained killing Peter Henderson.'

There are rules, Anselm. You can't just forget them and run. They make the world go round. They stop an archivist killing a beekeeper.

Bede seemed to have come running up the incline, panting and important, but Anselm ignored him and said: 'Which is one of the reasons that Ernest shot Albert, I suppose.'

The Prior had halted. His glasses flashed again.

'Albert?'

'Yes,' replied Anselm. 'The poor guy's foot was trapped. He couldn't escape. He couldn't speak.'

The Prior's face had settled into a mask of pale dismay. He'd made a monumental mistake in licensing Anselm's work beyond the monastery walls. He shared the fault.

'And Ernest shot him in cold blood, while Albert waved his arms around like mad. But everything worked out well in the end because, would you believe it—'

'Ernest?'

'He meant well, honestly . . .'

Anselm moved away, smiling to himself, waiting for his Prior to catch up.

The two monks had reached the low summit, giving an elevated view over the fields below. The Prior swished at conkers with a stick, brooding about the *Titanic*, while Anselm looked towards Larkwood. He could see the bell tower, the glistening cloister, the sleeping orchards, and the grove of poplars that hid the graves and his beehives. He was still thinking about law and morality. Because Bryan Ingleby had tried to find a way between the two.

'Timothy committed a grave wrong,' said Anselm. 'He doesn't know it, but he killed his mother against her will. And Doctor Ingleby has assumed all the responsibility.'

The Prior came to Anselm's side, placing both of his hands on the top of his stick.

'And we had this meal,' said Anselm. 'He wanted to know if Jenny had changed her mind. Because if she had done, it would change the quality of what he was about to do. It's as though he wanted to be absolutely sure about the exact offence that Timothy had committed, so that he knew what he was about to pick up.'

'But he gave you the truth,' observed the Prior, astutely.

'Yes, he did,' replied Anselm. 'He knew that the result would be controversy, attracting both denunciation and respect, but it would all arise from a total misreading of his actions . . . because he hadn't done it. And he wanted at least one person to know who he was, who he'd been and what he'd *really* done for Timothy.'

You silenced me, too, thought Anselm. With that promise not to repeat what you were about to say, except, if I wished, to my Prior. Because you knew I'd be deeply troubled by the cold territory you'd decided to enter: the use of a lie as a means to an end; the assumption of responsibility in someone else's stead. You'd thought it all out, hadn't you?

'He picked up all the weight,' murmured Anselm. 'Mine included.'

During the slow and gentle descent, the Prior took issue with Albert thanking God for the stutter. Apparently, Professor Bannon had left that aspect of the problem unexplored, so the Prior thought he might fill the gap. As they stepped out of the woods into the sunshine, the Prior, however, suddenly changed the subject. He stopped, frowned and looked at Anselm.

'I've just realised something,' he said, not very happy.

'What?'

'I gave you this job so that you could solve crimes . . . and all
you've done is conceal them.' He looked at Anselm, bewildered
at the turn of events. 'Your first case has been solved on a basis
that couldn't be further from the truth and you didn't even discover
who it was that wrote to me in the first place. That's an incredible
achievement.'

The two monks nodded slowly at one another, resuming their
measured return to Larkwood as strangely humbled men.

Epilogue

Mitch invited Anselm to tea. But not, it transpired, on the wherry. When Anselm arrived at the boat, he was taken on a short walk, past the Spinning Mule and along the lane that led to the Gate House cottage, the former outpost of a wool merchant's modest estate.

Mitch opened the front door without knocking and ushered Anselm along a corridor into a compact, sunlit room with French windows. They were open and the mild afternoon air seemed to swim in and out, bringing the scent of autumn from the garden. There were two people in the room: a stout square-faced elderly man sitting in an armchair, his legs covered by a green tartan blanket. A table on wheels had been rolled over his legs. He was doing a monumental jigsaw. A rural scene by Gainsborough. He looked over his glasses, smiled and swore violently . . . distress suddenly sweeping over his face, a hand raised to his mouth, wondering if he'd done something wrong.

'It's all right, Dad,' said Mitch, with a calming hand.

'He can't help it,' said the second person in the room, a somewhat frail, stooped woman in shapeless clothes whom Anselm had seen only once before, waving at Mitch through a window. 'He had a stroke, long ago when Mitch was a boy. Never got his speech back, just a few words. He swears like a trooper and he doesn't know he's doing it, do you, love?'

The man shook his head, still distressed; humiliated and

frustrated by his incapacity. His eyes were wide and glassy, not really comprehending.

Anselm walked over and took the man's hand in greeting. The grip was strong – he'd been a powerful man – and grateful. 'Say what you like, when you like and how you like. I live with people who'd just love to do what you do and can't.'

The man was called Jack, the woman Eileen. They were Mr and Mrs Robson.

'Mitch tells me you're the man who defended him all those years ago,' said Eileen after she'd come back with the fresh tea. She stood near Anselm, pouring carefully into old, chipped china. 'That was very nice of you.'

Anselm told her not to mention it and Mitch's father gave a wink. He looked at his son proudly and winked again.

'We lost faith in the law, didn't we, Jack?' said Eileen, sitting down. 'I hope you don't mind me saying that, Father?'

'Absolutely not.'

A selection of sandwiches had been prepared – ham, cheese, cress, tomato. They'd been laid on plates and brought to a table in the middle of the room before the guests had arrived. All the crusts had been removed. There was a cake, too. A Battenberg. The armchairs, upholstered in white linen with a pattern of red roses, stood close to the table. Anselm reached for a ham sandwich.

'Well, I won't bother you with all that,' said Eileen. 'Best forgotten.'

Jack, however, made a wave, nodding at his wife, urging her on.

'No, love, I should've put my foot in my mouth.'

Anselm urged her to speak. It sounded as if he was being polite but he meant it. He well understood the urge. People who've had a bad experience of the law can't help but mention it to representatives who cross their path; even ones who've left the fray. He urged her on, with a wink to Jack.

Mr and Mrs Robson had been driving home after a visit to

Warkworth Castle. Eileen was driving a bit too carefully. Jack was telling her to speed up, for God's sake. Only Jack was wearing a seatbelt. A drayman coming in the opposite direction veered round a bend, crossed the road and sent the Robsons into a field of sheep. Jack banged his head, broke a leg, an ankle and an elbow. Eileen broke a lot more. The absence of the seatbelt saved her life, because the steering wheel, pushed in by the impact, shoved her into the back seat. The drayman climbed out of his cabin without a scratch. Said it had all happened so fast and he was sorry. Jack smelled that hint of beer on his breath but passed out before he could tell the ambulance man. Turned out the police didn't breathalyse him – but Jack knew, and he'd seen the accident happen. It was an open and shut case. Then, six months later, Jack had his stroke ('didn't you, love?'). When he came home, he could only limp. Couldn't read, write or talk . . . not easily anyway. The big question was whether the stroke was caused by that bang to the head. If it was, the damages would be huge. If it wasn't, well, fair enough. Medical experts were called. London. Leeds. Bristol. First for the Robson side, then the drayman's. Funnily enough, the expert for the drayman said the stroke 'would, tragically, have happened anyway'; and the expert for Jack said it was caused by 'trauma to the cranium'. The insurers were getting ready for a big fight over how much to pay out, because Jack would never work again and he was the breadwinner and Mitch was only a lad. Eileen couldn't work any more because she was looking after her husband. Unfortunately, the solicitor had forgotten to take a witness statement from Jack about what he'd seen and smelled. Which was a bit of a problem because, in truth, Eileen couldn't remember a blessed thing ('could I, love?'). When the other side found out that memories were weak, they decided to call in a road traffic accident expert to examine the road and the vehicle damage. Same for Jack and Eileen's side. And funnily enough, the specialists just couldn't agree on anything.

'The case just dragged on and on,' said Eileen. 'I didn't know what was happening. I'd ring and write and no one ever got back in touch. And we were borrowing money against the house to pay the fees.'

Reading between the lines, Anselm guessed that someone in the office had been out of their depth. They'd let the case ride. It happened sometimes.

'Cutting a long story short, we changed solicitors three times,' said Eileen. 'And then, just as we were coming up to trial, we heard that the medical expert for our side had gone to France the year before. He'd retired, so we had to start all over again, didn't we, Jack, and . . .'

Anselm examined the frail woman. She was a fighter. All those broken bones had been put to work to get Jack his compensation. She'd done all she could, trusted and waited. The new solicitor found another doctor. In Cardiff. And – thank heaven – the expert agreed with the man who'd gone to Biarritz.

'Well, Father, I don't really want to talk about the trial, do I, Jack?'

Her husband made a tired wave of the hand, as if to say that was enough for everyone. He winked at Anselm and pointed at the sandwiches.

'It was a big case, Anselm,' said Mitch. He'd opened up a pine cupboard by the chimney breast, and taken out a bundle of papers. 'Here are the pleadings. Take a look.'

Anselm flicked through the Statement of Claim. Jack's Schedule of Damages claimed £263,400.38 – in effect a sum for the injury, lost wages and cost of future care. Eileen's sought £42,326.15. The grand total came to £305,726.53. The case had dragged on for seven years. Anselm began to have a premonition of where this tale was going . . .

'I was there for the trial,' said Mitch. 'It was unforgettable.'

The trial never got beyond the dispute between the road traffic experts. Two men who'd written their reports years earlier. It became a technical argument about skid marks, braking distances and the quality of the photographs, the judge lapsing at one point into Classical Greek when a dispute arose over some term or other that Mitch could no longer remember. Counsel for Mr and Mrs Robson had joined in the quick banter with a stab at Latin, before losing his place yet again in the bundle. In a cold, intellectually precise and devastating judgement, the judge accepted the expert evidence obtained for the defendant, though – to show his fair-mindedness – he threw a few biting remarks at the drayman, rejecting his account on matters incidental to the issues at stake.

Anselm had closed his eyes, wondering if Mitch and his family had ever realised that the question of liability (as opposed to damages) could have been sorted out years earlier while they were waiting for those first medical reports. Three firms of solicitors had let that slip.

'I found out afterwards that our barrister was a criminal specialist,' said Mitch. 'He'd picked up the case the night before from some personal injury hotshot in chambers who'd been double-booked. I could tell there was something wrong with his style . . . he kept making points as if he were trying to win round a jury . . . folk like my mum and dad. Didn't seem to realise that the judge didn't like it . . . that he might want to show, if only to himself, that his mind could work independent of feeling. That justice could be cold to be right.'

Shortly they moved on to the cake and Eileen moved on to lighter matters, though only marginally so.

'And then, to top it all, the police started going for Mitch.' She looked over at Jack with indignation, and the old man made a fist. 'Accused of crimes he'd never commit. We're just grateful he came to you, Father. Glad you were out there in the courts making sure justice was done.'

And she was so thankful that Mitch had done well in life. They'd been horrified when he didn't go to the Royal College of Music – 'the *RCM*, Father, one of the most *famous* colleges in the *world*' – but he'd made his way in life and got a decent, honest job. What else could his parents ask for? When you look at how some children grow to treat their own.

'He's looked after his mum and dad, hasn't he, Jack?'

A wink from Jack and another nod at the cake. There was a lot left.

'Given us what was lacking when he could' – she leaned towards Mitch – 'though we've never asked, have we, Son?'

'No, Mum,' replied Mitch, quietly. 'You've never asked for anything. Only what you deserve. That's right, isn't it, Dad?'

On the walk back to the boat the monk and the former insurance manager fell into step. They'd started out one in front of the other, but now they'd moved side by side. There was a heavy sense that important things had not been said. Truth is like that. It insinuates itself into the gaps of a conversation and then inflates like an airbag after a collision. Mitch, hands in his pockets and dawdling, said:

'They've never had much luxury, just the sort of life they might have had if there'd been no accident.'

So this was the mystery to Mitch Robson. He'd packed in music so he could target two insurance companies, stealing a substantial sum from each. But he'd taken less than the sum sought from the court so that no one could ever make the evidential link between his theft and his parents' loss. Not even Anselm.

'There are other ways of handling damage claims after a car accident,' said Mitch, as if Anselm might not know. 'It's called no-fault compensation. That's what they do in New Zealand. The insurers just pay out.'

This was the rationale, then: Mitch had made an extreme attack upon a flawed legal system that didn't match the situation on the ground. And this was where Anselm's scheme for atonement had ground to an ambiguous, inconclusive halt. The irony was acute: he'd set out intending to reveal the truth at any cost, only to uncover a murder that would remain secret, and concealing in the process a number of other grave offences. And, to cap it all – and not surprisingly – he'd failed to convince Mitch that his principled approach to theft ought to be exposed. Life, morality and the law had joined forces to rob him of the restitution he'd hoped to make. There was to be no new beginning as a servant of justice, free from the complications that had dogged his days at the Bar. But the argument couldn't end at this unhappy juncture. There was a great difference between leaving a crime unresolved and committing that crime in the first place.

'I'm sorry, Mitch,' said Anselm, diffidently, after a while. 'It was still wrong. Life can be terribly unjust, but we can't play God. We can't bring about outcomes, regardless of the law, just because we believe them to be right . . . because that's the road Jenny went down, at first. And Timothy followed her. Michael went somewhere similar. Ó Mórdha, too.'

Mitch wasn't hurt and he wasn't surprised. He'd expected Anselm to say as much. They'd taken differing views on the law a long, long time ago. But there was a quiet sadness in his face.

'I didn't expect you to approve,' he said, 'because I don't either. I'm not proud. I'm not pleased with myself. I live with the discomfort.'

When they reached the *Jelly Roll*, Mitch suddenly turned around, struck by the one unresolved question:

'I wonder who wrote to your Prior about Jennifer Henderson?'

Anselm looked back to the beginning; to be precise, a couple of days before that fateful letter had arrived.

'The article in the *Sunday Times* had quite an effect on my Prior,' he said, measuring his words. 'He vanished into himself and when he emerged I was sure that he'd decided to limit my work to beekeeping, washing bottles, waxing floors. Humdrum stuff. And then, all of a sudden, the letter arrived inviting him to change Larkwood's way of engaging with the world. As it happens – because of you – he'd been thinking along those very lines and the letter had served to remove any lingering hesitation. Now

– and this causes me some disquiet – if I'd knocked on his door to say what he'd read, I don't think he'd have listened; and yet after he'd opened that envelope, he did. Strange, isn't it?'

'Yes,' replied Mitch, with a dawning smile. For an instant, they were both tongue-tied: their working relationship was over; henceforth Anselm would be on his own. There was a need for a gathering in and a send off. Rising to the challenge Mitch held out his hand, Geordie mischief in his eyes: 'And now, troubled explorer, go forth into the wilderness and find another problem to solve.'

Anselm strolled home to Larkwood, the river murmuring at his side. He'd have to have another walk and talk with the Prior, at some point. He'd have to admit that he'd given his own vocation a bit of a shove. For the moment fish were jumping. Sudden and fleeting; appearances and disappearances; flashes of bright silver. Anselm barely had a chance to see them. They'd gone before he could acknowledge that they'd been there. And he thought if he could just speed up his discernment, or slow down their movement, he'd see that the wonder of their glittering existence was absolute; that they were what they were, regardless of whether anyone could appreciate them or not; that nothing was lost for the speed of their passing. And, elevating his mind above carp and trout, Anselm thought that the glory of life – even brief and trimmed down to the point of seeming insignificance – remained utterly breathtaking. That death, with all its power, would always be the one who came afterwards, the latecomer who'd missed the party. He paused, staring into the green water, past the flies skipping over the reflection of the evening sky.

'You came and you went, so quickly,' he said. 'But I saw your flight; and I'll remember you.'